T0158103

This Is How It Started

Books by Stacy Finz

The Nugget Series
GOING HOME
FINDING HOPE
SECOND CHANCES
STARTING OVER
GETTING LUCKY
BORROWING TROUBLE
HEATING UP
RIDING HIGH
FALLING HARD
HOPE FOR CHRISTMAS
TEMPTING FATE
CHOOSING YOU
HOLDING ON

The Garner Brothers
NEED YOU
WANT YOU
LOVE YOU

Dry Creek Ranch
COWBOY UP
COWBOY TOUGH
COWBOY STRONG

Published by Kensington Publishing Corp.

This Is How It Started

Stacy Finz

LYRICAL PRESS
Kensington Publishing Corp.
www.kensingtonbooks.com

LYRICAL PRESS BOOKS are published by

Kensington Publishing Corp.
119 West 40th Street
New York, NY 10018

All Kensington titles, imprints, and distributed lines are available at special quantity discounts for bulk purchases for sales promotion, premiums, fundraising, educational, or institutional use.

Special book excerpts or customized printings can also be created to fit specific needs. For details, write or phone the office of the Kensington Sales Manager: Kensington Publishing Corp., 119 West 40th Street, New York, NY 10018. Attn. Sales Department. Phone: 1-800-221-2647.

Lyrical Press and Lyrical Press logo Reg. U.S. Pat. & TM Off.

First Electronic Edition: February 2023
ISBN: 978-1-5161-1119-0 (ebook)

First Print Edition: February 2023
ISBN: 978-1-5161-1120-6

Printed in the United States of America

To my family, a never-ending source of inspiration.

Acknowledgments

First and foremost, I would like to thank my editor, John Scognamiglio, for helping me go deeper and realizing I was telling multiple love stories instead of just one. His insight was invaluable and working with him is a dream.

Thanks to Alex Nicolajsen for all the encouragement, cheerleading, and kind words over the years. I am so lucky to have her in my corner. Kensington is so lucky to have her, period.

To my agent, Jill Marsal, who is the best first reader a writer can ask for. I couldn't do this without her guidance.

To Wendy Miller, Leah Garchik, Miriam Morgan, Amanda Gold and Rebecca Hunter. They say the devil is in the details. Thanks for keeping me out of the weeds. They're the best.

Thanks to the entire talented team at Kensington. It takes a village.

And to my late father, Steven Finz, who instilled my love of writing from the time I was a kid. Dad, I think you would've loved this book.

Above all, thanks to my husband, Jaxon, who makes everything possible.

"Goodbyes are only for those who love with their eyes. Because for those who love with heart and soul there is no such thing as separation." —Rumi

Part 1
The Funeral

Chapter 1
Colma, California
Present Time

I think of my mother as I stand at the edge of block seven, lot two, section six, peering over the side of an empty hole. Oddly enough, the depth of a modern grave in the United States is a mere four feet deep. The whole six-feet-under thing is a misnomer, according to the funeral guy. He was a fountain of information during our first consultation, throwing out selling points about Eternal Home the same way I do when I'm trying to push a house that's sat on the market too long.

Despite the barren trench's shallowness, it looks dark and bottomless. And soon, they'll lower the most important person in my life into the freshly dug hole and cover him with dirt.

I shudder, angry with myself for giving in to my mother and not insisting on cremation. At least I could scatter Josh's ashes somewhere beautiful, a place that held meaning to him, instead of the so-called "City of Souls." Besides burial being horrifyingly claustrophobic, I don't want Josh here.

I want him home, alive, and making Saturday-morning pancakes, wearing his silly chef's hat and singing "Volare" at the top of his lungs in his best Dean Martin voice. And while I'm nowhere close to acceptance in the so-called seven stages of grief, I know that's impossible. Still, he deserves better than Colma, where two million dead people live.

The San Francisco suburb was turned into a necropolis in the 1920s because the city banished all its graveyards. No one can afford to live in San Francisco, let alone be dead there.

The town's motto is "It's great to be alive in Colma."

I can attest that it's not. It's depressing as hell.

But my mother is emphatic that Jews don't do cremation, that it's only for "the pagans." My mother's relationship with God and Judaism is based solely on convenience. That is to say, she wields both like a sword when she's set on getting her way. The last time we actually set foot in a synagogue was for my brother's bar mitzvah, twenty-three years ago.

But that's not why I'm thinking of my mother at this moment. I'm wondering whether my late father would rather be buried next to her than Brooke. She was, after all, his wife of thirty-seven years, the mother of his three children, and the love of his life. So, when the time comes, will he choose Mom over Brooke in the afterlife, knowing that you only get to take your one true love with you into eternity?

We'll never know, I guess. But in my own time of grief, I think about it a lot. I think about Josh and me and our enduring love for each other. How there's no doubt in my mind that when my turn comes, I will be Josh's plus-one in the hereafter.

"What are you doing?" My brother, Adam, pulls me away from the open grave. "Come on, Rach, everyone's waiting."

He ushers me inside the funeral home, where the rent-a-rabbi greets me with a sympathetic smile. My mother waves me over to the seat next to her. The front row has been reserved for family only, and I can't help but notice how alone Brooke looks amid the rest of the Golds. We're a clannish lot, and from day one she's been persona non grata for obvious reasons. But today I feel a smidgen of solidarity with my stepmother. After all, we're part of the same club now.

She takes her place on the right side of my brother-in-law, who is too absorbed with looking at his phone to notice. My sister pokes him in the arm, a not-so-subtle hint that he's being disrespectful. This is when I normally would turn to Josh, and a silent acknowledgment that Stephen is a douchebag would pass between us. For some reason that makes me laugh out loud.

My entire family is staring at me now with a mixture of embarrassment and pity.

Adam takes my arm. "You okay, Rach?"

I nod, but I'm not okay. I don't know if I'll ever be okay again.

Mourners are still filtering in, and it strikes me that soon the chapel will be standing room only.

My mother whispers, "I knew we should've gone with the larger sanctuary." She turns to Adam. "Ask the director if we can squeeze in more chairs along that aisle over there." She gives a Vanna White wave, indicating the space near the door.

"Ma, they're not going to block the exit. It's probably against fire code."
My mother shoots him a look. He rolls his eyes and goes off to do her
bidding.

The rabbi and the Ackermanns are huddled in a corner, speaking in
hushed tones. I look over at Hannah, but from her body language I can
tell she and Stephen are fighting. For a second, Brooke meets my gaze,
and I quickly turn away.

On the other side of the room, three rows up, Campbell and Jess scootch
through the aisle and grab two of the last remaining seats. Campbell
catches my eye and holds his hand to his heart. The gesture both warms
and angers me at the same time, which isn't fair. None of this is his fault.

I face forward, knowing I should probably join the Ackermanns and
the rabbi, but am unable to move. I decide to let the Ackermanns make the
final arrangements. I'm too checked out to contribute anyway.

By the time the rabbi takes the dais, I'm somewhere else entirely. A
bench in Fiji with Josh. We went there for our honeymoon, which was sort
of a strange choice given that neither of us are beach people. But Josh's
friend had taken a similar trip the year before, and Josh picked the same
hotel in Viti Levu on his recommendation. I'd never seen water that blue
or coral reefs so vividly colorful. The entire week had been blissful.

I relive every second of the trip as the rabbi recites the opening prayer.
Something from the book of Psalms, according to my program. A few
seats down, I hear Josh's mother sob. My mom reaches over Adam and
takes her hand.

When it comes time for the eulogy, I only half listen, lost in my own
grief. I've chosen not to speak, knowing that there are not enough words
for all the things I want to convey. Besides that, I'm feeling deeply selfish,
wanting to hoard my memories for myself.

One by one, friends and family tell stories that range from funny to
poignant. Adam has been designated to speak on behalf of the Golds.
Despite my mother nagging him to write out his speech, Adam does it
off the cuff. He talks about the first time I brought Josh home to meet
my family and how Mom made her famous roasted chicken—famous
because it's one of the few dishes my mother makes. The story has become
legend in our family. And when Adam tells the part about how my mother
mistakenly coated the chicken with cayenne pepper instead of paprika,
the room erupts in solemn laughter.

"It was trial by fire," Adam says. "We knew Josh passed the test when
he went in for a second helping."

Even I find myself smiling at the memory. Then I silently sob until my whole body shakes. Hannah stuffs a wad of tissue in my hand, and I surreptitiously blot my eyes. I don't want anyone to see me cry, which is patently ridiculous. But like I hoard my memories, I also want to hoard my sadness. It's mine and mine alone.

The eulogizing goes on too long, and the rent-a-rabbi signals that we need to wrap things up. We only have the chapel for ninety minutes. The *El Malei Rachamim* is first chanted in Hebrew, then English.

"God, full of mercy, who dwells above, provide a sure rest on the wings of the Divine Presence, amongst the holy, pure and glorious who shine like the sky, to the soul of Joshua Seth Ackermann, son of Saul Joseph Ackermann, for the sake of charity which was given to the memory of his soul...And he shall rest peacefully at his lying place and let us say: Amen."

"Amen."

Our family is whisked away to a private room in preparation for the funeral procession.

I chose four of Josh's closest friends to be pallbearers. Two of them are from Chicago, where Josh grew up. The other two are from Martin, Owens and Luckett, Josh's architecture firm. For a fleeting second, I wonder if Campbell will feel slighted that I didn't choose him.

The burial service goes by in a blur. For most of it, Adam's arm is slung around me as if to hold me up. It's not until the mourner's kaddish that I break down, though. It's not the prayer itself, which I don't understand because it's in Hebrew. It's the finality that it represents. Josh is never coming back. The thought of it squeezes my chest like a tourniquet.

Afterward, I ride with my mother and the Ackermanns in the limo (part of the Eternal Home package) to the house on Vallejo Street. Brooke has graciously lent it to us for the funeral reception. Josh's and my apartment is too small, and Mom's townhouse is in the middle of construction hell. She's been remodeling for the last six months.

The minute we walk into the Queen Anne, I'm embraced with a sense of warmth and familiarity. It's ironic because the home is the size of a museum and more than a hundred years old. It should be drafty and stodgy, but it floods me with so many happy memories that I'm momentarily vaulted back in time. Even Josh, who preferred steel and black glass and precise lines, loved this house. He used to say, "Oh the stories this Victorian could tell." It definitely knew our story. The story of the Golds.

My mother heads to the kitchen, where she immediately starts delegating. The caterers have arrived, and she's rifling through the china cabinet in the butler's pantry, handing them serving platters. I look at Brooke and my face heats. *This is not your house anymore,* I want to tell my mother. Brooke gently rests her hand on my wrist. "Let me make you up a plate before everyone gets here."

I'm not hungry, but I nod. My mother continues to bustle around the kitchen like a military commander, expediting the massive quantities of food she's ordered to the dining room. Brooke fixes me a bagel sandwich from one of the deli trays and leads me to the front parlor.

Today, she is warm and ingratiating, a side I've never seen before.

The parlor looks mostly the same as when I lived here, though I can't help but notice that the millwork could use a fresh coat of paint and the furniture looks a little worse for wear. The photos of my parents that once adorned the mantel have been replaced with pictures of my late father and Brooke. I'm sure they've been there for a while. But for some reason I'm just noticing them now, noticing how old my father looks standing next to Brooke in her simple sheath dress. On the sofa table is a wedding portrait of Josh and me taken in the backyard. My throat clogs just looking at it.

Hannah and Stephen are the first to arrive. Stephen pats my shoulder and disappears down the hallway.

My sister eyes the plate on my lap. "How you holding up, Rach?" She's at least the tenth person to ask me that today.

"Hanging in there," I say and make room for her to sit next to me on the sofa. But she heads off in search of Stephen.

Soon, the house is buzzing with people. The Ackermanns are surrounded by members of Josh's firm. I'm glad his parents are getting to see them again. Josh was a rock star at Martin, Owens and Luckett. His last project won an AIASF design award. I'm hoping his colleagues brag on Josh. I love his parents, but they never got over the fact that their only child didn't follow in Saul's footsteps by becoming a prominent Chicago lawyer. That, and not marrying his high school sweetheart, who now works for Saul's law firm. Instead, Josh settled for the adrift San Francisco girl who failed to give them a grandchild.

"What are you doing over here alone?" Adam grabs my sandwich and takes a big bite.

I shrug. "How long do you think I have to stay?"

"Probably to the end. Anything else would look weird, don't you think?"

Typically, Adam would be the last person on earth who I'd ask an etiquette question. But in this instance, I know he's right. Thank God I nixed the whole sitting shiva thing (my mother's idea, which the Ackermanns and I quickly nipped in the bud). Seven days of sitting on stools and mourning while friends and family call to pay their respects sounds like the seventh ring of hell. Besides, Josh would've hated it. Or maybe not. He did so love being the center of attention. Me? Not so much.

"Are the Ackermanns staying with you tonight?" Adam nudges his head in their direction.

"They've been staying at the Mark Hopkins and are going back to Chicago tomorrow." I'd invited them to stay with me but am secretly glad they chose the hotel.

"The Mark Hopkins, huh?" Adam lets out a low whistle, then glances across the room at Brooke, who is being held hostage by my late father's Aunt Rose. "What's up with Dad's child bride?"

"What do you mean?"

"Why is she being so nice?"

"I don't know." It isn't like Brooke is an ogre. But we haven't been all that kind to her over the years, starting with the fact that Adam, Hannah and I nicknamed her the child bride behind her back. My mother is less tactful. She calls Brooke the *kurveh,* Yiddish for prostitute, to her face.

Mom also hasn't gone unscathed in the name game. Little does she know that long before the divorce, her darling children gave her the moniker of Mommie Dearest. Adam used to run through the house, wearing her lipstick, screaming, "No more wire hangers."

"I suppose she thought Dad would've wanted her to offer up the house. We grew up here after all."

"Maybe." Adam takes another bite of my sandwich. "The place looks like shit. You see the walkway out front? I nearly killed myself tripping over the crumbling brickwork."

It is a big estate to keep up, especially for one person. "She probably hasn't had a chance to think about it." Dad had only been gone a year. I know it'll take me at least that long before I have the wherewithal to think about anything other than Josh and all I've lost.

Adam rolls his eyes. "Yeah, she's too busy counting Dad's money."

The general consensus is that Brooke is a "Gold" digger (see what I did there?). The late David Gold was twice her age and one of the most sought-after plastic surgeons in California, maybe even the country.

Adam takes the plate off my lap and rests it on the coffee table, then takes my hands in his. "What are your plans for tonight? You shouldn't be alone, Rachel."

All I want is to be alone. Over the last week, I've been surrounded by people and feel smothered. Though everyone means well, the platitudes only make me sadder. I've never felt this weary, not even when my father died, and plan to spend the foreseeable future curled up in a ball on our king-size bed, clinging to Josh's pillow.

"Mom will drive you crazy. And Hannah and Stephen..." He trails off but we both know what is being unsaid. My sister and brother-in-law are too wrapped up in their own problems to be of any help to mine.

"Stay with me, Rach," Adam continues. "We'll watch old movies and get high."

It's a sweet offer, but I don't want to stay with Adam. First off, I'm pretty sure he has mice. Last time I was there, I saw what looked like droppings. And second of all, I need space to digest everything that has happened. Space to mourn by myself.

"We'll see," I say because it's easier than simply saying no.

Across the parlor, in the hallway, I catch a glimpse of Campbell and Jess in conversation with my sister and my best friend, Josie, and am momentarily distracted. The last thing I want to do is talk to Campbell right now. So, I make an excuse to Adam that I have to use the bathroom and slink away through the dining room, then quickly climb the stairs to my old bedroom. It looks exactly the same as when I left it sixteen years ago. Same lavender walls, same antique iron bed, same appliqué bedspread, same tulle canopy from the Limited Too catalog.

I sit on the edge of the mattress and take in a deep breath, enjoying a modicum of calm for the first time since Saturday, which seems like a lifetime ago. I know it's only a matter of time before my mother, Hannah or even one of the Ackermanns comes looking for me. In the meantime, I plan to take advantage of the solitude. It's probably rude because everyone has come to mourn Josh and offer me condolences. But for once in my life, I'm going to ignore protocol and let myself hide for a little while.

I slip off my shoes, lie on the bed and promise myself that I'll only close my eyes for a few minutes. As I drift, I can almost feel the mattress dip and Josh moving next to me. His warm breath trails my neck like a feather as he wraps his body around me. A combination of his aftershave and soap soothes me like a lullaby. And then he whispers, "Night, Rach," as sleep claims me and takes me far away from grief and funeral parties.

Part 2
Before Josh Dies

Chapter 2
Seven Years Ago

This is how it started.

I met Josh at a bar. Well, I actually met him on the street in front of the bar. It's kind of a funny story.

Campbell had called earlier that day and asked to rendezvous at the Round Up, an old-man saloon turned gastropub south of Market. I hadn't seen him in forever—his fault, not mine—and he wanted to get together. It's complicated between us, and half the time I don't know where I stand with him.

It didn't used to be that way. Before I accidentally got pregnant and lost our baby to a miscarriage ten years ago at the tender age of seventeen, Campbell was my first everything. My first kiss, my first love, my first sexual experience. My first real heartbreak.

I try not to think about our past because what happened, what we lost, can't be changed. Funny how someone can go from being the center of your world to a casual friend. At least that's what we're trying for. Friends.

So, I'm circling the block, hoping it won't be weird tonight.

But anyone who has ever lived in San Francisco can tell you that parking on Folsom at seven on a Friday night is a bitch. The perfect time to snag a parking space is a skosh past six. That's when the meters stop running and everyone is headed home from work. The window of opportunity is short, though, as residents in the neighborhood vie for the now-empty spaces and fifteen hours of uninterrupted free street parking.

It used to be that I could wedge my MINI Cooper into the odd miniscule space between driveways. But now the entire city is awash in MINI Coopers.

I circle at least a half dozen more times until finally a BMW pulls away from the curb. It's only two blocks from the Round Up. Jackpot! I hang a quick U-turn in the middle of the street before anyone can snatch the vacant spot. I'm not an aggressive person by nature, but when I get behind the wheel, I become my mother's daughter, a raving lunatic.

It's not until I pull into the space that I realize the curb is marked yellow. A loading zone. Shit! I'm about to pull away and go in search of a real spot when I get lit up by an SFPD motorcycle cop.

"I see it," I call through my open window, indicating the yellow curb. Still, I'm unsure if he can hear me through his helmet with his motorcycle idling.

He kills the engine and approaches. "Do you know why I stopped you?" I give him a blank stare.

He stares back. "You made a U-turn in a business district."

Yeah, I think. *So what?*

He must read the giant question mark in my expression, because he says, "It's illegal."

Before I can try to talk him out of citing me, he's scribbling in his pad. Ten minutes later, I pull into traffic with a $234 ticket sitting on my passenger seat. Next month's rent is due on the first, and I have no idea how I'm going to pay it, let alone the extra $234. I'm barely scraping by selling real estate, a sad commentary on my skills as a salesperson in a city where the median home price is well over a million dollars and every agent I work with is making a fortune. My father says I just don't have that killer instinct, which I suppose is a nicer version of my mother's "You're wasting your life." Sort of rich coming from a woman who never worked a day in her life, but not exactly wrong.

I'm tempted to call Campbell and tell him I give up. The Prius in front of me has now circled the block twice in search of the holy grail. But the parking gods must sense that I'm at my wits' end, because mercifully a spot opens up when a Honda Civic pulls out in front of me. I parallel park my MINI with all the grace of a drunk, having to attempt it multiple times before I'm even with the curb.

It's three blocks to the Round Up. I grab my coat from the back seat and wait for traffic to ease up before I open my door.

I'm halfway to the Round Up when someone comes up behind me. "Hey, hold up."

My first instinct is to get to the bar as fast as possible. I'm somewhat mollified by the fact that there are quite a few people out walking, but I still lengthen my stride. A few weeks ago, a woman was attacked in broad daylight right in front of my mother's building. Or at least that's what she told me. Her penchant for exaggeration is legendary in our family. Still, a person can never be too careful.

The man is beside me now. And while he doesn't appear to be a homicidal maniac, one can never tell. I've seen too many true-crime shows to let a cashmere coat and a pair of perfectly creased slacks fool me.

"I saw what happened back there," he says.

I don't have the first clue what he's talking about. "What happened?" I pick up the pace, convinced that he's a well-turned-out nutjob.

"That cop that stopped you and gave you a ticket."

Oh, that.

"What was it for? Flipping an illegal U-turn?"

I stop. "Did you know you're not allowed to turn around in a business district?" Because it's the first I've heard of it. I'm wondering if the cop, worried about making his quota, made it up on the spot.

"Sure. Everyone knows that."

I shoot him a look, and he laughs. It's one of those deep, rumbling laughs that vibrates in his chest and makes me feel immediately at ease.

"How much?" He makes the money sign with his fingers.

"Two hundred and thirty-four bucks. Can you believe it?"

He whistles and shakes his head. "That sucks."

"Yeah, it does." It's my first ticket. Truth is I didn't get my driver's license until I was twenty-three and didn't own my own car until I started selling real estate two years ago. "What happens if I don't pay it?"

"San Quentin. They'll lock you up forever." He smiles, and my eyes are drawn to the cleft in his chin. "But seriously, you've gotta pay it. The fine accrues over time, and eventually they'll impound your car. I might be able to help you out with the two hundred and thirty-four bucks, though."

I instantly go on creep alert. Instead of waiting for what is sure to be a proposition, I continue heading to the Round Up, hoping to shake him once I get to the bar. Undeterred, he follows me inside, where a rush of warm air greets us. I search the place for Campbell, but he's nowhere to be found.

We both take a seat at the concrete bar. Everything from the live-edge wooden banquettes and wallpaper with meat-cut diagrams to the bare Edison light bulbs and Radiohead music in the background screams hipster. It's probably why I don't come here often.

He grabs a cocktail napkin off a stack in the far corner, scribbles something on it and slides it over to me. I look down where he's written "Born to Run" and stare up at him quizzically. *What does Bruce Springsteen have to do with my ticket?*

"It's a horse," he says. "He's racing tomorrow at Golden Gate Fields, and I got a hot tip he's a winner." He bobs his chin and says, "You're welcome."

I can't tell if he's joking, but I fold up the napkin and stuff it in my purse anyway. It isn't what I was expecting. I'll give him points for that. "Thanks."

"You bet."

"So, are you like a compulsive gambler?"

He laughs that really great laugh again.

"Nope," he says. "But a friend of mine is. He's the one who gave me the tip."

He attempts to flag the bartender over, but she's at the other end of the bar, flirting with a couple of businessmen. "You want a drink? I just landed my dream job and am buying. Figure it's good karma."

I don't think karma works like that, but who am I to turn down a free drink? "Sure." I study him for the first time since we've met and lose my train of thought as I stare into a pair of nice brown eyes.

Actually, nice is an understatement. They're gorgeous, the kind of brown eyes that have the power to mesmerize.

He also happens to have one of those perfectly proportioned faces. It's square with a forehead that's roughly the same width as his chin. His jawline—I'm a sucker for jawlines—is well defined. I once read that women subconsciously equate strong jawlines with high sperm counts and cringe a little at the objectification. Yet my mind still goes there.

He grins as if he knows exactly what I'm thinking. And for a second I can feel my cheeks heat. Then, just as quickly, my armor goes on. I still can't figure him out. Odds are he's either married or on the prowl for a hookup. I don't do married men—or hookups. Though I'd be lying if I said the latter isn't tempting. It's been a while, and this stranger is doing something funny to my insides. I turn away, afraid he'll read my thoughts.

The woman next to me is eating a soft pretzel that smells so good it makes my stomach rumble. As I remember, the place has good food, even if it is pretentious. Lots of elevated beer bites like truffled corn nuts, mini lamb corndogs and buffalo sliders. I consider ordering something because I'm starved but decide to wait for Campbell.

"So what's the job?" I ask him, half hoping, half not, to catch him in a lie.

"Martin, Owens and Luckett." He nudges his head at the door as if it's just outside.

I shrug. "Law firm?"

"Nope, only the best architecture firm in the city." He smiles again, and this time I notice his teeth and wonder if they've been capped; they're that freakishly white. "I was coming out of their building when I saw the cop pull you over."

"You're an architect?" I immediately think of George Costanza's alter ego, Art Vandelay, in *Seinfeld* and how he boasted about designing the new wing of the Guggenheim to impress a woman.

"I am," he says with a cocky nod that simultaneously turns me on and off. But mostly on.

The bartender finally makes an appearance and takes our drink orders. I get a glass of Prosecco, which is probably a weird choice for a gastropub. But they serve it, so it can't be that weird. Art Vandelay gets a beer on tap and doesn't so much as flinch when the bartender says, "That'll be $20.95."

"I used to be with JBR Design," he continues. "But their specialty is residential. My background is in commercial buildings. Restaurants, retail, that sort of thing. You ever been to Rabbits? That's my work," he says before I have a chance to answer. "The chef's a dick. I once saw him reduce a contractor to tears and can only imagine how he treats his cooking staff. I bet I'll open the paper one day and read that his sous chef hacked him to death with a meat cleaver and the cops ruled it justifiable homicide. But the dude's got impeccable taste. He pretty much let me do whatever I wanted. And it didn't come cheap.

"So what do you do?" He looks at me expectantly, and I'm struck by the fact that we're probably around the same age and he's already designed one of the premiere restaurants in San Francisco.

"I'm in real estate," I say, leaving it vague because my biggest claim to fame is that I once was the listing agent for the governor's best friend's sister. A flat in a tenant-in-common building in Cole Valley that I got through my father because he did the woman's nose.

"Oh yeah? Residential or commercial?" His eyes slowly drift over me, and I can't tell whether he's trying to assess the measure of my success from my clothes or if he's checking me out.

"Residential."

"Nice. Good market for it. You hungry?" He glances at the bartender, who's on her way from across the bar with our drinks.

I'm tempted to say yes, but Campbell will be here any minute. "I'm waiting for someone."

His gaze drifts up and meets my eyes. "I should've known you weren't single."

I can't tell if he's feeding me a line. But I don't bother to clarify the statement. I'm still trying to figure him out. As my father likes to say, "If it seems too good to be true, it probably is."

"I'm Rachel, by the way. Rachel Gold." I reach into my purse and hand him my business card, telling myself it's good networking, him being an architect and all and me being a real estate agent.

"Josh Ackermann." He riffles through his wallet for a card and writes his number on it. "The card is only good for two more weeks, then I start my new gig. But I'm always reachable by cell." He points to his handwriting and smiles again.

He has a smile that packs a punch, and for a second I can't breathe. I sip my Prosecco, trying to act unaffected.

"So, you planning to bet on that horse?" He points his chin at my handbag.

I've only gambled twice in my life, once on a family trip to Vegas when I was twelve and my father let me sneak a pull of the handle on a dollar slot machine, and again when I was at Century 21 and the office manager set up a betting pool to predict the date one of the agents would give birth. Both times I lost.

"I'll go with you...bring you luck," he says a little tentatively, like a puppy dog hoping for a treat.

I don't want to commit but have to admit I'm intrigued by the man. He's different than your average San Francisco guy. Not in tech, which is a plus. Doesn't wear the obligatory hoodie (how I long for a man who wears actual grown-up clothes). And more than likely, judging by the way he appears to be hitting on me, not gay, which is kind of huge in this town.

He looks away from me and eyes the menu. "What's good here? I'm starved."

He's left the ball in my court as far as the racetrack, which I'm still undecided about. I like that he's not pushy.

I gaze over at his menu and do a quick perusal of the appetizers. "I've only been here a few times, but everything was good."

"I'm thinking the nachos, fully loaded." Once again, he beckons over the bartender, who's moved on to a couple she seems to know and has been talking to for the last ten minutes.

She reluctantly leaves her conversation and takes his order.

"So where are you from, Rachel Gold?" He leans over and swipes a handful of the complimentary snack mix from one of the bowls scattered across the bar. To me, it looks like the Chex stuff my old babysitter used to make. But knowing this place, it's probably coated in truffle oil or made with lardo.

"Right here," I say and leave out the part that for most of my life I grew up in Pacific Heights. Call it middle-class guilt, though I have nothing to be guilty about. It's my father's money not mine. As my mother is fond of saying, I "don't have a pot to piss in." "How 'bout you?"

"Chicago. I came out when I got accepted to Cal's master's program and never left. I love this city." He stares up as if he's looking at the skyline but is just as enamored to find a trail of exposed ductwork.

"You don't have an accent," I say, thinking of Dan Aykroyd in *The Blues Brothers.*

"Neither do you."

"We don't have accents here."

"Yeah you do. Kind of a Brooklyn thing, just a little milder."

He's talking about the so-called Mission Brogue. According to urban legend, Irish and Jewish people from the East Coast brought their penchant for pronouncing "store" as "stawh" and "third" as "thoid" with them when they settled in the city during the Gold Rush. But in my twenty-seven years, I have never heard a native San Franciscan speak with anything close to a New York accent.

"It's a myth," I say. "We all speak like the Kardashians."

The bartender arrives with the nachos, and Josh pushes the plate toward me. "Share with me, Rachel Gold." Those amazing brown eyes meet mine, and he holds my gaze, which I feel all the way down to my toes.

Still, I'm apprehensive. I've never been a player when it comes to picking up guys in bars. And honestly, my parents' recent divorce has made me gun-shy. I look away and pluck a cheese-covered chip off the plate and pop it in my mouth.

"Mm, good." I point to the platter. "You should try one."

He swallows a smile as if he knows he's made inroads with those peepers of his. Then he props his elbows on the bar and rests his chin in his hands. "So, tell me about your day."

I laugh because he makes it sound like we're a couple. "Let's just say my traffic ticket was the coup de grâce."

"The coup de grâce?" He lifts a brow, and I'm not sure if he doesn't know what the phrase means or if he's mocking me for using it.

"That bad?" he asks.

I don't know why, but I start telling him about the morning I had with my father's child bride. "My dad twisted my arm to have breakfast with my stepmother."

"I gather you don't like her."

"Nope." I pop the *p.* "She's only eight years older than me, and I'm the youngest of three. My father's sixty."

Josh grimaces. "Wow. That's some shit right there."

Yes, it is. But he doesn't know the half of it.

"So why'd you go?"

"He told me she knows someone who wants to list their house."

This time, he raises both brows in censure. Now he thinks I'm a real estate whore.

"What?" I say defensively. "It's an Edwardian in Noe Valley with a garage."

He nods, clearly comprehending the significance of such a listing. "Did you get it?"

I roll my eyes because after having to suffer through an entire breakfast with Brooke, it turns out the person doesn't want to list until summer. That's nearly four months away, when the market is flooded. "Not yet."

"You will." He says it so confidently that I start to believe it myself. Yet that isn't the way life has been going for me lately. "How is it that your father wound up with junior, anyway?"

The whole thing is such a cliché I'm almost too embarrassed to tell him. But I think, *Why not?* I'll probably never see him again after today. "She works for him. He's a plastic surgeon, and she's his nurse," I say.

He chuckles. "Wow. Was he married to your mom when they got together?" he asks more soberly.

"Yep. Your classic midlife-crisis affair. He didn't even wait for the ink to dry on their divorce before rushing off to City Hall with Brooke. We keep expecting him to realize his mistake, but he's still with her."

Josh doesn't say anything, but I can see the wheels turning in his head. *Maybe he loves her.* I've actually thought it a time or two myself. But while there's no question that Brooke is beautiful—and young—what could a man who is nearly twice his wife's age have in common with her? My mother can be difficult, but she was his soul mate, his intellectual equal. Hell, they've known each other since they were twelve, for God's sake. How do you just throw that away?

I filch another chip from the plate and this time dip it in the chipotle sour cream.

Josh is watching me, a little smile playing on his lips. "What happened to the person you were meeting?"

And that's when I realize Campbell never showed up. And for once I don't care.

Chapter 3
Fast Forward a Year

My mother is about to lose her mind. I think she's more nervous than I am, and I'm the one getting married.

It's been a whirlwind since Josh proposed three months ago. It wasn't his first time popping the question. He'd actually gotten down on one knee at the racetrack of all places. It hadn't even been an official date. Just him trying to make good on our first meeting's promise to win me enough money to pay off my traffic ticket.

That hadn't worked out too well. His horse—rather his roommate's horse, which we razzed him mercilessly about—came in dead last. I literally thought the poor thing would collapse before making it to the finish line. It seemed to be hyperventilating, if a racehorse can hyperventilate. Foam was coming out of its mouth, and even from the cheap seats I could see its long muscular legs wobble like a toddler learning to walk. By the time the race was over, I was just happy that Born to Run didn't keel over in the middle of his lane.

A remorseful Josh knelt on the cold bleacher, took my hand in his, and said the only way to make it up to me was by asking me to be his wife. He would be my slave forever.

"Don't press your luck," I told him as a small crowd looked on, laughing. But even then, I knew the chances were good that he was the one.

Josh Ackermann took my breath away.

Then, three months ago, he proposed for real. It was your typical San Francisco day. In other words, gloomy and cold. On a clear morning, his apartment had a peekaboo view, real estate speak for if you smash your face against the window and crane your neck until it hurts, you might catch a glimpse of the Golden Gate's less famous stepchild, the Bay Bridge. But on this particular day, the fog hovered over the bay like a thick shroud, and you couldn't see anything except for a few neighboring buildings.

Josh, a Rat Pack revivalist, turned on some Frank Sinatra (vinyl only) and brought me breakfast in bed.

"So, Rach, are we going to raise our kids in the Jewish faith?"

Josh was as Jewish as I was, which was to say we enjoyed really good deli food, had memberships at the JCC because it had a fantastic gym, and had discussed attending services for the High Holy Days because Josh's best friend and his best friend's girlfriend were doing it. Apparently you had to get tickets months in advance. We'd also attended the Ackermanns' annual seder in Chicago, where I met his parents for the second time and managed to choke down four glasses of Manischewitz.

But kids...We'd never so much as broached the subject.

"I guess so," I said and popped a strawberry in my mouth, wondering if Josh was just screwing around or if there was deeper meaning to the question. "I never really thought about it," which was a lie. I thought about kids—mine and Josh's kids—constantly. But we never talked about it because it was one of those taboo topics. Not just because of the baby I had lost with Campbell. I've tried for years to move on from that, to lock it away, but it's always right there under the surface. That sense of loss, and even failure, never quite leaves you.

But I also feared that talking babies with Josh would make me sound desperate. The whole biological clock thing. By my count, I had roughly nine years left of prime child-bearing time. But if a person wasn't too careful, nine years could go by in a blur.

He got back in bed and stole a strawberry off the plate. "You think about us?"

"All the time."

"Me too," he said and took my hand under the covers, lacing his fingers through mine. "What do you say we get married?"

As far as proposals go, it isn't the most flowery or romantic. But it's us. Real. Not like those people who propose over a giant scoreboard at the baseball game or hide the ring in the dessert at the French Laundry or write "Will you marry me?" in an explosion of pyrotechnics. Not that there's anything wrong with that. It just isn't our style. Ours is Sinatra, strawberries, and turkey bacon on a cold June morning in bed.

And today, we're doing it. We're merging our two lives. Josh likes to joke that if we smooshed our two names together a la Brangelina (pre-breakup of course), we'd be Rash.

Dad's house—I refuse to call it Dad and Brooke's house—is decked out with a bazillion white roses. My mother insisted we hire Ran Gately, San Francisco's florist to the stars, to do the flowers. I'm pretty sure her ulterior motive was to cost my father as much as possible because he's picking up the tab for the entire wedding. The Ackermanns threw the rehearsal dinner at Rabbits. It was a nice tribute to Josh's work, and according to my mother, his parents *kvelled* all night.

I always knew I would someday be married here in my family home. I think I started planning my wedding when I was twelve. A few of those plans have changed, including the groom, who was supposed to be Campbell. But I'm surprised—and perhaps a little mortified—that a lot of my childhood fantasies about the perfect wedding have stayed the same. For example, Josh and I chose to hold the ceremony and reception outside. We put the chuppah, a white tulle canopy (okay, at twelve I envisioned it to be macrame but who does that?) covered in sprays of roses and hydrangea with two hundred white folding chairs on the lawn with a view of the bay in the background. It's even more spectacular than I imagined.

Yesterday, an event company set up a huge white tent in the backyard. Josh has quipped at least a dozen times that our wedding is like a mullet: "business in the front, party in the back." Honestly, it was barely funny the first time he said it. But I'm so happy, I refrain from socking him in the arm each subsequent time he brings it up.

Before the reception starts, someone from the company Mommie Dearest has hired has been tasked with lighting at least fifty floating tea light candles in the pool. With two bars—one for beer and wine and a second for mixed drinks and soda—and a labyrinth of buffet stations, it's the most bougie wedding known to mankind. But I've decided to let my middle-class guilt go for a day. Tomorrow, I'll let it fester, then donate to the food bank the commission from the Richmond studio I just sold.

Someone taps on the door of my parents' old bedroom, which Brooke has turned into a guest suite. She and my dad have taken one of the smaller suites as their bedroom. It's got to be weird for the child bride having the specter of my mother haunting every room of this big house.

My parents bought the Victorian before I was born. Back then it was a disaster, or as we like to call it in the real estate world, a contractor's special. The place had been a boarding house, then a halfway house, and eventually a rental. Rumor has it that one of the members of the Grateful Dead lived here before the band got famous. Then a sugar heiress purchased it with grand plans to bring it back to life. But she died in a yacht accident off the Amalfi Coast. The house just sat for years while her children and lawyers fought over her estate.

In that time, squatters had destroyed and stolen whatever charm was left in the home. The wealthy and irate residents of Pacific Heights welcomed my parents, the new owners, with open arms. But they had their work cut out for them. Back then, my father's cosmetic surgery practice was still in its infant stage, and the house had been way above my parents' means.

Still, my mother made it her full-time job to turn the Queen Anne into a showplace. She had the chipping walls replastered, the ornate cornices and medallions returned to the ceilings, and the missing millwork replicated and replaced. And that was just the beginning. The knob and tube electrical and iron plumbing needed to be brought up to date, and many of the windows had cracked.

I was not alive at the time, but my mother loves to tell the story of how she combed through every salvage store west of the Mississippi to find everything from period glass to a hundred-year-old chandelier that once hung in one of San Francisco's oldest bordellos. Who knows if the bit about the bordello is true? Shana Gold never let the facts get in the way of a good story.

But the house had always been their first child. From the time I was born, it was where every milestone of the Gold family was celebrated. Adam's bar mitzvah, Hannah's sweet sixteen, my high school graduation, my parents' numerous anniversary parties. Even our relatives and friends threw their special occasions at the house on Vallejo. My father's partner's daughter's quinceañera, my mother's best friend's third wedding, and my cousin Arie's coming-out party to name a few.

That's why we were all surprised when Mom let my father buy her out of the house during the divorce. While there was no way in hell she could afford to buy him out, let alone pay for the upkeep on an estate this size, we all expected her to fight dirty for it. Guilt is a great bludgeon when it comes to my dad. And my mother had the goods to send him to the poorhouse.

Instead, my father gave her half of everything they owned—including a note on his medical practice. She deposited her loot, bought a condo, and took art classes. We're still waiting for her to exact her revenge, knowing that when it happens, it'll be like Mount Vesuvius erupting.

I tell the person knocking at the door to come in, expecting it to be Whitney, the person who has been cutting my hair since I was sixteen and has promised to copy an updo in a picture I found on the internet. But it's not Whitney, it's Adam.

"I come bearing gifts," he says and waves a joint in the air. "I figure between Mom and Hannah, you could probably use this by now."

"You've got to be kidding?"

"Nope."

"I'm not getting high on my wedding day."

"Why not? Josh is."

My brother is a bad influence on Josh. He's a bad influence on everyone.

"Go in there and tell him to stop." I give Adam a little nudge, but he doesn't move.

"I was only joking, Rach."

"No you weren't." Adam always uses "I was only joking" whenever he's confronted with doing something inappropriate.

"He's fine. He says for me to say hi."

As tradition dictates, we haven't seen each other since early yesterday morning.

"Where's Mom?" I ask. Ten minutes ago, she went in search of Hannah. Now, both of them are missing in action. My best friend, Josie, went on the hunt for them, leaving me alone in the room. Until Adam.

"Probably eating the heads off small children."

"How about Hannah? Have you seen her?" Wasn't it just like my family to desert me on my wedding day?

"Last I saw her, she was giving Stephen a hummer in the pool house." Adam smirks, proud of his frat-boy humor.

"You're disgusting." It's the best I can do on short notice.

Adam plops down on the bed and sprawls out in his suit, not giving a care if it wrinkles. "You sure about this, Rach?"

"Sure about what?" I'm definitely sure I don't want to burn one with Adam only hours before I walk down the aisle. But somehow I know that's not what he's talking about.

"Sure about getting hitched?"

"Why would you even ask that?" I look at him like, really? Really, you want to do this right now? As if I don't have enough pressure. There are two hundred people milling around my father's yard, including the Ackermanns, who I'm pretty sure think their son could do better.

Adam shrugs. "It just seems sort of rushed."

"Rushed? We've been together a year. Besides, I thought you like Josh?"

"I do," he says. "This isn't about Josh. It's about you."

"What about me?" I stare at him, waiting for an answer, half hoping he won't say it, half hoping he will just so we can get it out in the open and dispense with it forever.

He shrugs again. "Nothing. Forget I said anything."

"Kind of hard to do now, Adam." I squint my eyes at him, then worry that I've smeared my makeup. The makeup that Josie, who used to work at the Lancôme counter at Nordstrom, painstakingly applied only an hour earlier.

"You're my baby sister, Rach. I just want to make sure you're happy and not under duress."

Yes, Josh has held a gun to my head to make me marry him. I shake my head because what the hell does that even mean? *Under duress.* "Please don't ruin the happiest day of my life."

He laughs. "You sound like Mom. Okay, I won't ruin the happiest day of your life. In fact, I place better odds on your marriage surviving than I do on Hannah and Stephen's. Hell, I place better odds on Mom and Dad getting back together than I do on Hannah and Stephen making it through their third year." Adam won't say it, but he's the one who is most bitter about Mom and Dad's breakup, though we all are.

But I'm curious what he knows about Hannah. From where I'm sitting, my big sister has the perfect life. She and her husband are both corporate lawyers, own a lovely Spanish revival in Redwood City, and are the epitome of a power couple.

"Why?" I ask and get up to stare at myself in the mirror, wondering what is taking everyone so long, including Whitney, who should've been here ten minutes ago.

"Just a gut feeling that trouble is headed to paradise. And there's the minor point that Stephen's a tool."

There is that. Though he's been supportive of Josh and me. "What do you know and why have you been holding out on me?"

Before he can answer, there's a light tap on the door and my mother and Hannah stroll in. Both Adam and I look at each other, worried that Hannah might've overheard our conversation.

But Josie and Whitney break the moment when they trail in behind my mother and sister. Jo's clutching a bottle of sparkling wine and two champagne flutes. Whitney's schlepping a duffel bag filled with hair care accoutrement and enough product to fill a salon.

"Look who I found?" my mother says and starts fussing with my dress, which is hanging on a hook on the back of the door.

"What took you so long?"

"I ran into Campbell and his new girlfriend downstairs. He came early to help his dad with the arbor and to make sure the sprinklers have all been turned off. He's such a good boy. And the girlfriend...Jessica...a real looker."

Adam sneaks a look at me, but I pretend not to notice, focusing instead on Hannah, who grabs one of the flutes and pours herself a glass of bubbly. Josie and I pass a knowing glance to each other. Isn't it just like Hannah to help herself to my wine without offering me a glass first? But I've promised myself that I won't be a bridezilla today. Despite the large guest list, I've vowed to keep everything low-key. The wedding party has been confined to just my sister, Josie, Adam and Josh's best friend. My father has been designated the sole Gold spokesman for the wedding toast. Otherwise, my mother is liable to say something bizarre and inappropriate:

"It seems like just yesterday when Rachel had her first period."

"Where is that little girl I caught in the pool house making out like a bunny in heat with Campbell?"

Likewise, Josh has chosen his dad to make the Ackermann toast. And that's it. No open mike night at the Ackermann-Gold wedding. For insurance, we've hired a DJ who moonlights as a bouncer at the Condor Club. No one is getting past him unless they're a sumo wrestler. He's also promised that all requests for the Macarena will be summarily ignored.

"Adam, don't you have groomsmen duties to attend to?" my mother asks pointedly and shoos him out of the room, calling, "And Campbell was looking for you."

Whitney commandeers one of the nightstands to set up her blow dryer, flat iron and brushes and pulls a chair in front of the full-length antique mirror that used to be in the guest suite that is now Dad and Brooke's room. Without a second thought, Hannah plops her ass into the seat and starts instructing Whitney on how she wants her hair. "Not too tight at the crown, with little whisps framing my face."

Josie and I exchange another look, and I resume my silent mantra of not turning into bridezilla. It doesn't stop me, however, from wishing my mother would remind Hannah that it's my day and not hers.

Josie hands me the remaining champagne flute and fills it until the bubbles spill over onto my robe. "Drink up."

We both stifle a giggle. Maybe a couple of tokes from Adam's joint wasn't such a bad idea. I wonder if Josh is in the other room lighting up a second doob with my brother. The thing about Josh is, even stoned, he'd slay at this wedding. I think of that Sammy Davis Jr. quote Josh constantly says: "I have to be a star like another man has to breathe."

My mother looks at her watch. "Rachel, honey, it's time to get ready. You don't want to be late for your own wedding."

I bob my chin at Hannah, whose curly hair has been tamed into a sophisticated version of a messy bun.

"Whitney, chop-chop, darling." Mommie Dearest actually snaps her fingers, and I feel a sting of mortification rise on my cheeks.

Whitney winks. "I've got this, Shana." She shellacks Hannah's hair with a tsunami of hairspray and gently pushes my sister out of the chair. "Be careful when you put on your dress not to mess up my masterpiece."

Hannah disappears inside the bathroom to change. Whitney whisks me into the spot Hannah's left while Josie pours me another glass of bubbly.

"Just a few sips," Mom tells me.

I bristle, but she's right. The previous glass has gone a little to my head. I barely ate at the rehearsal dinner and only had a small bowl of fruit for breakfast. But I feel a bit of nerves coming on—the idea of having two hundred pairs of eyes on me as I walk down the aisle makes my stomach roil like the first time I rode the Matterhorn in Disneyland—and the wine settles me.

And suddenly I wish we'd just gone to Vegas or to the beach or to the mountains, somewhere where it was just the two of us, our immediate families, and a few friends.

But then I think of Josh and how in less than an hour we'll be married. For some reason that song he always sings pops into my head. "I've got the world on a string...sittin' on a rainbow...what a world, what a life, I'm in love!" And a smile splits my face.

I must've checked out for a little while because my mother is saying, "Rachel, what's gotten into you? You're not even listening. I was telling you about Brooke."

The last thing I want to hear about on my wedding day is my father's paramour and my parents' failed marriage.

Hannah comes out of the bathroom and does a little twirl and my mouth falls open. Josie is staring too, and it takes a lot to impress my best friend. My older sister is about to upstage me at my own wedding. I let her and Josie pick their own dresses. My only rule was that they had to be the same shade of blue, something bordering on cerulean. Originally, I'd wanted black, but my mother said it was bad luck. I still don't know where she got that from, but who wants to risk it? So blue was my second choice.

And Hannah, who mostly wears blacks and browns and an occasional red power suit, is killing it. The dress brings out her blue eyes, which I've always been jealous of, mine being plain old brown. The bodice clings to her incredible rack, which is also a source of great envy. I barely fill a B cup. The only thing I have on her are my legs. They're long and toned and unfortunately will be hidden from view in my full-length gown.

As I stare at Hannah, I kind of wish I'd gone for a mini skirt. "Wow, you look amazing."

"You need a little bling. Everything is so plain," my mother says, and Hannah and I share a look before smothering a laugh. Good old Mom.

Whitney manages to copy my photo perfectly. And while I don't look anything like the model in the picture, I'm thrilled with the results. Hannah, Josie and Mom help me into my gown, which takes what seems like an eternity. Everyone is uber careful not to mess up my hair or get any makeup on the white satin crepe fabric. The dress is a knockoff of Pippa Middleton's bridesmaid dress from the royal wedding and clings to me like a wet T-shirt.

"Did you bring Spanx?" my mother asks, making me immediately self-conscious.

"No. I thought it would be good to breathe for the next four hours. Why? Do I look fat?"

"You don't need Spanx," Hannah says and shoots daggers at my mother. "You look beautiful, Rachel."

There are a million tiny buttons to do on the back of the dress, and Josie's nimble fingers have taken on the task. "You do look beautiful," she says. "I've never seen a more gorgeous bride. Oh my God, I'm going to cry."

And that right there is the reason Josie Blum has been my best friend since the fourth grade when the two of us bonded over s'mores at Ramah in the Sierra, otherwise known as Jew camp. She had me at "There are so many bugs here."

Unlike me, Josie has found her niche in the world (a saying I think my mother coined). Two years ago, she started her own personal shopping business, and now her clientele list includes a couple of Gettys, a former mayor, and a porn star. In other words, she's a big freaking deal while I'm still trying to launch. Not that I begrudge her the success. Just the opposite. Nothing makes me happier than for my people to reach the stars. But between Josie and Hannah, a girl could get an inferiority complex.

I turn to look at my reflection in the antique mirror and like what I see. I don't have Hannah's boobs or blue eyes. Or Josie's high cheekbones and bee-stung lips. I never did have Mom's bohemian style. But I look pretty and confident and, most of all, happy.

And why shouldn't I? Today I'm marrying Joshua Ackermann, the love of my life.

Chapter 4
Six Years After the Wedding

I'm not saying that Josh and I are perfect. Like any marriage, there are peaks and valleys. Times when the sex is perfunctory. Times when the sound of him slurping his cereal across the breakfast table makes me gnash my teeth. And times when he's a little too soft on me.

I've never told anyone this before, but sometimes I think Josh is relieved that I suck at my job. For example, a deal I'd been working on for a week fell through escrow yesterday. This morning, the seller fired my ass and is listing with another agent. Josh's reaction: "Rach, don't put so much pressure on yourself. It's not like we'll be thrown out on the street and have to move in with your mother." He says that last part with a shit-eating grin.

While I should probably thank my lucky stars that I have a supportive husband, I can't help but feel that his blasé attitude is more apathetic than empathetic. No, we won't wind up homeless. Nor will the loss of income put a dent in our grocery spending. But it will likely mean we'll have to put off buying a house for another year. And how about just the mere fact that it makes me feel like shit?

What if I told him not to let that bad review of 23rd Market Street he'd spent two years designing get him down? *Hey, it's only one review. So what if the reviewer was one of the premiere architecture critics in the country?*

Okay, to be fair, I've been phoning it in for the last five years of our marriage, selling only about three houses a year. But I can't help but think that if Josh didn't have such lovingly low expectations of me, I'd be doing more.

My father still insists I'm in the wrong vocation. And my mother says I'm not a people person, whatever that means. I suppose if I dug deep,

I'd realize that real estate really isn't my passion. Otherwise, I'd be better at it, right? But is there anything wrong with that? Millions—probably even billions—of people go to jobs every day that are just ho-hum, just a means to a living. No one blames them. No one thinks of them as sellouts or less thans.

So why can't I cut myself some slack?

"Back so soon?" I say as Josh walks in the door. I still haven't showered and am sipping my coffee, allowing myself to recover from the morning's debacle.

"I forgot my earbuds. I got as far as the Embarcadero when I realized they weren't in my backpack."

Most of the time, Josh rides his bike the four miles from our Marina District apartment to his office on Folsom. I have this horrible premonition that one day he'll have his music turned up too loud and not hear an oncoming car in time to avoid a collision. I read somewhere that an average of 742 bicyclists die a year in this country from fatal accidents.

Josh goes in search of his missing earbuds while I wash out the coffeepot and my dirty mug. I guess I better start my day, though I'd rather stay here and feel sorry for myself.

Our apartment is eleven hundred square feet, and I can hear Josh rooting around in our bedroom.

"You can't find them?" I call through the thin wall.

"Got 'em," he yells back. "They were in the dirty clothes." He comes into the kitchen and kisses me behind the ear, wrapping his arms around my middle until my back fits snugly against his chest. And for a while we just stand like that, our bodies so close that I can feel his heat.

"Don't get hit by a car," I say, breaking the moment. "You've got precious cargo on that bike of yours."

"Yeah, like what?"

"You."

He chuckles, then turns me around and kisses me again. This time he catches my lips with his mouth and takes his time, letting his tongue explore. It's such a good kiss that I still feel it on my lips an hour after he leaves.

Because I don't have any clients today, I leave the MINI Cooper in our coveted garage and walk to the office. Windham Real Estate. The company, which has three satellite offices, is independently owned and boasts 2.1 billion dollars in annual sales. I left Century 21, where I felt stifled, years ago. The other agents there were all a little too cutthroat for my taste.

Windham feels more like the city. Laid-back but at the same time exciting. The other agents, while hard chargers, are friendly and helpful. The fact that Windham has a state-of-the-art coffee bar (like seriously good coffee) and a generous eighty-twenty split is the cherry on top.

"Rachel, you're here." Janney, the office manager, is surprised to see me. I rarely come in these days, instead working from my laptop and cell phone from home.

"I'm here," I say with a weak smile. "Is Chip in?" I crane my neck around Janney to search the glass office at the rear of the agency for my broker. I want him to hear my side of the story before he gets the buyer's agent's version. Both of us happen to work for Windham, which puts Chip squarely in the middle.

"Niki's already here," Janney says, making it obvious she knows there's a conflict between us.

Despite Windham being a decent place to work, no one here is above watching a good catfight. The office staff, Janney and Chip included, trade on gossip like it's the opening bell of the New York Stock Exchange. In fact, before Chip got into real estate, he was a trader. Janney was an editorial assistant at the *San Francisco Chronicle* and was laid off two years ago when the newspaper downsized. Besides running the agency like a boss, she knows where all the bodies are buried.

"Is she in with Chip?"

"Yep." Janney clicks her tongue and gives me a look that says *You should've beaten her to the punch.* "I'd tell you to barge in, but I don't think Chip or Niki would appreciate it." She strides over to the coffee bar, pulls a shot of espresso, and hands me the cup. "Guess you better cool your jets until their meeting is over."

I walk over to one of the empty desks with my coffee and try to pretend I'm busy. The sad truth of it is I have nothing to do. I'm taking offers on my one and only listing, a janky two-bedroom, one bath in the Outer Sunset, next Tuesday. The market here is so obnoxious that even a shit box with bad plumbing that sits in the fog nine hours a day is enough to pit frenzied buyers against one another until they all offer well over the asking price. My seller is hoping for an all-cash offer with no contingencies from a buyer who is willing to waive the appraisal because God knows the house isn't worth what it will ultimately fetch. Josh, a pragmatist, would argue that a house is worth exactly what someone is willing to pay for it. Unfortunately, banks don't see it that way.

In any event, my seller will probably get everything on his wish list and then some. That's how crazy it is here. If I wasn't so upset about my other deal falling through, I'd probably be counting the commission in my head, prematurely spending it with wild abandon.

Chip's door swings open. From his chair, he holds it open with his foot and searches me out across the room. "Hey, Rachel, come in here for a sec."

I take a fortifying breath and a circuitous route to his office, passing the coffee bar, where I slip my cup into the dishwasher. Suddenly, I'm in no rush to have this conversation. Niki is still there, taking up Chip's blue loveseat with her Christian Louboutin tote bag, Burberry shawl, and larger than average ass. She's about my mother's age. The similarities between them stop there, though. My mother's attitude toward designer labels is, why should she pay an exorbitant price for a logo only to give the designer free advertising? Unlike Niki, who colors her hair an unnatural shade of red, my mother let hers go gray years ago. And unlike Niki's cosmetically enhanced face and neck—ass withstanding—Shana Gold has never gone under the knife, despite once being married to a renowned plastic surgeon. And still, everywhere my mother goes, she turns heads. She just has a certain style that's age defying.

But that's superficial bullshit. The thing about Niki is she's one of the hardest-working real estate agents in the business, continually named top salesperson in the city. She also has a client list that rivals Oprah's address book. Celebrities, athletes, politicians, billionaires, and tech moguls. Oh, and the occasional relative.

"Have a seat," Chip says.

I take the chair facing the window with a view of the gym across the street. There's enough tension in the room to start an electrical fire.

Chip breaks the awkward silence with, "Niki says you're a bad communicator."

"That's a nice way of putting it." Niki leans toward me, her hands on her knees and an almost bored expression on her face. Her bearing says, *You're not in my league, child, and now I'm going to bitch-slap you to kingdom come.* "What I said is that you cost this agency a hefty commission because of your incompetence."

What she really means is that her niece didn't get the house and I made her look bad.

"Niki, you know as well as I do that clients aren't always flexible, that they often believe their homes are worth more than the market will bear." It is a polite way of saying my seller was a greedy, delusional son of a bitch. He thought his Bernal Heights contemporary was an architectural masterpiece. Josh certainly didn't think so. He'd taken to calling the house "the toaster oven."

"Well, it's your job to make them understand what the market will bear," Niki says with a sneer. "For God's sake, Rachel, we were twenty thousand dollars apart. Twenty goddamn thousand dollars."

Really only ten when you take into consideration that Niki and I had agreed to scrape off some of our commission to close the deal. But at the last minute, Irving Toaster Oven Jones decided he wouldn't be nickeled and dimed for a home as significant as Fallingwater. He accused me of being "unscrupulous" and plotting with the buyer to "steal" his house out from under him.

"Niki, I did all I could do. It's not like I could force the guy to sell."

"Not force," Niki says through gritted teeth, "but a good agent"—she puts heavy emphasis on the word *good*—"has the power to persuade. You should've explained that this market won't last forever and that he should take the inflated price we offered and run."

As if I didn't say all those things. But when you think you own freaking Manderley, you don't listen to real estate agents. To Irving, I was no better than a worm.

"I have a listing for a nice house in the Outer Sunset your niece might like," I say, knowing it will provoke Niki beyond reason.

Before she can throw her Louboutin bag at me, Chip steps in. "Why don't we chalk this whole situation up to a learning experience and move on." Always the diplomat. Except Niki's hair looks like it's about to burst into flames.

She starts to say something when my phone rings. I glance at the caller ID. Mommie Dearest. Normally, I'd ignore the call, but it is an excellent excuse to extricate myself from Niki's wrath.

"Excuse me, I have to take this." I wave the phone in the air like it's Sam Zell on the line and hightail it to the conference room.

"Whassup?" My mother hates when I do that.

"Rachel?"

Who else would it be? It's my phone, for Pete's sake. "Mom, I'm in a meeting."

"Where are you?"

"At work...Windham."

"You need to get to San Francisco General as fast as you can. I'll call you an Uber."

"What are you talking about?" I'm waiting for her to tell me that Hannah has a hangnail or that Adam ate too many edibles. My mother is a bit of a drama queen and is never happier than when she's blowing up a minor incident into a mega tragedy. She can't remember what she had for breakfast but can recount the aftermath of Uncle Hersch's two-year-old hernia operation in excruciating detail. But today there's something in her voice that's different.

My mind immediately travels to Josh and his earbuds, and my heart races. "Mom, what's going on?"

"It's your father. He's had a heart attack."

Chapter 5
That Same Year

They say the dead come to you in your dreams. I keep waiting for my father, but he's a no-show. In hindsight, there are so many things I wish I'd told him. "Thank you for being the best father ever." And "Why did you leave Mom for a woman half your age and ruin our family?"

I've never cried so much in my life. But at least I got to say goodbye. We all did, even Mom. We stood around his bed, squeezing in between the life support machine, tubes and wires, telling him we love him until Brooke told the medical staff to pull the plug. And then, just like that, he was gone.

A half dozen times a day, I start to pick up the phone to call him before I remember. Despite how angry we were with him, he was still our rock. None of us made a move without consulting Dad first. Not even Hannah, the most independent and arguably the most successful of us Gold kids, was immune from leaning on him. Adam liked to say Hannah couldn't get dressed in the morning without Dad telling her what to wear. Yet Adam wasn't one to talk. My dad had been a key investor in Adam's startup and in some ways his business guidance counselor, though David Gold knew nothing about gaming or tech. What he did know was that his son liked to play more than he liked to work. Someone needed to crack the whip.

For me, Dad was...well, everything. My confidant, my reality check, my North Star.

I remember being thirteen and having my wisdom teeth pulled. The next morning was Heritage Day at school. I was bringing homemade mandel bread, the Jewish version of biscotti, to represent the food of my people. Most of the evening I labored with the dough from my grandmother's recipe only to realize that I'd dripped blood into the batter from my bruised mouth. The painkillers had begun to wear off, and the lower half of my face throbbed like it had been run over by a Mack truck. I sat, hugging the batter bowl to my chest, sobbing. I didn't have the wherewithal to start over. But I'd wanted to show off those cookies. For two days, I'd been mapping out my presentation with help from my *safta*. I spent hours on the phone with her at the nursing home, going over exactly what I should say during my speech.

My mother said she'd write me a note. My father took one look at the disappointment in my eyes and got to work mixing the ingredients for a new batch, sending me off to bed. The next morning, my mandel bread was wrapped and ready to go.

In those early days, when I was just starting out as an agent, Dad used to help me write the ad copy for my listings. Not only was his spelling and punctuation better than mine—he was the guy who carried a Sharpie with him into the supermarket so he could correct the occasional misspelled word on a sign—he had a knack for real estate lingo. "Cozy" was a home for a family of hobbits. "Needs a little TLC" was code for bring in a wrecking ball. And "Up and coming neighborhood" meant MS-13 was moving in.

The day before he died, we'd met for lunch at Original Joe's, his favorite restaurant, and he gave me a pep talk when I lamented that my career was a dumpster fire. It was an exaggeration of course. Dumpster fires are at least active. But I'd told him how I'd lost the deal on Irving Jones's toaster oven house. At that point, Irving hadn't canned me yet, but I could see it coming.

"Rachel," he said, tying a linen napkin around his neck the way he always did whenever he ate anything with red sauce. "You still haven't found what you're looking for." He grinned, realizing he'd just quoted Bono. "Things will work out with your client. But maybe you should go back to school, explore the things that make you happy. I never doubted that Hannah loved the law or that Adam would make a fine success out of his gaming company." He shook his head. "And to think I used to worry about that kid. But you...I don't think real estate is lighting you up, honey."

"Is plastic surgery lighting you up?" I asked.

Then he surprised me by saying, "No. I wanted to be a photographer."

It was the first I'd ever heard this. I couldn't recall him ever taking pictures with anything other than a run-of-the-mill old Nikon—and later an iPhone. The pictures were mostly of us kids. All the usual stuff. Us opening presents at Hanukkah, Adam in front of his first car, Hannah with her debate team, Josie and me at Jew camp. Not exactly the stuff of museums or coffee table books.

"Really? I didn't know that. What happened? Why didn't you pursue photography?"

With a wistful shrug, he said, "It made more sense for me to go to med school. It was the sure thing, you know?"

Only he would think fourteen years of college, medical school and residency was a sure thing.

I was still trying to wrap my head around this revelation, trying to picture my father as Ansel Adams. "What kind of photographer?"

"Photojournalist. At Yale I worked for the student paper. One of the photos I took wound up on the cover of the *New York Times*. A shot of a demonstration against William Shockley, who'd come to campus to spew his bullshit on eugenics."

"Wow. I had no idea. So do you have regrets? I mean, do you ever wish you would've done that instead?"

"I don't know. It was a long time ago," he said with a practiced nonchalance, which made me think he did.

"Was it because of Mom?" I blurted, assuming she wanted the luxuries a doctor's salary could provide. I didn't know how much photojournalists made, but my gut told me not as much as very sought-after cosmetic surgeons.

"Nah." He waved me off in a way that said she might've had something to do with his decision. "I chose stability over adventure. Back then it was the right decision."

"But not anymore now?" I pressed, intrigued by this new revelation.

"Rachel, I'm sixty-eight years old. You think I want to be running around in war zones a year away from retirement?" He laughed, but it sounded superficial, almost sad.

If I had known he was going to die the next day, I probably would've spent more time asking him about it. Instead, we moved on to Josh's and my plans to someday buy a house.

But when we parted ways after lunch, I couldn't help wondering if Brooke was my father's consolation prize for not becoming a photojournalist. Was she the substitute for all his regrets in life?

My buzzer goes off, snapping me out of my memory.

"I'll be right down," I say through the intercom.

Adam's Prius is parked in the loading zone in front of my building. His music is so loud I can hear it through his closed windows. I turn down the volume the minute I get in the passenger's seat. As usual, his car is a wreck. Fast-food wrappers litter the floor, and I have to lift up to clear away the stack of papers I didn't see when I first got in.

"You can toss those in the back," he says as he pulls out onto my street. "You ready to do this?"

"Not particularly. Better us than Brooke, though."

"I guess." There's a long pause, and then he says, "Do you think Mom wants anything?"

I take a deep breath because I've been wondering this myself. "I think she pretty much got everything she wanted in the divorce."

"Not the same thing," Adam says. "These aren't fragments of their marriage. This is Dad, man."

My mind immediately goes to the painting she got him for their last wedding anniversary together. It was a landscape of the giant redwoods in Humboldt County. When my father was doing his residency at Stanford, he was working around the clock. Even when he got time off, they were too broke to go anywhere. So they would drive up the coast to the redwoods and sleep in a tent under the stars. My father used to say it was better than the best Ritz Carlton because my mother was with him.

"I'll take the painting for her," I tell Adam, who nods.

"Is Hannah bringing Stephen?"

"I don't think so. He probably has to work."

"Stephen works a lot, doesn't he?" Adam doesn't have to spell it out because I know exactly what he's implying.

"So does Hannah," I say defensively.

"Hannah doesn't have dinner meetings with clients at ten at night."

"Hannah also doesn't work for Google."

Adam starts to say something, then stops. After a long pause, he says, "What about Josh? Is he coming?"

"He has a meeting but is coming over afterward."

Adam shoots me a sideways glance as if to say, *See what I mean? Josh is making the time because he knows this will be difficult, and you're important to him.*

"You think Brooke will hover over us?"

Adam laughs. "If she's not out looking for her next sugar daddy or at the bank, counting Dad's money. You see her pretending to be all broken up at the funeral?"

"Jeez, Adam, when did you get so judgy?" Of the three of us, my brother is the chill one, though you wouldn't know it from today. His hostility is permeating the car like one of those pine tree air fresheners.

He turns in his seat slightly, and I'm just about to tell him to watch the road when he says, "Sony made me an offer."

"What?" I do a double take. "To work for them?" I ask, confused.

"To sell them my company." He says this like he's angry, like how dare one of the wealthiest corporations in the world have the gall to approach him.

"Well, is it a good offer?" Because from his demeanor I'm thinking it's an insult. Maybe they've offered him a pittance of what the company is worth just so he'll go away. I've heard these kinds of things happen in Silicon Valley.

"Yeah, pretty good," he says, though there's no joy in it.

"Like how good?" I'm waiting for the hitch.

"Like never having to work again good, except they want to hire me as a consultant."

I throw my hands up in the air. "So what's the problem?"

"The problem is, Dad is fucking dead, and I need him to tell me what to do."

And that's when we pull into the driveway at the Victorian on Vallejo and both start sobbing uncontrollably.

Chapter 6
The Newsboy Cap

Brooke has laid out snacks, though none of us is in the mood to eat while we pack up my father's clothes, medical books, and keepsakes.

Hannah, who missed her calling as a drill sergeant, organizes our efforts by room. She has us starting in my father's study and working our way to the now main bedroom. Hannah has also brought boxes and packing tape, something Adam and I never would've thought of on our own. That's why she's an A-list lawyer. Ironic that Adam, whose idea of ambition is waking up before noon, is the sibling destined for triumph.

"Everything that goes to the Goodwill in this box." Hannah pushes the large carton she's whipped together at us. "Everything we're donating to the library over here." She points to a second box. "And everything we're keeping, we'll line up on the sofa and go through after we finish with the rest of it."

I suspect there will be a battle over a few of the most sentimental items. The framed photo of my father as a little boy with Safta at a resort that used to be their family's farm in Moodus, Connecticut. The Rolex my mother bought him with the proceeds from her pearl earrings when he finished med school. And my father's tweed newsboy cap. Him in that hat is probably my most indelible image of my father. I don't know where the cap came from, but he'd been wearing it since I was old enough to walk.

Hannah is barking more orders at us, which I can tell puts Adam on edge.

"Fuck off, Mussolini," he barks back and grabs an armload of the medical books and tosses them one at a time into the carton like he's shooting baskets. "I doubt Nurse Ratched has a need for any of these."

Brooke has left us alone, thank God. I don't think I could bear sorting through the flotsam of my father's life with her underfoot. It is just too damned personal. By the time she pops her head in to see how we're making out, I've noticed that the painting my mother gave my father is missing from over the fireplace mantel.

"Do you know where the watercolor of the giant redwoods is?" I ask her.

Brooke's face flushes with embarrassment. It reminds me of the time Josie's high school boyfriend, Chuck Tillerman, got caught stealing the tip jar at Swensen's.

"It's not valuable," Adam says, and I don't know whether to laugh or be mortified.

"It's in there." Brooke points her chin at the closet and abruptly leaves the room.

I open the closet door to find it wedged between an old set of golf clubs and a pair of crutches left over from when Adam broke his ankle in eighth grade, covered in a thin layer of dust. I gently pry it loose, careful not to rip the canvas, and set it against the sofa with the keep pile.

Hannah looks at me. "For Mom?"

"Yeah."

She acknowledges the gesture with a slight nod. Her way of saying, "Kudos to you for thinking of it."

"Is it just me," she whispers, "or does Brooke look ten years older?"

She still looks like my sister's age to me; she just doesn't have makeup on. Her long blond hair is tied up in a messy bun, and she's wearing glasses instead of contact lenses. Brooke's fashion choices have never been what you would call overly stylish, but she can rock a pair of jeans and a T-shirt with that svelte body of hers. This is all to say that even when she is slumming it around the house, she has an effortless beauty only found in soap commercials and Tommy Hilfiger ads. But today she does look like she's operating on little sleep, judging by the dark circles around her eyes and the brackets at the corners of her mouth.

I shrug. "She looks the same."

We go back to sorting until Adam finds a photo album, and for the next twenty minutes, we pore over the pictures.

"Nice hair." Adam pokes me in the ribs as we thumb through photographs of my junior high school graduation.

It was before keratin treatments, back when my hair looked like Howard Stern's.

"Nice jeans," I shoot back.

"Skinny was in then."

"Look how young Mom and Dad are," Hannah says.

The picture makes my heart jump. My parents' shiny faces staring at the camera. You can feel their love for each other emanating through the lens. Deep and real. The way they belonged.

A wave of melancholy washes over me. If only he'd had more time. They would've found their way back to each other, I'm sure of it.

Josh walks in as the three of us, gathered around the album, are caught up in a world of memories. "I see you're getting a lot done."

"Come look at this," I say and wave him over to show him the picture of my parents.

He gazes down at the photograph, then takes me in his arms, where I rest my head against his chest as he slowly sifts his fingers through my hair.

The room is quiet, except for the ticking of the massive grandfather clock near the fireplace. The clock was a rummage sale find that my mother had to have. She spent more money fixing the thing than she did on the clock itself.

Josh breaks the silence. "Give me a job to do."

"You can load the boxes into the trailer," says Hannah, who rented a U-Haul and borrowed Stephen's truck—the one he uses twice a year to tow his boat to Tahoe—so we can deliver the things we're giving away.

Brooke had offered to do it—or rather hire someone to do it—but we wouldn't hear of it. It wasn't so much an act of kindness toward the grieving widow as it was a territorial thing. We are dogs peeing on our domain. I wonder if Brooke realizes that.

Josh carts out the boxes while we move to the main bedroom.

It's the first time I've been inside my dad and Brooke's suite and it's weird, almost like we're in the room of strangers. Even the scent is different. My parents' bedroom always smelled faintly of my mother's perfume. Instead of the four-poster—another one of my mother's flea market finds—there's a modern platform bed that doesn't really go with the period of the house. Like the bed, the bedding has a modern vibe. Lots of bright colors and swirly designs. Maybe Marimekko. But Josh would know better.

The walk-in closet is half the size of the one in my parents' old bedroom, and my father's clothes take up most of the space. Brooke doesn't appear to have a whole lot. Just a row of jeans, a few dresses and skirts, some dress pants, and a small rod with blouses. A stack of sweaters is folded neatly on one of the shelves next to a higher pile of T-shirts and an even higher stack of scrubs. Compared to my mother's wardrobe, Brooke lives like a Buddhist monk.

"Let's do in here first and make our way to the bathroom," Hannah says. "Everything we're keeping goes on the bed. Everything else in a box for the Goodwill."

I want Josh to have something of my dad's, but Adam gets first choice. Unlike the stuff in his study, it feels a little ghoulish going through his clothes. Adam pulls out a black tuxedo, which I don't remember ever seeing my father in.

"Kinda cool." Adam holds it against himself and stares in the mirror on the back of the door.

Hannah and I erupt with laughter.

"Where will you ever wear it?" she says.

"Bond. James Bond," Adam says to his reflection, ignoring Hannah.

"You're an idiot," I say.

He chucks the tux in the Goodwill box, then changes his mind and throws it on the bed.

We sort through the racks of my father's suits, sport coats, and slacks. Most of it is a bit staid for my brother's and Josh's taste, though it's tasteful and expensive. A plastic surgeon has to look the part when he's meeting with prospective patients.

"You think Stephen might want some of these?" I ask my sister.

She shakes her head. "Doubtful. Maybe we could donate them to one of those organizations that help men get back on their feet."

I like that idea, and I know my father would have, too.

Josh returns, eyes the pile on the bed and joins us in the closet. "How's it going in here?" He looks at me with eyes that say, "I know this is hard."

"I want you to pick out something," I say and open the drawer where my dad has his cuff links. I look over at Adam to make sure this is okay, and he nods. "My mother got him these for his fortieth birthday." I hold up a vintage pair of Scholz and Lam square ones. They were made after WWII and are a modernist design that I think will appeal to Josh's architectural sensibilities. I have always loved them.

"You sure?" Josh turns to Adam and Hannah.

"Go for it, dude," Adam says.

"I know my father would've been honored," Hannah says.

"I'm the one who's honored." Josh hooks his arm around my neck and kisses the top of my head. "Thank you."

I finally find my father's newsboy cap on a hook next to his jacket and put it on the bed pile, figuring that when we're done, we'll hash out who gets what. But I want the hat more than anything else, even more than the photo of my father and my safta on the family farm.

We've cleared the closet and have made good headway on the bathroom when Brooke pokes her head in. "How's it going?" Her eyes, sort of a bluish green, search the room.

I give her credit for trusting us to invade her space. In the eight years she's been married to our father, none of us has put in any effort to get to know her. Besides it being disloyal to my mother, we decided from day one that we didn't like her. For the most part, we're cordial with her but stiff. Occasionally, Adam will throw out a thinly veiled insult, which she pretends to misunderstand. For all intents and purposes, we're strangers to her. Yet we've been pawing through her personal space like a nursery of racoons in a garbage can.

She steps in hesitantly, as if she's intruding on a private memorial instead of her own bedroom. Her gaze shoots to the piles on the bed and lands on the newsboy cap.

"You can't take that." She snatches it off the bed.

"It was my dad's hat," I say, stating the obvious, unsure what she could possibly want with the faded tweed cap that predates her by at least three decades. There are far more precious pieces in the home, not to mention the house itself, which is all hers now.

"I'm aware of that." Any pretense that we're all one big happy family is gone as she clutches the hat to her chest.

"I don't see why it would hold any importance to you," I blurt, immediately wishing I'd said it differently. But it's too late now, and I'm pretty sure it's true. The image of my father in that hat probably means nothing to her.

"No, I'm sure you don't," she says, her voice catching.

Josh steps between us. "Look, this is difficult for everyone. Rachel didn't mean what she said. The hat clearly holds sentimental value to her, but if it does to you, too, you should have it, Brooke."

He gives her a small hug, and I want to kill him. How can he take her side over mine? She's probably going to sell the hat along with the house and everything in it.

Brooke's face softens. "Thank you. I appreciate it."

From watching her, you'd think Josh had just granted her a stay of execution. She quickly excuses herself, taking the hat with her.

We wait until we hear her footsteps retreat down the hallway before Adam throws himself down on the bed.

"What the hell do you think that was about?" he asks.

"Community property state," Hannah says in her lawyerly voice. "Technically, everything in the house is hers. She just wants to make sure we know that she knows that."

"Or maybe the hat is a talisman for the husband she lost ten days ago." Josh shoves his hands in his pockets and walks over to the window and peers outside.

"There's that." Adam hops off the bed. "Then there's the possibility that she's just being a vindictive bitch."

Chapter 7
Dinner at the Restaurant

"Did you really mean what you said about Brooke and the hat?" I ask Josh as we pull away from the house on Vallejo.

We finished what we came to do and are on our way to Tino's Pizza Napoletana for takeout. I'm not in the mood to eat in a restaurant, but we're both hungry.

"Don't be mad at me, Rach. Brooke looked as if she was going to break down any second. I know you wanted the cap, but you got the picture and the painting for your mom."

"It's not the same." I know I'm pouting like a six-year-old but don't care.

"Can we please table this until we get home?"

It's been a long day, and Josh is battling traffic, so I accede. But I want him to take my side in this.

What's normally a four-minute drive takes fifteen. After circling four or five times, Josh finally finds parking on Stockton Street, close to the restaurant.

Together, we walk to Tino's hand in hand, taking in the sights and scents of North Beach. It's dinnertime, and the streets are starting to fill with people. The smell of Italian food wafts onto the street, and my stomach growls. The last time I ate was a container of yogurt for breakfast.

To my surprise, Tino's isn't that crowded. There are times when there's a line around the block to get in, and Tino, the owner and pizzaiolo, has a no-reservation policy. He won the best pizza margherita at the World Pizza Cup in Naples, Italy, years ago, and the restaurant has gotten write-ups in every food and travel magazine imaginable. This is to say, he doesn't hurt for business, even without taking reservations.

"Wanna just eat here?" I say.

Josh holds my gaze, surprised by my sudden change of heart. "You sure?" "The pizza will at least be hot when we eat it." Unlike Josh, I hate cold pizza. "I also wouldn't mind a glass of wine." Ten if I'm honest with myself. And all we have at home is a couple of bottles of Chardonnay. Not great with pizza.

He asks the hostess if we can eat our to-go pizza in, and she finds us a booth near the front window. It's a small place, so there's not a lot of privacy. But in a way, the hum of the cooks and servers moving around the restaurant is a welcome distraction.

Josh gets us each a glass of Cesanese, our favorite wine when we eat here. The days are getting longer, and it's still light outside. The bars are starting to fill up with the after-work crowd. Even on a Wednesday night, it feels like a party.

Original Joe's is less than a block away, and I think of my father and the last lunch we had there together.

"You okay?" Josh reaches for my hand across the table.

I blow out a breath. "It was harder than I thought. And I thought it would be pretty hard."

"I know. But it's done now."

"Yep, it's done now." I sip my wine, finally able to relax. "On another note, Adam got an offer from Sony for his company."

"No shit. A good offer?"

"I think so. Adam says he'll never have to work again, but coming from my brother, that could mean they're giving him lunch money and an Xbox."

Josh's lips curve up in that double-take smile that won me over the first time we met, and suddenly I'm not angry at him anymore.

"What's his plan?"

"He doesn't know. Maybe you could talk to him."

"Me?" Josh hitches his shoulder. "Rach, I don't have the first clue about the gaming industry. I wouldn't even know what something like Adam's company is worth. Doesn't he have people for that?"

"I'm sure he does, but he could use some moral support. I'd ask Stephen but..." I trail off because I don't have to say it. Josh knows. It's not that my brother-in-law is a bad person; he's just completely wrapped up in himself. Any advice he could give Adam would wind up being all about Stephen.

"I'll call him," Josh says. "I've been meaning to grab a beer with him anyway."

Our food comes. Josh picks the artichokes off his salad and slides them onto my plate. I in return give him my cherry tomatoes. We've been doing this so long that I can't remember when it started. You would think we would order a different kind of salad by now, one without artichokes and cherry tomatoes. But this one suits us just fine.

Something outside catches Josh's eye, and it's as if his body goes on high alert. I follow the direction of his gaze to a small group of people standing outside the restaurant. A line is starting to form for Tino's, but it looks as if these people—two women and two men—have already eaten and are either getting ready to part ways or have just met up. They're huddled together, talking.

Josh is still staring at them, riveted.

"Do you know them?" I ask and turn back to Josh.

He shakes his head at first, then suddenly utters, "I went to Cal with a couple of them."

"Why don't you go say hi?" I say, feeling a subtle shift in him as soon as the words leave my mouth.

"Nah." He scrubs his hand through his hair and seems uptight, which is uncharacteristic for him. "They wouldn't remember me."

I don't understand why, if he remembers them, they wouldn't remember him. As far as I'm concerned, Josh is pretty memorable. I turn back around to have another look, and they're gone.

When I face Josh again, he's still staring through the plate glass window.

Chapter 8
Our Seventh Anniversary

It's been a year since my father died, and life is slowly getting back to normal.

Adam wound up holding on to his company, determining the time wasn't right to sell. All the self-help and grief books say to avoid making big decisions after experiencing the death of a loved one, so I guess it was smart of him to wait with Sony. And it's not as if he needs the money. His latest game is a top seller, and his earlier one is a perennial favorite.

It's Hannah I'm most worried about. Her marriage seems to be unraveling. Despite it—or maybe because of it—my sister is desperate to have a baby. The problem is Stephen is never home. And when he is, he's working on briefs or doing whatever lawyers do, mostly ignoring her. Last week, my sister, usually Ms. Decorum, had a knock-down, drag-out fight with him over the phone in the middle of Nordstrom's lingerie department.

I know this through Josie, who is my sister's personal shopper (God forbid Hannah pick out her own clothes). Even though I consider the three of us Gold kids close—there isn't anything we won't do for one another—Hannah would die if she knew Josie had told me. Pretty dumb for a woman with an advanced degree from Stanford. Josie is my best friend, after all.

In any event, even though Adam and I are open books, Hannah has always been private. Especially when her life doesn't follow her neat little script. Even in high school when she was a senior and I was a freshman, she kept her boyfriends secret from the rest of us, going to such crazy lengths as having them pick her up down the street, where we couldn't meet them. Mom thinks she takes after my father. But Adam and I think Hannah is a chip off the old Mommie Dearest block.

No one does the secret life of Shana Gold like Shana Gold. After my dad left her for Brooke, Mom threw herself a sixtieth birthday party at the Log Cabin at the Presidio. The venue, built in the 1930s, was used as a clubhouse by the army and has this incredible rustic vibe with views of the bay that go on forever. To rent the venue, there's a waiting list two years long. I know this because at least three of my high school friends reserved the cabin even before they got engaged. But my mother has friends in all the right places. She managed to snag it with only a few weeks' notice just in time for her birthday. The only catch was the party had to be held on a weeknight. Here she was, on the cusp of a divorce, her husband with a woman half my mother's age, and she invited two hundred of her best friends to dance the night away.

My siblings and I sat back, watching the greatest charade in the history of the Gold family. No one seemed to notice that my father wasn't even there.

This is why I'm not surprised Hannah is pretending that everything Is fine with her and Stephen, even though I know it's not. Judging by all the time she's spending with Josie, shopping, she's either really bored (my sister is not a shopper) or trying to change up her appearance to impress her absent husband.

But today I'm not going to think about Hannah or anyone else in my family because it's Josh's and my seventh wedding anniversary. And instead of going to a fancy restaurant for brunch, we're celebrating by upholding our Saturday morning ritual.

"You ready for this?" Josh places the breakfast tray down and slides into bed next to me. "I used chocolate chips this time. The blueberries were moldy. These may be my best pancakes yet. Happy anniversary, baby."

San Francisco's legendary June gloom is hanging over the bay while we eat breakfast in bed. Of the two of us, he has the kitchen moves. My pancakes tend to look like crepes and taste like rubber.

I dip my fork in to test before I smother my pancakes with syrup. Chocolate seeps out into a gooey mess on my plate. I take a bite and close my eyes from the pure goodness of it. Just one forkful and I'm in heaven.

"Decadent, right?" Josh is watching me, a proud grin stretched across his face.

"Oh my God." I cover my mouth with my hand, afraid to drip chocolate on our new duvet. "Definitely your best. What's in here besides chocolate chips? Something is different."

His eyes sparkle like he's got a secret. "Try to guess."

Of the two of us, he's the foodie. My palate is rather unsophisticated. That isn't to say I don't like good food, but my taste buds can't distinguish between ingredients the way Josh's can. "I don't know. It's just...different. Come on, what is it?"

"Almond paste," he says. "We had some left over from when I made macarons." Josh got on a macaron kick after he did the design for a French bakery in Cow Hollow. The owner used to work at Ladurée in Paris and allegedly brought its macaron recipe with her to the States. She gave it to Josh as a thank-you with a promise that he wouldn't give it to anyone else.

I take another big bite to see if I can taste the almond paste. "They're so fluffy," I say on a mouthful.

He digs into the heaping stack—another one of our Saturday rituals is that we share from the same plate—and we fork fight each other for the last scrap.

"Mm, better than sex," Josh says, and I kick him under the blanket.

He looks at me, his brown eyes meeting mine, and says what we've both been avoiding for weeks. "I think it's time, Rach."

"I know," I whisper. "I just wanted it to be..." I start to say "normal," but that's not really the right word. I guess what I mean is that I wanted it to be natural, that one day I would simply wake up pregnant without having to focus all our energy on it. Without doctors and hormones and laboratories.

As if Josh knows exactly what I'm thinking, he says, "Sometimes people need a little help. That's all, Rach. It's not a big deal."

I blow out a breath. This isn't the way I want to spend our anniversary. But the truth is we're running out of time, especially if we want more than one child. Two had always been the plan.

"I know," I say, yet I feel a tremendous amount of guilt for not being able to give Josh and me this one thing. This one ultimate gift. I can't help but question whether there is something wrong with me, whether what happened seventeen years ago made me infertile. "But can we maybe talk about this tomorrow?"

"Or the day after. Or the day after that." He smiles that Josh smile, and it goes straight to my soul. "Whenever you're comfortable, Rach."

"Thank you," I whisper, a little choked up. God, I'm so lucky to have this beautiful man in my life.

"De nada, baby." He winks and moves over me and kisses me on the lips. He tastes like chocolate and coffee, and I love him so much I want to cry. "You got it," he says. "What do you want to do today?"

"Go for a walk, then make our list." We do it every anniversary. Instead of New Year's resolutions, we make anniversary resolutions. Usually, it's about ten things we want to do for our marriage. Last year, the big ones were to get pregnant and buy a house. I suspect those two will land at the top of the list this year.

We almost got the house. It was a duplex in Eureka Valley that had been stripped of all its vintage charm. Josh wanted to put the charm back in it and rent the second apartment until we had enough money to make it one large home. The only reason we could afford the neighborhood in the first place was because the building had structural issues. The floors were so unlevel that you could roll a marble from one end of the house to the other. We hoped that it was a settlement issue and that for twenty or thirty thousand dollars we could shore up the foundation.

Josh brought in an engineer who works for his firm, and it turned out that the only thing that would save the foundation was to start over. Given that the house was perched on the side of a hill and was three stories high, we were probably looking at half a million dollars. Needless to say, it wasn't worth it, not that we have that kind of money anyway.

If Josh wasn't so particular, we could probably get something in the Outer Sunset or Outer Richmond, or even pockets of the city that are less desirable. But he's looking for something that he can work his magic on, something architecturally interesting or at least something with architectural potential. I can't blame him, not when it's what he does for a living.

"You want to walk to Chestnut or go to the park?"

"What do you want to do?"

I'm hoping for Chestnut so we can look in the shop windows. It isn't the greatest day weather-wise for the park. And while I'm not a clothes horse like Josie, I like something new every now and again.

"I know you're voting for Chestnut," he says, and I smile.

He knows. He always knows.

* * * *

Two hours later, we are back at the apartment, our walk a rousing success. I have a new dress Josh bought me in one of Chestnut's trendy boutiques. And Josh got a fedora that he says looks exactly like the one Dean Martin wore in *Robin and the 7 Hoods*.

"Want to make our list now?"

I do and I don't, knowing that our top priorities from last year will once again top this year's list and make me feel like a loser.

"Let me print last year's list," Josh says.

I've never met a person more organized than my husband. Everything has its rightful place. Unlike me, he cleans his closet—and his computer—

frequently. His rule of thumb is, if he hasn't worn something in the last year, out it goes. He's equally as fanatical about cleaning out old emails. His architecture files are color coded. And his vinyl records and CDs are in alphabetical order.

He goes to the tiny alcove we use as an office, and I can hear the grind of the printer. I grab two cold sodas from the fridge and take them to the living room. The best thing about our apartment is the large picture windows with views of the bay and the Golden Gate Bridge. It's another reason Josh has been so picky about buying a house. While our place is small, it's got location, location, location.

Josh brings last year's list and his laptop and plops down next to me on the sofa. We set about marking off our accomplishments on the hard copy. That's my job. I find a pen in the coffee table drawer.

"New bed. Check. New car. Check." My MINI finally gave up the ghost, and we splurged on a plug-in hybrid for the reason that it was roomy enough to fit my real estate clients.

"Date nights. Check." Watching Hannah and Stephen's marriage go from bad to worse, Josh and I made a conscious decision to spend more time together. Every Wednesday night, no matter what, we go on a date, even if we just order delivery and watch a movie on Netflix. The point is not to take each other for granted.

I scan the list to see what I've missed. "Living trust. Check."

It was Josh's idea after my dad died. I thought it was premature. We're only in our midthirties and don't have kids. But after talking to an estate lawyer—a friend of Hannah's—she said it was never too early to "plan" for the future.

"What else is on there?" Josh stares at the list over my shoulder.

I hold Josh's gaze. "You know what's on there."

His hand gently rubs my back. "We'll get there, Rach. I promise."

"I guess you should add it to our new list."

"Yep," he says, but instead of starting a new list, he just deletes everything from our old one.

"What are you doing? Don't you want to keep that?"

He nudges his head at my hard copy. "Why? You've got that one."

"I don't know," I say. "Just to keep a permanent record, so that when we've been married for fifty years we can look back and say, 'Remember when...?' Tell me you have our old ones?"

He shakes his head. "I assumed it was out with the old and in with the new."

Maybe I'm being overly sentimental, but it bothers me that he's being so cavalier about it. This is our thing. Someday we may want to show our kids our lists.

"When we're done, send me a copy," I say, annoyed. "I'll keep a record."

"Sorry. Seriously, Rach, I didn't know we were keeping these."

"Whatever." I toss my head.

He kisses me on the back of my neck, and I feel my irritation slipping away.

"Are we doing this?" Josh says.

"Put that you promise never to delete any more of our lists as number one on the list. There is a limit to how anal you are about cleaning up your computer files."

"I promise," Josh says and pulls me onto his lap. And for the rest of the evening, the list is forgotten.

Chapter 9
Jessica Simpson

Campbell is getting married. It's nine in the morning, and I haven't yet had my first cup of coffee as I try to process the news.

"She's the one," he says, his voice almost reverent in a way I've never heard it before. In a way that, if I didn't know Campbell better, was designed to be mean.

I clutch the phone between my shoulder and my ear while scooping beans into the grinder. "So, Jessica Simpson, huh?" That's her name, I kid you not. Jessica. Freaking. Simpson. She even looks a little like the real Jessica Simpson. "When? Where?"

"Don't know yet. But save the date." He laughs, and I'm suddenly transported back nineteen years when that laugh filled me with an impossible giddiness.

"I'm really happy for you," I say, and I am. Everyone should be as in love as Josh and me.

"Thanks, Rach. Everything good with you?"

"Everything is great. A big restaurant group just hired Josh to do the plans for three new restaurants in the city. One's at the Embarcadero with incredible water views. He's over the moon."

"Very cool," Campbell says, but I detect something in his voice, something that says *I wasn't asking about Josh.* "What about you, Rach? What do you have going?"

"Same old," I say cheerily. Too cheerily. "You know, working on a couple of deals."

"Yeah, anything interesting?"

"Just the uzhe." I try to sound as if the usual is juggling a dozen listings at a time, while brokering a sale between a Russian oligarch and the Zuckerbergs. "How 'bout you? I mean workwise."

"I'm doing the kitchen cabinets for this sick apartment in Russian Hill and a built-in entertainment center in the Castro. Other than that, working on some furniture. I guess you can say *just the uzhe*." His voice is teasing.

In reality, I think he finds my shortening of words annoying, even childish. But Josie and I have been doing it since we were thirteen. Old habits die hard.

"Jess and I want to do some sort of party in a couple of weeks to announce the news. We're still working on the details, but I want you there, Rach. You, Josh and all the Golds."

"Of course," I say. "Just give me a day and time. I'd offer up Dad's house but...well, you know how that is." If anyone deserves to have a party at the house on Vallejo, it's Campbell.

For more years than I can count, his father tended my parents' gardens. While his landscaping company had grown to the point that Mr. Scott rode a desk more than a tractor mower, he still saw to every detail of our gardens until the day he retired.

As a boy, Campbell used to come with him and do his homework in our kitchen. He and Adam were the same age, and an everlasting friendship grew out of those days Campbell waited for his father. I, of course, followed them wherever they went, having decided even as young as thirteen that Campbell was my destiny. It took him a little longer to come to that conclusion, regarding me for the most part as a tagalong pest.

I don't know exactly when or how it happened, but as the both of us got older, he started spending more time with me and less time with Adam. First, it was longing looks when Adam wasn't paying attention. Then it was kisses. Then clandestine meetings whenever and wherever we could. In my junior year of high school, I got pregnant. We were always careful but apparently not careful enough. And for seven weeks we kept it a secret, plotting our future with all the naiveté of children.

"Yeah, don't sweat it," he says. "We'll probably do it at Jessica's folks'. Or maybe at a restaurant. Nothing too fancy."

Campbell eschews all things fancy. He plays up his blue-collar roots like a Bruce Springsteen song.

"I'm so happy for you," I say again. Yet I feel ambivalent about his news. It's just that there is so much history between us, and Jessica, who I actually like, feels like a trespasser.

"Thanks, Rach. It means a lot to me." He pauses for a beat, then says, "I'll let you and the rest of the Golds know as soon as we hammer out a party date."

"What was that about?" Josh asks after I hang up with Campbell.

"Campbell's getting married."

"To the blonde? What's her name?"

"Jessica. Jessica Simpson."

Josh laughs. "That's right. How could I forget that name?"

"They're planning an engagement party. We're invited."

"Okay," he says but is sorting through the mail, his attention already on something else.

Josh pretends to like Campbell, and Campbell pretends to like Josh. But the two of them are like oil and water. The logical reason for that is me. But even without me as the common denominator, Josh and Campbell are polar opposites. The best way I can describe it is Campbell leads with his heart, which bugs the shit out of Josh, and Josh leads with his head, which bugs the shit out of Campbell.

It's one of the things I loved most about Campbell, his passion, his fire, his constant desire to create and build things with his hands. I think that's why as kids he and Adam became best friends. As different as they are—Adam a computer nerd and Campbell a master carpenter—they're both dreamers. Together, there isn't anything they can't do, like the tree house they built in the towering oak in our backyard on Vallejo that they even wired for internet.

It's still there.

Funny that I should go from loving a romantic to loving a pragmatist. Then again, I was just a girl when I fell for Campbell. Things change, people change.

I look at the time on the enormous schoolhouse clock Josh hung on the wall over our minuscule pantry. "I thought you had a meeting at the Ferry Building at ten." It's the only reason he's still here and not at the office.

"Cancelled." Josh takes over the chore of making the coffee. "I thought I'd go with you to the doctor."

I wonder if the so-called meeting was a ruse to go with me in the first place.

"Um, okay." I grab the cups from the dishwasher, which I'd started to empty when Campbell called.

"You don't sound that into it."

"Not into you coming with me or having a stranger inspect my uterus?" I'm definitely not into having my private parts probed six ways from

Sunday. Or having Josh watch the probing. But the truth is I don't want Josh to come for a different reason.

The whole run-up to in vitro fertilization involves me talking about my medical history. While Josh knows about the miscarriage and what happened with Campbell and me all those years ago, I'd rather not revisit the topic with him present. It's a piece of my life that belongs only to Campbell and me. And while I do believe that all things happen for a reason and that Campbell and I were better off not bringing a baby into the world when we were just kids ourselves, losing the baby left a hole in my heart that has never completely healed. To think we might've had a seventeen-year-old right now. To wonder whether he or she would've had Campbell's eyes or my hair...well, it's something I'll never know.

It started with a sharp pain in my midsection, and before I knew it, a thin line of blood trickled down my leg. I think I subconsciously knew I was having a miscarriage but didn't want to believe it. So I waited three hours before going to urgent care, where I got the official confirmation.

"There was nothing you could've done, sweetheart," the kindly nurse, who reminded me of my great-aunt Beverly, told me. "It's just nature's way of saying chromosomally life wasn't viable."

I waited another ten hours to tell Campbell. We climbed up to the tree house, and I cried my eyes out in his arms.

"Are you sad?" I asked him.

"I'm a little in shock. Why didn't you call me, Rachel? I should've been there for you. I should've gone with you to the doctor's."

"I don't know. I guess I didn't want to believe it was happening. I kept telling myself that it was a mistake. That the bleeding was normal."

"Ah, Jesus." Campbell pulled me against his chest and stroked my hair. "Are you in pain?"

"No, not really. I'm just very, very sad. Even though I was only seven weeks, I feel different, like sort of empty inside." I snuggled my head against Campbell's chest, wishing I could burrow there forever, and whispered, "At least we don't have to tell anyone now."

Campbell didn't say anything, just rocked me back and forth.

"And now you can go to school." In a few months, Campbell was supposed to leave to attend the University of California at Santa Barbara, almost six hours away by car. We hadn't made any firm decisions in that regard, but Campbell had said he would stay and work for his father until we had the baby if that's what I wanted.

In hindsight, I hadn't known what I wanted. But at the time, I spent a lot of time in my head, playing house.

"You good with that? With me going away to school?" he asked.

"Of course." But I was sort of surprised that he'd jumped on it so quickly. Even though pre-pregnancy, him going away to school had never been in question, I felt a stab of rejection. I suppose I'd wanted a space of time where we suspended reality and continued to play house. "Business as usual," I said dryly.

He kissed the side of my neck. "I'm sorry, Rach. I'm so damned sorry." But was he?

I don't know what I wanted out of him, but I knew it was more than he was giving. The truth was, from the minute we climbed into the tree house, I could feel a heaviness lift off him. He was suddenly lighter, freer. It made me resent him, even though there was a part of me who felt lighter too.

That was the only day we ever spoke of what we'd lost. And maybe that's why we lost each other. Because from that day forward, something intrinsically changed between us. We used to be inseparable, but we began to spend less time with each other and more time with our friends. They say even the strongest relationships come unglued by tragedy or death, but for Campbell and me, I think it was more about liberation from the secret fear that a baby would have stolen our youth.

Anyway, the whole situation has got to be uncomfortable for Josh, especially because Campbell is still very much a part of the Golds. I know it would be awkward for me if the tables were turned. Why rub my husband's nose in it?

"When you say it like that..." Josh moves away from me, and I feel the distance like a sharp edge.

"It's just an exam. Just an exam to make sure I don't have fibroids or anything else. No different than a Pap smear. You don't come with me for those."

"Not the same, Rach. Not the same and you know it. But if you don't want me to come, I won't come."

Now I feel guilty, like I'm being a bad wife. "It's not that I don't want you to come. It's just that I don't want to make a huge deal out of it. When I go for the ovarian reserve testing, I'll want you there. But this is just routine stuff."

"You're making this all about you, and it's about me, too. But whatever." He grabs his pack and bike helmet and heads for the door, slamming it closed before I can stop him.

Chapter 10
Fly With Me

Two weeks later, we're in the car, driving to Campbell and Jessica's engagement party. It's in Jess's parents' backyard in San Mateo, and my whole family will be there. We're running late because at the last minute, Josh had to take a call from a client who was flipping out over how much he was being "overcharged" for change orders on his project.

Josh had to talk him off the ledge. I know it's his job, but I'm still peeved that it ate up so much time. The bottom line is that Josh doesn't really want to go to the party and used his client as a handy excuse. He could have just let the guy go to voicemail and dealt with the issue tomorrow or Monday. By the time we get to San Mateo, which is forty minutes away, the party will be half-over.

"Sorry." Josh gives me a sideways glance. He knows I'm irritated.

"Avoid Van Ness, or it will take us all day to get to the freeway." Saturday isn't as bad as a weekday, but still, the traffic seems to get worse every day.

"Aye, aye, Captain."

"You're not funny," I grumble.

At least the day is gorgeous. You can't beat August in the Bay Area. It's the first month that truly feels like summer here. June is usually overcast and cold. And July isn't much better. But August and September—mostly September—is perfection.

Josh manages to circumvent Van Ness, taking Cervantes instead. The traffic is lighter here, but there are still a good many cars on the street. He turns on the music, and Frank Sinatra blares through the speakers. Soon we're singing along to "Come Fly with Me," and I almost forget I'm angry at him for not wanting to go to Campbell's party.

I roll down the window and stick my hand outside as if I can catch the sunshine. We've taken the hybrid with its padded leather seats and new-car smell. Although we're only going thirty miles, it feels like a road trip. And suddenly I'm excited to be leaving the city. It's as if the music reads my mind, because the next song in the queue is "It's Nice to Go Trav'ling." Josh turns it up before he hangs a right on Fillmore and a left on Chestnut.

"Did you bring the champagne?" I suddenly have a vision of the expensive bottle I bought as a gift still sitting on our kitchen counter.

"Of course," Josh says smugly. "It'll be lost on Campbell, though."

He's right, but I don't give him the satisfaction of agreeing. I bought it for Jess anyway. She'll appreciate it.

"It's here." Josh reaches his hand around the console to the mesh organizer on the back of his seat and holds up the bottle.

"I don't think you're supposed to use that to store your booze."

Josh laughs. "Hey, it works."

"I guess I should've wrapped it or put it in a gift bag."

"Didn't you get them something else, too?"

"Not yet, but I'll have something shipped." They haven't registered yet. Who knows if they ever will? Somehow, I can't picture Campbell standing in a department store, picking out china. At the same time, I can't see myself sending Campbell, the man who taught me how to kiss and how to love, a butter dish or a salad bowl. Then again, stranger things have happened. For instance, Campbell getting married in the first place.

I cringe when Josh turns onto Gough. Talk about slowing us down, Gough is steep with a million stop signs. "Really?" I say.

"What do you want me to do? Drive halfway around the city to catch the freeway?"

"Yes, because it'll actually be faster."

"Fine." He hops onto Pacific.

It happens so fast that I don't see it coming. All I hear is metal on metal and something so loud it sounds like a gunshot. I lurch forward only to be caught by my seat belt, then punched in the gut so hard it knocks the breath out of me. I struggle to breathe, lost in a fog of confusion. Everything seems to be happening in slow motion.

I try to move but am pinned tightly against the back of my seat. And I can't see. Everything is white, and for a few heart-stopping moments, I think I'm blind. No, that can't be right. If I'd lost my sight, wouldn't it be dark? That's the way I've always imagined it. And I can see daylight squeezing through the top of the windshield.

Then I realize all that white is the airbags. I frantically shove at them, trying to free myself. From the corner of my eye, I see a flash of red. It's on my hands. It's everywhere.

"Josh," I call, frightened. "Josh?"

But there's no answer. No answer at all.

Part 3
After Josh Dies

Chapter 11
The What-Ifs and the Whys

They say Josh died instantly, that the impact from the Tesla that T-boned us snapped his neck. Even still, the paramedics rushed him to San Francisco General. I think they did it for my sake, as I stood in the middle of the wreckage, keening like a wild animal, begging them to bring Josh back from the dead.

I walked away with a few cuts and bruises from the glass and the airbags, wishing it was me instead of him.

Even weeks later, there are so many what-ifs running through my head. What if I hadn't told him to avoid Van Ness? What if I'd insisted he get off his call and leave a few minutes earlier? Or inversely, what if I hadn't rushed him and we'd left a few minutes later? What if he'd forgotten the wine and we'd gone back home to get it? What if I'd been driving instead of Josh? What if Campbell hadn't gotten engaged? What if I'd given Josh the free pass he'd really wanted to miss the party?

But mostly it's the whys that haunt me. Why hadn't I told him I loved him that morning. Why hadn't I told him how much he made my world a better place? Why was he taken from me so early?

Why? Why? Why?

I vacillate between denial and fury. And my mind is constantly swirling with questions that have no answers. My family wants me to go to grief counseling, but I'm not ready yet. I'm too busy staying in bed, making up excuses for why I can't get out. Yesterday, I was positive ticks from the cemetery gave me Lyme disease. Adam of all people has convinced me that I'm crazy.

"Rach, this isn't healthy." Hannah stands at the foot of my bed in one of her power suits. "I'm not saying you can't be sad, but you can't continue to hole up in this apartment. When was the last time you ate? Or showered, for God's sake?" She opens a window, and a blast of cool air rushes in, bringing with it the briny smell of the bay.

"Don't you have to be in court?" I say, desperately wanting her to leave. It's bad enough that my mother was just here a few hours ago to stock my fridge with foods I hate. You would think that after thirty-four years she would know that I don't drink milk and peas give me hives.

Hannah's phone pings with a text, and she is momentarily lost in her screen.

"What's that about?" I swing my legs over the bed in hopes that I might catch a peek of the message. But she quickly stashes the phone in her suit jacket and regains her resting lawyer face composure.

"Nothing. I have to go. But Rachel you really need to get dressed, maybe go out for a walk. Mom said she left you food. Eat!"

I nod just to get her off my back. As soon as I hear the snick of the front door lock, I crawl back under the covers. I only have six hours before Adam shows up. He's apparently drawn the night shift and has been coming every day for a week, often sleeping over on my couch. If I didn't know better, I'd think the Golds have me on suicide watch.

The Ackermanns call every day since they went back to Chicago. I probably should be the one calling them. Outliving your own child is unfathomable. A good daughter-in-law would be the one to see to their well-being. But I just don't have the bandwidth.

I'm about to nod off when the intercom jolts me upright, and Josie's muffled voice wafts its way into the bedroom.

"I know you're up there, Rachel. Let me in."

I consider ignoring her, rolling over, and pulling my pillow over my head. The Golds have obviously sent reinforcements. More than likely it was Hannah who dropped the dime. I must really be pathetic. Guilty, I drag myself to the front door and buzz her up.

Five minutes later, she breezes in looking like a fashion plate in a creamy shift dress and a chunky coral necklace she got at Gumps at its so-called closing sale. Last I looked, the department store was still open.

I gaze down at my coffee-stained T-shirt but can't muster any shame. Not even a modicum of disgust.

She takes my hand and leads me to the bathroom. "Take a shower, get dressed, and fix your hair."

"Why?" But I have a feeling I know the reason, and I don't like where it's going.

"We're stepping out for a little while."

"Not today, Josie. I don't feel well."

"Of course you don't feel well. You haven't had fresh air in days, and you probably have bed sores. Come on, Rach, a walk will do you some good."

Ultimately, I agree on the corner café for a cup of coffee with her. It's a tiny restaurant with only a few tables and counter service. The only reason I'm able to tolerate the place is because Josh and I never came here. We preferred the café two blocks down because it had booths, and Josh loved booths. He used to joke that we should open a restaurant that only had banquette seating and call it "Booth." My response: "You mean a diner?"

"Did you hear that Ashley Birnbaum is getting divorced?" Josie asks, and I give her credit for pretending that this is like our millions of other coffee dates pre–car crash.

"No." Ashley is part of our Jew camp clique. There's six of us in total, and we're spread across the country. We try to get together twice a year to relive our childhood glory days, which looking back on it weren't all that glorious. But it was a rite of passage, and despite having very little in common, we still enjoy one another's company. "I can't believe she didn't say anything at Josh's funeral."

Josie stares at me as if I have two heads. "Right, because that certainly would've been the time to talk about her marital issues."

Despite myself, I laugh. "I guess not." I mop up the coffee that spilled on the table when I topped off my cup with too much cream. "I was under the impression that Eli was the perfect husband." According to Ashley, he was a saint, taking over the midnight feedings of their twins, taking charge of their copious amounts of laundry, all while overseeing a Fortune 500 company.

"There is no perfect husband, Rach."

I don't have the heart to tell Josie she's wrong. Of all our friends, she's the only one who isn't married or in a committed relationship.

"Apparently Eli has a porn problem."

I rear back a little in surprise. "Eli? Seriously? He always seemed so..."

"Straitlaced," Josie finishes. I was going to say prudish, but straitlaced is right on the money.

"It's so bad he lost his job over it," she continues. "His assistant saw it up on his screen and went to HR. Ashley says it wasn't the first time."

"Can't he get help for it?"

"Maybe, but I don't think that's going to save their marriage. Ashley's humiliated, and although Eli swears he never physically cheated on her, she feels betrayed, not to mention totally skeeved out."

"I can see that. I'm sorry for Ash."

"It would be great if you called her. She could use all of our support right now." Josie looks at me pointedly. The fact that Ashley flew all the way from New York to attend Josh's funeral is not lost on me.

"I will," I say but secretly don't know if I have the stamina to go through with it. I usually think of myself as a good friend but can't seem to think about anyone else but myself these days.

As if Josie reads my mind, she reaches out and takes my hand. "Rachel, maybe it's time to go back to work. Get out again. You need...something to occupy your time." What she means is something to keep me from dwelling on the past.

On some level I know she's right. It doesn't help that in the apartment, all I see is Josh. I refuse to wash his pillowcase for fear that I'll lose the scent of him. I can't bear to remove his clothes from the closet we share. And two nights ago, I cried myself to sleep on the floor in front of his neatly organized vinyl records.

"I don't know if I'm ready." Selling real estate to happy couples right now sounds about as appealing as a mammogram.

"I know, but it's time, Rach."

I want to be angry with my best friend. She doesn't get to decide when it's time, only I do. Ultimately, though, there's a part of me that knows hiding in my bed for days on end is unhealthy.

"I'll try," I say, hoping it'll put an end to the conversation.

But Josie won't let it go. "I think Campbell would like your help finding him and Jess a place."

I flinch. Since when are Josie and Campbell buddies? "You've talked to Campbell?"

He's called me more times than I can count since the funeral, leaving repeated messages. He even sent Uber Eats to the apartment with burritos from Arturo's, which used to be our favorite.

I didn't even have the good grace to thank him for it.

"He reached out." Josie tries to sound nonchalant. "We're worried about you, Rach."

"I'm fine."

Josie throws me a look like *you're not even close to fine.* "Why don't you call him? It'll be a good way to ease back in. Campbell and Jessica won't be demanding clients, and they'll be so happy to have a friend, someone who truly has their best interest at heart, advocating for them."

"I'll call him." It's become my mantra along with "I promise." One thing Josh's death has taught me is to become a very adept liar.

Chapter 12
Harry Asia's

Adam is holding watch today, sprawled out on my couch as if my entire apartment is his domain.

"Move in with me, Rach. A change of scenery will do you good."

"I don't think that's a good idea," I tell Adam. It's an understatement, of course. Within a few days, we'd be at each other's throat. "But thank you for the offer."

"Well, you can't stay here." Adam does a visual turn around the room.

Pictures of Josh are scattered across the coffee table along with the photo albums and scrapbooks I've been making. I feel a bit like Miss Havisham, stopping the clocks and living in my wedding gown.

"It's not working for you."

I nod. "I wish I could go home." For as long as I can remember, the house on Vallejo has always been my refuge.

"How about Mom's?"

We both look at each other and bust out laughing. It's the first real laugh I've had since the funeral, and it feels foreign. Yet at the same time good.

"Besides the obvious, I don't want to live in a construction zone." After Mom tore out the kitchen, she decided to redo her two bathrooms. Sometimes I think she's remodeling out of boredom rather than necessity. Her townhouse was perfectly lovely when she bought it.

Regardless of all the reasons it's a bad idea for me to stay with her, it's not home. It's the place Mom went when our family was irreparably shattered. Home is what I need right now. Unfortunately, it's an impossible ask.

"I'll figure something out," I tell Adam.

"You sure you don't want to stay with me? We could have slumber parties with Josie." He waggles his brows, and it takes all I have not to tell him that Josie is out of his league.

"What's going on with your company?" I'm tired of talking about myself. It seems like it's all we ever do. *How are you, Rach? Did you get out of bed today, Rach? Are you ever planning to go back to work, Rach?*

Adam stretches out, warming to the subject. He can clear a room when he starts talking about Switchback. At this point I don't care that I know nothing about gaming or the technology that goes into creating a video game. I simply want a normal conversation, though nothing having to do with Adam is ever normal. Still, I'll take it.

"I might sell."

It's the last thing I imagine him to say. "I thought you wanted to wait."

"That was after Dad died. Now...well, it seems like the right time."

"Why?" I'm perplexed by his sudden pivot. Or maybe it's not that sudden, and I've been so wrapped up in myself that I wasn't aware Adam was revisiting a sale.

"The money is good, and I'm thinking it's time to move on."

"Is the offer as generous as it was last time?"

He grins his big Adam grin, the one that had all my girlfriends in high school drooling over him, and says, "They've sweetened the pot."

"Really?" Why didn't I know this? "Did you talk to Hannah and Stephen about it?"

He shakes his head, vaults himself off the couch, and rummages through my refrigerator.

"Why not?" I ask. "They're lawyers, for God's sake."

He returns to the sofa with two forks in one hand and a pan of my mother's kugel in the other. Did I mention that Mom is a terrible cook? But she does make a mean egg noodle kugel. It's always been my go-to comfort food. Adam tosses me one of the forks and digs in as if he hasn't eaten in weeks. I run my fork along the edge of the pan, going for the crispy bits. I'm not hungry, but eating is a competitive sport in our family, the only one I'm remotely good at. Adam's better, though. In no time at all he's mowed through half the pan.

Between mouthfuls, he finally gets around to answering my question. "Because Stephen's an asshole and Hannah is too busy taking his shit."

"What am I missing here?" Stephen has always been self-absorbed, and everyone in the Gold family is aware of it, except of course Hannah. And all of us know he and Hannah are having issues, mostly because he works too much. But Adam, usually so easygoing he could be mistaken for comatose, sounds different today. There's a hostility in his voice I've only heard him reserve for Brooke. "Why the sudden vitriol toward Stephen?"

Adam responds with a stony silence. It's clear something significant has happened during my three-month mourning fog. Something that no one bothered to clue me in on.

"Adam?"

"A few weeks ago, I bumped into Stephen at Harry Asia's." Harry Asia's has the distinction of being the world's first fern bar. Supposedly, the owner invented the lemon drop. It's gone out of business more than a dozen times, then pops up again out of nowhere. Nowadays, it's a tourist trap, and the lemon drops are crappy.

"What were you doing at Harry Asia's?"

Adam shakes his head like that's beside the point. But I have a feeling I know where this conversation is going, and a part of me doesn't want to hear the rest.

"He wasn't alone, Rachel."

"Who was he with?" I ask hesitantly.

"A woman who wasn't Hannah."

"What happened when he saw you?" I tell myself we're jumping to conclusions. Stephen has meetings all the time. If Stephen was having an affair, why would he do it in such a public place?

"That's the thing, he acted like he'd been caught...came over to where I was sitting and started sputtering bullshit."

"Like what?"

"Like how the woman was a colleague and they'd decided to grab a drink after work. Except the Google campus is nearly an hour away."

"Maybe they were in San Francisco that day. Isn't that where the federal courthouse is?"

Adam looks at me like I'm Pollyanna's more gullible sister. But I don't want to believe Stephen's cheating on my sister. For all his faults, I know Hannah loves him. And I believe he loves her too.

"It's not as if finding Stephen in a bar is a smoking gun," I say. "Never mind that conducting an illicit affair at Harry Asia's is kind of like taking out an ad on the side of a bus." Especially because the bar is close to our old house on Vallejo. Any one of us could've happened by. "I'm sure Stephen was telling the truth. It was a work thing, Adam."

"All I'm saying is I felt a very weird undercurrent. I'm serious, Rach, it was like déjà vu with Mom and Dad," he says as if he was the one to have caught our father with Brooke.

Unfortunately, that was my mother. She decided to surprise Dad at an American Academy of Cosmetic Surgery conference at the Westin in San Diego. She hadn't thought it strange that he took his nurse with him until she found out they were sharing a room. She took a red-eye home and two days later made appointments with every top divorce lawyer in the city. Her best friend, Diane, an expert in divorce, taught my mother all her dirty tricks, including the convenience of conflict. All Shana had to do was pay for a brief confidential consultation with all the best attorneys to make them ineligible to represent my father, leaving him with the equivalent of *My Cousin Vinny*. As it turned out, Dad gave her everything she wanted anyway.

"Did you tell Hannah?"

Adam gets up and sticks the pan back in the fridge, even though there's nothing left of the kugel but crumbs. I start to yell at him to put it in the sink, but I want an answer to my question. Did he tell Hannah?

"Well?"

Adam blows out a breath. "No. You think I should?"

"No...Yes...God, I don't know." On one hand, we Golds stick together. On the other, Adam's sole evidence is that he spotted Stephen at the world's douchiest bar with a colleague. Hardly conclusive.

He flops down on the sofa again. "You're the first person I've told."

Great, now I'm an accessory if it turns out to be true that Stephen is schtupping some floozy he takes to '80s fern bars. "What did she look like?" Not that it matters, but I'm curious.

Adam hitches his shoulder. "Your run-of-the-mill vapid blonde." He shakes his head. "That make you feel better about it?"

"So nothing like Hannah?" I say.

"Give me a break, Rach. A guy doesn't go around comparing women to his sisters. I couldn't even pick her out of a police lineup. But she was hanging on Stephen's every word, which tells me she's pretty hard up."

"Or they were talking shop because...uh...lawyers. Cases. Work. You ever think that perhaps that crazy little gamer brain of yours is working overtime?"

"Maybe," Adam says, stuffing two throw pillows under his head and throwing his legs over the back of the couch. "But it wasn't the first time Stephen was out with a woman not Hannah."

"Oh?"

Adam comes to a sitting position. "Right before your wedding."

Memories of a conversation Adam and I had on that day come flitting back. But like everything about my life now, the conversation is hazy. Of course, it was the happiest day of my life, so I wasn't paying all that much attention to Hannah and Stephen's marital issues. But I do remember the queasy feeling I got when Adam mentioned that there might be problems. It was as if I'd already sensed that something wasn't quite right, and the fact that Adam felt the same way confirmed it.

"Where?" I ask, grabbing the throw blanket over the chair and wrapping it around me.

"Coming out of the Fairmont."

"As in the Fairmont Hotel?" It's the only Fairmont I know but am hoping there's another one that doesn't include beds and six-hundred-thread-count sheets.

"The one and only." Adam hitches his brows in challenge. "Smoking gun enough for you?"

"Not necessarily. There are restaurants in the Fairmont. What time of day was it?"

"Afternoon."

"Maybe he was entertaining someone from out of town, and he wanted to show them the Tonga Room. It is a San Francisco institution."

"And maybe I'll get drafted by the 49ers. No one goes to a tiki bar for lunch. It's a little early for mai tais."

We could go round and round, me disputing everything Adam saw as purely circumstantial. What I wanted was details, something concrete that I could base an informed decision on and decide what to do.

"What did Stephen say when he saw you?"

"I don't think he did. I was coming out of a coffee shop across the street on Mason."

"Are you sure it was even him?"

Adam pierces me with a look. "As sure as I am that I'm looking at you now. He was holding the leather briefcase Hannah gave him that year for his birthday."

"Did you recognize the woman?"

"Nope. She was blond. That's all I can tell you."

"You think it was the same woman you saw him with at Harry Asia's?" That would mean Stephen had been seeing her for nearly seven years. The length of time Josh and I were together. For some irrational reason, I decide that infidelity is better if it's multiple partners instead of just one.

"I couldn't say. But the fucker clearly has an affinity for blondes."

Or a blonde. My stomach roils the way it does when I have indigestion. Hannah's a brunette, like the rest of the Golds.

"What do we do?" I ask, dreading the answer.

"Beats the hell out of me."

Chapter 13
Going Home

Today I did something absolutely insane, like completely bonkers. That's the thing about losing the love of your life, you feel like you have nothing else left to lose. Not your pride. Not your loyalty. Not even your sanity. Life simply becomes a succession of ways to survive the pain, using as little energy as possible.

This morning, I held my nose and called Brooke to ask if I could take up my old bedroom until I'm strong enough to find a place of my own, a place where Josh and I have no history, a place that won't bring back a flood of memories of us.

Granted, it was a strange—and humbling—thing to do, given that Brooke and I aren't close or even friendly. But I need the safety and familiarity of the house on Vallejo like a sick child needs her mother. I guess you can call it my shelter from the storm. And the house is large enough that Brooke and I never have to see each other.

Weirdly enough, my stepmother is being surprisingly accommodating. Perhaps it's my imagination—or I'm that pathetic—but she sounds almost eager for me to spend time there. Maybe she's lonely, though from the little I know of Brooke, she has lots of friends. Other nurses, doctors, members of her hiking group, and a crowd of friends she's still in touch with from college. I know this because they surrounded her at my father's funeral like a protective wall. At the time, I wondered if they were protecting her from us, the Golds. Needless to say, I don't think she's in want of company. Whatever her reason for letting me stay...well, I'm not going to question it.

Josie says she'll help me pack. And Adam has volunteered to clean out Josh's side of the closet, a chore I should've done months ago. My landlord is more than thrilled to break the lease, knowing he can jack up the rent another thousand dollars in this market. So, there's no reason I can't be out of this apartment and in my childhood home by the end of the week.

All I need is a truck to move. The only people I know who own trucks are Stephen and Campbell. I could ask Hannah if I can borrow it, but ever since Adam told me about Stephen, I've been avoiding her. And Campbell...I haven't talked to him in more than four months.

I pick up the phone at least a dozen times, only to put it back down. On my tablet I do a quick Google search for moving truck rentals. The closest one is ten miles away. If I ask Mom for a ride to the rental place, I'll have to explain that I'm moving into Brooke's. I sort of want to wait on that until I've had time to work on my story. It'll take some crafting. Two months ago, I probably could've used the pity chip. But I've more than likely used up the my-husband-is-dead card.

Believe it or not, there is a statute of limitations on grieving. I've learned that the hard way. Besides Josie, none of my friends call anymore. The only reason my family does is because they're stuck with me.

I could ask Adam, I suppose. But he's already doing the closet, and things are crazy with him at work, especially now that he has to get his company's books in tip-top shape for the sale. So I pick up the phone again and rehearse a short speech in my head before I dial.

Campbell picks up on the third ring. "Hey, Rachel. Good to finally hear from you." He doesn't say it as a rebuke. He says it like he's genuinely happy that I've called.

For some reason, that makes me break down. The speech I've carefully prepared turns to racking sobs, and now snot is dripping down my nose onto my upper lip. My throat clogs, and everything that comes out of my mouth sounds choppy and nonsensical.

"Rach," Campbell says in a soft voice, "you want me to come over?"

"No," I manage, trying to get control of myself. "I'm good."

"You don't sound good," he says in that even, steady deep voice of his.

And that makes me cry even worse. "No, really, I'm good," I blubber. "But I need to borrow your truck."

"Okay. When do you need it?"

"Tomorrow." I wipe my nose on my sleeve and try to get hold of myself.

For a long time, Campbell doesn't say anything, but I can hear him breathing on the other end of the phone.

Finally, he says, "What do you need my truck for?"

"I'm moving home."

Another long silence. Then, "Home? You mean Vallejo Street?"

"Uh-huh." I choke on a sob.

"Okay," Campbell says, and I can hear him mulling over the sheer bizarreness of it. He was there when things fell apart between my parents. He watched me...all of us...lose our collective shit. "Does Brooke know you're moving in?"

"Of course."

"Wow," he says, obviously thrown. "Yeah, okay. What time tomorrow?" I manage to pull myself together. "Morning, I guess. Does that work for your schedule?" I look for something to blow my nose into, but I'm in the bedroom and my tissue box is empty.

There's another long pause from Campbell, and then, "Yeah, I can make it work."

So, another thing about losing a spouse is it apparently makes you a self-centered bitch. For more than four months, I've ducked Campbell's phone calls, pretended not to be home when he rang my buzzer, and couldn't be bothered to reply to his many emails. Yet, when I do finally contact him, it's for a favor. A favor to drop everything on a dime and help me move my crap across town.

"How are you?" I ask in an impossible effort to redeem myself. "How is Jess?"

"Good. We're both good."

I can't bring myself to ask about the engagement party. As far as I know, it went on as planned. By the time they found out about the accident, about Josh, they were probably waving goodbye to their last guest.

"I'm glad." Conversation between Campbell and me has never been this awkward. There was a time when we used to talk for hours about everything under the sun. Even before he became my everything, when he was still just my big brother's best friend, he was the one I went to with all my secrets.

There was the time I lost one of my mother's favorite sterling silver earrings. She'd lent them to me to wear to Mary Bixby's fourteenth birthday party and would've killed me if she knew that somewhere between Rock 'n' Rollarena and Yank Sing for dim sum, it fell off my ear. Campbell, holding my hand the whole way, rode with me on two Muni buses to the gift center on Brannon Street to have a jeweler perfectly replicate the one I didn't lose. To this day, he and I are the only ones who know.

"How 'bout you, Rach? I'm worried about you," Campbell says.

"Nothing to worry about." What I want to say is my husband is dead, killed in the blink of an eye by a twenty-eight-year-old, texting while driving, whose only punishment was a few scratches and community service. I'm entitled to not return phone calls. But I know that's not why he's worried about me. Adam, Josie and probably even Hannah have likely exaggerated my state of mind, which, granted, isn't good but not as bad as I'm betting they told him.

By the time he buzzes my intercom the next morning, I've actually showered and put on real clothes, even a bra. Josie brought by a couple of wardrobe boxes the other day, and I spent much of the night loading them up with my clothes. I'm only bringing the bare essentials. The rest, I'll hire movers to put in storage until I come up with a plan.

"Did you find parking?" I call down.

"A loading zone, two buildings down. You got coffee up there?"

"Of course. Come up."

Campbell is in his lumberjack attire. For as long as I've known him, he's dressed the same. Kind of a retro grunge vibe, jeans and flannel shirts. It's a good thing it never gets terribly warm in San Francisco.

I get him down a mug and fill it from the fresh pot I've made. "You want something to eat?" I can probably scrounge up an egg or two. There's also leftover Russian coffee cake—another gift from Josie. I don't know what I'd do without her.

"Nah, I ate earlier." He looks around the apartment. "We taking all this?"

I shake my head. "Just the stuff in the bedroom."

He wanders through the apartment, sipping his coffee, perusing one of the bookshelves where Josh's architecture books are lined up according to height. Without even looking up, he says, "You've lost weight."

"A little bit," I say without meeting his eyes. Ordinarily, I'd take his statement as a compliment, but that's not the way he means it. His tone is filled with concern.

"This move, you think it's wise?" Now he's just being downright polite, because we both know the real question is "Are you out of your goddamn mind?"

I drop the act and let out a long sigh. "I can't stay here anymore." My eyes well up, and Campbell nods in understanding. He starts to reach for me, then immediately lets his arms drop to his sides.

We both pretend like it didn't happen.

"My mother is redoing her two bathrooms, so her place is out of the question. And Adam and Hannah have their own stuff going on. Brooke works nights, and I work days, so we'll keep out of each other's hair." It is true that Brooke works nights. After my father died, she left his practice and went to San Francisco General.

"Josie says you and Jess are looking for a house," I toss out, hoping to change the subject. It's been at least a month since Josie mentioned Campbell's real estate hunt. For all I know, they've already bought a place and have moved in.

"We gave up." Campbell wanders back to the kitchen, tops off his coffee, and watches me over the rim of his cup. "Nothing in our price range that Jess is willing to live in."

I can't really blame her, especially because they have a cute rent-controlled apartment with a small yard that's walking distance to great restaurants and BART. To buy something equivalent would cost a fortune.

"You could buy a fixer, flip it, and get something better," I say and then tell myself, *Thanks, Captain Obvious.* Campbell is a gifted carpenter. He can build or repair anything. And if that's what he wanted to do, he would've done it by now.

"Yeah, I've thought about it. But anything worth fixing has half a dozen bids on it before a for-sale sign even goes up. I need an agent who's tapped in." He continues looking at me. This time, pointedly.

I'm so out of the loop that I'd be doing Campbell a disservice. Not only that but I'm still not ready to dive in yet. "I could recommend someone really good, someone who knows everyone in the city who is even considering selling and does a lot of pocket listings." I'm thinking of Niki. While we've never been on the best of terms, there's no one better I'd trust to help Campbell.

"Been there, done that." Campbell rinses out his cup and sticks it in the dishwasher. "If I have even a ghost of a chance of convincing Jess, I need you."

I'm pretty sure this is all a ruse to get me back amongst the living again. I like Jess, but we're certainly not close enough for me to have any kind of power of persuasion over her.

"You'd be better served by someone who's been paying attention," I say, knowing that this will never go anywhere, and I should just leave it alone.

"I'd be better served by a friend who's got my best interest at heart." Campbell gives me another sharp look.

"Can we move now?" I'm wondering how long someone can remain in a loading zone without getting towed, and the last thing I want to talk about is real estate for more reasons than I care to count.

"Yep. Show me what you've got."

Over the next hour, Campbell lugs a closet load of clothes, a small dresser and a bathroom full of toiletries to his truck while I wait at the curb, making sure no one steals anything. Whatever he doesn't fit in the bed of his pickup, I'll schlepp over in my car, even if it takes a few trips.

Campbell still turns the ladies' heads. Twice now, women have stopped in their tracks to watch him load or stare at his butt. Oblivious to being ogled, he's quick with a smile and a classic dude nod.

"You want to meet me over there or ride in the front?" My overly large suitcase occupies the passenger seat, so I have no idea how I'll fit.

"I'll meet you." I look at my watch. It's a little after noon and I worry that Brooke is sleeping before she has to start her shift. I don't want to get off on a bad foot with her. I'm there only by the grace of her goodwill. The minute she revokes it, I'm out on my ass.

I watch Campbell secure the load and drive off before I go into the garage for Josh's old Accord. I haven't driven since the accident, and I suddenly wish I'd taken up Campbell's offer to ride with him.

You can do this, I tell myself even as I break into a sweat. It takes me ten minutes to work up the nerve to start the ignition. I'm not having any kind of flashbacks, but just sitting in the driver's seat gives me palpitations, and the air seems too heavy to breathe.

I inch my way to the automatic gate, lurching forward every time my foot presses the brake. As a carrot, I remind myself that it's only a five-minute drive to Pac Heights. I make it onto Fillmore without hyperventilating, but traffic is denser than I would've thought for this time of day. Still, I soldier on.

Someone cuts me off and flips me the bird. I look down at my speedometer, and I'm only going eight miles an hour. Wow, it feels faster. I don't speed up, though, and behind me someone leans on his horn. I have a mind to slam on my brakes, get out of the car and ask the driver if he's ever watched a person he loves die of a brain hemorrhage. I don't, of course. It takes all my concentration to make it to Union. By the time I pass Wildseed, I'm considering stopping the car in the middle of the lane, leaving it there, and walking away. There are too many vehicles on the road, and everyone seems to be speeding.

I somehow make it to Vallejo without having an aneurysm. When I finally pull into the driveway, my heart is beating a hundred miles a minute, but I'm intact and the Honda is no worse for wear.

Campbell has already unloaded the bulk of my boxes and is leaning against the garage, waiting. Until now, I hadn't noticed what a beautiful day it is. Crisp and clear and cold enough to see my breath in the air. If I hadn't been petrified, I would've taken the time to admire the holiday decorations on my way over. Hard to believe that Hanukkah is only a week away, Christmas only two.

"What took you so long?" Campbell pushes himself off the wall.

"There was a lot of traffic." I rummage through my purse, looking for the key.

When my father was alive, I would've let myself in. But now, I'm not so sure about the etiquette of such things. Do I ring the bell? Send Brooke a quick text that I'm here? Or go in quietly so as not to disturb her?

Campbell is looking at me like *Where do you want all this stuff?*

I opt for the text and shoot her, "I'm here. Is it okay if I come in and unload some boxes?"

My phone dings a few minutes later with a response from Brooke. "I'm out. Go in and make yourself at home."

"You get the green light?" Campbell looks over my shoulder.

"Yep. She's not here." Thank God. "Let's take everything up to my old bedroom."

Campbell knows the way, as he's been there many times.

Chapter 14
Guilt Trip

"Of all the places you could live, you move in with her?" my mother says over the music at Marigolds. Despite how loud the restaurant is, it has the best Shrimp Louie in the city. "I told you, you could stay with me. Jesus, Rachel, I'm your mother."

Of course this has to be about her.

"Your place isn't livable, Mom." Which is only half of it. Not even the important half.

"It's a couple of bathrooms, not a hovel in Siberia. This is your father's fault. He always spoiled you kids. We were lucky to have a roof over our heads when we were growing up."

My mother grew up in Greenwich, Connecticut. Enough said.

But next, she'll tell, in great bloody detail, the stories of how her people fled Russia during the nineteenth-century pogroms.

I sigh in relief when Adam joins us at the table. I called him last night and begged for backup. Though he's forty minutes late, I've never been happier to see him in my life.

"You're late, but we waited." Mommie Dearest pulls him in for a hug. He always was her favorite.

"What did I miss?" Adam kicks me under the table, and I kick him back.

"Mom was telling me about her remodel."

Shana shoots me a look. "Fine. We won't talk about the elephant in the room." The elephant's name is Brooke, and my mother won't last the rest of the evening without getting in a couple of digs at both of us.

No question I'm on her shit list.

"How's the sale going, Adam?" Adam and I already talked about how everything is moving at a glacial pace, but better he be the center of attention than me.

"I'm letting the lawyers handle it from here," he says, flipping through the cocktail menu. "Drink, anyone?"

I raise my hand like a schoolgirl.

"I'll try one of those mojitos they're famous for," my mother says.

Adam and I exchange glances. A) Marigolds is not famous for mojitos. And B) We try to keep Mommie Dearest away from liquor as much as possible. She's a lightweight and a bad drunk. I guarantee she won't stop at one mojito, and by the time we leave she'll be telling everyone from the bartender to our server how much she loves them and how her youngest daughter betrayed her. Just like Judas did Jesus. Yep, a real shit show.

Thanks, Adam.

He flags over the server, and we give her both our drink and food orders. If we're lucky, Mom's Cobb salad will only trail the cocktails by minutes. Best if she has something to coat her stomach before the booze sets in.

"Did anyone think to invite Hannah and Stephen?" she asks, her voice slightly accusatory.

"Mom, you set this dinner up. It's your job to invite your other children."

She scowls at me. "Well, since you all plot behind my back, I figured one of you would've said something to her."

"We don't plot behind your back," I say.

"Then why is it that I'm the last one to know that you're moving in with...her." After all this time, Shana still won't speak Brooke's name. Just *her.* Or the kurveh.

"Rach is only telling people on a need-to-know basis," Adam says, and I stifle a laugh.

Shana's legendary sense of humor appears to be on hiatus tonight. We'll see what happens after that mojito.

"Well, don't be surprised when she sells the place out from under you." My mother purses her lips in that know-it-all way that never fails to irk me.

While the thought of Brooke selling makes me shudder, I sort of half expected her to put the Queen Anne on the market shortly after my father died. It's too much house for one person, and Brooke has never struck me as an aficionado of old things—except of course my father.

"Don't worry, Rachel. There will always be room for you with me. I am your mother."

"No, I am your father," Adam says in his best James Earl Jones voice.

Our drinks come, and Mommie Dearest is off to the races.

Adam sneaks another glance my way, silently conveying that we should let her drink. *It will go easier on you that way.*

Our salads come—Adam got a burger—and for a while we eat in companionable silence with a side of hostility. Midway through her pile of lettuce, Mom starts in on the whole Brooke thing again.

"I simply don't understand why you're doing this to us."

"I'm not doing anything to us. Can't you see that I'm having a hard time? Can't you see that a part of me died in the car with Josh? I'm trying to catch my breath here, Mom. I'm trying to make myself whole again. And the house on Vallejo will always be our house. The house where every nook and cranny doesn't hold remnants of Josh. The house where I can just be."

Except for the music in the background, our table goes silent. Mom puts down her mostly consumed drink and reaches for my hand. "I want you to get better, Rachel. If you have to stay with that woman to get there, I support you."

I don't bother to correct her. She knows the last person on earth I'd run to is Brooke. She knows damned well that I'm running to my childhood, to the way things used to be before my parents split up, when life was filled with possibilities. With love. With hope. With happiness. I don't have to tell her because she knows.

With a slightly crooked smile on his face, Adam looks at the both of us, waves over our server again, and orders Mom another mojito.

* * * *

I've been here two weeks now and have only run into Brooke four times. Her schedule at the hospital is nuts. What's even nuttier is she appears to have turned the guest cottage into a Vrbo or Airbnb. Twice, I've run into strangers on the property. The first time, I was just about to call the police until I got the 411 from Brooke via text.

The cottage has apparently been rented out for much of the holidays. With all the extra cash, you would think Brooke would devote more resources to caring for the grounds. The house, gardens, and even the brick walkways look more worse for wear than they did at Josh's funeral. I keep reminding myself that it's none of my business. I'm only a guest here.

The doorbell is ringing, and I'm not sure if I'm supposed to answer it. Brooke is either asleep or at work. I roll over and stare at my nightstand, where the same Kitty Cat Klock I had as a teenager still sits. It's eleven in the morning. I should've been up hours ago at least pretending to work. I've given myself until the new year to start in earnest. But in the meantime,

I've been rejiggering my business cards, organizing my contacts, and researching the market.

Unfortunately, none of those tasks has inspired me to get back out there again and beat the pavement. But without Josh's healthy paycheck, I need an income. Our savings, the small inheritance from my dad, and Josh's life insurance won't last forever, especially in a city where even milk is more expensive than the rest of the free world. And I can't sponge off Brooke forever.

The doorbell rings again. I get out of bed, throw on a robe, and pad down the staircase. Through the peephole there's a portly man with thinning hair staring back at me. I open the door a crack.

"Can I help you?"

"I'm here about the pool house." He seems to think I should know what he's talking about.

"Uh, Brooke...my stepmother...isn't home right now." Frankly, I don't know if she is. But if she was expecting someone, I'm sure she would've answered the door. "Did you have an appointment?"

He's scrolling through his phone and shows me an entry on his calendar with the house's address. For all I know, he stuck it in there five minutes before he rang the bell and he's Ted Bundy's cousin.

"I don't know what to tell you."

"She said it was unlocked. I'm just here to take a few measurements."

My eyes go to the tape measure clipped to his belt. His truck is parked in the driveway, and Bleu Construction is written in bold red letters on the side. Looks like he's legit. I point him in the direction of the pool house. It only dawns on me as he's halfway around the house that I didn't ask what the measurements were for.

I race upstairs and throw on jeans, a hoodie and a pair of shoes, then cross the wet grass to the pool. None of the patio furniture has been covered, and everything has taken quite a beating. I find the man walking around the pool house, taking measurements with one of those surveyor's wheels. I only know what it is because of Josh.

"What are you measuring for?" I ask, trying for friendly rather than nosy. This is no longer my family's home, and what Brooke does or does not do with it is none of my concern. But I'm wildly curious.

"Your stepmother wants a bid for expanding it and adding heat."

It sounds to me as if Brooke is considering Vrboing the pool house now. It's just a studio with a bathroom and a tiny kitchenette. When I was a kid, my parents would let me have sleepovers in there with a few girlfriends. We'd make popcorn in the microwave and stay up all night, watching movies. On hot summer mornings, we'd wake ourselves up by diving into the pool and letting the cool water from the rock fall sluice over us and pretend we were in a remote lagoon in Hawaii. Sometimes, Campbell and I would rendezvous there while his father weeded and trimmed the lawn.

And now Brooke wants to open the studio, a perfect replica of the Queen Anne, to perfect strangers. Not my business, I remind myself. But it's so bizarre. Is she planning to turn the entire place into a boarding house?

The question sticks with me until dinner, a cobbled-together meal of carrot sticks, smoked almonds, and Reese's Peanut Butter Cups. I'm sitting at the center island, waiting for the water to boil for tea, when Brooke walks in. It's the first time since I've moved in that we're in the same room together. Typically, on the few occasions we've come face-to-face, it's been in the hallway or the staircase, like two ships passing in the night.

I instantly freeze up, feeling awkward. Brooke, on the other hand, breezes in, wearing a pair of green scrubs and white clogs. Her hair is pulled back, and there's not a stitch of makeup on her. She looks tired and, yes, even a little old.

She grabs an apple from the fruit bowl on the counter and joins me at the island. For a long time, we sit there without speaking.

Finally, I break the silence. "A man was here today to measure the pool house."

"Shit. The guy from Bleu Construction. I totally forgot." She rubs her temple and mumbles, as if she's alone, "I'm working so many shifts I don't know if I'm coming or going."

"Why?" I blurt. She can't possibly need the money. But between the guest cottage and the pool house, I'm starting to wonder.

Brooke looks at me and shakes her head. "Why? Because I enjoy having a roof over my head." She says this as if someone with my privileged upbringing wouldn't understand, which to be perfectly honest isn't altogether untrue.

I know I've led a charmed life. First, with my parents, who made sure Hannah, Adam and I had the best of everything, including top-of-the-line orthodontia work and first-rate education, which I'm very thankful for. And second, with Josh, who did the heavy lifting as far as our finances were concerned. But Brooke wasn't exactly married to a pauper. She's sitting on millions of dollars' worth of real estate, not to mention all my father's other assets, including part of a lucrative cosmetic surgery practice.

So, save me the woe-is-me pity party.

"Do you know how much it costs to keep up this place?" She stares up at a brown spot on the tin ceiling, which is original to the house, or so my mother says. As far back as I can remember, the stain has been there. But it does seem to be spreading.

We go back to being silent until the whistle of the kettle rends the air. I pour myself a cup of chamomile.

"You want one?"

She appears to think about it for a beat, then says, "Sure."

I find another bag in the pantry and fix her a cup.

She blows on the top of the mug, then tests it by taking a small sip. "Did the guy from Bleu say how much?"

"No. He took measurements and left. If you don't mind me asking, why are you expanding it?"

"The cottage brings in four-hundred dollars a night. I figure with a little work, the pool house could bring in at least two fifty, even three."

A quick calculation in my head says even if the two apartments are only occupied half the year, it's roughly more than a hundred thousand dollars in income. Not bad if you don't mind strangers roaming around your backyard.

"Why not just sell?" I ask, wondering if I'm crossing a line. I have no idea how private Brooke is about her finances. And I certainly hope she doesn't think I'm angling for the listing, because I'm not. This house means everything to me, and to watch hordes of people walk through these halls, talking about all the things they'd like to rip out, change and refinish would make me physically ill.

She sucks in a breath and takes another sip of tea before resting her cup on the counter. I can tell she's choosing her words. *Mind your own business, Rachel Gold. What I do with this house is none of your concern.*

"Your father wouldn't want me to," she says after a few seconds.

Okay, not what I anticipated. I want to say that I don't think he'd be particularly thrilled that she was turning it into a youth hostel either but hold my tongue.

"What are your plans for the pool house, then?"

"Add a bedroom and expand the bathroom, make it more luxurious. Maybe modernize the kitchenette, add a small stove, and a dishwasher. That way I can do longer-term rentals. I know a few traveling nurses who are always looking for something inexpensive...safe."

It sounds as if she's given it a lot of thought. I can't say it doesn't make sense, though the whole thing gives me the creeps. But the cottage and the pool house are just sitting here, empty, I rationalize.

Still, I can't help believing there's something Brooke isn't saying. Obviously, Dad didn't leave her as much money as we thought he did.

"I've got to go to work." Brooke gets up, puts her cup in the dishwasher, and swivels around to face me. "I would love it if you could run the project for me."

At first, I have no idea what she's talking about. Then I realize she means the conversion of the pool house to an efficiency apartment.

"My hours are crazy in the ER, and if you don't ride these guys, they'll run roughshod over you. Would you be willing to take it on?"

I know absolutely zero about remodeling. While my mother isn't happy unless she has a major construction project going on in her home, the sound of power tools sends me into a homicidal rage. Furthermore, I like the pool house just the way it is. The idea of changing it makes me sad. And nostalgic. But Brooke is letting me live here free. And there is the minor detail that I'm here all day long—until I get my act together—without making any real contribution. So, how do I say no?

"Sure," I tell her. "If you trust me to do it. It's not like I have any experience, though."

"All you have to do is make sure the contractors show up every day and do the work. I'll send you inspiration photos of what I have in mind. You can use those to guide you. The sooner I get this done, the sooner I can get a tenant in here."

I don't see the rush, but I'll do my part. Perhaps having some purpose will motivate me. I really should be focusing on selling real estate and finding a permanent place to live. At least for the first time since Josh died, I've been sleeping through the night and eating better. I credit being home in my happy place for making the difference. It's probably why I'm gripped by paralysis every time I start to scroll through the rental ads on craigslist. I could let Janney at Windham know that I'm looking. She would put out the word to the office in case any of the agents have a lease listing. But I can't seem to launch.

Same goes with work.

Campbell has called a few times about picking up his and Jess's house search again. My response has been radio silence. Deep down inside, I can't help but question whether it's my lack of ambition or if I'm simply resistant to helping Campbell find his happily ever after. It's not that I don't want him to be happy. I do. But maybe not with Jess...or anyone. *It would be different if Josh were still alive,* I tell myself. Ugh, this makes me the worst kind of person.

I empty my half-filled cup of tea into the sink and wander to the living room. The house creaks, which ordinarily, alone, would scare the hell out of me. But the sounds of this old house's squeaky bones are so familiar to me that I find comfort in them. My untouched laptop sits on the coffee table. I reach over it for the remote control and flick on the television, surfing through the channels, looking for something to watch. Josh and I used to love snuggling on the sofa after a long day and binge watching a series—usually a crime show—on Netflix.

My heart is not really into anything that takes real commitment, so I settle on a network sitcom. After a few minutes, though, the annoying laugh track forces me to switch it off. I consider checking in with Hannah, then remember that she and Stephen took a few days off and rented a house in Sea Ranch. I suspect she's ovulating and they're using the time to get busy.

Josie's on a date with one of her clients—a tech guy she's had a thing for going on more than a year. I'm keeping my fingers crossed for her. No one deserves to find love more than Josie. We've been with each other through every crush, every breakup, and every ugly cry over a guy. She knew Josh was the one even before I did.

In the end, I settle for Adam, but he doesn't pick up his phone. I mentally shuffle through my Rolodex of friends but am too embarrassed to call any of them after ignoring their repeated attempts to reach out to me over the last five months. I've basically alienated everyone I know, becoming one of those sad sacks who walks around her apartment all day in a stained housecoat that once belonged to her grandmother.

The good news, I suppose, is that I have any desire to call them at all. And that's when it hits me. I may in fact be slowly returning to the land of the living.

Chapter 15
Company Is Coming

It's eight o'clock in the morning, and there's a buzz saw running loose through my head. At first, I think I'm dreaming, and then I remember the contractors are here. It's their first day on the pool house job.

It took the portly man from Bleu Construction three weeks to finally send his bid. I had to prod him, which I'm not terribly good at. But Brooke is relying on me, and I would very much like to continue living here. As it turns out, every construction company west of the Mississippi is booked out for years thanks to California's four summers of wildfires. We're lucky to have Bleu, though the fact that the company is the only builder available isn't exactly a ringing endorsement. Then again, the pool house isn't what you would call the Great Mosque of Djenné. How bad can they screw it up?

I take a quick shower and dress, figuring I should probably show my face. Act like an overseer or whatever I'm supposed to be. The crew, five guys in hard hats and steel-toed boots, are ripping out what used to be the kitchenette and bathroom. One of the men introduces himself. He's Kyle Wright, the foreman. Apparently, the portly man I've been dealing with only does the bids. Kyle, who is about my age, is anything but portly. I slip a covert look at his ring finger. Naked. I'm thinking about Josie and if things don't work out with the tech dude.

"How long do you think this will take?" I ask. We're already behind Brooke's schedule, and it's my job to make the trains run on time.

"The demo or the whole project?"

"The whole project."

"Five weeks if we don't run into problems."

"Problems? Like what kind of problems?" It's a freaking square box that we're expanding by three-hundred square feet. I'm no builder, but it seems like something that could be knocked out in a few days.

"Dry rot, structural integrity, hang-ups with the city permitting folks." "But we have a permit." I'd hired an expediter for that very purpose. Josh used to call them schmoozers. Basically, it's government corruption at its finest. These expediters all work for the city planning department by day and moonlight as "construction consultants" by night. All you have to do is write them a big fat check, and they grease the wheels to get your permits through the system with no fuss or muss. Believe it or not, this is a perfectly legal and accepted practice in San Francisco. Meanwhile, on Planet Earth, it's called bribery.

Kyle The Unportly shrugs as if to say *Shit happens.*

Well, it better not, I say to myself because I'm tough that way. "Alrighty then." I bob my chin for them to carry on and walk back to the house, where Brooke is eating gluten-free toast at the center island. The only reason I know it's gluten-free is because I've seen the package. Maybe she has celiac disease or is a health nut. I watch her nibble around the burnt edge of her toast, and in that moment it strikes me that I know very little about my stepmother. Not where she's originally from (although I think somewhere in the Midwest) or even her birthday. Until I moved in, I didn't even know she was an emergency room nurse. I'd always assumed her specialty was in cosmetic surgery.

"Hey," she says, noticing me for the first time as I come further into the room. "You're up early."

I'm not sure if it's a veiled jab or just a conversation opener. Our cohabitating together continues to be awkward. Thank goodness we rarely see each other.

"I was in the pool house, talking to the contractors."

"I heard them." She pulls a face, and I realize she's still in her pajamas. White flannel with little scottie dogs.

Weird, because I would've taken her for a negligee girl. The kind from Victoria's Secret with scratchy lace, plunging decolletage, and a hemline that comes up to her *pupik,* as my mother would say. There are a few streaks of gray in her mussed hair I hadn't noticed the last time we talked. And her eyes are puffy and bloodshot.

"How long before your shift starts?" She should go back to bed and catch a few more hours of sleep.

"I'm off until Friday."

It's the first time Brooke has had time off since I moved in. Either that or she's staying elsewhere on her days off. We, as in the Golds, have always assumed that without my dad, she'd move on with the next man who came her way. So far, though, there's been no sign that she's seeing anyone. No new car parked in the driveway, no strange voice coming from her bedroom, no extra coffee mug in the sink in the morning. But who knows, she could be going to his place, and I'd be none the wiser.

"I'm having a few people over tonight," she says. "Want to join us?"

Her invitation catches me by surprise, and I feel like a deer caught in a pair of high beams. No, I don't want to join a group of strangers. But it's not like I can lie about having other plans and then hang out in my bedroom all night. I don't have anywhere to go. But the idea of spending the evening with Brooke and her friends...well, I'd rather have a colonoscopy.

"I don't want to be rude, but I'm not quite ready to socialize yet." It's the truth, though lately I've been venturing out more. Yesterday, I even went on a broker's caravan to check out new listings. Lord knows why, since I don't have any clients. But it felt good to at least pretend to be working again.

"That's fine," Brooke says. "There's no pressure. Just know that if you change your mind and feel up to it, you're always welcome."

It is beyond generous of her, and I'm filled with guilt for resenting her for it.

* * * *

I can hear them downstairs. Out of curiosity, I loiter in the hallway just outside my bedroom door and peer over the banister, hoping to catch a glimpse of Brooke's friends. Presumably they're from the hospital where she works. I wonder if she's sleeping with any of their husbands, which is wholly unkind but where my mind wanders when it comes to Brooke.

Their conversation is coming from the direction of the dining room, which means I'll have to go downstairs if I want to spy. I deliberate on whether to snoop or stay cloistered in my room. Ultimately nosiness wins out. Brilliantly, I've come up with the excuse of needing a drink of water, transporting myself back to when I was eight years old, trying to crash one of my parents' fancy dinner parties.

I find them gathered around my parents' old Duncan Phyfe dinner table. My mother used to brag that she spotted the mahogany table at an estate sale and knew instantly it was an original. Always shined to a high polish, that table saw the Golds through many a holiday and celebration.

Not so much tonight. The wood finish is dull and the lion feet dusty. And some of Brooke's guests look as old as the table.

For some reason, I was expecting a rowdy group of nurses. Instead, it's a diverse crowd of about a dozen people, drinking coffee and eating bakery-bought pastries, wearing solemn expressions like their dog just got run over by a truck.

"This is my stepdaughter," Brooke announces to the gathering, making my cheeks heat. She looks more like my older, thinner, blonder sister.

"I just need to make a pitstop in the kitchen and will be out of your hair in a minute. Sorry for the interruption."

"You're not interrupting, dear," says an older man with an Indian accent. "Brooke says you've lost a spouse too."

The word *too* is momentarily lost on me. I'm too busy reacting to the knowledge that Brooke has shared my personal tragedy with people I don't know. People I've never seen before. Then, like remembering an early clue in the mystery book you've been reading, the *too* word comes floating back to me. And it becomes clear. These are not Brooke's work friends. They're a bereavement group here to grieve the loss of a husband or wife.

"You should join us," says a woman who can't be more than forty.

I feel cornered. I don't want to be impolite, but I also don't have the capacity to share my heartache with strangers. The same goes for advice. I have nothing to offer, except to tell these people that the pain of losing the most important person in your life never goes away. It festers like a gaping, infected wound. Which I'm sure is not helpful. Not helpful to anyone.

"You don't have to say anything," Brooke says, making me think she's telepathic. "You can just listen."

Now I'm stuck. If I leave, I look like a total bitch. One of the members of the group, a brawny guy with sad brown eyes, drags over an extra chair from the wall and makes space for me at the table. A cup of coffee magically appears, and someone slides me an almond croissant with an assurance that "it's from Tartine."

The room goes momentarily silent. Then the woman—Vivian someone else calls her—says, "I'll go first."

"Yesterday, Matthew wanted Rich's stuffed fish to bring to show-and-tell. It's a huge blue marlin Rich caught in Cabo a few years ago and insisted we mount over our fireplace. The thing is hideous. Like seriously disgusting. I can't tell you how many times we fought over that goddamn fish. But my baby wanted to show off his daddy's trophy at school, and I was going to move heaven and earth to make sure that happened. I climbed up on a foot ladder and pried the son of a bitch off the wall. It probably weighs as much as I do. Still, I managed to wrangle it to the floor, cursing the entire way down. Words my darling Matthew has never heard before."

The room breaks into laughter, but I sense there is more, that she hasn't yet delivered the punchline to a heartbreaking story.

"The awful thing is lying on my good rug, and in my head I'm strategizing on how to get it to the car without breaking my back in the process. Its bugging eyes are staring at me. It feels as if the fish is following my every move. And like a crazy woman, I say, 'Rich, are you in there?' And then for no damned reason, I start blubbering over the piece of shit, hugging it to my body like it's a living thing, uncontrollably crying. And when I finally get a hold of myself, I start all over again, petrified that I won't be able to get it back over the mantel after Matthew's show-and-tell. I've always hated the thing, and now all I can think about is how much I miss it looming over our living room."

The Indian man reaches over and takes her hand. "It's okay. We all have those moments."

I think about Brooke and my father's newsboy cap and am astonished to wonder if that was her blue marlin moment. There are so many things I don't know about her. I think about all the silly items I'm still unable to part with because they meant something to Josh. All the books and records and hats that embody his memory.

The stories move around the table. The Indian man is Raj, and he lost his wife of thirty years to breast cancer. Vivian's husband was killed by a drunk driver. He'd survived two tours in Afghanistan but, yeah, a fucking drunk driver. Doris's husband died from complications of sickle cell on his seventy-fifth birthday. They were high school sweethearts and best friends.

Each testimony is more heartbreaking than the last. But there's something uplifting about them, too. Their stories of undying love, their resilience, and their will to move forward, alone, fills me with hope.

When the group leaves, I help Brooke clean up. We don't say much, as I'm still digesting the revelation that she's part of a grief group to mourn the death of my father. It's not anything I saw coming. So far, nothing about Brooke is. She's definitely an enigma.

After the last coffee mug is loaded into the dishwasher, I climb the stairs to my room. It's too early to go to bed, but I want to give Brooke space. It's her house, after all. I'm just a guest here.

To while away the time, I open my laptop and scroll through emails. Most of it is spam, including an ad for enlarging my penis and a congratulatory note that I've won the lottery in Malawi.

There's a message from Chip that says it was good to see me on the brokers' tour. That it looks like I'm getting back into the swing of things. And if there's anything I need...blah, blah, blah. The one that catches my eye, though, is from Martin, Owens and Luckett. I haven't talked to anyone from Josh's architecture firm since the funeral. A few of his friends have tried to stay in touch, but like everyone else, I've blown them off.

I open the email to find a nice note from Josh's old boss. He hopes I'm doing well and says he thinks of Josh all the time. "The firm isn't the same without him." He asks how my real estate "business" is going and says someday soon he'd love to take me to lunch, which is very sweet. But it's clear that the real reason he's written is he's looking for a set of plans Josh was working on right before he was killed. Do I have access to his laptop or know how to get into Revit?

I definitely have access to his laptop, but Revit is another story. I know it's the software program Josh used for his job but have no idea how to work it. It's late, so I decide to tackle it first thing in the morning.

Except, Kyle and the boys are back at the crack of dawn with their power tools. Again, I go traipsing across the lawn to inspect their work and pretend to know what I'm doing. They're still in demo phase, ripping out the walls to the bare studs.

Kyle says they expect to start pouring the concrete footings for the expansion sometime next week. Then they can begin framing. He assures me that everything is running on schedule.

Although Josie is still seeing tech boy, I make some discreet inquiries into Kyle's romantic status.

I guess they're not as subtle as I think, because he responds, "Why? You want to go out?" He does a slow turn over my body.

I'm slightly mortified, even though he appears highly amused. And I think truly interested, because he makes sure I know that he's single, straight and "really into" brunettes with brown eyes.

I hightail it out of the pool house as fast as I can before Kyle gets any more ideas. Only a few feet from the back door, the gray sky opens, and I'm caught in a downpour. I cover my head with my arms and make a run for it, my flip-flops squishing in the sodden grass with every step I take. It's the first real rain we've had this winter, and it feels like it's going to be a soaker.

I had plans to go into the office today but don't want to drive in this weather. As it is, I'm hesitant to drive even when conditions are good. I could call an Uber or Lyft, or even take Muni, but these days I look for any excuse not to go in, despite promising myself that in January I would hit the ground running. I tell myself I will work from home today but not before I wash down one of the leftover Tartine pastries from last night with a cup of coffee. First, I strip out of my wet hoodie and toss it into the washer and slip into a pair of fuzzy slippers.

Brooke's nowhere to be found, so I assume she's still sleeping. I run up and grab my laptop and scroll through emails while I munch on a morning bun. *See, I can be productive.* Nothing stands out in my inbox, except an email from Campbell. I pretend to ignore it, then can't help myself and open it.

"You up for showing us some real estate? Jess likes this one." It's a link from Realtor.com.

I click on it, gaze at the price, and suspect it's already gone. I sort through the pictures anyway. It's a Craftsman bungalow in Dolores Heights. Great neighborhood, but the house is a dump and that's with good lighting and a flattering camera lens. There's no telling what it really looks like. According to the description, there's only one bathroom. From the photograph, I'd call it circa 1970 prison cell. Just a wall-mounted sink, old toilet, and a rust-stained tub. The original built-ins in the living room have been modified and not in a good way. And unless the camera was held at a weird angle, the floor appears unlevel. Not a good sign. In my experience, it usually means a bad foundation. But Campbell would know better. The kitchen is a total gut job, though in this price range they typically are.

Still, it's a steal of a deal. Which makes me question whether the house has more wrong with it than just aesthetics. I switch over to the MLS and check the house's status. There's nothing that says pending, but the Multiple Listing Service isn't always up-to-the-minute correct. I grab my cell off the counter and dial the listing agent.

"Hi, this is Rachel Ackermann from Windham. Is the Craftsman on Liberty still available? I have a client who may be interested."

"Why it absolutely is. But I'm sure it won't last. It's priced to sell," the agent trills.

I don't know her by name, but she's from my old shop. "Okay. Let me get back to you."

"Don't wait too long."

That last line annoys me. It's pushy. And that's probably why she's better at her job than I ever was. I don't do pushy. Hell, I don't even do passive aggressive. I'm not a natural-born salesperson. But I have nearly ten years invested in selling real estate, so to have this epiphany now... well, it's a waste of time. *Just get out there, Rachel.*

But Campbell...I grimace and consider calling Niki to give her the referral. Let her make Campbell and Jessica's dreams come true.

"What's up?" Brooke's in her scottie dog pajamas again.

She puts on a fresh pot of coffee, which I should've done the minute I drained the old pot. I'm a crappy houseguest as well as a crappy real estate agent.

"Campbell wants to look at a house." I turn my laptop so she can see the pictures I have on my screen.

She looks over my shoulder. "Nice."

"Really?" Because it's not. But if anyone can save it, Campbell can.

"Sure." She reaches in the drawer on the other side of the center island and puts a pair of glasses on before pulling the monitor closer and examining the house. "It's a little run-down, but Campbell's a carpenter, right?"

"Yep." I'm surprised she remembers. I don't think she's met Campbell more than twice. Three times max.

Her glasses slip down on the bridge of her nose as she reads the property details, then does a double take. "Holy shit, the price is fantastic." She turns to me. "You better hurry."

She's right. I dash off a text to Campbell, and twenty minutes later, I'm running down the driveway in the rain to get inside his truck.

"Thanks for picking me up." So far, my driving phobia is a well-kept secret. Anyway, it'll be easier as far as parking to go in one car. "Is Jess meeting us there?"

"Nope. She got caught up at work. But you made it sound pretty urgent that we look at it now, so you've got me." He grins, showing off a pair of dimples. Those dimples used to turn me inside out.

For some reason, they make me flash on my sixteenth birthday. Campbell took me to Arturo's, and in a red Naugahyde banquette in the back of the restaurant, he slipped a promise ring on my finger, making us official. The ring, an eighteen-karat-gold band with a rainbow of gemstones, must've cost Campbell two years' worth of lawn-mowing money. Little did he know he already had me with those dimples. Still, I've kept the ring all these years stashed in the back of my jewelry box.

We find parking right in front of the house, wouldn't you know it? The Craftsman is wedged between two contemporaries that look like twin space stations. Who knows what they were before? Dolores Heights' architecture is all over the map. I'm sure Josh would've loved these gleaming glass-and-steel monstrosities. Me, not so much. I've always been drawn to vintage. The painted ladies in Alamo Square, the Spreckels Mansion on Washington, anything Julia Morgan. It's probably because I grew up in a Queen Anne where you could smell the history. And I mean that in a good way.

I much prefer the Craftsman, though it's tiny and in need of lots of tender loving care. The grass is grown over in what passes for a front yard, the paint is the color of baby poop, and any charm it once had has been stripped away, starting with the columns on the front porch. Who knows if it's even structurally sound?

I glance over at Campbell to see his reaction to the place, but he's looking at me. His green eyes are filled...with something. Longing. Grief. I tell myself I'm wrong. How can it be? His life is so full. Here he is looking at a house, at his future. And just like that, that damned Frank Sinatra song pops into my head.

I've got the world on a string, sittin' on a rainbow...

I open the door and climb down from his truck, hoping that a little damp air will make it stop.

Campbell comes over to my side. "Come 'ere," he says and doesn't wait for me to walk into his open arms. He just pulls me in and wraps me in a hug so warm and tight that I want to stay burrowed in his chest for a thousand years.

It's the first time since Josh died that anyone has held me. Until now I didn't realize how much I needed that kind of human contact. And Campbell is like memory foam, everything about him is familiar, and my body instantly comes to life. For a moment, I revel in it. But there's a niggling at the back of my head that it's wrong. It's Campbell, not Josie or Adam or Hannah or even my mom. He's Jessica's now. And I'm Josh's, always and forever.

I slowly pull away. "You ready to take a walk on the wild side?"

He chuckles and glances at the house over my head. "It's a real piece of shit, isn't it?"

"Yep." I fuss with the lockbox until it finally opens, realizing how rusty I am. "But possibly a jewel in the rough."

We go in, and I'm immediately hit with the smell of something dead.

"Don't look," Campbell says and shields my eyes.

And with that, it doesn't take hyperosmia to know what the stink is.

Campbell takes me by the shoulders, turns me around, and walks me outside. "I'll take care of it." He is well acquainted with my fear of rodents. Live, dead, cartoon characters. It doesn't matter. I loathe them all.

It's merely misting now, and that horrible odor is replaced with the smell of fresh rain and newly tarred streets. This block of Liberty is really quite pretty with its mature trees. I spy a porta potty down the street, which means there's construction going on. Not great for quality of life, but gentrification is good for property values. And don't I sound like bougie scum?

Campbell leans out the door, gives me a thumbs-up, and beckons me back inside. I don't even want to know what he did with Mickey Mouse or, given the stench, Rizzo the Rat.

We stand in the living room, taking it all in.

"The floor's not level." It's even worse than in the photographs.

"It's either a bad foundation or busted floor joists."

"Is that bad?"

"Well, it's not good." Campbell goes to the worst spot, a dip the size of a sinkhole, and jumps up and down. "Feels spongy. But I'd have to get under the house to see."

"It's good space." For a house this small, it really does feel open and airy.

Campbell turns in place. "There were columns there and probably bookshelves." He points to the transition between the living and dining rooms. "You can see where someone feathered in new flooring to cover the holes."

The dining room still has the original wainscoting, but some of the windows have been replaced with hideous louvers that don't fit the period. Whoever lived here before was a smoker because there's a brownish yellow film on all the walls. And unlike the living room, it has a cottage cheese ceiling.

Campbell follows my gaze upward. "Could be asbestos, which won't be cheap to get rid of."

We move into the kitchen, which bizarrely enough is the only room that shows better in real life than the pictures. It's still a gut job, but there's plenty of light and the layout is decent, even good.

Campbell walks into the adjoining bedroom and examines the wall that separates the two spaces. "I'd open this up and expand the kitchen. Maybe add a breakfast nook."

I can see it. The second room has views of the overgrown backyard. If the grounds were cleaned up and landscaped, that little space could be the best spot in the house.

I nudge my head to the outside. "Your dad could make that yard a showplace."

"Yep. The place definitely has potential. Let's see the bedrooms."

They're on the other side of the house. Just two rectangles equivalent in size with enough room to squeeze in queen-sized beds.

"I'd make this one ours," Campbell says. "Maybe add French doors here and put in a deck."

I nod as a wave of melancholy hits me like a punch to the gut as I picture the room filling with light in the morning as Campbell and Jessica sleep. A small child pads into the room and climbs into bed with them, snuggling between mother and father.

My eyes fill with tears, and I go in search of the bathroom so Campbell won't see me crying.

"Rach, where'd you go?"

"I'm checking out the bathroom," I manage to call in a coherent voice.

He's there, standing beside me, and I quickly turn away, pretending to examine the tub. "You'll have to replace this."

"You okay?"

"Of course. Why wouldn't I be?" I surreptitiously try to blot my eyes dry. "What do you think?" I wave my hand at the bathroom.

Campbell steps back and assesses it. "Worst room in the house, and the others ain't good."

I laugh because he's right. But it's not as bad as it could be. "It's a steal, Campbell. Almost too good to be true. If you consider the neighborhood, the benefit of having a real backyard, and a driveway where you can park at least one car—maybe even two small ones tandemly—it's basically a pot of gold at the end of the real estate rainbow. If you're interested, we'll need to do a thorough inspection. And if everything checks out, be prepared for multiple offers." There's a reason why it's priced the way it is. To drive up interest and fuel a feeding frenzy.

"Jess'll need to see it. But out of everything we've looked at over the last few months, this one has the most potential. It's more than we wanted to spend. To fix it up will take more than we have. But at least it's something substantial. Something we can grow into. Maybe even add another bath at some point." He steps out of the bathroom and examines the casing around the door. To my inexperienced eye, it doesn't look original to the house, but Campbell can fix that.

"Let's check out the yard."

We walk around the side because the back door won't open against the heavy overgrowth. My shoes, a pair of high-heeled booties, are no match for the weeds. But Campbell walks the property. It's large enough for his deck and possibly a second bathroom with enough room to spare for a grassy area, patio furniture and a grill. There's no doubt in my mind that Mr. Scott can design something great. According to my mother, whose bar is as high as the sky, Mr. Scott could tame a jungle into the royal gardens.

The inside...well, there's nothing Campbell can't do. He'll bring back the charm and then some.

"There's a lot of dry rot." He's returned to the house now and is poking the wood siding with a stick. "I wouldn't be surprised if it needs to be torn down to the studs. If that's the case, it might not make sense. But I like it. I like the challenge."

"We can't wait too long. This place isn't going to last. When do you think Jess can see it?"

Campbell pulls his phone from his jacket pocket and walks over to the dilapidated fence, another thing that needs rebuilding. I step away to give him privacy, which in and of itself is weird.

He finds me on the sidewalk in front. "Does tomorrow morning work for you?"

I go through the motions of checking my calendar. Why the pretext, I don't know. It's Campbell, for goodness' sake. There was a time when he knew everything about me, even the things I didn't know about myself.

"That'll work," I say, scrolling through days with no entries. "In the meantime, I'll call the listing agent to see when she's taking offers." My hunch is that she'll wait the usual two weeks, enough time to drum up a bidding war.

"Sounds good. I can do the inspection myself. Save time and a little money, though I'd like to get a roofer and a foundation expert in here."

Ordinarily that would be my job, but I don't know any roofers or foundation people. "You have anyone in mind, or would you like me to get them?" I can always ask Chip or someone else at Windham for recommendations.

"I got a buddy who's a foundation guy, and I'm sure my pop knows a good roofer. I'll handle it." He reaches over and touches my shoulder. "Thanks for doing this on such short notice. Jess and I can't tell you how happy we are to have you looking out for us."

"Of course," I say and turn away. "Should we get going, or do you want to go back inside for another look?"

To my relief, he says I can lock up. I do a quick walk-through to make sure the lights are out and the windows are closed, leave my card on the kitchen counter, and put the key back in the lockbox.

The first half of our trip back to Pacific Heights, we ride in silence. Then Campbell asks about the construction crew that was parked in the driveway when he picked me up.

"Brooke is expanding the pool house."

He lifts a brow, and I know exactly what he's thinking. Everything he knows about Brooke he's heard from me and Adam.

"She wants to rent it out to traveling nurses or put it on Vrbo," I say.

Now both brows wing up. "Why?"

"I don't know for sure, but I think she's strapped for cash. Either that or she's entrepreneurial. She's got the guest cottage rented out almost every weekend."

"I guess it's a big house for one person...two..." He smiles, and those dimples make another command appearance. "May as well put it to work."

"I guess," I say but still feel a little creepy about it. I'll always think of the house as my family home, not as a hotel. "How are the wedding plans coming?" I ask, partly to change the subject and partly because I haven't asked and I know I should.

"That's Jess and her mom's bailiwick. I'm just along for the ride." He gives me a sideways glance. "Are we ever going to talk about the day it happened?"

At first, I think he's talking about seventeen years ago, and my heart stops. Then I quickly realize he's referring to the day Josh died.

"There's nothing really to talk about." Other than the fact that it was the worst day of my life, worse than even the other worst day of my life.

"You sure?" He slides me another glance. "Because these last months, I feel like you've gone out of your way to avoid me."

"Not just you, Campbell, everyone." Which is the God's honest truth. "My husband died," I say with a tremor in my voice, as if he needs reminding.

The cab of his truck fills with silence. The only sound is the purr of the heater.

"I wanted to be there for you," he finally says.

Like you were when we lost our baby?

I silently berate myself for being unreasonable. We're both to blame for the way things ended between us, though I guess at the back of my mind, at least then, I'd thought our breakup was a temporary thing. That we were fated to be together and were simply spreading our wings. But the more time went on, the more he felt lost to me. And I missed him. I missed what we used to be. By the time he'd left for school, the gulf between us had deepened to the point where I didn't even know him anymore.

He'd come home some weekends and on holidays and go out of his way to avoid me. The only reason I knew he was home was from Adam. I'd leave him messages, asking if he wanted to meet up at our favorite pho place or go out for ice cream, and he wouldn't return the calls. Twice, I got Hannah or Josie to drive me to his house, where Mr. Scott told me he wasn't home, even though I knew he was.

Once, I saw him at the Westfield Shopping Centre downtown. And for a second, it was like seeing the old Campbell, the boy I'd loved since I was twelve years old, the boy I'd given my heart. I started to go toward him, and that's when I saw what made me know that we were never getting back together again. He was with a girl, which alone wouldn't have been enough for me to give up on him. It was the way he was looking at her. It was the same way he used to look at me. And that's how I knew that we were over. That what we once had was history.

I remember crying for a month straight and climbing into the tree house so many times that I could navigate the crude wooden ladder in my sleep. For hours I would sit in the branches, writing Campbell letters. Love letters, hate letters, and everything in between. My pride kept me from mailing them, thank God. But it was a long time before I could even so much as glance at another guy, my heart never stopped beating for Campbell.

Around my sophomore year at San Diego State, I reluctantly began to date again, but nothing ever stuck until Josh.

It wasn't until after college that Campbell and I started talking again. I was studying for my real estate exam, and he came over to the house to hang out with Adam. I wouldn't say we picked up right where we left off, but we fell into that easy way that people who have grown up with each other have. I was seeing a guy named Warner at the time and was pretty into him. Still, a part of me wasn't over Campbell. You never get over your first. Isn't that what they say?

After that, we would occasionally meet for drinks or he, Adam and I would go to dinner and catch a movie. There was always something a little off between us, though, like we knew there were things that had gone unsaid, but we'd been too young to know how to say them. And now we were old enough to know better than to dredge up things that were probably better left unsaid. But it made the air heavy around us. And we could never just be, if that makes any sense.

And then I met Josh. And eventually Campbell met Jess. And being in separate relationships seemed to smooth out the harsh edges between us. But I suppose those edges never really went away. We just became more adept at hiding them.

I think about this as we drive home. I think about fate and destiny and how everything that happened between Campbell and me was part of my journey to Josh, like I had to experience one to find the other.

"I just needed to fall off the map for a while," I tell Campbell. "That's all."

"Are you back on it?"

It's a good and fair question, so I answer it the best way I can. "I don't know yet."

Chapter 16
Love Letters

As I suspected, the listing agent on Campbell's house (that's what I'm calling it now) isn't taking offers until the first week of February, which gives us ten days to get our ducks in a row. I've set up another showing for tomorrow morning and have nothing left to do.

Kyle and his men are making a racket, so I give up on an afternoon nap. Before Josh died, I never slept in the middle of the day, not even on weekends. It just seemed too frivolous.

Brooke is gone, and I find myself at loose ends. It's too dismal of a day to go on a walk. So, I call Josie. Just when I think the call will go to voicemail, she picks up.

"Hey," she says in a hushed voice.

"Why are you whispering?"

"We're at the movies. It's just about to start."

I've never known Josie to go to a matinee, and I'm encouraged that things are heating up in the romance department. "Are you with tech guy?"

There's a long pause—too long—and Josie finally says, "No, Hannah."

"My sister?" I ask as if it's possible that it's another Hannah because I don't want to believe they've left me out.

"Uh-huh. It was a last-minute thing," she sputters, which tells me it wasn't.

I want to say, *When did you start choosing my sister over me?* And since when does Hannah leave work early to catch a movie (never)? But I don't say any of those things, afraid I'll sound like a jealous ass. Instead, I tell them to have a good time in a feigned upbeat voice that sounds nothing like me.

Then I wander around the house aimlessly, suddenly remembering the email from Josh's old boss.

Up in my room, I find Josh's laptop in a box of his things I've brought with me and set it up on the white Pottery Barn desk of my youth. I used to spend hours here, doing homework, but now find it a bit cramped.

I flip up the lid of the computer and watch it come to life with sound effects. I know Josh's password by heart—it's our anniversary date.

His desktop is as neat and organized as was his side of the closet. Unlike mine—mostly an odd collection of memes and photographs downloaded from my phone—each folder is carefully labeled. There's one that says "plans," and I click on it because, duh, it's a logical place to start.

I scan the contents, looking for anything called High Top, the two-story restaurant he was designing for a Marin County chef and Food Network personality. I remember Josh talking about it and how the funky space was causing him all kinds of challenges. It used to be a shoe factory that sat vacant for five years. But when the Chase Center sports arena went in on the adjacent street, the empty factory became a highly sought-after piece of real estate.

Two stories for a restaurant isn't ideal, but Josh wanted to take advantage of the amazing bay views from the top floor. He was planning to cantilever a patio over the water to make diners feel like they were eating on a yacht. Those last few weeks of his life were consumed by the restaurant. I hope whoever takes over the project sticks with Josh's blueprint. It really was going to be spectacular.

I don't see anything labeled High Top and click on a few plans just to make sure I'm not missing it. The first is Rabbits, which makes my chest swell. It was Josh's first project, and he was so proud of it. I think back to our rehearsal dinner there, and my eyes cloud up. He wore that blue suit, a combo of hipster and rat pack, that I loved.

After sorting through everything in the file, I click out of it and continue my hunt. There's nothing promising on his desktop, so I move to his documents. There are so many that I'll be here all day, scrolling. Rocket scientist that I am, it dawns on me to just punch in "High Top" in his computer's search bar. Boom! Within seconds, I find what I hope I'm looking for, open it, and voila, I unlock pages of notes, elevations and three-dimensional drawings that to my untrained eye look like a two-story restaurant.

I switch over to Josh's email, attach the file and shoot it over to Martin, Owens and Luckett, feeling rather proud of myself.

While I'm in his Gmail, I decide I may as well deal with that too. No one tells you when you lose a loved one whether you're supposed to close his email accounts or how to answer correspondence from people who don't know the person they're writing to is dead. His parents and I bought obits in the *San Francisco Chronicle* and the *Chicago Tribune,* but people our age don't read those pages.

Because you're not supposed to die when you're thirty-five.

I scroll through his unopened mail. It seems my late husband was popular. I try to prioritize, discarding anything that looks like junk mail or spam. Most of the emails are work related, and judging by the sent dates, those people are now up to speed on Josh's untimely death.

There's an invite to an architecture conference, a note from the landlord of our old apartment that at long last he's replacing our hot water heater (I had two months of uninterrupted hot water before I moved out), and a call to action from our neighborhood association to block a Panda Express from coming in (for the record, I wanted it).

There's a number of other emails that don't require responses. And some that do. I try to make those as short and to the point as possible without completely breaking down. But of course I do. By the time I finish, my cheeks sting from a flood of salty tears and my tissue box is empty.

Next, I do a Google search to figure out how to delete a deceased person's account. It appears easy enough. But before I close Josh's account for good, I cull through his email folders to make sure there isn't something important I need to hold onto. His Gmail account is as organized as his desktop. Everything has a place, even seven years' worth of Verizon bill invoices. *Well, we don't need that anymore.*

There's a folder titled "Texts/Beth" that piques my interest, and I click on it. It's a text conversation between Josh and someone named Beth Hardesty, who I never heard Josh mention. I deliberate on whether to open or delete them, ultimately deciding they must be important for Josh to have moved them from his iPhone to his Gmail account and to have kept them all these years. From a cursory glance, they look like they date back to before Josh and I met.

I scroll down to the first one, hover, then click.

"Meet me at Sproul Plaza at six. We can grab dinner or whatever." It's signed Beth.

Sproul Plaza is on the UC Berkeley campus. I've been there many times to hook up with friends. I assume Beth attended Cal the same time Josh was there, doing his graduate studies in architecture.

Impatient, and yet a little hesitant, I open the next one to see where this is going.

"Last night was fun. And by the way, I think I'm in love with you."

Josh: "You tell me this over a text. Seriously? Want to come over tonight? And for the record, I'm in love with you too."

Beth: "I'll see you at eight. Can't wait."

Okay, I'm full-blown nauseous now.

The texts are from a long time ago, I tell myself. A woman Josh knew in graduate school. It's not like I didn't have boyfriends...or a history when we began dating. The difference, though, is Josh knew every bit of my history, including what happened with Campbell. Yet Beth, the woman whose texts he saved for nearly a decade, is a complete mystery to me.

I should shut this down now. But like one of those people who joins the crowd to watch a bar fight, I can't seem to look away. I open the next text.

"Got to cancel tonight to work on my resume. There's an opening at JBR Design for a junior architect. Getting in there would be a dream. Speaking of dreams, I had an X-rated one of you last night. Come over tonight after the party. I'll make you pancakes in bed in the morning."

Beth: "Ugh, that's two nights in a row you've bailed on me. Unacceptable. You can make it up to me with those pancakes...and...something X-rated."

Josh: a smiley face emoji.

I scroll to the next text, which is dated eighteen months before Josh and I met.

Josh: "My final thesis is in, and I could use a drink. You up for a nightcap...or two? Can't stay out too late 'cause I've got a presentation at work tomorrow. I know it's been crazy lately. The sad truth is I don't see my schedule lightening up anytime soon, which leads me to a proposition. Meet me at Triple Rock and I'll tell you all about it."

Beth: "Give me thirty minutes. Just got back from the gym. A proposition, huh? Sounds interesting."

The next text isn't until a week later. I assume Josh's proposition was made in person but open the message, hoping for a clue. Intuitively, I know I'm not going to like it.

Beth: "San Francisco is so freaking expensive. You sure we can't just get a place in Berkeley and commute?

Josh: "The whole point of this is to spend more time together. Can't do that if I'm commuting back and forth. Keep looking, we'll find something. If not on craigslist, I'll put the word out at JBR. Love you."

Beth: "Love you too."

My heart is hammering so hard I think I can almost hear it pounding against my chest. I open the next one, praying it's not what I think. What I know.

Beth: "It's perfect! Hurry up. I can't wait for you to see it."

Josh: "Stuck on BART. Will be there as soon as I can. Is anyone else looking at it?"

Beth: "Someone at three. We can't lose this place. Hurry."

Included in the text is a photograph of a cute living room with a period fireplace and hardwood floors. From the window is a view of a busy street. I can't tell which street, but I think the two spires in the distant background is Saints Peter and Paul Church in North Beach.

"Rachel, are you home?" It's Brooke.

I slam down the lid of Josh's laptop and push away from the desk like a kid who's just been caught rifling through her mother's change purse.

Shell-shocked, I'm slow to answer Brooke. I'm too busy reeling.

"Rachel?"

"Yes," I croak. "I'm here."

"Can you come down for a minute?"

"Uh, yeah sure."

I do my best to pull myself together, almost happy for the interruption, and tell myself I'm going to delete the messages and pretend I never read them. The whole thing is silly. Just an old girlfriend, that's all.

"Coming," I call, wondering whether I forgot to turn off the coffee maker or some other small infraction that has Brooke in a dither. Though admittedly she's the most chill roommate I've ever had.

Brooke is standing at the foot of the staircase dressed in jeans, a bulky sweater, and a pair of knee-high worn leather boots. Nothing about her outfit is special, yet she looks like she just walked off the cover of one of those British countryside magazines.

"What's up?"

"I wanted to talk if you have time."

Uh-oh. She's going to kick me out.

"Sure," I say, mentally preparing myself to move in with Adam until I can find a place.

She leads me into the kitchen and motions for me to take a seat.

I'm tempted to tell her to just get it over with and quit dicking around. If she wants me out, I'll move. It's as simple as that.

Out the back window I can see the Bleu Construction crew packing up for the day. It's hard to tell from this vantage point how much they got done. Perhaps Brooke is unhappy with their work and plans to lecture me about it. That would be better than the alternative, I suppose.

It's getting dark, and the rain seems to have stopped. There's a thin layer of fog hovering over the pool, making it look like smoke on the water. Brooke really should've covered it. Come summer, the water will be green as split pea soup.

"I have an offer to rent the house out for a week in March," Brooke says.

Okay. Not as bad as I thought. But she's dreaming if she thinks this can happen that soon.

"When? Because the guys said they need five weeks until completion." I've lived through enough of my mother's projects to know that really means two months. So even March is cutting it close.

"Not the pool house. This house."

I stare at her, not sure I'm understanding correctly. "What do you mean this house?"

"I stuck it on Airbnb with an obscene price tag just to see what would happen. And I actually got a serious hit. A group of mystery authors are planning a writing retreat in the city, and this fits their needs."

She can't be serious. I hold eye contact to see if she's messing with me.

"It's ten thousand dollars. Twelve if I include food and maid service. That's roughly seven times what I make in a week. You and I can bunk in the guest cottage. I'll do the cooking if you do the cleaning."

I think the British call it gobsmacked. And I can't tell for certain, but I'm pretty sure my mouth is hanging open. "Brooke...are you...like...broke?"

I suppose there's always a possibility that she has a gambling problem or a shopping addiction, though you'd never know it by her clothes.

"Not broke." She shakes her head. "I make a good living, even by Bay Area standards. But this house...property taxes and insurance alone are killing me. And that doesn't cover upkeep."

"Didn't my dad leave you money for that? Life insurance?" My father was loaded. Hannah, Adam and I were each left a generous sum. Not enough to make us rich by any stretch of the imagination, but enough to start college funds for our kids if we had any. Or in my and Adam's case, a start toward buying a home.

Brooke drops her gaze to the floor. "He left me this house, which has a mortgage."

A mortgage? My parents owned the Victorian free and clear. My father paid off the loan when my safta died with the money from his inheritance. "I thought it was paid off."

"How do you think your father bought out your mother's share when they got divorced, Rachel?" Brooke is looking at me like I live in la-la land. "He had to take out a second."

I feel the sudden urge to remind her that he wouldn't have had to if she hadn't come along and inserted herself into my mother and father's marriage. But that isn't really fair. My father was just as much to blame as Brooke. As the cliché goes: it takes two to tango.

"You're a real estate agent, Rachel. I'm sure you have a fairly good idea how much this house is worth. Now divide that by two." She waits as if she's letting me do the math. "Your father didn't have that kind of cash."

"What about his half of the practice?" It was probably worth more than even the house and a cash cow to boot.

"What about it?"

"You could sell it to his partners. I'm sure they wouldn't pass up a chance to buy."

Again that look. "Your father's piece of the business went to your mother when he died. It was part of your parents' divorce settlement, as was the bulk of his investments."

I'd never spoken to my parents about how they had gone about dividing up more than thirty years of a life together. I was too busy mourning the loss of my broken family. My mother, however, was entitled to every cent. It may have been my father's money that bought this house, but it was my mother who made it a home. It was my mother who raised his children. And my mother who made sure my father lived in the lap of comfort. And his thanks was to run off with another woman.

Maybe it was hearing the condescension in Brooke's voice or finding Josh's love letters that makes me throw whatever loose hold I have on tact right out the window. "You must've known California was a community property state when you got involved with my father in the first place."

She shoots me a look, then, in a voice I can only describe as facetious, says, "I had hoped he was so rich it wouldn't matter."

I don't know what to make of this woman. I've only ever been rude to her, and yet she lets me live here and is even nice about it. The revelation that she's part of a grief group could've knocked me over with a feather. And here she is willing to give up her house and wait on a group of rich writers for...okay, it's a lot of cash. But still.

"Brooke, why don't you just sell the house? You said it yourself. It's worth a fortune." Take your ill-gotten gains and run.

She squints at me. "The hell I will. Your father loved this house. He wanted it for you guys. If you ever needed a place to land." She emphasizes that last part, her meaning clear. *Like now.* "Eventually, I'll pass it on to the three of you. That was his fervent wish, his legacy." Her eyes mist, and I look away, having nothing to add.

It seems that Brooke, my father's child bride, has won this round.

Chapter 17
Who is Beth Hardesty?

I forgot to set my alarm and, as I stare at the Kitty Cat Klock, realize I have exactly forty minutes to meet Campbell and Jessica at the house on Liberty.

Shit, shit, shit.

I get out of bed so fast I get tangled in the blankets and nearly fall into the desk where Josh's laptop still sits. I don't have time to think about that now. Later.

I take the shortest shower known to mankind, throw on a pair of black pants, a white sweater and suede booties, then rush down the stairs. As much as I don't want to, I force myself to drive. The problem is that Kyle's work truck is parked behind me in the driveway. I don't have time for this.

I march to the pool house, where I find him up on the roof.

"Hey, Kyle, you're blocking me," I call up to him and motion that he needs to move his truck.

"Give me a sec," he yells down.

I don't have a sec, but I wait anyway, my anxiety building over having to get behind the wheel. This time of the morning, there will be traffic. Even on a non-traffic day it could take fifteen minutes, and I'm up against the clock as it is.

Kyle finally comes down the ladder, stops to scoop his coffee thermos off the ground and saunters over to his pickup like he's got all the time in the world.

By the time I make it down the driveway and onto Vallejo, I'm a bundle of nerves. Thankfully, Divisadero is light today, and I manage to arrive at the Craftsman unscathed with four minutes to spare. I'm still shaking when I snag a parking space a block away and use the extra time to collect myself.

Campbell and Jess are waiting for me on the sidewalk in the front of the house. Jess is nauseatingly adorable as usual. She's in a winter-white fitted knit cowl-neck dress and a pair of gorgeous suede boots. Campbell says she has a meeting at noon at the Serena & Lily campus in Sausalito, so we don't have time to waste. She's been working for the furniture company for two years, and except for the commute to Marin County every day, Campbell says she loves it.

Jess greets me with a giant hug. "Hey, stranger. How are you?" She rubs my arms, steps back and assesses me. "You look great," she says in a way that lets me know that I don't. "You okay?"

Until a few seconds ago, I felt pretty good. I'd made it here in one piece. I didn't have a heart attack behind the wheel of Josh's old car. And Brooke was still asleep when I left.

"I am," I say and turn to the house. "What do you think?"

Jess bites down on her lip and waggles her hand from side to side. "Campbell says it just needs some spit and polish. But I don't know. What do you think?"

"I think it's a hell of a deal as long as we don't find anything significantly wrong. But you're the one who's living in it, so it's a really personal decision."

"I like the neighborhood." But even that she sounds iffy about.

Hey, I get it. It's their first house, and she wants everything to be perfect. Unfortunately, to get perfect on their budget, they'll have to move to Bakersfield.

"Let's go inside," Campbell says.

The smell isn't as bad today. But it's stuffy, and with the morning light the nicotine stains on the wall are more evident than they were yesterday. But damn does the house have potential.

I sneak a look at the kitchen counter, where the pile of agents' cards has quadrupled in size. We're going to have to come in with an aggressive offer if Campbell and Jess want the house.

"Did you talk to your friend about looking at the foundation?"

"Yeah. He can do it this weekend. I'm still on the hunt for a good roofer. But if Jess likes it, I'll have someone here by next week."

"I just hope we're not biting off more than we can chew," Jess says and looks up at the popcorn ceiling in the dining room and grimaces. "I mean, with the wedding in summer and all, we're stretched pretty thin."

I slide a glance at Campbell, who rolls his eyes.

"I'll give you two some privacy to check it out on your own. If you have any questions, I'll be out front."

Unlike yesterday, there's no sign of rain, only the promise of sunshine.

I lean against Campbell's truck—wouldn't you know he got a space right in front of the house—fish my phone out of my purse and scroll through emails. Adam wants to go to dinner. Josie is just saying hi, which I know is a mea culpa for not inviting me to the movies with her and Hannah. And Hannah wants to know if she can borrow my old ski pants. She and Stephen are going to Tahoe for the weekend. Why not? She already borrowed my best friend. At least she and Stephen appear to be getting along. Mom, who doesn't do email, left me a voicemail, which I'll listen to later, after I've had coffee.

For shits and giggles, I do a Google search for Beth Hardesty, of whom there are legions. I start to tailor my search to the Bay Area when Jess comes out of the house.

"What did you think?" I push off Campbell's truck.

She puffs out a breath. "I don't know. Campbell thinks it's a good investment. He's in there taking measurements. I've got to run." She pulls me in for another hug. "Let's go to dinner soon. We've missed you, Rachel." She says it like I've been locked away in a mental institution for a while.

"Absolutely," I say and watch her walk down the block to her car, then go in search of Campbell.

"We're doing it," he says. "I've still got to crawl under the house and climb up to take a look at the attic. Can we do that tomorrow? Hopefully I can get my foundation expert and roofer here at the same time."

"I'll see what I can do. But, Campbell, Jess didn't seem too thrilled with the house."

"Jess still thinks we have a shot at finding something in Pac Heights or Cow Hollow. Hell, while we're at it, maybe Sea Cliff, right next to Robin Williams's old place."

I laugh because that's the way of all first-time home buyers. They want to shoot for the stars. At least Campbell is realistic.

"I get it. But is she going to be okay with you moving forward on this?" To be a good real estate agent, you sometimes have to play marriage counselor. But I don't want that role with Campbell and Jess.

"Yeah, she'll come around. It's the best thing we've seen since we started looking, and I don't want to lose it."

Pressure much? "It's going to be competitive, Campbell. This is the kind of property that could easily go tens of thousands over asking. Are you prepared for that?"

He holds my gaze and grins. "I'd rather not. But yeah, if I have to."

He comes closer and tucks a strand of loose hair behind my ear, the gesture a little too intimate for two people with our history. But I don't step away.

"I'm sorry if Jess was weird before," he says. "Neither of us know what to say. What to do. But we're here for you, Rach."

"I know." I nod because I really do. Over the last six months he never gave up on me, persistently calling and emailing.

An agent I recognize with a young couple comes through the open door, which I should've shut when I came in. If for no other reason than to lock in the funky smell as a deterrent to other buyers.

"We've got to skedaddle," I whisper to Campbell as the new visitors wander the house, their voices echoing through the empty rooms. "Put away the measuring tape and don't look too interested."

"Gotcha." He tucks the tape measure in his pocket, and we walk out together. "Where you parked?"

I point down the block, and he walks me to my car.

"I'll let you know what time we can get in the house. And if you have any trouble finding someone to assess the roof, let me know. I might be able to scrounge up someone for you." Worse comes to worst, I can ask pool house Kyle if he knows anyone.

"Thanks, Rach. I feel good about this. I knew our house luck would change once you got involved."

Campbell is the one who found the listing, not me. My only contribution so far has been a lockbox code. But it's nice of him to give me credit.

"I'm keeping my fingers crossed. But it'll help to make the offer as clean as possible. You have your financials in order, right? A preapproval letter from the bank?"

"We're good."

For a second, I consider confiding in him about Brooke and her plan to rent out the house but decide for now to keep it under wraps. I'm not even planning to tell my family until I've had time to absorb it. Because the whole thing is crazy. Although I can't help but think that if I'd been paying more attention, I would've known.

But the thing about the Golds is that my siblings and I were never looped in on matters of money. My parents, the descendants of good Russian peasant stock, were firmly of the belief that their finances were none of our business. We knew my father had given my mother everything she'd asked for in the divorce settlement. We just didn't know he'd given her everything he had.

Which proves to me one thing. He knew. He knew he loved Mom best and that deep down inside she would always be his one and only. It's not because he threw cash at her that I come to this conclusion. No, it's because my father understood the legacy of the love, the home and the life they'd built together. The legacy that belonged to them and no one else.

The confirmation of this cheers me as I navigate the city streets on my way home. Though I never had any doubt that Brooke was nothing more than Dad's midlife-crisis Porsche Carrera to Mom's reliable Toyota minivan, there were times when I wondered whether my parents would ever find their way back to each other. Call it a crisis of faith.

But now I know. If my father had lived to see another day, he would've eventually left Brooke and spent the rest of his life with my mother, which brings me to Josh. What if Beth Hardesty was his Shana Gold and I was his Brooke?

* * * *

Brooke is vacuuming when I walk in the door. She has on a pair of purple scrubs, and her hair is up in a careless messy bun that looks like it took hours to achieve. Except I know better.

"Hey." She turns off the vacuum. "You give any more thought to the mystery writers?"

Not really, given everything else I've learned in the last twenty-four hours. But I nod anyway. "Yeah, sure, go for it." As soon as I say it, I realize how presumptuous it sounds. Who am I to be giving her permission? But in her own way, wasn't she asking for it?

As far as cleaning up after a bunch of novelists, I have no problem with that. It's the least I can do. For all her faults, Brooke is trying to save the house for Hannah, Adam and me. And for the next generation of Golds. It is laudable, even heroic of her, which makes me ask myself, *What's the catch?*

"I can take over if you've got to get to work." I bob my head at the vacuum cleaner. It's a handy chore to keep me from running upstairs and reading the rest of Josh and Beth's text messages.

"That would be great." She leans the vacuum against the wall. "There's leftover pizza in the fridge if you're hungry."

I realize it's already noon and I haven't eaten breakfast. "Thanks. I may take you up on that." I can't tell whether we're forcing being pleasant to each other or if we're falling into a sort of truce-like cohabitation situation. Either one is good. The less drama, the better.

"Please do," Brooke says.

And that's when I notice the silence. "Where's the work crew?" I crane my neck to look outside the window for their trucks, which are conspicuously gone. "Did they leave for lunch?" Usually, they bring food and eat around the pool.

"They had an emergency at another job site. Said they'd be back tomorrow."

"Okay." I'm not going to argue with a day of peace and quiet.

"I'm grabbing my purse and taking off," Brooke says as I head to the kitchen.

"Have a good day."

After I scarf down two slices of pizza, I go out to the pool house to check Kyle's progress. The place looks exactly as it did yesterday, which is troubling, especially now that I know why Brooke is anxious to get every last room rented out. I rationalize to myself that maybe a lot of work has happened here that isn't evident to a layman like myself. Anyway, they'll be back tomorrow, and I can quiz Kyle on where they're at as far as timing and perhaps mention my gorgeous blond friend, Josie.

I take up where Brooke left off with the vacuum, running it through the entire first floor. Growing up, Ester, our housekeeper, came once a week to clean. That didn't mean the Gold kids were off the hook. Hannah and I were responsible for making sure all six bathrooms were spic and span. Adam was in charge of cleaning the cat boxes for our three beloved kitties. Mom wouldn't let us have a dog but at one point allowed us to keep a bunny in the garage (also Adam's job to clean up after). On top of that, we were responsible for dusting, doing the dishes, and keeping our rooms tidy. If our beds weren't made, there was hell to pay, and everyone had to do their own laundry. Mommie Dearest ran the house like a naval ship, and we were her little swabbies.

To show Brooke that I can earn my keep, I give the downstairs powder room and the kitchen a good scrubbing. While Ester retired and moved to the Napa Valley a long time ago (we threw her a bon voyage in the backyard), Brooke has someone come in once a week. I plan to start contributing to that fund as well as stocking the fridge and pantry.

I put away all the cleaning supplies when my phone goes off. "Tubular Bells," otherwise known as the theme song to *The Exorcist,* the ringtone I chose for my in-laws the second year into Josh's and my marriage. Needless to say, Josh was not amused. In retaliation, he chose "Mother in Law" for Shana. One time, she butt-called him while they were in the same room together. She either pretended to not get the joke or she really had no clue the song was meant for her.

I find my phone at the bottom of my purse. "Hi," I say, sounding breathless to my own ears.

"Rachel, darling, how are you?" my mother-in-law asks like we haven't talked in years when in fact it's only been two days.

"Good," I say. "I was just cleaning and raced for the phone."

"Cleaning what, dear?"

I have to keep from snorting aloud. Unlike mine, Josh's parents are not the descendants of fine Russian peasant stock. According to Pauline Ackermann, she's related to Sephardic royalty, though I have my doubts. And so did Josh. But she's a good mother-in-law in spite of her delusions of grandeur.

"How are you?" I say to move the conversation along.

"Oh, you know, getting by," she says with a great sigh. "I wanted to talk to you about *yahrtzeit*." Yahrtzeit is the one-year anniversary of Josh's death. "We'd like you to come to Chicago. Can I have Saul book you a flight?"

But that's more than five months away, I think. "In August, right?"

"Of course in August," she says impatiently, like she thinks I'm sketchy on the month of my husband's death.

The date will forever be engrained on my soul. What I'm sketchy on is Jewish mourning traditions.

"I can book it, Pauline. You just tell me when you want me to come."

"It'll have to be in accordance with the Hebrew calendar. I think Saul said it was sundown on August 15th. Let me check with him. But you'll come?"

"Of course. I think it'll be wonderful for us to be together, to light a candle together." And I do because Josh would've wanted it that way. He loved his parents, and I love him.

"We miss you, Rachel. Josh loved you so much."

It comes to me in that moment that I could ask her about Beth. Did Pauline know her? Had Josh ever talked about her. Did he ever bring her home to meet his family?

I don't, of course. Because it's silly, and I'm making way too much out of a couple of text messages. People fall in love a half dozen times or more in college or grad school. It's easy when you're young and your body hasn't yet experienced the ravages of gravity. Everything is new and the sex is exciting. Then you move on, and those once-shiny new relationships quickly fade to distant memories, like the trip you took to the Grand Canyon or the summer you spent as a foreign exchange student in Italy. The pictures and journal entries are eventually relegated to a dusty drawer or attic where the mementos yellow and tear and disintegrate.

Or in Josh's case, transferred from his phone to his email to a folder to a safe place on his computer where they can live forever, preserved, and just within reach.

Chapter 18
Go Big

The first thing I notice Monday morning is the silence. No power tools, no hammering, no curse words, no nothing. The pool house is as quiet as a library. I glance at my bedside clock (I really have to get something more mature). It's 8:35 in the morning. *Okay, Kyle and the boys are probably just a bit late,* I tell myself. But by the time I'm out of the shower and dressed, there's still nothing.

Just to make sure, I check the driveway for their fleet of work trucks, then hike across the lawn to the pool house. *Nada, nichts, nichto.* The worst part is they've opened up the roof, and rain is in the forecast.

I go back in the house and scroll through my phone for Kyle's number. The call goes directly to voicemail.

"Hey, Kyle, this is Rachel Ackermann. You know, the pool house on Vallejo. Where are you guys? You left the roof wide open, and it's about to pour. Please call me. Or just show up."

I put up a pot of coffee and search the fridge for a breakfast option. I'm halfway through my cereal when my phone rings. Thank God. Kyle.

"Where are you guys?" I say by way of a greeting.

"Sorry. My boss sent us to another project across town. I guess he's shorthanded. A lot of folks out with the flu. I'll send someone over to throw a tarp over the roof. It should be fine."

I hope so. Otherwise, you're paying for the damage, bucko. "When will you be back to finish the job? Brooke says you left early on Friday to deal with an emergency. Are we still on track to finish in five weeks?"

"Yep. No problem."

Why is it, then, that I think it's a problem? "Okay, just please send your tarp guy. And I'm expecting you to be here bright and early tomorrow morning."

"Roger that, boss lady."

After he clicks off, I reevaluate setting him up with Josie. *Roger that, boss lady?* Who even talks like that? I glance at the clock. Campbell is stopping by to go over the offer for the house on Liberty.

Last time I spoke to the seller's agent, there'd been twenty requests for disclosure packets. That doesn't mean all twenty are making offers, but it's a good indication of what we're up against. Chip thinks we should go ten percent over asking, but it sounds low to me given the market. I don't want to squander Campbell and Jess's hard-earned money but also don't want them to lose out on the house.

I hold my nose and dial Niki's number. We haven't talked since the Bernal Heights debacle. The woman can hold a grudge. But I suspect she'll be nice to me because of...Josh. She did, after all, send flowers after the accident, a huge arrangement from a fancy florist on Chestnut.

"Hi, Niki, this is Rachel Ackermann. How are you?"

"I'm fine. How are you, Rachel? I haven't seen you in the office in a while. Are you still with Windham?"

I can't tell whether it's a dig or a genuine question. To be fair, I would probably think the same of a colleague who hadn't sold a home in close to a year.

"I'm still there. In fact, I'm calling for some advice." I pause, trying to gauge her reaction. All I get on the other side of the phone is crickets. "I have clients making a bid on a house on Liberty Street in Dolores Heights. There's a lot of interest. Chip thinks we should go ten percent over asking. I'm worried it won't get it done. What do you think?"

"First of all, don't you think it would've been a good idea to ask me if I have a client who may be bidding on the same property?" she says, her voice so withering I have to check the houseplants to make sure they're still alive.

Give me a break. Everyone knows Niki Sorento doesn't get out of bed for anything less than a hundred-grand commission. And this ain't that kind of house.

I hear her tapping on a keyboard in the background. "The one near the intersection of Sanchez?"

I can almost see her brows wing up in distaste as she flips through the house photos. "That would be the one. Do you have an interested party?" I ask just to be a bitch.

"You've got to be kidding." She continues tapping. "Does that third bedroom even have permits?"

"Yes." I'm tempted to tell her to shove it and hang up. But I trust her opinion more than I do Chip's. He's not out there every day like she is.

"The house two blocks down, which is about the same size, went for two thousand a square foot. But that one was fully renovated." She lets out an audible sigh. "It's a popular neighborhood, and if your clients fix up the place and this market holds, they'll make a pretty penny when they decide to sell. I'm guessing at this price point, they'll be no fewer than fifteen offers. Possibly more." She continues tapping in the background. This time I can tell she's working a calculator. "Go fourteen percent over. Not a penny more. You're welcome." With that, she hangs up.

I get out my own calculator and do some mathematical gymnastics. Whoo, that's a lot of money, especially for a house that's barely livable. But Niki's right. If Campbell works his magic on the place, it'll be worth a hefty sum in the future.

There's a tap on the French doors, and I nearly jump out of my skin. It's Campbell, who I think in his whole life has only used the front door once or twice. None of the Golds did.

He comes in and makes himself at home at the center island. "You got more of that?" He tilts his head at my coffee.

I pour him a cup and slide it down the counter. "I've been crunching numbers for your offer."

I tell him about the twenty disclosure packets that have already gone out and that I'm expecting at least fifteen offers not including ours.

"Ah jeez." He rubs his hand down his face.

I stare past him at the pool house. The wind has picked up, and the sky looks ready to open up any minute in a blast of thunder and rain. And still no one from Bleu Construction to batten down the hatches.

"What's wrong?" Campbell turns around and follows the direction of my gaze.

"Rain. The guys working on the pool house were a no-show today. The foreman promised to send someone over to cover the roof, but here it is"—I look at my watch—"almost noon and no one is here."

Campbell gets to his feet. "Let me take a look."

We walk out together. The water in the pool is rippling from the wind, reminding me that it should've been covered months ago. The electric motor no longer works, and the cover has to be manually closed. No easy feat. Campbell reads my mind and single-handedly wrestles the heavy vinyl across the pool. I help him fasten down the straps. I'd drag the patio furniture into the pool house but, uh, no roof.

The first drop hits me on the nose. A big wet blob. Soon, the sky is spitting raindrops onto the brick pool deck. Campbell makes a beeline for the garden shed, which is more the size of a two-car garage. He knows his way around the outbuilding better than I do and goes straight for a storage cabinet at the back of the room, where he pulls out a folded silver tarp.

"Grab me some bungie cords from the peg board." He leaves before he can point me in the right direction.

I find the cords over the workbench and chase after him. By the time I get to the pool house, he's up on the roof, spreading the tarp over the spot where the crew ripped off the shingles for the expansion.

"Be careful up there," I call up, hoping he can hear me. The wind has picked up, and it's gone from sprinkling to full-on raining. I think about my father and then Josh. Neither was the type to climb up on a roof in a downpour. I correct myself, neither was the type to climb up on a roof period. Even Josh, who spent a good fraction of his job on construction sites, left the physical stuff to the contractors.

"Toss me up those bungie cords."

I throw them as hard as I can, only to have them bounce off the roof and onto the ground. "Hang on." I try it again, only this time, one at a time.

Campbell catches the first one and attaches it to the tarp and manages to strap it down MacGyver-style on one side.

"Toss me the other one."

I throw up the second cord, but this time it doesn't even make it as far as the roof.

"Put a little English on it," Campbell calls down.

I throw it again, this time with more power. He catches it in midair and securely buckles the other side of the tarp down.

"This should do it," he says and walks to the edge of the roof.

I hide my eyes as he does a tightrope walk along the roof's slope so he can scramble down. "For God's sake, Campbell. You'll kill yourself."

"Nah." He gets to the bottom of the slope, grabs the edge, lowers himself onto the ladder, and drops down. "Who are these assholes?" He could only mean the construction crew.

"Someone Brooke hired. Bleu Construction."

He shrugs, indicating he's never heard of them. "They shouldn't have left you in the lurch like this."

No, they shouldn't have. "Thanks for saving the day."

"No problem." He ducks inside the pool house to check his handiwork.

I follow him inside, and we both stare up at the ceiling. No leaks. Hopefully it'll keep until the crew returns.

Campbell gives the interior a once-over. "Wow, they took it down to the studs."

"Brooke wants to add a bedroom, enlarge the bath, and reconfigure the kitchenette." I leave out the part about how she's planning to rent out the big house too. I'm still digesting her admission that she can't really afford the place and is only hanging on to it for the sake of the Gold kids and our nonexistent offspring.

"Does it look like they know what they're doing?" I ask. Even though Campbell is a master carpenter whose work is more art than construction, he understands the fundamentals of building. Even as a kid he could fix anything. A fence, a rotted windowpane, a door that wouldn't close right. A kickass tree house.

"It's just demo," he says. "Anyone can do it."

By the end of the week there will be more progress, I assure myself. It's not like they have anything left to rip out.

Without the insulation, the construction site is chilly. I can hear the rain pattering down on the tarp, and it reminds me of the one time Josh and I went camping. It was the first summer we met, and we decided to do a weekend in Yosemite. The original plan was to stay at the Ahwahnee, not realizing it books out a year in advance. We wound up staying in a campground in a two-person pup tent during a summer storm, the only summer storm in the history of California.

"Let's go work on your offer," I tell Campbell, who's continuing to examine the bowels of the pool house.

We run across the yard, trying to dodge the rain, only to go inside soaking wet. I jog upstairs for a couple of towels so Campbell can at least dry his hair. He's always had really great hair, dark and full with just enough curl to give him that slightly disheveled look everyone is going for these days. The difference is Campbell comes by it naturally.

I toss Campbell one of the towels and spill out our cold coffees and make a fresh pot. "You hungry?"

"I could eat." He hops off his stool and opens the fridge. "What've you got?"

Having grown up with this being his home away from home, he's as comfortable here as I am. We used to spend the summers in the pool, letting our bodies turn copper in the sunshine. And winters, playing in this house, building forts or anything our imagination came up with.

Then Campbell, Hannah, Adam and I used to climb up on the stools at the center island while my mother made us triple-decker peanut butter and sugar sandwiches.

"How 'bout a triple-decker?" I ask, wondering if he still eats them anymore, wondering if they bring back a flood of memories that at once makes him smile and his chest ache, like it does me.

"Yeah, I could go for that." Campbell grins. "Can't remember the last time I had one."

Probably here, eighteen years ago. But I don't say it. These days, Campbell and I avoid talking about the past, pretending that our history isn't fraught with complications. The fact that we're still friends at all is a minor miracle.

"Grab me the peanut butter." I go in search of a loaf of bread in the pantry and wrap my arm around the sugar canister, dropping everything on the counter.

Ten minutes later, we're back at the island, enjoying the most decadent sandwich in the history of sandwiches.

"It's better than candy, right?"

"It is candy," Campbell says. "We're eating candy for lunch, and I'm totally down with that."

We crack up, and it feels almost normal to be laughing again, the way Campbell and I used to.

"It's my dirty little secret," I tell Campbell and grab the jar of peanut butter. "I bet this isn't even organic."

"I bet the bread is filled with GMOs. And guess what?" Campbell says. "It's freaking delicious."

I choke on my soda, which goes up my nose. Well, it's actually Brooke's soda. For a nurse, her diet is pretty crappy, except for her gluten-free toast. But who am I to talk? I'm eating half a C&H factory. Campbell at least is drinking milk. As a kid, he used to drink it by the gallon. My mother used to make weekly trips to Costco for milk alone and send one container home with the Scotts.

Campbell lost his mother when he was just three to metastatic breast cancer, and Shana Gold never met a tragedy with which she didn't become absorbed. She likes to think of herself as Campbell's surrogate mother.

"So I've got some bad news," I say. "You want it now or after we're done eating?"

"We're not getting the house?"

"That depends. An agent I trust, who's been doing this a long time and knows the market like no one else does, thinks you need to go fourteen percent over asking."

Campbell lets out a sigh. "That's more than a hundred thousand dollars. Holy shit."

"Yeah, I know. We could go less and take our chances. We can even look for something else."

He pushes his plate away and looks at me. "What do you think we should do?"

I let out a breath, uncomfortable with being thrown into this position. It's probably why I suck at real estate. I can hear Niki saying, "Everyone needs a little push. Clients don't know what they want. They're relying on you to tell them."

But this is Campbell we're talking about. And while I'm sure he and Jess make a nice living, this is a lot of money even for a millionaire.

"I can't tell you what to do, Campbell. Only you and Jess can make that decision."

"What would you do if it was you?"

Ugh, it's such a hard choice. Josh and I agonized over whether to wait until the market calmed down but at the same time worried that it would only continue to get worse and we'd be priced out of the city. It was a legitimate fear. For as long as I've been in real estate, the prices have continued to soar. Case in point: my parents could never have afforded this house today, even though my dad made six times the salary he had when they bought the house.

"If I loved the house and I thought I could make the payments without being miserable, I would do it," I finally say. "Especially if I was an amazing carpenter with the talent to make it a dream home. But that's just me."

If a face can shine, his does, and I instantly know I've said the right thing.

"Yeah, I can make it pretty outstanding. Jess will be impatient, though. She's not exactly a roughing-it kind of girl, and it's going to be a mess for a while. She wants something that's move-in ready, so we can focus on having—" He stops, and we both look away, cognizant of all the things we're not saying.

"Sorry," he says in a low voice and reaches for my hand, which I snatch away.

"You want to go ahead with the offer, then? We don't have to do fourteen percent. We can do whatever you feel comfortable with." My tension is cloaked in professionalism.

"Let's go big." He drums his fist on the marble countertop.

"Let's go big," I repeat but feel three inches tall.

Chapter 19
Legally Blonde

It's been six days since any work has been done on the pool house. No one, not even the guy who eventually came to tarp the roof (a little late, fellow), has been back. Kyle has stopped answering my calls. And I'm almost certain he's blocked my texts. I've left repeated messages at Bleu Construction, including a threat of legal action, all of which have gone ignored.

Apparently this is not uncommon in the construction world. My mother, who appears to be over her snit about me living with Brooke, swears all contractors have attention deficit disorder.

"What do we do now?" I ask Brooke, who's painting her toenails while watching television in the den.

"Find someone else, I guess. What we're not doing is paying Bleu. Fuck them."

It's the first time I've ever heard Brooke use the F-word, and I kind of like it.

"Okay, do you have anyone from your original list I can contact?" Considering the shortage of contractors, it won't be easy finding someone to take over the job in the eleventh hour.

"Bleu was it. You've got to have some good contacts."

Wrong. The people Josh dealt with specialized in commercial buildouts. Restaurants, retail stores, tech companies. None of them would stoop so low as to take on our five-hundred-square-foot pool house redux. Chip might know of someone, but the likelihood of anyone being available at this very moment is about as good as me getting a reservation at the French Laundry before summer.

"I'll see what I can do, Brooke. But I'm not optimistic."

She looks up from her feet. "I've got it rented out for most of April. So if we have to do it ourselves..." She flashes me a tight smile that in the immortal words of Tim Gunn says, "Make it work."

Jeez, the woman is relentless. But she hasn't once so much as hinted that I'm reaching my expiration date here at Chateau Sharing Economy, even though she could probably sublet my bedroom.

"I'll soldier on," I tell her. "I have to say, you're really taking preserving Dad's legacy to the next level." I'm still befuddled about why. We've been nothing but dismissive of her. Not overtly, mind you. But we made it clear that she wasn't accepted. That came in various forms but most notably that we rejected any and all invitations from my father that included Brooke. That meant that all holidays were spent with Mom and that my dad had to leave Brooke out if he wanted us to go on any family vacations with him. For a while after the breakup, in solidarity with Mom, he was dead to us. But at the end of the day, he was still our father, the man who brought us onto this earth, kissed our booboos, and was there for every one of our milestones. In other words, we took him back. And there's not a day that goes by since he died that I don't wish we hadn't wasted time disowning him, even if it was only for a short time.

"You going out?" Brooke eyes my outfit, a pair of good jeans, a cashmere sweater that I've never worn before and my favorite boots. Compared to my usual attire, yoga pants and hoodies, I'm dressed up.

"Adam and I are going to dinner." It occurs to me that I should invite her, but I don't, telling myself that Adam wouldn't like it and that it would eventually get back to my mother. The real reason, though, is that I'm not quite ready to face the possibility of an inconvenient truth. Brooke may have actually been in love with our father.

"Have a nice time." She waves, then goes back to her pedicure.

I meet Adam at the foot of the driveway. It's a nice evening, and I can use the exercise, such as it is. But mostly I know Adam would want me to save him from having to run into Brooke. Thank goodness she's gone most of the time, working, or I'd never get to see my brother.

Our dinner date is ostensibly to celebrate my first home sale since Josh died. Yes, Campbell and Jess got the house. Yay! The second runner up came in two thousand dollars behind them. So Niki, bless her bitchy heart, was right on the money.

If I'm being completely honest, the news of them getting it was bittersweet. On one hand, it made me ache for Josh. This could've been us buying our first house together. On the other hand, it made me proud that I could do this for Campbell. He wanted the house so badly I could feel his excitement as if it was my own. Yet a part of me (and it doesn't make me feel good to admit this) is jealous. Jealous that he gets the happily ever after and I don't.

Adam squeals up to the driveway and slams on his brakes. "Why are you waiting here?" he asks as I get in his car.

I cock my head at the house.

"The child widow is home?"

"She's home, and while it wouldn't kill you to say hello, I decided that because you're paying for dinner, I would cut you some slack."

"I'm paying for dinner? You're the one with a big fat commission check."

"You're the one selling a multi-million-dollar business. Why's it taking so long, by the way?"

"It's not. We're done."

My mouth goes slack. "When? Why didn't you tell us?"

"I'm telling you now." He hangs a U-turn. "Where do you want to go?"

"Do Mom and Hannah know?"

"Yep. Where do you want to go?"

"Wait a minute. You told them before me?" My brother and I have no secrets between us.

"It happened at the same time Campbell got his house. I didn't want to steal your thunder."

Is that how pathetic I've become to my family that one stinking sale—to a friend no less—trumps my big brother closing out the deal of a lifetime? "Seriously, Adam, this is huge. How could you not tell me?"

"I'm telling you now." He slaps my leg. "I've got an idea since we're both celebrating. Let's go to Frank Dina's and have lobster pot pie."

"We won't get in. Not on a Friday night. Not unless we eat at the bar." I'm not feeling a sitting-at-the-bar vibe tonight. I was hoping for a quiet dinner and was even considering telling Adam about Josh's text messages.

Over the last two weeks, I've shown great restraint by not reading the rest of them. A couple of times I came close to deleting the entire file but couldn't do it, holding out hope that his last text to Beth goes something like this:

Beth, I've met someone. And while you're amazing—cute, sweet, and a great dancer—this new woman, well, she's the one. I mean like seriously The One. It's still early in our relationship, but I already know she's going to be the mother of my children and the love of my life. I hope we can stay friends, but if we can't, I'm cool with that too.

Wishing you all the best —Josh

"We'll get in," Adam says. "Frank is a big fan of the *Legend of Zena*." That's the first video game Switchback ever made and to this day one of the most popular—in the world.

"Really?" I ask surprised. Frank Dina is a renowned chef with restaurants all over the globe. Somehow, I can't picture him lying on a crusty couch with a bowl of Cheetos on his stomach, manning a joystick. But there are stranger things known to happen.

"Yep. He's catered two of Switchback's parties, and we're sort of friends."

"Okay, as long as we can get a table, because I don't want to sit at the bar. Wow, I can't believe your company is sold. What are you going to do with all that loot?" I know a Victorian he can buy as long as he lets me continue to live there.

"Probably reinvest it in another startup. Buy a Tesla." As soon as the words leave his mouth, he stutters, "Shit. Sorry, Rach."

"It wasn't the Tesla that killed Josh, it was the dumbass behind the wheel. Get one if you want."

When we get to the restaurant, Adam doesn't even bother to look for parking, just pulls up to the valet stand and hands one of the attendants his keys. Fancy.

"Watch me work my magic." Adam cracks his knuckles.

Why do I have a terrible feeling that my brother is going to make a fool of himself? Ordinarily, it would be fun to watch. But I'm hungry, and lobster pot pie sounds so good right now that I don't want to leave disappointed.

As I suspect, the host doesn't have a table for us. When Adam asks to talk to Frank, I cringe. It's the equivalent of "Do you know who I am?"

"Is he expecting you, sir?" The man, who's a caricature of a haughty maître d', is actually intimidating as he stares down his long nose at us.

I want to say, *Lighten up, Francis. This is the city by the bay, not Paris.*

"Tell him Adam Gold of Switchback wants to say hi." My brother jams his hands in his pockets, way more confident than I am that Frank Dina will deign to make an appearance.

But five minutes later, much to my surprise, Dina comes sauntering out from the kitchen. He's got on a white chef's jacket, chef's pants, Prada sneakers and a smile a mile wide.

"Adam!" He gives my brother a fist bump and then some kind of weird shoulder knock handshake thing.

Adam introduces me. Dina's polite, but he only has eyes for Adam, who he definitely has a man crush on. Who knew my nerdy brother was so popular?

"You guys here to eat?" Frank asks.

"Yeah, if you've got a table."

Frank motions us to follow him across the dining room. Tucked in the corner, next to a window facing California Street, is a quiet little two-top that the restaurant obviously reserves for VIPs who wander in without a reservation.

"I'll send some apps out," Frank says. "Good seeing you, Adam. Nice meeting you, Rachel. Bon appétit."

As he walks away, I mouth to Adam, "Oh. My. God."

Adam laces his hands behind his head and leans back on two legs. "It's good to be king."

Normally, I'd tell him he was a jackass but...lobster pot pie coming my way. And apps. And maybe, since Adam is buying, some really good French champagne.

"We should've invited Campbell," Adam says, and I note that Jess is conspicuously missing from the sentence.

"And Jessica too," I add, if for nothing else to read Adam's face. My brother has no game when it comes to hiding what he's thinking.

But tonight he's playing poker. "And Jess, too," he says.

"They're probably having their own celebration."

"Probably." Adam is watching me over the rim of his water glass. "So are you back at Windham full-time now?"

The thing is I've never been full-time even when I was. But I nod because my family will be relieved that I'm finally coming out of my grief and getting on with my life. Let it be my secret that I don't have any clients waiting in the wings or any leads on listings. Campbell was the only one.

I consider telling Adam that I'm helping Brooke save our family home but intuitively know what she told me was in confidence. She never said it was, but something passed between us that day. A camaraderie of sorts. Her confession couldn't have been easy. *Your father gave everything to your mother, his first wife. I got sloppy seconds and a house that's more of a burden than a benefit.*

A server brings us plates of wood-fired asparagus with smoked pork shoulder and lentils and ahi tartare. Everything looks too pretty to eat, but I'm digging in. Adam orders a bottle of champagne. The good stuff, though honestly, I wouldn't know André from Cristal. The sommelier pops the cork and pours Adam a taste. Adam gives a thumbs-up, even though his idea of living large is a blue raspberry Slurpee. The sommelier pours us each a glass and leaves us to enjoy.

I dip into the asparagus. "My God, this is so good." When I take a gulp of the champagne, I get bubbles up my nose.

Both Adam and I bust up laughing.

"We have to do a real celebration," I say while going in for the ahi.

"This is a real celebration."

"I mean with the fam. I can't believe you sold your business, Adam. Dad would *plotz* as Mom would say."

"It would definitely have blown his fucking mind. I'm sure he thought Switchback was a losing proposition."

"No, he wouldn't have invested if he thought that."

Adam pins me with a look. "If he thought it would keep me from being homeless, he would."

"There is that. But he never believed for one minute you'd be homeless, just penniless, living in the Tenderloin in one of those single-room-occupancy hotels where everyone shares the same cracked toilet."

Adam laughs, nearly knocking over his champagne flute. "Thank God it never came to that."

The server comes to take our order, and we both get the pot pie, though I'm already full from the appetizers and bubbly.

"Campbell says the house is a dump with promise."

I nod. "He'll make it great. Mr. Scott will do the landscaping, and it'll be gorgeous when the two of them are finished."

"I can't believe he pulled the trigger."

"Why?" I ask, surprised. If anyone would buy a vintage Craftsman in sore need of renovation, it would be Campbell.

"I just thought he'd wait a little while, that's all." Adam shrugs in that noncommittal way of his, but it seems like there's more he isn't saying.

I want to pin him down on it when I see Stephen sitting across the dining room by himself. "Look who's here." I nudge my head in Stephen's direction. "I bet he's waiting for Hannah. We should go over and say hi. Invite them to eat with us."

Adam follows the direction of my gaze and puts his hand on my arm as I start to get up from the table. "Let's wait."

"Oh, for goodness' sake, you don't—" I stop short as a blonde joins him, and for a second I can't breathe. "Is that her? The woman you saw him with coming out of the Fairmont?"

Adam gives the woman a hard look. "I can't tell."

"Could you tell if you got closer?"

"I don't know. I don't think so."

"Should we go over there? Confront him without actually confronting him?"

Adam throws his hands up in the air. "We're not going over there. We're staying here, finishing our dinner, and watching them."

"Do you think they can see us?"

"If we can see them, they can see us. So try not to call attention to yourself."

Our pot pies come, and I use the opportunity to glance around the server to see what Stephen and the blonde are doing. Nothing terribly revealing. Then again, it's not as if they're going to start groping each other in the middle of a Michelin-star restaurant.

Adam clears his throat. "Thanks," he says to our server. When he leaves, Adam turns his attention to me. "Can you be any more obvious? Chill."

"I just want to see what they're doing. Maybe I should take a picture of them." I reach in my handbag for my phone.

"Why? So you can blackmail them later?" He rolls his eyes.

"So I can show Hannah, you idiot."

"And what the hell would that accomplish other than to destroy her? Let's keep calm and watch them. Discreetly." Adam holds up a finger. "Maybe you're right, maybe it's just a business meeting. Two lawyers eating at an expensive restaurant on a Google expense account, talking about legal shit. As you pointed out, it happens all the time."

"He just got on his phone," I whisper.

"How do you know that?"

I point to the mirror on the wall behind our table, which gives me an unobstructed view of Stephen and Legally Blonde. "Do you think it's Hannah, looking for him?"

"How the hell would I know?"

"Call her. See if she's on her other line."

"Bad idea. You and I both know that one of us will wind up saying something."

I steal another glance of them in the mirror. "Stephen's off the phone now. They're ordering."

"Eat your lobster before it gets cold."

How can he think of eating at a time like this? "Oh my God, it's so good." I fan my mouth with my hand as I try to swallow a huge bite full without scalding my tongue. "Hot. Be careful."

"Jesus Christ, I can't take you anywhere."

"What's he doing now? You look."

Instead of using the mirror, he turns slightly to get a view of their table. "I can't tell. The sommelier is standing right in front of them."

"Are they ordering wine? Do you think that's suspicious?"

"No. Why would it be?"

"I don't know. If it's a business meeting...it just seems weird."

Adam shakes his head. "Boy, you don't get out much. Every business meeting I've ever had involved some kind of alcohol."

"You're not an attorney," I shoot back.

"Thank God for that."

I catch Stephen's reflection in the mirror. The sommelier is gone, and it's just my brother-in-law and Legally Blonde. They're making conversation, but because I can't hear what they're saying, I have no idea whether it's work related or sexy-time talk. She's dressed professionally. Wool pants, white blouse, a blazer, and sensible loafers. Nothing that says "I'm a home-wrecking whore." But who knows?

I dig into my lobster pot pie again because eating is better than watching the possible demise of my sister's marriage. And this really is the best thing I've ever tasted. Adam is almost done with his and is eyeing mine, so I pull my plate closer. "Keep your hands to yourself."

"I'm thinking of getting another one."

Unlike the rest of our family—we veer into the curvy category—Adam can afford the extra calories. He's not as lanky as Josh was but is thin enough to go back for seconds.

"Knock yourself out," I tell him. "It'll help us stall to watch Stephen."

"I don't need to see more, Rach. It's a done deal in my mind. Stephen's got himself a mistress. The question is, what do we tell Hannah?"

I don't want it to be true. Besides it breaking my sister's heart, I'm left to wonder whether most men cheat. My father, for instance. And although I don't believe Josh ever cheated on me in the classic sense, he never told me about Beth, who he clearly loved. One of the things I thought was special about us was that we didn't keep secrets from each other. Finding out I was wrong about something I considered to be the hallmark of our relationship makes me feel cheated. Perhaps it's unfair to Josh. But I can't change the way I feel, and Josh isn't around to explain it.

"I think we have to tell her, Adam. If we don't, we're complicit."

"I was afraid you'd say that. How 'bout you do it?"

"No way. It has to be the both of us." Safety in numbers.

We simultaneously glance over at Stephen, who is sticking his spoon into Legally Blonde's bowl of soup.

Adam pivots back to me and holds my gaze. "Should I call her? Or should you?"

* * * *

After watching Stephen slurp soup out of another woman's bowl, not his wife, I'm more curious than ever about the rest of Josh's text messages. Yes, obsessed is more like it. Up in my room, I try to convince myself of all the reasons it's wrong to read them. *It's no different than pawing through someone's diary,* I tell myself. If Josh had wanted me to know about Beth, he would've told me.

But he's dead.

I'm not sure whether that gives me free license to go through his private communications or makes it even more forbidden. It's a conundrum to be sure.

For a long time, I sit on my bed, staring at his laptop. I can swear I hear it say, "Read me, Rachel. It'll put an end to this nonsense once and for all."

The more I think about it, the more convinced I am that I'm making a big deal out of nothing. *Just read them and get it over with and move on, Rachel. Stop being a big baby and working yourself up over nothing,* I tell myself.

Yet I continue to vacillate, recognizing the whole Pandora's box situation. If I simply nuke the folder now, I can put this whole *mishigas* to rest. The worst thing that will come out of it is the knowledge that Josh once loved a girl and didn't tell me about her, even though we shared all our secrets and stories, including my saddest one.

I can live with that...I think.

But maybe I don't have to. What if I read the rest of the letters and realize that Josh and Beth didn't wind up moving in together and that their relationship was nothing more than a short-lived romance? So short-lived that Josh didn't even remember it, or the texts. He just stored them away like one does old receipts. *Hey, I might need to make a return one of these days.*

It's this last bit that moves me toward his laptop. And before I can stop myself, I fire it up, click on Josh's Gmail account, and find the Texts/Beth folder.

Ah, where did we leave off?

Josh: "Just got a call from the rental company. We checked out. Can move in next Friday."

Beth: "I have my last Diego Rivera class Friday afternoon. Can't miss it. Ugh. Let's wait until Saturday."

Josh: "Don't want to wait even a minute to start our new life together. I'll borrow Sergio's truck and move a bunch of boxes over Friday. Will pick you up for dinner in our new place."

My stomach churns, and I force myself not to throw up. It's like the time Hannah and I took the ferry to Larkspur. The bay was so choppy that I had to stand in the middle of the boat and stare at the horizon to keep from getting sick.

My tears drip onto the monitor, but I don't stop. June...July...August...I keep reading about my husband's other life, the one he hid from me.

I now know that Beth Hardesty was an art history major, she worked at the gift shop at SFMOMA, her favorite flowers were red roses (how boring) and during her and Josh's fifth month of living together, they adopted a Pomeranian mix from the pound (I hope its insane little bark drove Josh crazy). Their favorite takeout was Zuni's roast chicken for two. They talked about buying a house but wanted to wait until Beth finished school.

It's three o'clock in the morning, and I'm bleary eyed. I want to find out how this story ends. More than anything I want to understand why Josh never told me that he was in love with a woman named Beth, who he lived with, and from what I can ascertain, quite happily. But there are so many more texts, and I can't stay awake any longer. I could skip to the last one, like I sometimes do with a book when I'm impatient to see how the plot plays out. The problem with that, though, is I might miss something. Something important.

Just one more, I tell myself.

Beth: "Don't forget I'm going to be late tonight."

Josh: "Right, Jacob's show at that gallery in Berkeley. Is someone giving you a ride home?"

Beth: "Probably or BART. If it gets real late, I'll stay at Jamila's."

Josh: "Call me. I'll get you."

Beth: "No need. I'll figure something out."

Josh: "Love you."

The next one isn't until three weeks later, which seems odd to me given how prolific their texting has been. Okay, one more, then I'm calling it quits.

Beth: "What do you think?" It's a selfie of Beth in a slinky cocktail dress in what looks like a department store dressing room.

She's so lovely that my heart folds in half. Brown hair, fair skin and blue eyes. She looks familiar, like a prettier version of me. But as I study her closer, I realize I know her. Or at least I've seen her before. Yet I can't put my finger on where.

Hers is the last face I see before I nod off to sleep and the first face I see when I wake up.

But it isn't until three days later that it finally hits me where I've seen Beth before. She was part of that small group at Tino's that time after we cleaned Dad's closet and Josh and I went out for pizza. She was standing outside the restaurant with three others. Josh said he knew some of them from Cal and that they wouldn't remember him.

Who knew what an accomplished liar he was?

Chapter 20
Revelations

I'm at my wits' end. I've tried every contractor I can find, and no one has an opening in their schedule to do the pool house. There are only four weeks left until Brooke's traveling nurse is supposed to occupy the place. She's staying five days at two hundred bucks a night. And I'm pretty sure the woman is expecting walls and running water.

Next week, Brooke and I move into the cottage—things are going to get cozy fast—while we play housemaids to the mystery writers.

"Can you even cook?" I ask her as we share the kitchen island over our morning coffee because I realize I don't know this about my stepmother. And if our paid houseguests are expecting meals, it's a little late for culinary school.

"I worked my way through nursing school, catering." She laughs at the expression of surprise on my face. "My ex and I owned the company."

I didn't know she had an ex, let alone a catering company. "As in ex-husband?"

"Yep." She doesn't elaborate, but I'm dying to know if she and my dad were cheating on him, too. "So when are you going to break down and call Campbell?"

"Huh?"

"About finishing the work." Brooke aims her chin in the direction of the pool house.

I'd be lying if I said I hadn't considered Campbell. But the work is so beneath his pay grade that I don't want to insult him. At least that's what I keep telling myself. The real reason is petty and shameful. I just can't be around happy right now, not while I'm still reeling from death and secrets and inconvenient truths.

"It's not what he does," I say. "He's a finish carpenter, an artist."

"Didn't he just buy a house that he can't afford?"

I don't know how she knows these things. It's not like we sit up at night in our pajamas by the fire, trading gossip.

She drills me with a look. "I'm sure he could use the money. Most artists can. We need the work done, so call him."

The woman has *chutzpah,* I'll give her that. I'd always gotten the impression that she was milquetoast. Opposite of my mother. I suppose I assumed that part of the reason Dad left Mom was because he needed a break from her domineering. So far, it seems that Brooke could give Shana a run for her money.

And for no reason I can quantify, this sudden discovery makes me want to confide in her. "Stephen is having an affair on Hannah," I blurt.

Brooke stops buttering her gluten-free toast. "Stephen's a piece of shit. Your sister would be better off without him."

I jerk back, a little stunned by her bluntness—and her keen observation. From the day Mom found out Stephen was a six-figure lawyer with Google and a Harvard Law grad, he could've killed kittens in his free time and she would've looked the other way.

"Adam and I don't know whether to tell her."

"What evidence do you have?"

I tell her about Legally Blonde and how they shared soup out of the same bowl, about Adam seeing Stephen and a woman coming out of the Fairmont, and of course my brother-in-law's rendezvous at Harry Asia's.

"Was it the same woman?"

"Adam isn't sure."

She appears to be deliberating. Kind of ironic that I'm asking her advice in connection with a cheating spouse. Then again, why not go to an expert?

"Sounds pretty circumstantial to me," she finally says. "Either way, Hannah isn't going to appreciate the interference."

"So you're saying I should keep my sister in the dark about her slimeball husband?"

"Nope, not saying that at all. I'm saying don't expect her gratitude and be prepared for her to throw a lot of hostility your way."

"Is that what happened with you when someone told your husband about you and Dad?" I'm going out on a limb here. Until today, I was unaware that Brooke had been previously married.

To her credit—or discredit, depending on how you look at it—her face stays neutral. Not so much as a blink of an eye. If she's angry, she hides it well. And she should be angry because I crossed a line.

"There was no husband," she says calmly. "Only an ex-husband."

Unable to stop myself, I say, "But there was a wife," and stare at her in challenge.

"Yes, there was a wife. I can't change history, Rachel. I am sorry that it caused your mother, your sister, your brother, and you pain. I could say that I never intended for that to happen, but it would sound hollow and, frankly, idiotic. So I won't insult your intelligence."

Her lack of defensiveness throws me off guard, and I find myself temporarily speechless.

"I don't like Stephen," she continues. "Never have. And I especially don't like him for Hannah. But it's obvious that your sister cares for him a great deal. Or at least the idea of him." She meets my eyes to see if I'm following. What's not to follow? The idea of him, meaning he's handsome, powerful, and successful. In Hannah's eyes, the perfect husband. Except, I get the feeling that's not what Brooke is talking about, that she's talking about something entirely different, and is one step ahead of me.

"All I'm saying is if it were me, I'd tread lightly. But you, Adam and Hannah are close. Maybe she'll listen."

She spills her cold coffee out in the sink and puts the butter in the fridge. "I've got to get to work. Do me a favor." I wait for her to say "Don't ever talk to me like that again" or something equally stepmotherish. But all she says is "Call Campbell."

As soon as I hear her car wind down the driveway, I swipe my phone off the counter and go outside. It's the first nice day we've had since February, the azaleas have bloomed early, and I can use the fresh air. I sit in my mother's old tree swing, use the trunk to push off with my foot, and let myself sway back and forth. Why is it that the gentle movement of an old swing can soothe your blues away? And to think it's a thousand times cheaper than a shrink. Maybe I'm onto something and can quit real estate and sell therapy swings.

I close my eyes, count to ten, and punch in Campbell's number on my phone.

"Yello," he says. "We still set to close tomorrow?"

"Yep. Everything is running on schedule. But that's not why I'm calling."

"No? What's up?"

"How would you like a quick side hustle to help you with the remodeling budget on your new house?"

"Sounds interesting. Whaddya got?"

"Remember that thing we were doing with the pool house? Well, the construction company Brooke hired is MIA, and we're sort of on a deadline."

"Hmm, what kind of a deadline?"

I pinch the bridge of my nose, knowing it's a big ask. "It needs to be done by the second week of April. I know it's below your usual pay grade, and I wouldn't ask, but we're really in a bind. Brooke has already booked the place out for most of next month and currently it isn't...well, you saw it."

"Yep."

"Yep, you saw it? Or Yep, you'll do it?"

"Both. I cleared my decks for the new house but can squeeze you in."

"Really?" I don't know what I was expecting, but I didn't think it would be this easy. "You don't mind that it's not carpentry?"

"Nope. How 'bout I come over tomorrow to get the keys to the new place and you show me what you want done?"

"I was going to meet you and Jess at Liberty. I have a gift for you guys." Closing day is usually a big production. I meet the clients at the house, present them with the key and take lots of happy pictures that I can later use in promotional mailers about how I make dreams come true. It's also standard operating procedure to give the buyers something for the new house. In Campbell and Jessica's case, it's a home warranty. I'm figuring most of the appliances that come with the place are circling the drain. At least the warranty will pay for replacements.

"You didn't have to do that, Rach. But if you want to meet at the house first, that works. I've got to motor, but I'll see you tomorrow."

"Thanks, Campbell. You're a lifesaver."

I click off, relieved that I can check the pool house off my list. Although I have my reservations about being near Campbell every day—things never feel resolved between us, like we're always walking on eggshells—I know he'll get the job done and finish on time.

It's cooler outside than I thought, and my arms prickle with goose bumps. That's what I get for not wearing a jacket. I try to brave the chill in my short sleeves so I can let the swing take me away for a while, but the cold eventually sends me scurrying inside.

It's been a few days since I checked in with Mommie Dearest and should probably give her a call. Instead, I linger in the kitchen, considering the wisdom of a second cup of coffee. Ultimately, I go in for the second cup but reject Mom. There's too much for her to wheedle out of me, and I'm still not ready to share.

Instead, I shoot Josie a text and ask her what she's doing for dinner. Suddenly I feel restless. It's hard to believe it's been nearly eight months since the accident. My life has changed in ways I never could have predicted. Here I am in my childhood home, running it like a Motel 6 with my father's child widow, who I've actually come to respect. And maybe even like (the jury is still out on that one). My brother-in-law is no doubt schtupping half the blondes in the city. And my husband had a whole other life he kept from me. Maybe it's not infidelity in the classical sense, but I feel cheated. It doesn't mean I love him any less, but it has made me question everything I thought I knew about us. And that's not a good place to be when I can't ask him for answers.

In other news, my professional life is still in the shitter. So at least some things have remained the same for consistency's sake. This morning, though, I did get a referral from Zillow. A middle-aged man looking for a house in the Inner Sunset, who seems like a serious buyer and not just a lookie-loo.

After finishing the rest of my coffee, I drag my ass upstairs for my laptop. I should probably start searching the MLS for him since we're scheduled to go out Saturday and I have nothing to show him.

But instead of searching for homes, I grab Josh's laptop, plop down on my bed and return to his Gmail account to spend more quality time with him and Beth. I realize that this is unhealthy, bordering on obsessive compulsive. That some things are better left in the dark. But I can't seem to help myself. I have to know how it ends.

Where did I last leave off? Oh, Beth, the slinky dress, and the fitting room. I find it interesting that Josh never responded to Beth's selfie picture. No you-look-incredible return text. It could be that he was simply too busy to reply. But that doesn't seem to be his MO as far as their texting history.

I skip to the next one, which is a few days later.

Josh: "I'm at the store. Should I get milk? Or did you?"

Beth: "Get milk."

Next day.

Beth: "I'm two doors down from the dry cleaners. You want me to pick up your suit?"

Josh: A thumbs-up emoji.

Hmm, it appears the honeymoon is over. Yet the fact that they've fallen into a domestic rhythm makes me feel worse rather than better. They may as well be a married couple, which is like a dagger in my chest.

I sort through the perfunctory—i.e., boring—texts and hunt for the ones that will shed light on why Josh was single the day I met him. What if Beth died and Josh was so crestfallen he couldn't say her name without having to be rushed to the hospital? Or what if it turns out she was married and living a secret life with Josh, and he feels so foolish about the way she duped him that he vowed to erase her memory for all eternity?

It does occur to me that maybe he wasn't single after all, and the reason he never told me about Beth is because he was still with her while he was in a bar, flirting with me. I don't really know how to feel about that.

I'm through more than a year's worth of texts when I come to one in September, just five months before Josh and I met.

Beth: "I'm going out for drinks tonight with Jamila and Jacob. Don't wait for me for dinner because we may go out and grab something."

Josh: "Where? I may get off early tonight, in which case I'll meet you."

Beth: "We haven't chosen a place yet. I'll text you as soon as I know."

Four hours later.

Josh: "Do you know where you're going yet? I'm off in ten."

No answer.

Two days later.

Beth: "I don't want to fight with you anymore."

Josh: "Really? Because it seems like you do."

Beth: "No, I don't. I love you and I want us to get along."

Josh: "I love you too and will endeavor to do better. Date night tonight?"

Beth: "I have Jacob's thing. But I could cancel."

Josh: "Don't cancel. We'll do it tomorrow night. Or better yet, let's go away for the weekend."

Beth: "Ooh, that sounds wonderful. Surprise me with somewhere good."

Josh: "Okay, one surprise coming right up." Heart emoji.

My years with Josh had been filled with heart emojis. Now, I want to ban them for life and fine anyone a million dollars who dares to use them in anything other than a Valentine's card. And even that is questionable.

In for the long haul, I stretch out on the bed and prop a few pillows behind my head. I'm now in October, which from a quick glance is off to a rocky start.

Beth: "You embarrassed me last night. I don't know what's wrong with you lately."

Josh: "What's wrong with me? Take a wild guess, Beth. And by the way, taking off this morning before we had time to talk and forcing us to have this conversation by text is beyond fucked up."

Beth: "No, what's fucked up is you making a scene last night in front of all my friends at Jacob's opening. You know how important the night was to him."

Josh: "This is the thing, Beth. I don't give a flying fuck about Jacob or his goddamn opening."

Beth: "You made that quite apparent. I'm going to class now. I hope you spend some time today thinking about how childish you sound."

I can't get a read on November. It's cryptic at best. But there's definitely trouble in paradise. I skim through the highlights.

Josh: "Next time you decide to be out until four in the morning, have the decency to call. If you're still home, or even awake, I forgot to turn off the coffee maker when I left this morning."

Beth: "I'm sorry. We were studying and the time got away from me. I'm sure midterms weren't that long ago for you that you can't remember how it was. But it was inconsiderate of me. I promise to do better."

Josh: "I was just worried, that's all. Let's carve out some time for dinner tonight."

Beth: "Can't. More study group. Jan van Eyck is a bitch. I swear he'll be the death of me. I don't even like Netherlandish painting." Barfing face emoji.

Josh: Laughing face emoji. "You'll get through it. Have a presentation in ten, so gotta go. Love you."

Next day.

Josh: "Had a meeting on the Peninsula, so snuck out before you were up. How'd you get home last night?"

Beth: "Jacob gave me a ride. How was the meeting?"

Josh: "Not bad. I think the Ryans liked the design. It was mostly Bill's, but the fireplace was all mine. And that's what they went crazy over."

Beth: "That's great. FYI: a bunch of us are going out to celebrate after the midterm. You're welcome to join us, but I doubt you want to come all the way to the East Bay. Wish me luck."

Josh: "May the force be with you. Seriously, good luck. I know you've got this."

Later that night.

Josh: "Beth, where the fuck are you?"

Ten minutes later.

Josh: "Please call me and let me know you're all right."

Two hours later.

Josh: "Beth, answer your goddamn phone."

Forty-five minutes later.

Josh: "I'm beyond panicked now. Don't know if you're lying dead in a ditch somewhere or just too inconsiderate to answer your calls."

Josh: "Jesus Christ, Beth. It's five o'clock in the fucking morning and I finally got a hold of Jamila, who says you're okay. I'm going to bed."

It appears that it was the beginning of the end. By late November, things were getting pretty dicey between my late husband and Beth.

Josh: "Can we talk before you do this?"

Beth: "There's no more that needs to be said."

Four days later.

Josh: "Don't do this, Beth. Can't we please try to work things out. I love you."

Beth doesn't respond.

Eight days later.

Beth: "I'll be there at four to pick up the rest of my stuff. I'll leave the key on the counter. I think it would be best if you weren't there. The landlord says he has the place rented. You can just mail me my half of the deposit when you get it."

Josh: "I won't be there. Please leave me a forwarding address to mail the check."

The last recorded text is December 10th at two in the morning.

Josh: "I mish you so moch. Come back to me, bootiful Beth. I will always loooove you."

Clearly, Josh is drunk. Beth doesn't even bother to reply.

The air is too heavy to breathe because I've already done the math. A mere two months later, Josh was trolling bars, looking for a new Beth. Me. It makes me question everything I thought I knew about us. Was I his rebound woman or the true love of his life, who made him forget Beth the minute he laid eyes on me?

This is the thing, either he didn't love Beth as much as he thought he did, or I was her flimsy replacement. Because you don't get over the real thing in sixty days. It took me years to move on after Campbell. I didn't even date until a year after we went our separate ways. It took college, a career and an assortment of boyfriends before I could even consider being his friend again. It hurt that much. And I don't think I really banished him from my heart until I fell for Josh, almost a decade later.

This all brings me back to why. Why didn't he tell me about her?

"Hey, Rach, you know how you loved Campbell? Well, I loved a girl named Beth once. I thought she was the one until I met you."

It would've been that simple. But instead I'm stuck in this place where everything I thought I knew feels like a lie. And the one person who'd always been my go-to reality check is gone.

There's only one thing to do, I tell myself. And I grab my coat and white-knuckle it in the car all the way to Colma, the land of graveyards, dead people, and Josh.

The day is gray at the cemetery as I wend my way around the headstones, looking for Josh's gravesite. It's the first time I've been here since the funeral, which probably makes me a bad wife. But I don't associate anything about this place with Josh.

The artificial flowers placed at many of the graves would've made him cringe. And the sound of traffic from the nearby freeway doesn't exactly lend itself to serenity. It may be called Eternal Home, but it sure the hell isn't Josh's. *He's somewhere beautiful,* I tell myself, *like Barcelona, where his spirit is gliding through Gaudi's neo-Gothic buildings or strolling The Bund, taking in the beaux arts architecture.*

I find his marker easy enough, take off my coat, lay it on the ground and sit cross-legged at the foot of his headstone.

"Hey, babe," I say, reaching out and tracing the Hebrew lettering on the marker with my finger. Here lies Josh Ackermann.

I'm angry and confused but somehow feel better just sitting here next to him. It's as if his love for me rises from the earth and envelops me like a winter shawl.

"I miss you," I say. "I miss us." I pause almost as if I think he'll respond.

"I miss you, too, Rach." Then I'll tell him I'm okay, that he shouldn't worry about me, even though I'm not.

"Josh? How come you never told me about Beth Hardesty?" I ask foolishly, hoping that he'll at least send me a sign from beyond. A breeze, a whiff of his scent, a small earthquake. Something. "I found her text messages in your email and don't understand why you kept her a secret from me. Why you never spoke of her. It's weird, don't you think? I mean, we shared everything with each other. I told you about Campbell and my miscarriage. Not even my parents or Hannah know about that. If you loved this Beth Hardesty woman, you should've told me because now I'm faced with wondering if the reason you didn't is because she means more to you than I did. Were you afraid to tell me the truth? I would've loved you no matter what. You know that, right?"

I move closer to Josh's gravestone, ridiculously believing that he's trying to talk to me, and I can't hear him over the din of the 280. But there's nothing. Not so much as a whisper of wind.

I leave as confused as when I came, but my heart is full having talked to him.

Chapter 21
Fate and Destiny

I wrap Campbell and Jess's home warranty along with a bottle of wine, a loaf of bread, a box of salt and a bag of sugar in a big basket and tie it with a bow. I also include a card to explain the bread, salt and sugar, a weird thing to give someone in the twenty-first century but a Jewish housewarming tradition just the same. It was my mother's idea.

"Bread, so you will never know hunger. Salt, so your life will always have flavor, and sugar, so your life will always have sweetness."

I stuff the basket into the back seat of my car and get to the Craftsman on Liberty before Campbell and Jess.

Driving has become better for me. I don't flinch every time I see an oncoming car. I also don't slam on my brakes every five seconds, which gets me to where I need to be a lot faster. Am I ready to drive the Autobahn? Probably not. But at least I've made progress since the accident.

I leave the basket in the car but grab my purse and wait at the front door. Campbell arrives a few minutes later.

"Hey!" I wave, wearing my big real estate smile as he comes down what can loosely be called the walkway. It's so overgrown with weeds that the flagstone is mostly hidden. "Where's Jess?"

"She can't make it. She has a work thing."

Something about the way he says it makes me think there's more to the story. Besides that, it seems weird that she would miss this. It's their first home purchase together. A pretty damn big deal if you ask me.

When Josh and I got our rental apartment, we could barely contain our excitement. Even before the lease was a done deal, we bought all new furniture for the place. On the day we got our keys, we went first thing in the morning, sat on the floor in the empty apartment and celebrated with a bottle of champagne before the movers came.

I rearrange my face to hide my surprise and pretend that a lot of clients do it this way. And to be fair, the house is such a wreck that it might be more meaningful to Jess when Campbell fixes it up.

"Then we'll take lots of photos for her," I say in a chipper voice. "You ready to go inside?"

"Sure." But he doesn't seem as excited as I thought he'd be.

I hand him the key and get ready to snap the first picture of him going inside. He opens the door, and I get the shot. For promotional purposes, it would've been better if Jess was there too. A gorgeous, young couple, looking ecstatic as they enter their new house is the money shot of course. But it is what it is.

That funky smell assails us as soon as we get inside. Campbell certainly has his work cut out for him. But when he's done, the place will be stunning. I know it.

I snap a few more pictures of Campbell holding the keys, standing in the center of the living room, and then coerce him outside so I can shoot him next to the sold sign. He's a good sport about it, though I can tell he isn't thrilled.

"Let's go back inside," he says, his hand toying with the tape measure clipped to his belt. He's anxious to get going on a plan.

"I have to get something from the car. I'll meet you inside." I go back for the basket. Jess probably would've appreciated the pretty cellophane wrapping more than Campbell. Oh well.

"You see this?" Campbell asks when I find him in the kitchen, fidgeting with a long narrow cabinet.

"What is it?"

He opens the door and pulls down an ancient ironing board. "Pretty cool, huh?" His lopsided grin does the thing to my insides that it used to do.

I chalk it up to how excited I am for him. "It's very cool. This is for you and Jess." I hand him the basket, suddenly wanting very much to leave. I tell myself that Jess should be sharing this moment with him, not me.

"Mazel tov. Here's to many wonderful years in your new home," I say. "I've got to run. But you've got the keys, and the house is all yours now."

"Thank you, Rachel. We couldn't have gotten it without you. And though it wasn't necessary, thank you for this." He holds up the basket, then comes over to me and kisses the top of my head.

"Ah, shucks, it was nothing." I try to joke this moment away, but I'm seconds away from crying and need to get out of here before I break down and make a fool of myself.

Campbell must sense it, because he lifts my chin and in a soft voice says, "I know it should've been you."

For a second, I'm confused. But no, he means Josh and me. He must mean that it should've been us buying a home and starting the next phase of our life together. Of course that's what he means.

"I've got to go, Campbell."

"Okay." He nods. "I'll be over in a little bit to take a look at the pool house."

I don't say anything, just turn around and bolt out of there as fast as I can.

Chapter 22
Traces of a Happy Marriage

Brooke and I are back to the daily cacophony of power tools. The mystery writers are coming tomorrow, at which time Campbell will have to stop working in the pool house. For twelve thousand bucks, our guests deserve some semblance of peace and quiet. Unfortunately, it's going to put us behind schedule on the project. Despite the hiatus, Campbell still believes he'll finish in time for the traveling nurse.

I'm looking forward to a break from the noise but not to rooming with my stepmother. The cottage is tight for two people. And Brooke is taking the week off from work so she can get her side hustle on as a home chef, which means we'll be tripping over each other.

Other than to show my new client a couple of houses, I don't have a lot to do. Oh, except to clean toilets and scrub showers. I'd almost forgotten that that was part of the deal until Brooke reminded me this morning.

Luckily, we're having the house professionally cleaned before the writers show up. Brooke has made it known to them that our bedrooms are off limits. Yesterday, upon her request, Campbell installed key locks on both our doors.

The whole thing is very strange. But I'll give Brooke credit; she's not the prissy little trophy wife I thought she was. The woman gets shit done. The other day, she fixed the downstairs powder room toilet to keep it from constantly running. I've heard her on the phone, booking the cottage and the pool house like she's been in property management as long as I've been in real estate. The only difference is she's actually making money.

Tonight, she wants me to go with her to another grief group meeting. This time it's at Raj's house. Everyone takes turns hosting. I haven't decided whether to go yet. Honestly, I'm trying not to think about Josh for a while. How is it possible to miss someone so much but at the same time want to kill him?

Yesterday, I bit the bullet and deleted the Texts/Beth file. I'm not sure if it was to absolve Josh of his perfidy or to hide the evidence. I thought destroying the file would give me a sense of peace. Ironically, it had the opposite effect. I'm spending every waking hour dwelling on all the unanswered questions.

Like now, what I really want to do is find Beth Hardesty. I grab my laptop from the nightstand, close out the MLS program I'm in and turn to my trusty friend, Google.

There are more Beth Hardestys in the world than you would think. And for all I know she's married now and goes by a different last name. I narrow my search to Beth Hardestys in the Bay Area. Since Josh and I saw her at Tino's that time, it's a safe assumption that she still lives here.

There are still too many to choose from, so I widen my parameters by plugging in "art" and "SFMOMA" in the search bar. At the top of the first page is a link to the San Francisco Museum of Modern Art, which is having a Calder exhibit I wouldn't mind seeing. The rest of the pages involve links to artists that either have Beth or Hardesty in their names, none of whom appears to be her.

This isn't working.

I decide to go the social media route. For some reason I get a strong LinkedIn vibe from her and try that first. There are lots of Beth Hardestys. And since I don't know what she does for a living, I try to match profile pictures with the dressing room selfie. My dirty little secret is that while I purged the file, I kept the picture. It's been more than eight years, so who knows if she looks like that anymore.

It doesn't take long before I realize this isn't a good use of my time. I move on to Instagram, where everyone seems to be hanging out these days. Once again, I turn up a shitload of Beth Hardestys. Apparently, it's a very popular name. Again, without knowing her occupation, hobbies, or associations, it's one of those proverbial needle-in-a-haystack situations. I consider TikTok but wouldn't know what to do once I got there, so I fall back on the oldie but goodie. Facebook.

Like everything else I've tried, there's a ton of Beth Hardestys. I search for Beth Hardestys from Cal, hoping that it's somewhere in her profile. When that doesn't net me much, I try Beth Hardesty, Cal and Bay Area. Also a bust. I go back to the list of Beth Hardestys and try to match the face I now know by heart with the other Beths' profile pictures. There's one that looks like a match. But when I click on her information, I see she's an alum of Ole Miss and lives in Natchez.

Back to the list.

There's a Beth Hardesty Jones who has a Cal bear as her profile picture. Bingo, I think I've found her. But when I click over to her profile page, her birthdate shows her to be fifty-two and her last profile pic is of an African American woman.

Ugh, do I have to hire a private investigator?

In a burst of sheer brilliance and then pure trepidation of what I might find, I hop over to Josh's profile page. He set it up long before we were married. But as far as I know, he only used it sporadically in recent years to post pictures of his architecture projects.

Sure enough, there's not much here. The last thing he posted was four years ago, a picture of us in front of the Western Wall during a vacation to Israel. I click over to his list of friends. There's only about five hundred. Toward the bottom of the list is good old Beth Hardesty. I hover over her name and then do something really stupid. I sign out of Facebook as me and sign back in as Josh. Luckily, he used the same password for just about everything. I go straight to the messenger icon at the top of the page and think of Ashley Birnbaum and her soon-to-be ex-husband Eli.

When I finally called her, she told me the whole sordid story. Not only did Eli have a porn problem, but he used Facebook to hook up with women who shared his particular proclivities. They spent their days on Facebook Messenger verbally reenacting the Kama Sutra. Ash snuck into the twins' bedroom in the middle of the night, broke into Eli's account and read every filthy thing he and these women ever wrote, then summarily vomited her guts up.

Josh did not have a porn problem. I feel I can say this with a hundred percent certainty, though I'm learning that you never really know a person, even one you were with for eight years. And even though I tell myself every day that Josh was never unfaithful to me, I can't help but wonder whether he was still in touch with Beth Hardesty while he and I were together. So I hold my breath and click. And...there's nothing there. Not even one message. I don't know whether to sigh with relief or be skeptical. Does Facebook come through Messenger every couple of years with a digital Zamboni to sweep the place clean? Hide the bodies, so to speak? Mark Zuckerberg lives on the same street in Palo Alto as one of my mother's dearest friends. Perhaps I could get her to slip the question to him.

For now, though, I'll have to be satisfied cyberstalking Beth. I jump to her page. Unlike Josh, she appears to be quite active on "The Facebook," as my mother calls it. The first thing I notice is Beth's profile picture is of two little clones—a girl and a boy—of herself. That same dark hair, fair skin, and blue eyes. So pretty.

I scroll first through her pictures. There are lots of her and what I presume is her family. A handsome man in his thirties with unruly brown hair and the two mini-mes. They're at the beach, on a farm, in front of the Golden Gate Bridge, windblown and fabulous. There are also shots of just her and the brown-eyed handsome man. On horseback with what I believe are the Grand Tetons in the foreground. Dressed up in formal attire at what looks like a gallery opening.

Her posts are filled with the kind of crap that's designed to make everyone else feel bad about their life. Stuff like: "We got the house in St. Helena! Does anyone know a good interior designer? Someone who can make the place feel like a home and not a museum." Or my personal favorite. "I'm honored and humbled that Les Puces made *San Francisco* magazine's best places to shop in the city. Thanks to all our loyal customers for voting. You guys are the best."

It appears that Beth owns not one but two gift shops (or as my mother calls them *chotchke* shops). One on California Street in Laurel Heights and one in, oh, surprise, surprise, St. Helena. Because the Napa Valley needs another store that sells wooden bowls and olive oil decanters.

Oh, would you look at that. Les Puces has its own page. I click over to scroll through posts upon posts of shiny objects and pithy comments like "Isn't this darling?" when in fact it looks like something you can pick up at Home Goods for half the price.

There's a photograph of a well-merchandised wall of signs, like the cheeky "Mama needs some wine" and the more subdued "Gather" in festive cursive letters.

There's a blanket made from giant yarn and the caption "Doesn't this look cozy?" Pet bowls that cost as much as Royal Copenhagen. And the obligatory collection of wine paraphernalia.

There's a post with a picture of Beth standing next to a new shipment of bath products, looking California casual in a pair of ripped jeans and a chunky off-the-shoulder sweater reminiscent of the 1980s. The tagline says, "Come and get them before they're gone."

I switch back to Beth's profile page (so much more interesting) and leaf through her life like a peeping tom. I ask myself whether Josh did the same, whether he visited Beth here and yearned for a life that could've been.

After I mine everything I can from her posts, I tap on her About page. She's a business owner, which I've already ascertained. She graduated from UC Berkeley. Yep. She's from Westport, Connecticut. Didn't know that. She's married to Jacob Fry. Jacob. Hmm, how about that?

The last thing I think as I close out of the page is, *I wonder if Josh knew.*

* * * *

That night, I let Brooke drag me to Raj's. He lives in a lovely old home in the Haight. And everywhere there are traces of a happy marriage. Pictures of Raj's beautiful family line the wall, including a portrait of him and his late wife, Brinda, on their wedding day, vibrant and so, so in love you can see it shining in their eyes.

"It was an arranged marriage," Raj tells us as we fan out in his living room, sipping tea and eating fantastic cream puffs from a nearby bakery. So far, the food is really good at these things. "We didn't want it at first. But our parents pushed. And it turned out that we were perfect for each other." He looks at Vivian and me. "The moral of the story is listen to your parents. They know what's good for you."

Vivian and I plaster on smiles. He's such a well-meaning sweet man. And so sad you just want to hug him.

Doris starts us off. "I don't have any friends anymore. Before Elias died, we socialized with a lot of couples. People from our church, from the neighborhood, from the time our kids were in school. But little by little they've stopped calling. I don't know if it's because they find me pitiful or because there's no room for a widow at their gatherings. I've got a sister in Atlanta, who I talk to on the phone a few times a week. And the kids check in on me, but they've got their own lives. It's doggone lonely. I find I turn the TV loud just so the house doesn't feel so empty inside."

I tear up and make a mental note to take Doris to dinner. No one should be lonely.

A woman who I don't remember from my first meeting says, "Have you thought about joining some clubs? There's a senior center on Beach Street that I go to and would be happy to introduce you around."

There's a few approving nods, and Doris and the woman, Sylvia, exchange phone numbers. By now, I'm a soggy mess. The humanity in this room is more than I can take.

Brooke clears her throat. "Yesterday would've been David's and my ninth wedding anniversary."

Ah jeez, that's right. I'd completely forgotten, though it wasn't a date I was likely to mark on my calendar. The day Dad made it official that he'd chosen Brooke instead of the mother of his children. In protest, none of us went to the wedding. From what I understand, it was a small ceremony with a few close friends followed by a cocktail party at the house. As I recall, Mom took a cruise, and Hannah, Adam and I went to a bar and got drunk.

"I still can't believe he's gone." Brooke blots her eyes with a tissue.

Ordinarily, I would've considered her rare show of emotion crocodile tears. But her misery is palpable. I can feel it across the room.

"He was planning to retire, and we were going to take a trip. He'd always wanted to backpack in Alaska and see Denali. But we never made it."

Backpack? Alaska? Denali? This is news to me. I'd never known my father to be much of an outdoorsman. Except for the med school camping forays in Humboldt, he and my mother preferred five-star resorts, golf courses and fine dining. The last time they got remotely close to roughing it was glamping on an African safari. But then again, I hadn't known he'd wanted to be a photojournalist.

"I've thought of making the trip myself as an homage to him, but I can't bear the idea of doing it without him." She sniffles into her tissue. "If the grief is supposed to get better as time goes on, why is it getting worse?"

There are hushed murmurs around the room, and Vivian gives Brooke a hug. I probably should be the one consoling her. We lost him together, after all. My father. Her husband, though it's only in this moment that I've started to think of him that way. Before, he was always my mother's husband, even in divorce. Even in death. It was always Shana and David Gold. Our family, not hers. She was merely an interloper, a temporary nuisance, who would eventually go away.

Now I'm not so sure. The truth is I'm not so sure about anything anymore.

Chapter 23
The Mystery Writers

I never realized how small the guest cottage was until I had to share it with Brooke. It's not that she's a space hog or anything. It's just that we can no longer hide from each other. It's impossible in nine hundred square feet.

The mystery writers are due to arrive any minute, and Campbell is cramming in as much hammering and drilling as he can before they get here.

I put away a week's worth of clothes in the bedroom I'll be using. It's not much larger than a prison cell, not that I know much about prison cells. Just enough room for a full-sized bed, a nightstand, and a tiny closet. Brooke's room is slightly larger and has a queen-sized bed and a dresser, in addition to a closet. We'll share the bathroom, which is the cottage's best feature because it has an antique clawfoot tub and an RV-sized stall shower.

The guest cottage was here before my parents bought the house. At one time, it was probably a carriage house for a nearby stable.

According to my mother, the cottage was stuffed with everything from old furniture to tens of dozens of empty wine bottles when she and my father moved in. The best she could figure was one of the previous tenants from the 1970s used the old bottles for their candle-making business. My parents cleaned out the place, updated the bathroom and tiny kitchen. Other than that, though, they left it pretty much as is.

Every summer, Aunt Barbara, Uncle Al and my cousin Arie would stay in the cottage when they came to visit from Brooklyn. When Arie moved to San Francisco after college, he lived in the cottage until he found a job and an apartment. For a short time, I remember one of my father's medical partners staying here. I was too young at the time to get the full story, but on reflection, I'm pretty sure his wife threw him out of the house. In any event, the cottage was used on rare occasion and for the most part was where my mother sent discarded pieces of furniture to die.

Brooke "redecorated"—she painted, had the floors refinished, got rid of all the junk, added window treatments and a few rugs—so she could turn it into a Vrbo. The finished product is charming with a touch of old-world and a sprinkle of quirk (very San Francisco). And you couldn't get a decent hotel room in this city for the price Brooke is charging. A whole apartment? Forget about it.

I'm secretly impressed with her entrepreneurial spirit. And in a weird way, I'm kind of looking forward to this week. I've never met a published author before. I Googled some of the guests, and a couple of them appear to be big deals. Not Gillian Flynn–level but bestsellers just the same.

Even though it's still not warm enough to swim, I had Campbell help me open up the pool in case some of the writers want a pretty place to lounge outside. I also made sure all the twinkly lights strung in the trees are working.

Living in a place like this was never taken for granted by the Gold family. Every day, we counted having this estate as a blessing, which instilled a sense of pride as well as a certain kind of responsibility to share it with others. So in a way, Brooke is carrying on that tradition. And I feel it's incumbent on me as one of the stewards to make the house and grounds as pretty and comfortable as possible for guests.

After I stash my toiletries in the bathroom, I wander over to the pool house to check on Campbell's latest progress. In just a short time, he's made significant headway. He's gotten paper and siding up on the new addition and has roughed out the windows. It's only him, and he's still faster than Kyle and his crew. I don't know what those guys were doing all that time. Probably updating their Tinder accounts.

"Hey." Campbell gives me one of his signature head nods as he cuts a piece of wood. "Is Stephen King here yet?" His mouth curves up in a smile.

"Not yet. You're good. Anything new to see?"

"I got half the siding on." He walks me around to the addition.

"Wow, it looks great." Now that I have a vision of the finished product, it's more seamless than I thought it would be. I was afraid it would be out of proportion with the original footprint. Josh used to say that scale was the definer between success and failure, and Campbell nailed it. Though to be fair, it was Brooke's design.

"Yeah, it looks pretty good. I know you're pissed at those other guys, but they did a decent job framing it out...left me a clean slate to work on."

"At least they were good for something." I scoff. "You still think we'll make the deadline?"

Campbell nods. "It would be better if I didn't have to stop working. It'll be tight, but yeah."

"What about your place?" I ask. "Have you gotten any work done over there?"

"A little. Mostly demo. I'll need to pull some permits, and that'll take some time."

"Have you guys moved in yet?" I'm not sure whether they are planning to fix the house up before giving up their rental.

"Nah, not yet," Campbell says.

I detect something telling in his economy of words and am torn on whether to ask him about it. I hope he's not having buyer's remorse. A lot of clients do, especially when the purchase is as big a project as the house on Liberty is. And I'm taking him away from working on it with the pool house. It's not clear whether he signed on because he needs the money or as a favor to me.

"It's going to be the best purchase you ever make," I say, and mean it. "There's a reason there were fifteen offers. You'll see."

"You don't have to sell me, Rach." He winks. "I'm going to make it shine."

"Is this keeping you from doing it?" I bob my head at the addition, guilt stabbing at me.

"Nope. I need to spend some time with it, let it speak to me."

I presume he's talking about the other house, his house. "Well, don't let it talk to you for too long. Jess is probably anxious to get in."

"Yep." He pulls the trigger on the drill he's holding in his hand, a subtle hint that he wants to get back to work. "Let me know when they show up."

"Will do." I make two guns with my fingers. "Good talk."

He shakes his head at me and goes back to work.

At one o'clock, a shuttle van pulls into the driveway and six people get out. Four women and two men. They look fairly prosaic for people who write about murder. I would say most of them are middle-aged. Two of the women, younger, maybe in their thirties. It's hard to say. They're dressed in comfortable clothes, nothing flashy or black (for some reason I expected a lot of black).

Brooke rushes out of the house and greets them. While she takes them on a tour of the house, I play bellhop. I load up the luggage in the never-used elevator and take everything up to the second and third floors, following Brooke's elaborate room chart.

I can hear them downstairs, cooing about how beautiful the house is, and my chest swells with pride. Maybe this won't be as awkward as I thought.

In the dining room, Brooke has put out a charcuterie board with salumi, cheeses, dips, fruit, veggies and crackers. On the sideboard, she's set up bottles of wine and stemware. The whole presentation looks like something you'd see at a posh resort in wine country. She wasn't kidding about owning a catering company.

I introduce myself to the group. Brooke, bless her heart, doesn't mention that I'm her stepdaughter. We're just two women running an inn, entertaining famous mystery authors, who love the house I grew up in. Maybe one of them will even write about it in one of their books. Isn't the scene of the crime always in a fabulous old ancestral home? Oh my God, Adam will die, except I haven't told anyone from my family yet. Still waiting on that. Lately, I'm as bad as Josh with all my secrets. Even Josie doesn't know about Beth Hardesty.

We leave our guests to enjoy their snacks and head out to the cottage. Campbell has already packed up and left. I have no idea if he's coming back tomorrow, but I can't see why. Pretty tough to build an addition without making noise.

"So how does this work?" I ask Brooke. "Are we supposed to be available to them all day?" Not that I have plans. The Zillow guy has dropped off the face of the earth, and seeing as he was my only client, I have lots of free time on my hands.

"As long as you're here to help me clean up after meals and make the beds and clean the bathrooms in the morning, you're good to go."

"What about you?" I don't want to stick her with all the work.

"Same. We're contracted for three meals a day and an evening snack. The rest of the time, they're on their own."

The rest of the time? It would take me all day just to make dinner. I've seen Brooke's meal plans. We're not talking hot dogs and canned beans. Tonight, for instance, she's making tutto mare. There's enough fresh seafood in the garage fridge to feed the entire Gold family, and that's saying a lot.

"Just out of curiosity, are you going to break even on all the food you bought?" It's probably a stupid question to ask a former caterer, but for days she's been shopping and prepping. I feel like I should be pitching in on the expenses.

"Ohhh yeah, and then some. Nothing I'm making is terribly expensive. It's all in the preparation and the details. The key here is to make them so happy they want to book again next year."

Seafood is far from cheap, but she lost me on "next year." The cottage and pool house I can see. They're just sitting there empty, after all. No reason they shouldn't be earning some extra coin. But the house? "You're planning to make this a full-time thing?"

"If I want to keep the house, I'll have to. And that's the goal...to keep the house."

"Do you want to do this? Or are you doing it because you feel a responsibility to Dad?" There is a distinction, and I don't know how I feel about her laboring to preserve the house for Hannah, Adam and me. She isn't our mother and doesn't owe us anything. I know my siblings would feel the same way.

She thinks about it for a beat. "A little of both, I suppose. It's too much house for just me, and I'm finding that I kind of enjoy this new venture."

"Just as long as you enjoy it." I love this house and hated to lose it when my father died. But it's hers now.

* * * *

After Brooke and I sling the evening's hash for the mystery writers and clean the kitchen, I take off to meet up with Josie.

There's a little café on Fillmore Street that has killer desserts and good coffee. I'm stuffed from Brooke's tutto mare, which was amazing. If food is truly the way to a man's heart, Brooke has that in her favor over my mom. But I'll take that sentiment to my grave.

Josie is waiting at a table when I get there. It's late for dinner, so the restaurant isn't too crowded. As usual, Josie is adorable in a maxi dress, a cute little sweater and a pair of chunky platform shoes (her knocking-around-after-hours look). It makes me wish I would've worn something better than jeans and a battered SDSU sweatshirt.

We do the four-kisses-on-the-cheek thing. We've been greeting each other this way ever since Jew camp. It started out as us making fun of two fellow campers, these pretentious snotty girls from Beverly Hills. Rumor had it that one of them was Steven Spielberg's niece and the other was the daughter of some French fashion designer. Anyway, every morning at breakfast they would make a big show of kissing each other's cheeks twice on each side. So, it became our inside joke to mimic them. As time went on, it just became habit.

"You look so good, Rach."

I do a double take. "Are you making fun of my outfit?" I tug my sweatshirt down and stare at the letters. "It's college chic."

"Not your clothes, which look like ass. You should let me shop for you. This." She circles the air around my makeupless face with her finger. "You look like your old self again."

I don't exactly feel like my old self again. But I'm sleeping and eating, which is probably making a difference. And today, I actually got some exercise taking all that luggage up two floors in the elevator. I laugh to myself.

I tell Josie about the mystery writers.

"Whoa, whoa, whoa, back up. You didn't tell me the child bride was taking in boarders. What the fuck?"

"They're not boarders. They're only staying for a week. Brooke has kind of sort of put the house on Vrbo. You'll die when I tell you how much these people are paying."

Josie leans closer to the table. "How much?"

"Twelve thousand bucks. But that includes meals and light housekeeping."

Her eyes grow wide. "You're kidding me. Then again, I'm not surprised. The house is on the national register of gorgeousness, so yeah."

"Get this, Brooke is doing all the cooking. She used to own a catering company with...wait for it...her ex-husband."

The server comes to take our order, and against my better judgment I get the lemon soufflé. Hey, I earned it today. Josie gets the flourless chocolate cake, my second-favorite dessert on the menu. We both get lattes, which I know is déclassé after eleven a.m., but we're not in Italy. So suck it!

"Okay, go back to the ex-husband," Josie says once the server leaves. "What do we know about him?"

"Nothing. I didn't even know he existed until a week ago."

"Do you think your dad knew?"

"Probably." A month ago, I would've said with absolute confidence, "Of course he did. Who doesn't know about their spouse's exes?" Now, all I have are two words: Beth. Hardesty.

I give Josie the rest of the skinny on Brooke and her Vrbo side hustle, the grief group sessions and how my stepmother is practically broke. I make her swear on her dog's life that she won't tell Hannah—or any of the other Golds.

"The grief meetings are good for you, Rach. You should keep going."

I don't argue with her, but attending the meetings with Brooke feels surreal—and to be honest, a little creepy. Hearing about her and my dad's wedding anniversary was uncomfortable to say the least. Next, she'll describe their sex life. All right, I sound incredibly childish, but it's strange to hear her talk about her and my dad as a couple when I've spent their entire marriage waiting for him to go back to my mother.

Our desserts and coffees come, and I'm thankful for the reprieve. I don't want to talk about death and grieving tonight. I just want a good old gossip session.

Josie dips her fork into the chocolate cake and takes a dainty bite. "You got Campbell to work on the pool house?"

Now she's onto another topic I don't want to talk about. "It was Brooke's idea. Extra money for his new house and all that."

Josie holds my gaze across the table, then slowly nods. "Right."

I flip her the bird and do the opposite of dainty as I inhale soufflé. "Let me ask you something," I say with my mouth full. Between this and Brooke's pasta, I'm riding a carb high that's better than sex. "Has Hannah said anything to you about Stephen?"

"Like what?" Josie pushes her plate at me in a time-honored tradition. We go halfsies on all our desserts.

I slide my soufflé her way, finding it difficult to part with it. "Like maybe he's having an affair." Or multiple affairs.

"No, she hasn't told me anything." Something flickers across her face, but it's gone before I can read it. And to cover it up—because I know she's covering up something—she quickly says, "Wait a minute, who would have an affair with Stephen?"

We both laugh.

Stephen is actually a nice-looking guy. Tall, toned (he works out with a personal trainer every day), dark hair with a few strategic streaks of gray and brown eyes that kind of remind me of a puppy dog turned shark. It's his personality that could use work.

I tell her about Adam's sightings at the Fairmont and Harry Asia's and how he was eating out of Legally Blonde's bowl at Frank Dina's.

"Wow," she says, but her surprise seems feigned. "What are you planning to do with that information?"

If only I knew. "Adam and I keep going around and around on it. Brooke in so many words said we shouldn't tell Hannah."

"You told Brooke?" Josie's eyes go wide.

"I guess it just kind of slipped out. Anyway, what do you think we should do?"

"I'm not sure."

I get the feeling that Josie has a Stephen story of her own but is keeping it to herself. Perhaps it's out of loyalty to Hannah. My sister is her client, after all.

I put my fork down and blow out a breath. "Maybe you can tell her. She likes you better than us."

"No, she doesn't. She loves you and she loves Adam, and on some level, she has to know that her dickhead husband is cheating."

"On that note, there's more." In that split second, I decide to tell her, even if it does sully her memory of Josh, who she adored. I go through my texts and show her the picture of Beth, which I've now sent to my phone because I'm a glutton for punishment.

And after all that, Josie's response is, "So what? So he had a girlfriend? You had boyfriends. My God, you had Campbell."

"Hello, he lived with this woman? He was obviously brokenhearted when she dumped him for the dude she was probably doing while she was still with Josh. He begged her to come back to him. Are you paying attention? For all intents and purposes, they were married. The fact that he saved all those text messages for all these years—you know how he is about cleaning out unnecessary stuff—and never once mentioned her to me proves her importance to him. For all I know, he was still in love with her right up until the day he died."

"Okay, you have a point. But he loved you, Rach. Please, don't let this ruin what you had. We all have someone in our past"—she pins me with a look—"that we don't talk about. Don't make this more than that."

"That's the thing, Jo, Josh knew everything about Campbell and me. I could tell him because I had moved on."

She doesn't say anything, just looks at me, silently calling me out.

Chapter 24
The Stephen Affair

The mystery writers are leaving today, and I'm actually sad to see them go. Not that I won't be happy to get my bedroom back, but the group was fun.

It's not every day that you walk past the dining room and hear someone say, "Just kill him. He's gratuitous anyway." I'm still laughing over that one.

And they were incredibly complimentary about the house and how comfortable they were staying here. I can't say I loved cleaning up after them—they weren't the neatest people—but they made up for it by being so genuinely appreciative. I'll also miss Brooke's meals. I can't remember ever eating this well.

Now that the coast will be clear of houseguests, Campbell is returning to finish the job on the pool house. Brooke has already booked the guest cottage for the next week to a couple relocating to the Bay Area who need a place to stay while they house hunt. That's where I hopefully come in. By now, I'm sure Chip is wondering if I've been abducted by aliens.

While Brooke's in the kitchen making the group's farewell breakfast, I load the luggage onto the elevator and take it down to the mudroom. The airport van will be here in an hour or so to shuttle the writers to SFO.

"You need any help in here?" The kitchen smells like baked apples and fresh bread.

"You can start on the dishes."

I roll up my sleeves and get to work rinsing and carefully stacking everything in the dishwasher. As much as I hate to admit it, Brooke and I make a good team. All week we've been a synchronized machine.

"What are you making?" I'm still full from last night's dinner, baked salmon, couscous and roasted baby carrots that melted in my mouth. Whatever is going on in the oven, though, is making me salivate.

"German apple pancakes. I made the batter last night."

I finish the dishes and look around for something else to do. Brooke's already set the table. She doesn't have my mother's artistic flair, but her spare workmanlike style comes off as elegant rather than plain. "Want me to get going on the coffee?"

"That would be great." She slides the bacon into a skillet, and I hear it sizzle on the range, filling the kitchen with even more delicious smells. "I got a call from a guy who wants to rent the house for a bachelor party in July. Friday through Sunday. But I'm on the fence about it. He sounded young and...a bachelor party could get rowdy."

Uh, you think?

"I'm worried about the house getting trashed."

"What did you tell him?"

"That I was away from my desk and had to check the schedule." She laughs. "I just hate to turn away good money. What do you think?"

"What's good money?"

"Four thousand."

For two nights, hell yeah it was good money. But a bachelor party does sound risky. I know guys who I went to college with who had some raunchy ones. According to legend, Kit Markides had hookers at his and an orgy in the swimming pool. Though the nearest neighbors are a good football field away, it seems wrong, like we're turning the block into a frat house.

"I vote that it's a hard pass."

"Agree. I just needed to hear it from someone else." Brooke lays the bacon on a thick cloud of paper towels to drain.

The writers are getting restless in the dining room. I can hear them shuffling around and check on the coffee. Almost done.

Brooke takes the German pancakes out of the oven and places them on a heat-proof tray. "It's showtime."

* * * *

Josie and I are in her bedroom, which is also her living room, dining room and office. She lives in a large studio over a tortilla factory in the Mission District. You can't come here and not get hungry. The aroma of baked corn wafts up through the floorboards and fills the air.

She's just a hop, skip and jump away from Valencia Street, where all the trendy restaurants, shops and galleries are. It used to be a working-class neighborhood but has become popular with hipsters and tech brats, thus pushing out everyone who makes an hourly wage. It sucks, but at least she got in before rents hit a tipping point.

The apartment is quintessentially Josie. Everything is pale pink and white with occasional splashes of black. Her furniture is ultra-glam with lots of high-pile fabrics, geometrical designs, and metallics. Every time I'm here, I think of cotton candy.

"Try this on." Josie throws a halter mini dress on the bed next to a sleeping Poochini, her dog. The shih tzu looks like a small pile of rags.

The alleged purpose for my visit is to help her clean out her closet. But we both know the real reason is she desperately wants to dress me.

I peel off my jeans and sweater and slip into the dress. In front of the full-length mirror, I turn front and sideways, admiring my legs, which haven't seen the light of day in a long time. "Where would I ever wear this?"

"I don't know," Josie says and pulls the dress tighter in the back so that it clings to my breasts and waist. "It's a great date dress."

I turn and glare at her. "Not happening."

"So this is it, you're going to grow old alone?"

I'm thirty-four, soon to be thirty-five. Not exactly senior-citizen territory. "It's only been eight months, Jo. I'm not ready." Nor may I ever be.

Josie lets out a long sigh. "Take it anyway. It's fantastic on you, and I'd like to see you in something other than jeans and a frumpy top."

"This isn't frumpy." I tug on my sweater, which I bought for a trip to Seattle with Josh two years ago. "In fact, you helped me pick it out."

She eyes the sweater. "I did? God help me."

Her phone rings. She checks her screen and declines the call.

"Who was that?"

"No one important." She waves her hand in the air dismissively, which makes me think it was absolutely someone important, but she's protecting the sanctity of our time together.

"Was it that guy you're dating?"

"God no." She pulls a face. "That's over with a capital *O*. I'm still looking for my Josh."

I don't have the heart to tell her there's only one. And he was mine. Maybe. I force myself to banish any thoughts of Beth. From here on in, I decide to give her no meaning, none whatsoever.

"Why don't you just date Adam already?" He's had the hots for Josie since we were kids.

"Because he's like a brother."

We've had this conversation so many times that there's no use belaboring it.

She tosses me another dress to try on. This one is a summery number with pink and white polka dots. Definitely Josie's style but not mine.

"Pass," I say. "What else have you got?"

Josie sorts through the pile, handing me a gorgeous faux-leather bomber jacket, which I don't even have to try on to know it's a keeper. There's a peasant skirt, which conjures prairie life circa 1870. That's an obvious no.

I pick a white wrap blouse that still has its tags from the mound. "This is cute. How come you're getting rid of it?"

"I have too many white blouses. It was a freebie from one of the designers I rep. It's all yours."

I hold it against me and check it out in the mirror. "With a black pencil skirt, don't you think?"

"Absolutely. It'll look great on you."

I add it to my takeaway pile. This is better than Nordstrom and a hell of a lot cheaper.

While Josie ducks into the bathroom, I leaf through her closet. Her rods are so heavy with clothes, they're warping. Her phone rings again, and I glance down at the nightstand to see Hannah and Stephen's number flash on the display. They're the only people I know besides my mother who still have a landline.

"Hannah just called," I tell Josie as she comes out of the bathroom. My sister is probably having a fashion emergency. Or wants to go to the movies again without me.

Josie can tell I'm bothered. "I'll call her later," she says. "Are the mystery writers gone?"

"Yep, they left this morning. It's so quiet now." Except for Campbell and his power tools. "Brooke goes back to work tomorrow." I let out a sigh. "And I guess I'll have to try to sell real estate again." It was great having an excuse not to make cold calls and all the other things I hate doing to scrounge up business.

"I still can't believe she's renting the house out."

"She got a call for a bachelor party but nixed the idea. Not the clientele we're going for."

"*We're?*" Josie cocks her head to one side.

"Yeah. It was fun. The group was as kind as it was appreciative of everything we did. And they had such great stories about their careers. Do you know some of them write more than two thousand words a day?

Crazy, right? We have a couple staying in the guest cottage next week. In April, the pool house is pretty much fully booked. And I think for the right money and the right people, Brooke would definitely consider booking the big house."

"What about a wedding? It just occurred to me that one of my clients is looking for a venue for her wedding. It's her second marriage, and she's planning something low-key, like just fifty or so guests. I told her about the Log Cabin where your mom had her birthday party, but it's booked for the next year. Your parents' place...I'm never going to get used to calling it Brooke's...would be perfect. If she's really serious about pimping the house out, I could see if my client is interested. But if you'd rather me not, then my lips are sealed." Josie pretends to zip her mouth.

"Let me talk to Brooke first. But I bet she'd be into it. She might even be willing to cater it if your client doesn't already have someone."

"I'll ask her as soon as you give me the word."

On my way home, I think about my own wedding and how beautiful it was. How Josh had helped me plan it down to the linens and the silverware. He was a hands-on guy when it came to that kind of stuff. He wanted to be involved every step of the way. He wanted our big day to reflect all the pieces of us.

It's a good memory, one I'll cherish forever. Still, the dreaded Beth Hardesty is never far from my mind.

That's why despite myself I make a pit stop in Laurel Heights and am lucky enough to find a parking spot across the street from Les Puces. I don't know what I hope to accomplish by sitting here, but it doesn't stop me from spying on the shop like I'm on surveillance duty. All I need is a white van and some bad coffee.

It's getting late, but I suspect the store stays open at least until eight or nine to catch the dinner crowd. California Street has quite a few good restaurants. I wonder if Beth is inside or if she's at the St. Helena store, or at her new home amid the vineyards, sipping a glass of cabernet on the veranda while her two little kids play in the front yard.

I wonder if she knows Josh is dead.

And then I'm suddenly sobbing. Bawling so hard that I'm making awful choking noises and there's snot dripping down my nose. My whole body is shaking, and I'm unable to stop or even control myself. I'm literally hysterical, hiccupping on sobs, making animalistic sounds that are ugly to even my ears.

I want this all to be a bad dream. I want Josh to be alive and life to be the way it used to be. Before the accident, before I found Josh's text messages, before Beth Hardesty. I miss him so much that I wish it was me in the driver's seat instead of him. Why? Why was he taken from me? What did he ever do to deserve dying at thirty-five? It's so fucking unfair.

There's a tapping on my window, and I jump at the sound of my name being called. Then I look, and it's Campbell standing there. I try to wipe my eyes with the back of my hand, try to erase the tracks of my tears before rolling down the window.

"Hi," I manage in a croaking voice.

"Rach?" He tilts his head to the side. "What's going on?"

"Nothing. Just sitting here having a good cry."

"Unlock the door, okay?" He comes around to the passenger side and slides in next to me. For a long time, he doesn't say anything, then takes my hand. "Something happen today?"

"Nothing in particular." I sniffle. "Just the usual. What are you doing here...on California Street?"

He points to the bakery on the corner. "I'm meeting Jess to taste wedding cakes. And you?"

Just stalking my late husband's ex-lover. Nothing to see here. "Uh...I was picking up a gift for a friend."

"Hang on a sec." He gets out of the car, and I watch him in the rearview mirror go to his truck, which is parked a few spaces down from me. He returns a couple of minutes later and hands me a stack of napkins. "Best I've got."

"Thank you." I wipe my nose and face, vowing to keep a box of tissues in my car from now on. "I'll be okay."

"Did you get your gift?" His voice is so gentle that it makes me tear up all over again.

"Yep," I lie. "It's in the trunk."

"What do you say I drive you home? Jess can pick me up at your place."

"Thank you. But I'm fine."

"I hate to break it to you, Rach, but you don't look fine."

I start to cry again, unable to help myself. "I guess...I'm having...a bad day."

"You're entitled." He reaches behind me and gently squeezes my neck. "Let me take you home."

"Okay," I say as I choke on another sob.

"Jess is in the bakery. Give me a couple of minutes to let her know."

While he's gone, I crawl over the console into the passenger seat. Even though it's only a five-minute drive home, Campbell's right, I probably shouldn't be driving in this state...or any state. Even on a good day, I'm a menace on the road.

He's back in a flash and takes the wheel, nosing onto the street, which is full of traffic now.

"Is Jessica upset?" I should feel awful about pulling him away.

"Nah, she'll wind up picking it anyway. It's cake. They're all good, right?"

"Yeah." I wipe my nose. "You can't go wrong with cake."

He slides me a sideways glance and grins. "Remember Adam's birthday cake?"

I laugh, but I'm still crying, so it comes out like a baby being strangled to death. "I'd almost forgotten about that." My mother had brought home a St. Honoré cake for Adam's seventeenth birthday celebration. It was his favorite. But it's not the kind of cake you write Happy Birthday on. When I found it in the fridge, I assumed it was up for grabs. By the time my mother set it on the table with seventeen lit birthday candles, half of the cake was gone. Campbell and I had eaten it. "Man, was my mom pissed."

"Your mom? Adam cried."

I laugh again, this time snorting mucus up my nose. "He did, didn't he? It may be the reason why he turned out the way he did. We scarred him for life."

"Poor Adam. Always getting the short end of the cake."

It feels easy between us the way it used to, and I'm disappointed when we pull up the driveway so soon.

Campbell lightly touches my leg. "You want me to put your car in the garage or park here."

"Here," I say. "Thank you for taking me home, Campbell."

"Hey, that's what friends are for."

Maybe it's my imagination, but I hear a bit of wistfulness in his voice. For a long time, we just sit in the car, silent. Neither of us need to speak. We both know what the other is thinking, what neither of us need to say. Because the bond we shared is always there between us, even if we don't want to admit it to each other—or even to ourselves.

"I forgot something in the pool house. May as well get it while I'm here, before Jess comes, which I'm sure is any minute." Suddenly he's rushing to get out of the car, like he's afraid we'll get caught in a compromising position when all we were doing was talking.

It's my cue to go inside. I get out of the car, but before I turn to leave, I say, "I hope she's not mad."

"Of course not."

The house is empty when I get inside. Brooke is at work, and I should be delighted to have the place to myself. But I'm not. I go upstairs, wash my face and consider taking a hot bath, then abandon the idea. I go down to the kitchen and poke my head in the fridge, but I'm not hungry. I could call my mom, but she would know instantly that something is wrong. And I don't want to taint her memory of Josh. Not now. Not ever.

I could always call Hannah. But for obvious reasons, I've been maintaining my distance. I'm still deliberating on what and when to tell her. Besides, Adam and I need to do it together, and he's out of town at a gaming conference.

I settle for TV, but there's nothing on I want to watch.

Outside, I hear a car pull up. It's Jess's little BMW. I stand by the window and watch as Campbell folds himself into the passenger seat. They sit in the driveway for a while, and I can see Jess's arms flailing in the air. I don't have to hear them to know she's yelling. A few minutes later, Campbell gets out of the car and slams the door. Jess takes off down the driveway. Even from here I can hear her tires squealing on the pavement.

For a long time, Campbell stands in the driveway, staring off into the distance. I start to go to him but stop myself. Then I watch him walk down the driveway to Vallejo Street.

Chapter 25
We're a We Now

Today, I'm showing homes to Richard and Charles, the couple staying in the guest cottage. They're retired and are moving here from Ashland, Oregon, tired of the rain and willing to trade it for the fog. They're lovely.

Twice, we've shared coffee out in the garden, and they've told me all about their lives. Richard owned a dog grooming business, and Charles managed the neighboring hardware store. It was love at first sight, Richard says. But when Charles thinks Richard isn't looking, he shakes his head at me.

"No?" Richard huffs.

"You hated me at first."

They laugh, love shining in their eyes, and for a second, I bask in their coupledom, remembering what it used to feel like.

I've got three houses on our tour. They wanted the Castro, but their budget might get them a tree house there. And not much of a tree house at that. Instead, we're looking at the Outer Sunset and Richmond district and a small condo by the ballpark.

Charles has volunteered to do the driving because Josh's old car is too small for the three of us to fit comfortably. I've been meaning to replace the plug-in hybrid we lost in the crash but can't bring myself to do it.

The first on the list is a tiny pink stucco row house with the garage on the ground floor and the living quarters a flight up. Pastel row houses are the architectural vernacular of the Outer Sunset, which used to be a working-class neighborhood. But like everything else in the city, prices have gone sky high. It's close to the beach, which I thought Charles and Richard would like for their dog.

"This is cute." Charles beams up at the place.

Richard looks less enthusiastic. "I was hoping for something all one level."

Good luck with that in San Francisco. Maybe in the burbs.

I get the key from the lockbox, open the door to a small foyer and climb the stairs to the landing, which opens to a living room. The inside isn't half-bad. Plain with white walls, beige carpet and a big picture window that looks out onto the street below. With a little creativity, the house could be adorable. The kitchen is small but workable, and there's a sunny breakfast alcove with enough room for a café table and two chairs. If it were me, I'd expand the kitchen into the alcove and do an island with stools. Better resale value. The dining room is surprisingly large.

"Check this out." I pull down what looks to be a paneled wall, and a Murphy bed pops down.

"Would you look at that?" Charles says. "How did you even know it was there?"

"They're pretty common around here where space is at a premium. So I know 'em when I see 'em."

"It's definitely smaller than we wanted," Richard says and heads off to the bedrooms.

Charles and I follow. Both rooms are about the same size and share a bathroom, the only one in the house. Like the living room, the bedrooms are a dull combination of whites and beiges. The room I would use as the main bedroom has a window with a view of the backyard, a small patch of grass with just enough room for a patio table and a barbecue.

Richard has left no doubt that he is underwhelmed, so I suggest we move on to the next place.

This one is a ground-floor Victorian flat in the Richmond district, not far from Golden Gate Park. Unlike the first, which was empty, this one is cluttered with the current occupants' dark oversized furniture, making it difficult to visualize the space. I hope Charles and Richard have a good imagination. At least the location is primo. A quiet street, walking distance to shops and restaurants. The negative is there's no garage and the upstairs apartment gets the tiny sliver of driveway, which means Charles and Richard will have to park on the street.

The apartment has more square footage than the first house we saw but has had little in the way of updates. As is classic in homes of this era, the bathroom is in two separate rooms. The sink and tub in one and the toilet in another. Victorian-era residents were early adopters of indoor plumbing and were obsessed with hygiene. Basically, they didn't want to shit where they bathed. Ironically, they didn't take into consideration washing their hands.

Richard seems interested in this place, taking more time than he did in the first to explore each room. The floors are a gorgeous red oak, patinaed a rich golden color. The millwork needs a good coat of paint but is intact, which isn't always the case in these older homes. Often, new owners strip out every inch of charm.

The kitchen is a train wreck, with appliances that appear to date back to the 1980s. The countertops are white tile with stained grout lines, and the dark oak cabinets have seen better days. One of them is missing a door, and a couple of the drawer fronts don't hang right.

"This is a big job," Charles says, a slightly horrified look in his eyes.

"I don't mind a project," Richard replies as he turns in place, taking in the work that will need to be done.

"Babe, for the price of this place, we won't have anything left."

It's too early to tell them that the listing price is merely a suggestion. By the time offers roll in, the flat will go for well over asking.

The main bedroom is a nice size with French doors that open to a wooden deck that appears to be a recent addition. The second bedroom is also fairly spacious. There's a third room, but because it doesn't have a closet, it can't legally be called a bedroom.

"This would make a great hobby room," Charles says, and Richard agrees.

"It's definitely an improvement over the first one." Richard takes another look at the split bathroom. "What would you do about this?" he asks about the room with the toilet.

"You could take down the wall and make it one. But what a lot of people do is squeeze a toilet in the room with the sink and tub and add a tiny corner sink in here for a powder room. Then the unit becomes a bath and a half. If you can pull it off, it adds more value."

Richard looks dubious about fitting a toilet. "I suppose we could steal a little space from the hallway."

"That would be ideal. Should we move on to the condo?" I hate to rush them, but our appointment is at noon, and in traffic it could take thirty minutes. If there's a Giants game, it could take even longer.

"Do we have time for me to snap a few pictures?" Charles pulls out his phone.

"Absolutely."

He quickly walks through the apartment, taking pictures, then we race across town to a sleek six-story building that's just six years old. The South Beach–Mission Bay area is a hot spot for the young, single upwardly mobile crowd, but there's more available here in the way of condominiums and apartments that fit into Richard and Charles's budget. It's newer and shinier than the rest of the city, and the more I get to know Charles and Richard, the more I realize it's probably not their style. But I would be remiss in not showing them all their options.

The lunch crowd is swarming the restaurants, and the vibe is millennials on parade. One look at Charles and I can tell he's thinking the same thing.

"I know," I say. "But I wanted you to at least see what you can get here. It's by no means cheap. But there's a lot of new construction, which means move-in ready. To some people that's worth the price of admission."

"I don't even think this was here the last time we visited San Francisco," Richard says.

"It wasn't much before. But with Oracle Park coming in, it started the gentrification. Not far from here is the new Warriors arena, which is only bringing more shops, restaurants, and construction. It's a great investment."

Charles lets out a long sigh, and I laugh.

"If you want, we can skip the apartment, and I can try to find something closer to the Castro." Though I don't know what. That whole area is way out of their price range.

"No, we're here," Richard says. "We may as well look."

I haven't been in any of these newer apartments and am kind of anxious myself to see what they offer. Ten minutes later, we're taking an elevator up to the fifth floor. The building has lots of glass with views of the bay. Unfortunately, the apartment for sale faces the wrong side, and the only views are of other buildings. *At least it's bright,* I tell myself.

It's contemporary, with concrete floors, an electric fireplace, and big black steel-framed windows. It's so clean I can see my reflection in the quartz countertops.

It's also the size of a two-car garage. I don't know how you can fit regular-sized furniture in here. Judging by the current occupants' couch, they had it custom made. The listing in the MLS says everything is "smart," which I guess means you can turn on the oven from your lilliputian sofa by voice control without having to walk the two feet.

"I don't even think it'll fit Pup Tart's doggie bed," Richard says.

"It is gorgeous, though." Charles is examining the Viking appliances.

We follow the narrow corridor to the main bedroom, which will accommodate a queen-size bed but not much else. The walk-in closet is nice, and it's an en suite, which the others didn't have. There's also a second bathroom. It's small but a bonus.

"I don't even think you could fit a double bed in here," Charles says as we walk through the second bedroom. "It's more like an office or a nursery."

The more I see of it, the more I think Campbell and Jess got a steal on their place.

"You want to know the truth," I say. "This place is overpriced. But they'll probably get every dime and then some."

"Out of the bunch, the second one had the most potential for our needs," Richard says. "But I wasn't in love with it."

"I'll see what else I can find. But the pickings are slim." If they could bump up their budget by a hundred thousand, it would open the door to more listings. But they're on a fixed income, and I don't want them to be house poor.

"You showed us three wonderful homes," Charles says. "They may not be right for us, but they were lovely. You're a doll, Rachel."

What a sweet thing to say. If only all my clients were Charles and Richard.

Over the next three days, I show them a few more houses in their price range. With the exception of one, which will probably sell for well over the asking price, they were hovels. Small, dark and definitely not handsome.

"We've decided to rent," Richard says while we're enjoying our coffee-drinking tradition in the garden. It's only been a week, but I've become attached to these two charming men. "We desperately hope you're not disappointed and feel like you've wasted your time with us."

"Of course not," I assure them, though I'd be lying if I said I wasn't a little disappointed. It's already the beginning of April, and I've only had one sale this year. "I want you guys to be happy." Which is the absolute truth.

"Maybe when the market cools down, we'll start our search anew." Charles rubs my shoulder reassuringly.

This is where, if I was a decent agent, I would tell them the market is never going to cool down. It hasn't in all the years I've been selling real estate. It just keeps getting more absurdly expensive. This is where, if I was a decent agent, I would push the Victorian flat in the Richmond because it is the best thing we saw, and with a new kitchen and a little fluffing, it could be a great little place. And at least they would be building equity instead of throwing their money at rent, which by the way isn't cheap here either.

But I don't say any of those things, even if every bit of it is the God's honest truth, because I find it uncomfortable. Pushy. And that's why I'll never be Niki Sorento, who would've said all those things—and closed the damn deal.

So like the wuss that I am, I say, "Let me make a few calls and see if anyone knows of a rental in the Castro."

* * * *

Yesterday, I cried as I waved goodbye to Charles and Richard. They flew back to Ashland to pack up their stuff and retrieve Pup Tart before moving everything to their new apartment. I'm going to miss our coffee dates in the backyard. But they'll be back next month for good and have promised me breakfast in their new place.

Chip came through on helping me find them an apartment in a cozy duplex up in the hills within walking distance to Castro Street if they don't mind the climb on the way home. It was love at first sight, and they quickly made friends with the neighbor, who also has a dog.

This morning, Brooke and I cleaned out the cottage for the next guests, a mother-daughter pair from Arizona, taking a girls' weekend to see the sights.

"At some point, we'll have to hire housekeepers for this," Brooke says as we're pressing sheets in the laundry room. I don't miss the "we" in her statement, so it's not just me. Clearly, we're a quasi-team now, which reminds me of Josie's client.

"I may have a bride who wants to book the house for a small wedding. What do you think?"

Brooke stops what she's doing and turns to me. "Is the bride a friend of yours or someone you know?"

"She's a client of Josie's and is having trouble finding a venue that she likes. She'd like to see the property if you're into it. I mean, no pressure. I just thought if you were considering a bachelor party, this might be a better bet. And possibly more money. But a wedding might be more—"

"Hell yeah," Brooke cuts me off. "Have her come see the place."

I nod, worried that I may be getting her hopes up over nothing. This is a home, not a wedding venue, and there's no guarantee that Josie's client won't decide to go with something with all the proper amenities. You know, the little things, like a staff and a commercial kitchen.

"We should probably work out pricing and what exactly we'll provide," I say because those are the first things a bride-to-be asks about.

"Agree," Brooke says. "Can you do that? I've got shifts all this week at the hospital."

"Umm, okay, I guess. But I have no idea what I'm doing. At least you used to be a caterer."

"You're a smart girl. Figure it out. I've got to run. Can you make the beds in the cottage? These are ready to go." She pushes the freshly pressed sheets into my hands.

Making a bed? That I can do. "Sure."

As she starts to walk out, I call, "Would you be willing to do the food?"

She's momentarily flummoxed, then says, "For the wedding? For the right price, you bet ya."

I guess I'm a wedding planner now.

After Brooke leaves, I make the beds in the cottage. I can't compete with Brooke's hospital corners, but everything looks crisp and fresh. It wouldn't hurt to bring in a few floral arrangements for an added touch, which could help get us good reviews on Vrbo and Airbnb. I'll talk to Brooke about it.

On my way back, I make a detour to the pool house. While Charles and Richard were here, Campbell stuck to the quiet stuff. Drywall, mudding, taping, and painting. Today, he's finishing the floors. I find him in front of a chop saw.

He stops what he's doing, flips up his goggles, and smiles at me. "What can I do you for, lassie?" He affects his father's thick Scottish accent, and it sounds like he's saying something in Gaelic when it's just plain old English. It's what he used to do when we were teenagers, when we were in love.

"Nothing," I say. "Just checking in." We never discussed what happened between him and Jess that day he took me home. By now, I'm sure they've patched things up. I sit down on the old floor, pull my knees up and tuck them under my chin. "Can I pick your brain for a second?" I want to know what the going rate for a wedding is these days.

"Yep." He takes the spot next to me, and his familiar scent—a combination of wood, laundry detergent and something distinctly Campbell—takes me back.

And while I momentarily bask in the resonance of it, I notice how tired Campbell looks. His green eyes aren't twinkling the way they usually do. And there are brackets around his mouth that I don't recall from a week ago. He seems thinner too.

That's what you get from burning the candle at both ends. "Are you killing yourself to get the new house done before you and Jess get married?" I feel like an inconsiderate jerk. What kind of friend asks a man to remodel her pool house right before his wedding?

He's quiet for a long time. And for a minute I think he didn't hear the question. Then he says, "Jess and I broke up."

I'm too stunned to say anything. And even if I wasn't stunned, I wouldn't know what to say anyway. *Why? I'm sorry. Are you sure?* I mean, it could just be pre-wedding jitters, right? But somehow I know it's for real. He and Jessica aren't getting married. And even more than that, my intuition tells me it was Campbell who called it off and not Jess.

I'm feeling all kinds of things about this news that I don't want to explore too closely. And when I finally find my tongue, I say the one thing you probably should never say in circumstances like this. "It'll be okay."

He nods his Campbell nod, a sort of *yeah, maybe*. Then he blows out a breath. "Bailing two months before your wedding is a shitty thing to do. Bailing on your wedding period is a shitty thing to do," he amends.

I want to ask him why he bailed, but that's the answer I'm most afraid of. I ask anyway because despite myself I want to be a friend to him in the same way he's been a friend to me since Josh died.

"What happened, Campbell?"

He doesn't answer, just looks at me like *you know what happened*. And nearly two decades of history pass between us as if it were yesterday.

"How's Jessica taking it?" Stupid question but worse if I didn't ask at all.

"Better than I would've predicted, which shows that it was probably for the best."

"The breakup?"

He nods again. "It was inevitable. But it would've been worse if we were married."

"Why inevitable?"

He gives me the look again, and I play dumb.

"What about the house?" All things considered, the house is a minor sticking point. Sort of a deck chair on the Titanic in the scheme of things. But it's a safe topic. Safer than "You know what happened."

"My down payment, my house. She never wanted anything to do with it."

That was abundantly clear and why I was surprised that Campbell bought it anyway. My suspicion is he knew it was the beginning of the end. Or the house was his torpedo. I refrain from raising my theory, though.

"I'm sorry," I say, and before I can stop myself, I slip my hand into his. His palm and fingers are callused and work worn, at once strong and unbelievably gentle. Even when I was a young girl, Campbell's hands had the power to make me feel safe.

"Thanks," he says without letting go. "This'll make me sound like a jackoff, but I'm glad it's over with. Jess deserves better. She deserves the goddamn world."

I want to say that Campbell *is* the "goddamn world," but things didn't end between him and Jess because he has an inferiority complex. That much I know.

We grow quiet, knowing better than to say more. For seventeen years, we've managed to navigate the slippery slope of conversation without ever discussing anything that would take us back to that painful place and require self-reflection.

"How 'bout you? You feeling better than whatever was going on that day I found you in your car?"

"I am." Which isn't exactly the truth. Then I blurt out of nowhere, "What happened to us?"

It's a wholly inappropriate time to revisit our own breakup. This should be about him and Jessica. But he started it with his inuendo. And I'm sick of secrets, secrets about Beth Hardesty, secrets about Stephen's affairs, secrets about a miscarriage that changed the trajectory of my life when I was seventeen.

He looks at me, pretending that he doesn't understand the question. All it takes is a glare from me for him to drop all pretense, and a flicker of resignation crosses his face.

We're doing this. Seventeen years and we're finally going to talk about it.

"I was barely eighteen, Rach." He scrubs his hand through his hair. "I was a stupid, scared kid."

"But we used to be so close, so in tune with each other. Why didn't we grieve together? Why did we drift apart?"

There's a long pause as Campbell chooses his words. I know him well enough to know he'll tell me the truth, but he'll do it with utter and complete kindness. It's one of the things I've always loved about him, his thoughtfulness, his desire to never hurt anyone he cares about.

"Because I couldn't fix it," he finally says. "I didn't have the tools at that age to know what to say or what to do to make it better."

"I didn't expect you to fix it. A miscarriage isn't anything anyone can fix, Campbell. What I don't understand is why you stopped loving me. It's like you went from being the most important person in my life to a complete stranger overnight. Do you know what that was like? In one fell swoop I lost our baby and you. I need you to help me understand why."

Campbell lets out a long sigh and squeezes the bridge of his nose. "Because secretly I was relieved." He fixes me with a look, waiting for me to respond, and when I don't, he continues, "I was fucking relieved, Rachel. The idea of giving up school, my youth, to bring a baby into this world...Jesus, I could barely take care of myself. I lived in fear of seeing the disappointment in my father's face, my father, who'd worked his whole life so that I could make something of myself. The disappointment of your parents, who trusted me...the disappointment of Adam. But none of that came close to how I felt about disappointing you...So, when you came to tell me that you'd lost our baby, it was like a giant weight had been lifted. It was as if fate had given me a second chance, fate had given me my freedom. How was I supposed to tell you that? How could I be a man for you when I couldn't be a man for myself? The guilt burned me up inside."

I reach out and take his hand. "I was relieved too. Relieved but at the same time wrecked, a lethal combination. It just would've been good if we could have shared those feelings. If we could've leaned on each other instead of walking away."

The silence stretches between us. Then he says, "You think if we had, we'd be together now?" There's something in the lilt of his question that sounds sad and hopeful at the same time.

To answer yes would mean forsaking Josh and our precious time together, so I say nothing, not a word.

Chapter 26
The Kiss

A mere two weeks after I learn that Campbell has canceled his wedding, I am planning my own. Or more accurately Shireen Ali's. Josie's client. She loves the house, the property, the pool, the views, so much that it only took her five minutes to say, "Where do I sign?"

Now, Brooke and I are in the wedding business.

The learning curve is steep. I've spent days calling around, finding out the average price for wedding venues and what we should include. It runs the gamut, let me tell you. Everything from just the room to the whole enchilada. Shireen wants us to take care of everything. The tables and chairs, the china, the food, and the lodging, leaving the music, flowers and photographer in her hands.

We have a little over two months to pull this thing together. It turns out Shireen is ten weeks pregnant and would like to walk down the aisle without waddling. Her words, not mine.

In the meantime, both the cottage and the pool house are booked through June. Brooke's traveling nurse arrived two days ago to break in the new renovations.

I haven't seen Campbell since he finished the work. Twenty times, I've picked up the phone to call him and stopped before punching in his number.

Just when I consider calling him—really calling him—my phone rings. It's Mom.

"Whassup?" I can't help myself.

"You need to come over here right now and talk some sense into your sister."

"What's going on, Mom?"

"She's left Stephen."

These are the last words I think I'll hear, which is silly because it's wholly predictable. Even inevitable. "I'll be there in ten," I say.

I race across town, my fear of driving temporarily suspended, and command Siri to call Adam as I weave in and out of traffic.

"I'm on my way," he says instead of hello.

"Mom called you too?"

"Not too. First. I'm her favorite."

So true. When we were kids, we used to ask her which one of us she loved best. Her answer was to hold up her hand and say, "That's like asking which finger is my favorite."

Hannah, a born litigator, would reply, "The middle one of course, just like Adam is your middle child."

"You think Hannah knows?" I ask.

"I'd say it's a pretty good possibility. If she was going to leave him for being an asshole, that would've happened years ago."

"Good point. What's your ETA?" I don't want to go in the house without backup.

"I'm about five minutes out. See you there."

My mother's townhouse is nothing like the Queen Anne on Vallejo. When she was forced to start over, she didn't want anything to be the same. Now it's clean, simple lines and large open spaces without the warrens of nooks and crannies. Everything smells like fresh paint and newness. Perhaps a metaphor for her life.

Hannah is sitting at my mother's large kitchen island, eating pistachios. She must've been at it for a while because there's a large mound of empty shells in front of her. Adam is already here and hasn't wasted any time scrounging through my mother's refrigerator. He is so far submerged inside her Sub-Zero that all I see is his ass and a pair of denim-clad legs. Shana is stirring a pot of chicken noodle soup (Progresso, not her own), which I see for the cliché that it is.

No one is talking, which is an anomaly for the Golds.

I go straight to my sister and give her a hug. She sits there stiffly but doesn't back away. I know she's humoring me. But maybe, just maybe, she needs a hug from her baby sister.

"What happened?" I ask, breaking the weird silence.

She gives a half-hearted shrug. But if you know Hannah the way I do, you can see that below the surface she's losing it.

"I don't love him anymore. Maybe I never did," she announces. Her blue eyes meet mine, and there's a hidden warning there. Okay, not so hidden. She knows about Stephen. She knows I know about Stephen. She maybe even knows Adam knows about Stephen. But she doesn't want my mother to know.

I never gave much thought to whether Stephen was Hannah's One, like Dad was Mom's or Mom was Dad's, or Josh was mine. Perhaps because deep down inside I knew Stephen wasn't. On paper they look good together—two attractive upwardly mobile lawyers—but there was never that "I can see his heart in her eyes." Or vice versa. Not like I saw it with my parents. Or with me. I stand certain that Stephen is not Hannah's plus-one in the afterlife. Her story isn't finished yet. There's more to come.

"What happens now?" I ask.

"She thinks long and hard about what she's about to lose," my mother says. "Do you think it's been easy for me to give up the lifestyle I once had with your father?"

Hannah, Adam and I look at each other, then gaze around Shana's three-thousand-square-foot townhouse with a view of the Golden Gate Bridge and laugh. The three of us, laughing until we can't breathe.

* * * *

On my way home, I swing by Campbell's new Craftsman and find him in the backyard, building a piece of furniture. A chair maybe, though at this point in the process it's hard to tell. The wood is white oak, and judging by the straight horizontal spindles he's cut, he's going for a Mission style that would complement the house.

"Hey," he says but doesn't look up from what he's doing.

"I came by to see your progress."

"Take a look." He nudges his head at the back door, which has been cleared of weeds and appears usable now.

I wait for him, and when I realize he's not going to follow, I let myself in. I wander through the laundry room to the kitchen. Nothing much has changed here other than there's now a stack of boxes against one wall and a cheap plastic bistro table with a single lawn chair taking up a corner on the opposite side of the room.

It appears Campbell has begun scraping the cottage cheese (not asbestos, thank God) from the dining room ceiling. There are drop cloths on the floor and an assortment of buckets and ladders.

More boxes are in the living room, which hasn't been touched. Though the floor appears leveler, which might be a trick of the eye.

I take the back hallway to the bedrooms. I can't see the floor in the second bedroom. It's filled to the brim with clothes and moving boxes. The main bedroom has a box spring and mattress on the floor and little else.

Except for a new shower liner in the bathroom, it's still the worst room in the house. It seems crazy that Campbell is outside making furniture when the inside needs so much work. But I suppose there's a method to his madness.

A door creaks, and suddenly Campbell is standing behind me. The faint smell of sawdust, salt and sweat fill the air.

"Is it my imagination, or did you level the floor?"

"Not your imagination. It was a few days' worth of going under the house, jacking it up with a level and sistering the old joists with a bunch of two-by-twelves."

"It looks good." I move back into the living room and inspect the floor closer. No more sinkhole. "How's the cottage cheese going?"

Campbell follows me into the dining room. "It's going. I'm about half done."

It's a start, I think. "What are you making?" I glance outside at his makeshift workstation.

"A chair."

That's what I thought. Weird priorities, but whatever.

"How are you?" He still looks like he can use some sleep. Perhaps the chair is his way of working out his and Jess's breakup, the equivalent of me writing letters in a tree house.

"Other than feeling like an asshole, I'm holding up."

We both sit on the dining room floor with our backs against the wainscoting. I draw up my legs and rest my elbows on my knees, like the last time we were together. "Hannah is divorcing Stephen."

"Wow. Yet I can't say I didn't see it coming. Stephen's a dick. What happened?" Campbell scootches closer to me.

I have the sense he already knows and is stringing me along so as not to give away his source. "Did Adam already tell you?"

"Tell me what?" Campbell has no game, so I know he's telling the truth. No one has told him about Legally Blonde, Harry Asia's or the Fairmont.

"Nothing, never mind," I say. "Why do you think Stephen's a dick? I mean, besides the obvious."

"Isn't the obvious enough? He's so caught up in his own world, half the time he doesn't know Hannah's alive. I figured it was just a matter of time before she got sick of it."

"Or she got sick of him running around."

"Ah." Campbell leans the back of his head against the wall. "The plot thickens."

"The plot thickens."

"Stephen's got himself a side dish, huh?"

"It might be a side dish and couple of desserts. But yeah, it kind of looks that way."

"Tell Hannah I'm sorry."

"Hannah's not talking about it, so please keep it just between us."

"Our secret, then."

In that moment I consider telling him about Beth. About how betrayed I feel that Josh kept her a secret from me. About all the reasons he should've told me. About the lingering questions that still haunt me. Did Josh love her more than me? But I don't because to say it makes it all the more real, and it's not how I want to remember Josh and me. It's not how I want Campbell to remember Josh and me.

"I should go," I say but don't move to leave.

"Yeah, I should get back to building my chair." But like me, he doesn't stir either.

Instead, we sit on the floor, watching the shadows play across the wall, feeling the way it used to with us. I don't know if it's him or me, but one of us tucks our hand into the other's.

And that's when he leans over and kisses me. His mouth on me feels at once familiar but also electrifying, bringing back a rush of memories, some happy, some devastating, like the last time he kissed me in the tree house seventeen years ago. His hands cup the back of my head, and he takes the kiss deeper, filling me with a renewed yearning for him, for what we had, for what we gave up. As I lose myself in his arms, I think maybe the yearning is not new, maybe it never went away.

And then I see Josh's beautiful face and pull away.

Chapter 27
Elijah's Not Coming

Mom insists that this year we celebrate the first night of Passover. It's the one Jewish holiday we occasionally observe. Never for the full eight days because no one in the Gold family has the willpower to forgo bread, pizza or pastries for that long. But one night a year we can handle.

Besides, Hannah could use the family time. Stephen has moved out, and they're seeing a marriage counselor during their "trial"—Stephen's word, not Hannah's—separation. Although he's asked to join us for the seder, Hannah has said no. There's a reason my father used to call her "Hard-Hearted Hannah" after the Ella Fitzgerald song when we were kids, even before she got a Stanford law degree. I, for one, applaud her steadfastness.

Fuck Stephen and his multitude of blondes.

In any event, it'll just be the four of us tonight asking Moses to set our people free. And since tradition dictates that the youngest asks the four questions, that responsibility will fall on me.

Adam is at Mom's when I arrive, stretched out on her living room sofa, watching something on TV. Mom is in the kitchen, making up the seder plate.

"Mm, it smells good in here." I dip my finger in the horseradish (the bitter taste of slavery) and my mother slaps my hand away.

"Mom got one of those premade Passover meals at Whole Foods, so it should be good this year."

My mother shoots Adam a dirty look. "Just for that you can set the table. The *Haggadahs* are over there." She points to the side table, where a stack of the Passover booklets sit. They're the same ones we've been using since Adam's bar mitzvah.

"Where's Hannah?" I ask.

"She got caught in traffic." Mom checks the oven to see if the brisket is warm. "Campbell didn't want to come?"

Secretly, I didn't invite him. Ever since our kiss three weeks ago, I've been keeping my distance from him and avoiding his phone calls. Even though it was only an impulse kiss, like standing in line at the grocery store after a bad breakup and grabbing an armfull of chocolate before getting to the cash register, it was confusing. Better to give it time before it takes on more meaning than it should.

"Nah, he had something else going on tonight."

Adam slides me a glance. "He seems to be doing well with the breakup. I must be a relationship genius, because I predicted it wouldn't last past three years. Four years max."

"Why's that?" I ask despite myself.

Adam shrugs but looks at me like *You know why.*

"I thought she was a very nice girl," my mother says. "Not the sharpest tool in the shed but a figure to die for. And she's a real go-getter. Do you know she's had three promotions at Serena & Lily? You could learn from a girl like that, Rachel."

Hannah walks in just in the nick of time. "Sorry I'm late." She hands Mom two bottles of wine.

"Are they kosher?"

Hannah looks at Mom in puzzlement. "When have we ever been kosher? No, they're not kosher."

Hannah's in a black sleeveless shift dress and high heels, and her hair is done. She's also wearing makeup. The rest of us are in sweats. My mom's are really expensive sweats but sweats nonetheless.

"You look great, Hannah," I tell her.

"I don't know why everyone wears so much black these days. The world could use a little color."

Way to be negative, Mom. Hannah and I look at each other and roll our eyes.

"Can we open one of those bottles now?" Adam grabs the wine and starts searching through my mother's drawers for a corkscrew.

"I want to show you what I did in the powder room." Mommie Dearest takes the wine from Adam and herds us into the bathroom off the entryway, her latest project. The old toilet is gone, and in its place is a toilet that comes up to my belly button, I kid you not.

Adam stares at it for a few seconds. "All you need to do is build a counter in front of it and you can eat your breakfast in here."

"It's called a comfort toilet," my mother says. "Isn't it fabulous?"

"Other than it being much higher than your average toilet, I don't get the appeal." Adam again.

"When you're my age you'll understand," my mother says. "What do you think of the wallpaper?" It's a shiny blue that kind of looks like foil with big colorful butterflies.

It's not really my vibe, the translation being it's ugly as sin. But I gush, "It's amazing," in the hopes we can open that bottle of wine now.

"Something smells like it's burning," Hannah says. I catch a whiff of it too. Melting rubber.

"Oh my God, I forgot the carrots." My mother runs back to the kitchen, leaving the three of us alone with her giant toilet.

"Let's put it to the test, shall we?" Adam flips the lid up and sits on it, lacing his hands behind his head and stretching his legs out. "You know, I think she's onto something."

Hannah grabs his arm and pulls him up. "You're being obnoxious. Let's help Mom or there'll be nothing to eat."

Like good soldiers we follow Hannah into the kitchen.

"It was my good oven mitt." Mom holds up a charred silicon potholder. "I left it too close to the flame."

"At least it wasn't the carrots," Adam says.

Hannah takes charge, moving pans around in the oven, pulling out the dishes that are ready, and transferring them to the serving platters my mother has laid out on the counter. It at once feels familiar and foreign. It's our first big holiday without Josh. Without Stephen. And I miss Dad so much it makes my heart fold in half.

Hannah, who is about as good a cook as my mother but organized as hell, gets everything on the table while Mom hustles around the kitchen like a chicken with her head cut off. We sit down, open our Haggadahs, and start the seder.

"What makes this night different from all other nights?"

Mom, Hannah and Adam take turns answering the four questions. We sing a couple of songs in bad Hebrew and call it. We've managed to conduct the entire seder in less than fifteen minutes, which is a record breaker even for the Golds.

Adam is eyeing the goblet we've filled for Elijah, the prophet who is supposed to show up to herald in the dawn of the messiah.

"Don't you dare," my mother says.

"Why? It'll just go to waste. Elijah's not coming. He's got a previous engagement."

Hannah grabs another bottle of wine off the counter, opens it, and fills Adam's glass.

Adam was right, the food is delicious. I go in for seconds of the brisket and add a heaping spoonful of mashed potatoes to my plate.

"How's Brooke?" my mother asks, her voice filled with fake genuineness. I know full well her seemingly innocuous question is a prelude to a rant about the kurveh.

"I don't know. I hardly see her," I lie, hoping to cut my mother off at the pass.

But Shana Gold is undeterred. I can see it in the gleam of her eyes. Where's Elijah when you need him?

"How can you hardly see her when you live under her roof?"

"She works a lot." More than anyone I know, even Hannah and Stephen.

My mother snorts. "She could sell that house and live the rest of her days on a sunny beach in Acapulco."

"Except she wants to save the house for us and future Golds," I blurt vindictively, even though I've said the same thing to Brooke multiple times. And now, because I've gone this far, I figure there's no reason to hold back. "She has to Vrbo the cottage and the pool house just to support the damned place. In June, we're renting out the entire property for a wedding." I can't tell if I'm being mean or honest.

Three pairs of eyes stare at me in shock. Well, make it two pairs. Hannah doesn't appear surprised in the least, which surprises me. The townhouse gets so quiet that all I hear is the hum of the kitchen fan.

Adam breaks the stunned silence with, "Who's getting married?"

"Does Brooke even have the right kind of insurance for that?" Hannah is in lawyer mode now. "One slip and fall and she could lose the house."

I make a mental note to ask Brooke about this because Hannah raises a good point. But my sister doesn't stop there and continues to pepper me with questions.

Do the neighbors know?

Have we checked city zoning codes?

Are we setting up an LLC?

Throughout the entire conversation, my mother is conspicuously quiet. I can't tell if she's upset by the news that I'm working with Brooke to turn her and my father's marital home into the Disneyland Resort or is simply reorganizing for a counterattack. She's stealthy that way, the original B-2 Spirit.

"Mom?" I look at her, really look.

"What do you want me to say? We all do what we have to do. Do you think it was easy to bring that house back from the dead with three small children at my knee and a husband who was never home? Do you think we had the kind of money back then to own a place like that? Of course not. We had to scrimp and save just to keep the lights on. For days at a time, we ate nothing but meatloaf and lentils and rice just so we could afford to redo the plumbing and replace the old knob-and-tube wiring. No one knows better than I do that the house is a money pit."

Either her strategy here is to out-martyr Brooke—no contest there, my mom would win hands down—or she's tacitly agreeing not to turn this into a federal case. Whatever it is, I'll take it. I don't have the energy to pretend that Brooke is the enemy. I'm not saying I've forgiven her. What she and my father did was wrong. Atrocious. They were no better than Stephen, skulking around behind Hannah's back. But there has to be a statute of limitations on resentment. Mine has slowly begun to ebb away, and I'm trying hard not to feel guilty about that.

Adam, who is not as stupid as he looks, feels my pain. I can tell by the way he's reading the room, flicking his gaze from Mom to me, waiting for it, Shana Gold's ambush. She usually goes straight for the heart.

But all my mother says is, "How about dessert?"

* * * *

Brooke is home when I get there, sitting at the center island, eating her gluten-free toast. It crosses my mind that in all the months I've been living here, I haven't seen her eat anything else. Just diet soda and her special bread, slathered with butter.

"How was the seder?" she asks.

"Nice. Hannah seems to be adjusting well." I've continued to update Brooke on my sister's marital status, which in and of itself is freaky. Occasionally, Adam and the sale of Switchback will creep into the conversation. But anything having to do with my mother is off-limits. I do that out of respect for Mom's privacy. But I suspect Brooke is thankful for my discretion. There's no love lost there.

"Good. I'm glad to hear it." She goes back to nibbling on her late-night toast.

"She did mention that we should make sure your homeowners insurance covers the rentals and events."

Brooke lets out a breath. "Yeah, I've been thinking about that. I'll call David's insurance agent in the morning."

"She also said something about an LLC."

"Yep, I've been thinking about that too. Will you ask her about it? Maybe it's something she can do for us if it's necessary."

"Yep. I'm seeing her next week for lunch. I'll ask her then." I start to head for bed when Brooke stops me.

"Next Friday, the sorority sisters are coming for their city getaway. That's another six thousand in our coffers. I'm now able to pay a maintenance crew and a handyman to come in here and fix the walkways, freshen up the house...patch the leak in the kitchen. The revenue from the wedding will put us ahead. I just wanted to say how much I appreciate all the work you've put into this. Thank you."

I stare at her, taken aback. I never expected her gratitude, only to earn my keep, and in her words, to protect my father's legacy to his children. But it's a really nice thing to say. Furthermore, I believe she means every word of it. Maybe, just maybe, I'm good at something.

"Later this week, I'm meeting with that event planner. Hopefully it'll be advantageous."

Brooke crosses her fingers. "Night."

"Good night."

I climb the stairs up to my room, sit on the edge of the bed and kick off my shoes. It's been nearly ten months since the accident, and my world seems to have found some semblance of balance, though there are days I feel so lost that it's a wonder I don't have to be taken away on a stretcher.

Perhaps it's the calm before the storm.

But it felt good today to finally come clean with my family about Brooke's and my little enterprise. I laugh at how easily I include myself in this strange adventure. It's not Brooke's enterprise, it's ours.

As I so often do, I wonder what Josh would think of it. It isn't exactly real estate, but in a way the outcome is the same. Brooke and I are selling a dream. For the mystery writers, it was an escape in a house that served as their muse for a week. For Charles and Richard, the cottage and backyard set the opening scene for a new beginning. For Shireen and her fiancé, it will be the place where they fuse their two lives together.

Yes, I think. Josh, who also made people's dreams come true with his beautiful designs, would've loved the idea.

My thoughts drift to Campbell and the kiss. I reach for my phone, start to dial his number but quickly hang up before the call goes through. I'm still not ready to have a conversation about what happened in his new house or about us. I've tried not to think about it, about him, but it's proving difficult. Or, if I'm being a hundred percent honest with myself, impossible.

* * * *

Two days later, I see him at the Live Wire, a dive bar near the water that Adam is a big fan of. I could take it or leave it. The crowd is fine, kind of old San Francisco before the tech crowd took over. But it's always drafty and not the cleanest.

Hygiene doesn't stop Campbell and Adam from partaking in the happy hour's special on fried calamari and on-tap Pabst Blue Ribbon, though. I settle for a bottle of Sierra Nevada and give the neck and lip a good swipe with a napkin before I raise it to my mouth. Campbell catches me, shakes his head, and laughs.

He and Adam grab a four-top before the place gets crowded. Campbell plops a quarter on the rail cushion of the pool table closest to us. He's the best pool player I've ever seen. We used to have a billiard table at the house on Vallejo, and he and Adam would play for hours. Adam can hold his own, but he doesn't have Campbell's moves or coordination.

Both of us are trying to pretend that nothing happened the other day, yet it's still thick in the air. Judging by the way he keeps sneaking glances at me every couple of minutes, he wants to talk about it but won't because Adam is here.

"You cold, Rach?" he asks me, because like an idiot I didn't bring a sweater and am hugging myself like I'm in the frozen arctic dressed in a tube top. He slips off his jacket and drapes it over my shoulders. I immediately feel his leftover body heat and pull the jacket tighter to get more of it. To get more of him.

Adam follows with his eyes a redhead in a mini skirt who squeezes by us. I can't tell if he's interested in her or her basket of onion rings. The mystery is solved five seconds later when he announces that he's going to the bar to order onion rings, and does anyone want anything? Campbell and I shake our heads.

The minute we're alone, Campbell pulls his chair closer to mine and says over the music, "We gonna talk about it or pretend it didn't happen?" He's looking straight at me, approaching the kiss dead on, and I'm faced with the fact that Campbell Scott is no longer a boy. He's a man. A direct, take-charge man.

"Pretend it didn't happen." I take the easy way out. These days I'm all about easy. It's really all I can do right now.

He holds my gaze for what seems like an eternity, and I can see the wheels turning in his head. *But it did happen. And it meant something.*

"Okay," he finally says and lets out a sigh. "But why? Why do you want to pretend?"

"Because it shouldn't have happened. I'm grieving my husband, Campbell. And you're grieving Jess. We reached for each other because we're vulnerable. That's all."

For a long time, he doesn't respond and just looks at me. Really looks. And then, as if he's made a decision to lay it all on the line, he says, "I didn't reach for you because I'm vulnerable, Rachel."

I look away because I don't want to think about Campbell or the kiss right now. I don't want to think about second chances. Or love. Because all it's ever gotten me is loss.

Chapter 28
The Fleas

The next morning, I make the ninety-minute trek to Napa to meet with Shelby Dumas, an event planner who comes highly recommended by Josie. Shelby organized a charity auction for Josie's parents, who own a small share of a winery on the Silverado Trail. According to Jo, Shelby represents lots of vintners looking for small, unique venues to throw parties where they can wine and dine their San Francisco clients. I can't think of a better place than ours.

Shelby's office is off the beaten path in an old repurposed stone farmhouse with views of the rolling hills and vineyards of the Stags Leap District. I am at once smitten by the place. The receptionist, who sits at a live-edge wooden desk, offers me a glass of sparkling wine, which I of course accept. When in the Napa Valley...One sip and I'm in heaven. I know zip about wine but am certain I detect hints of pear and apple.

I get comfortable on the overstuffed leather couch that sits in front of an enormous stone fireplace and pretend to scroll through my phone—*look at me, so many emails, so little time*—instead of ogling the lobby, which Josh would've loved for its rustic simplicity.

A woman with long blond hair, dressed in black ponte leggings, a silk tunic top and a pair of beautifully tooled cowboy boots (very Napa chic) appears, takes one look at me and says, "Rachel?" I rise, and she folds me into a hug like we're old friends. "Let's go back to my office."

I follow her down a short hallway into a large open space with more comfy leather seating and views of Stags Leap. The ceilings are tall with chunky wooden beams. The whole setup reminds me more of a living room in a resort than an office.

"Josie says you have a spectacular event space in Pacific Heights." Shelby motions for me to take one of the chairs (Restoration Hardware's Wine Country Collection if I had to guess) by the coffee table, which appears to be made out of a reclaimed oak barrel.

I nod, questioning whether to tell her it's actually my family's home and decide to hold off.

"Can I get you something to drink? Coffee, water, wine?"

"No thank you. I had champagne in the lobby."

"I'm sure Josie told you that we're always looking for unique venues in the city for charity events, vintner parties, even retreats, and it sounds like you have something special."

"I took some pictures," I say, suddenly self-conscious that I snapped them myself instead of having them professionally taken. Shelby is probably expecting a leather-bound portfolio with photos of the house, grounds, and of events we've held. Other than family and friends' parties, I don't have any. I suppose I could've included pictures of Josh's and my wedding, but I didn't think of it.

I cue up my gallery and sheepishly hand her my phone. While she swipes through the pictures, I flip through an album on the coffee table that is filled with pictures of their events. Weddings, charity auctions, wine galas, concerts, and parties of all stripes and colors. Everything is uber classy and professional, and I'm starting to realize that she's out of our league.

"This looks lovely," she murmurs as she takes a second slide through my handful of snapshots.

I can't tell if she's just being polite or really likes the house.

"What's the capacity?" she asks.

I should've been prepared for the question, but I'm not. There were two hundred guests at my wedding. That's the most people I suspect we've ever had at once in the house on Vallejo. But it's not like we checked with the fire marshal or adhered to any kind of city safety rules, which I'm sure there are. That's when I decide to come clean with Shelby and not waste any more of her time.

"Can I be honest? This is my family home. My stepmother owns it now, and until recently it was strictly residential. That's not to say we didn't have lots of events there. My parents were not only proud of the home, they knew how fortunate and privileged they were to own a piece of San Francisco history and felt a karmic responsibility to pay it forward. Because of that, the house was always open to friends and family to use for their special celebrations. In the last year, though, my stepmother, Brooke, and I have decided to turn it into something of a small business. So, I guess what I'm trying to say is that I don't really know what the legal capacity of the property is, only that we've entertained up to two hundred guests at once at my wedding. I know it's not the most professional answer, but it's all I've got."

Shelby surprises me with an ear-to-ear smile. "We like that. We like properties to have a story and to have lived a life that's full. Most of our clients are vintners and farmers. Their homes are their businesses, and as good stewards of the land, they share them with the public. They'll love the idea that you and your stepmom are doing the same thing. But we do have to comply with city ordinances and ask that you have the proper permits and insurance. In the meantime, I'd love to set up an appointment for me to come see the property in person and get a feel for the kinds of events that fit best there. Would you be amenable to that?"

"Absolutely," I say, cheered by Shelby's reaction to my confession. From everything I've seen, they're a top-notch company with a respectable clientele. In other words, no bachelor parties with hookers.

Shelby walks me out into the bright Napa sunshine. No fog here, not even an ozone layer. Just clear, beautiful, blue skies.

I'm so excited about the meeting that I call Brooke from my car while still parked in front of Shelby's office. The call goes to voicemail, and I leave Brooke a long, rambling message that I hope she can decipher. After I hang up, it hits me that in the years she was married to my father, I never once called her. Not even after my father died to see how she was doing. When Josh died, she called me at least a dozen times.

The realization dampens my good mood. Whatever I thought of her, she was my father's wife. Anyone with even a speck of humanity would've called her. I can't make up for it now, but I'll try to do something nice for her.

I hop onto the Silverado Trail and at the last second turn the opposite way from San Francisco and head northwest to St. Helena, which is only fifteen minutes away. It's a scenic drive with rolling vineyards, stately wineries and ornate gate signs, beckoning visitors to tasting rooms. And to think this is right here in my backyard, yet another world entirely.

I'm not quite sure how to get where I'm going but miraculously wind up on Main Street. I park at the foot of the commercial district and wander from shop to shop, peeking in the windows. The quaint town once catered to farmers. Now, the utilitarian stores have all been replaced with high-end clothing boutiques, wine shops, gourmet restaurants and art galleries.

When I get to Les Puces, I cross Main and sit on a street bench where I have to turn backward for a bird's-eye view of the store. I don't know what

I hope to see or why I'm here. All I know is that there's likely a restraining order in my future.

The store has more presence here than the one on California Street in the city. Though the calligraphy—big black swirly cursive letters—is the same, the sign is bigger. Actually, everything about the store is bigger. Larger footprint, larger door, larger display window.

It's pretty, like a wannabe French bakery. Think Ladurée on steroids. The outside trim is painted a pistachio green and the awning is black-and-white stripes. I wonder if Beth picked out the color scheme or if she hired someone to do it.

A long time goes by, and I'm starting to get a crick in my neck, but I can't seem to pull myself away. It's as if just staring at the store might give me answers. A few more minutes go by, and I work up enough nerve to go inside.

A little bell over the door jingles, and a girl behind the cash register lifts her head up just long enough to grace me with a smile that says *why are you bothering me?* before going back to looking at her phone. It appears that it's just her and me, alone. That doesn't rule out that Beth might be somewhere in the back, out of sight.

I stroll up and down the narrow aisles, pretending to browse. The shop is as pretty on the inside as it is from the street. Pale pink and pistachio walls, light wood herringbone floors and Leucite shelving. Edith Piaf plays in the background. How original.

The merchandise is what you would expect to find in all the bric-a-brac shops with names like Nest and Home and Abode or anything with the word *magnolia* in it. Les Puces, "the fleas" in French (I looked it up), is a real divergence. At least in the US. In Paris, *Les Puces de Saint-Ouen* is the name of a world-famous flea market, which I learned from Wikipedia. I'm assuming the store was named after that. Yes, I've spent a great deal of time researching the name of Beth Hardesty's home décor stores. I'm not proud of it. But it is what it is.

I continue to wander, picking up various items as I go, fearing that the shop girl has found me out and is only seconds away from calling the cops. In reality, she hasn't lifted her gaze off her phone the entire time I've been here. By now, I could've walked off with enough Riedel stemware to open my own shop.

Everything is displayed and organized beautifully. A row of blown glass candlesticks. Drawers of Provencal linens. Shelves filled with handmade pottery. Racks of gorgeous lace. I flash on Beth and Josh's apartment and wonder if it looked like this. If every object was curated to reflect their exquisite taste.

Our apartment, with the exception of Josh's records, hats and books, was a dusty mishmash of things accumulated over our seven years together. None of it looked like this.

I make my way to the back of the shop, half fearing, half hoping that I'll bump into Beth. If I do, would I have the courage to talk to her? *Hey, didn't you used to date my late husband, Josh Ackermann? Hey, aren't you Beth Hardesty, my late husband's ex?*

Did Josh love you more than he loved me?

There's a door that looks like it goes to a storage room. But a painted wooden sign says otherwise. "Garden, come outside." I turn around to see if shop girl is going to stop me and half expect an alarm to go off as I turn the handle on the door, which opens onto a delightful courtyard that does indeed remind me of my one and only visit to Paris. I was twelve, and my parents took us for their twentieth anniversary. The things I remember most were Adam insisting that the food sucked and that we should eat all our meals at McDonald's, that all the women wore beautiful scarves, and the courtyard at the hotel where we stayed in the Marais. Green ivy clung to the walls, and red geraniums spilled from big terra-cotta pots. Instead of a lawn, the ground was covered in ancient-looking brick-colored tiles. There was a small iron table and two gloriously rickety chairs. Even as a child, I could feel the magic.

It's the same way I'm feeling now as I walk through Les Puces' small oasis with its ornate iron arbor and babbling, moss-covered fountain. Although everything from the patio furniture to the plants displays discreet little price tags, the space is so reminiscent of that courtyard in Paris, I want to stay and never leave.

Over the stucco wall, I spy an alleyway where there's a line for a taco truck. And just like that I'm back in California.

I turn to leave and hear the voices of a woman and two small children.

"Not today, Kingsley, Daddy's making paella for dinner. Mommy's got thirty minutes of work to do. Can you and Rivers sit here and color until I'm done?"

They turn the corner, and I come face-to-face with Beth. I'm pretty sure my heart stops, and by divine intervention I am still able to breathe. She is even prettier in real life than she is in pictures. Her brown hair is tied back in a high ponytail, and her face is bare of makeup. She's wearing a colorful peasant top, cropped jeans with ragged edges, and a pair of red platform sandals. Very Napa Valley casual. The worst part—Kingsley,

Rivers, and paella aside—is she looks down to earth and like the type of friend you can rely on. The one who never gets angry that you drunk-called her in the middle of the night. The one who throws the best bridal and baby showers. And the one who will drop everything to whisk you away for a spa day when your boyfriend dumps you.

She smiles at me, and I stand there, paralyzed. All the questions I've prepared in my head since I read the texts are lodged in my throat. There's no sign that she recognizes me. Then again, why would she?

"Can I help you with something?" she asks as her two perfect children climb up on one of the patio tables.

Yes, you can help me unravel the mystery of why my late husband never spoke of your existence yet saved every text message you ever wrote him.

"I was just browsing," I say, stunned to hear my voice so steady.

"Is this your first time in Les Puces?" I imagine her French pronunciation is spot on.

"It is. Lovely store." The urge to flee is so strong that if Beth wasn't standing in front of me, I'd sprint across the shop and out the front door as fast as a gazelle.

"Thank you. I'm glad you think so. And please let me know if you need assistance with anything."

Before I can say I will and force a smile on my face, she's at the patio table with her kids, unpacking a box of crayons and coloring books from her enormous handbag.

I race to the front of the store. Shop girl is still immersed in her phone as I duck outside. I make it all the way to the car before throwing up in my passenger seat.

A mess, I unearth my cell phone from the bottom of my bag and start to call Campbell, knowing he'll come all the way to St. Helena and get me if I ask him to. But I stop myself before his phone rings. This thing with Beth is a piece of my life that belongs only to Josh and me.

Chapter 29
Edinburgh

May is a whirlwind, and June rolls in with the fog. I spent a good portion of last month fighting City Hall for permits. Thank goodness for Hannah and the Esq. after her name. Between the two of us, we redefined the meaning of take no prisoners.

The Queen Anne on Vallejo is officially a party house now. Our permit allows us to hold events with up to two hundred guests twice a month, and ten times a month as long as we entertain no more than fifty people at a time. The only requirement is that we provide private parking and adhere to the neighborhood's noise restrictions.

For the last week, we've been running around the property in preparation for Shireen's big day. The wedding is only a week away.

Shelby has booked us for two winemaker dinners later this month. The first is to showcase the Grenache Blanc of a vintner from a Yountville winery. Shelby's bringing in a fancy chef to cook dinner for twenty of the winery's gold club members. The second is being billed as a night of chocolate and wine. That's all I know, but I'm definitely down for it.

In the meantime, the cottage and pool house are booked solid until November. And to add to the chaos, I'm on my way to meet with an old client who wants to sell his house. It's a small apartment in Nob Hill. The apartment isn't much but the location stellar. It's right on the cable car line with breathtaking views of the bay and Yerba Buena.

It's my first nibble since I sold Campbell his house, which according to Adam is coming along nicely.

On my way to the appointment, I call Mom. "I've only got a few seconds to talk." Which is never a good way to start a conversation with Shana. But if I don't, she'll talk my ear off, and I'm crunched for time.

"Well, that's a nice way to greet your mother."

See?

"Sorry, but I'm just about to meet someone about a potential listing." That'll hopefully shut her up. "Do you know where those glass balls are that we used to put in the pool that look like bubbles?"

"Why?"

I grit my teeth. "For that wedding I told you about." I've only been talking about it for the last week to anyone who will listen, including Mommie Dearest, who pretends not to be interested but is constantly adding her two cents to my plans for the party.

"Rachel, honey, I don't live there anymore. How would I know where the glass balls are? Did you ask Brooke? It's her house now." She says that last part like it's a news flash, like I needed her to tell me that.

"Yes, Mom. She doesn't remember ever seeing them."

"For all I know, your father threw them out." *Like he did me* is what she's implying.

Ugh, I don't have time for this. "All right. I thought it was worth a shot. Thanks."

"You might check the attic. I'm not saying they're there, and it'll probably take you a year and a day to sort through the mess up there. Your father was a hoarder."

I start to say that hoarders don't throw things away. But the contradiction would be lost on her. "I'll go up there later. Thanks, Mom. I'm here now, so I've got to go."

I'm five minutes late and decide it'll be faster to take six flights of stairs rather than wait for the slowpoke elevator that's probably a remnant of the Gold Rush. I'm not entirely sure they even had elevators during the Gold Rush, but if they did it was this one.

By the time I get to the sixth floor, I'm out of breath and trying not to pass out. I wait a second to recuperate, then knock on the door.

Wade answers in a pair of faded jeans and bare feet. "Rachel!" He gives me a great big hug, then a long assessing glance. "You look fantastic."

Not as fantastic as you, Dr. Booth.

He's an anesthesiologist who occasionally used to work with my father. Half my dad's staff panted after Dr. Booth. It's those broad shoulders and laid-back attitude. He looks more surfer than he does doctor.

He was married to his college sweetheart, an archeologist who died in a plane crash on her way home from a dig. It was their tenth anniversary. A year after her death, he needed a change of scenery and decided to buy a home. I was just getting started in real estate. My dad gave me a sterling recommendation, and Wade gave me a chance.

"How are you?" He tilts his head to one side, his eyes meeting mine, silently saying, *I know what you're going through. I've been there.* "It never really gets better, does it?"

"No," I say and sigh. "It just gets different."

"Don't knock different. Different can be good. Come take the tour, see what you think."

I follow him into the living room. Other than the fantastic view, it's rather bland. Lots of white walls and nondescript furniture. But it's nothing that a good stager can't fix. The dining room is more of the same. The kitchen, on the other hand, is outstanding.

"You remodeled." I turn in place, noting the high-end appliances, the Carrara marble countertops, and the custom white shaker cabinets. He took white subway tile all the way up the wall. The look is clean and sleek but also in keeping with the 1920s-era building.

"Pretty killer, huh?"

"Oh yeah. You added a lot of value here."

"It's the only thing holding me back from selling."

"We'll find you a new kitchen with all the bells and whistles."

He laughs. "I thought you might say that."

"Want to see the bedroom?" He arches his brows, and there's a hint of suggestiveness in his voice. Nothing pervy, just playful.

"Yes, take me to the bedroom." Jesus, I'm flirting.

He's at least eight years older than me. Maybe even ten. Which makes him harmless. And I'm so out of practice that it's fun to see if I still have it.

We take a small hallway off the living room to the one and only bedroom. I'd forgotten how large it is. There's a king-size bed, a small seating area and a fireplace.

He comes up behind me, close enough that I can feel his breath on my neck. "What do you think? You like?" His tone is sexy. Too sexy.

"Very nice."

Before this gets completely unprofessional, I hand him the folder I've filled with listings of comparable apartments that have sold in the area over the last three months. "Should we go back in the dining room and talk price?"

"If you insist," he says in a long-suffering voice.

I spread the comps on the table for him to look at.

"Can I offer you a drink? Sparkling water, coffee, juice, wine, a cocktail?" It's a little early for booze, so I ask for a glass of sparkling water.

"You want something to eat?" he calls from the kitchen. "Oysters, chocolate?"

I laugh. The man is bad. "No thanks."

He returns with waters for each of us, hands me one, and clinks my glass with his own. "To us and new beginnings."

"To us and new beginnings," I say, not entirely sure if he's talking about selling his home or something completely different.

After my meeting with Wade, I convince myself to swing by Campbell's. It's kind of out of the way, but I'd like to see what he's done with the house and...I miss talking to him. I miss him.

I don't see his truck parked on the street when I get there and start to leave. Then at the last minute, I decide it wouldn't hurt to see what I can see on my own.

I walk around the side and let myself into the backyard. Wow, Adam wasn't kidding. All the weeds and overgrowth are gone. Sod has been laid, flowers planted, and there's a small flagstone patio where there used to be a concrete pad. Mr. Scott has been busy. The old rotten fence has been replaced with a new redwood one, and Campbell has started building a deck off the main bedroom. When it's done, it'll be beautiful.

"Ma'am, you're trespassing. Do I need to call the police?"

I swing around, and my lips curve up. "I wasn't trespassing, I was snooping. There's a difference. Did you just get home?"

"Yeah. When did you get here?"

"Five minutes ago. I was in the neighborhood and wanted to check out your progress. This is like a totally different place, Campbell. I can't believe how much you and your dad accomplished out here."

"It was mostly him. Retirement is driving him crazy. Come inside and see what I've done in the house."

"If it's anything like out here...Oh my God, Campbell." The kitchen is completely gutted, and the wall separating it from the small back room has been taken down. The space is huge and filled with light.

"It's a mess right now. But later I'll take you through the garage and show you the cabinets I'm building for it."

He leads me to the dining room where the rest of the cottage cheese is gone from the ceiling. The walls have been painted dove gray and the trim a crisp white. The tobacco stains are gone, and all I smell is fresh paint.

"It looks great. Are you planning to build a table and chairs for in here?"

"You see what I did over here?"

I turn around to find that he's built two columns and a pair of bookcases with wavy glass doors to go back in their rightful place. "It's as if they were always here."

"It's probably what was original to the house. One more coat of paint and they'll be good to go."

"I can't believe how much you've accomplished in such a short amount of time."

"Yep, been burning the midnight oil. That's for sure. Hey, I'm glad you came by because I've been meaning to call you."

I take a fortifying breath, knowing what's coming. The kiss. He still wants to talk about the kiss. He still wants to talk about us, even though there is no us. Good, I say to myself. I came here to clear the air, so we could go back to being friends. Real friends. Not the kind I make small talk with at bars with my brother.

"I've got one chair," he says and motions for me to take it. It's the one he was making the day I was here.

I run my hands over the beautiful oak arms, caressing the wood. When I say Campbell is an artist, I'm not kidding. "Ah, Campbell, this is like a museum piece."

"It's okay." He shrugs. Not out of modesty but because his heart isn't in it. I know this instantly. Because I know him. "There's a folding chair in my bedroom. Let me get it."

No more sitting on the floor, apparently.

I test out the new chair while he's gone. The cushions are the same color of Campbell's eyes. Green.

"Where did you get the upholstery for the chair?" I call to him in the other room. Then it hits me like a sucker punch, and I suddenly can't breathe. Jessica. Serena & Lily. That's where he got the cushions. He's preparing to tell me that he and Jessica are back together.

He returns a few minutes later with the crappy folding chair that looks like it's seen a few too many trips to the beach. Some of the webbing is coming loose. He unfolds it and sits in it anyway.

I should insist we trade, since I'm half his size, but I'm too busy freaking out about the news he hasn't told me yet. The news he's about to tell me.

"How have you been?" he asks, which I know is a stall tactic. He doesn't want to tell me, so instead we're back to inane pleasantries.

"I've been fine," I hear myself say in a tight voice. I realize I'm not making this easy for him.

He lets out a breath. "I'd like to finish the house and put it on the market."

There's a long silence, and I finally say, "Why? You're making it so beautiful." And it's perfect for him.

Because Jessica doesn't like it, and we're planning to buy something else. Together. Where we can raise our babies.

"I'm going to do some traveling," he says. "Afterward, I have a cousin in Edinburgh who owns a furniture manufacturing company. He's asked me to work with him."

This is out of left field. I'm still trying to digest what he didn't say instead of what he did say. Which is much worse. Campbell is going away.

"Edinburgh as in Scotland?"

He grins. "The one and only. It's an amazing city. I was there with my dad a few years ago, visiting family, and have been meaning to go back ever since. This is my chance."

"This is your chance," I repeat because I'm struggling for what else to say, even though we both know why he's leaving.

"I've got about two more months of work on the house. But when it's done, will you take the listing?"

I'm suddenly lost for words.

Finally, when I get them back, I hear myself say, "I'm not really doing much real estate these days. I've sort of dedicated myself to this new venture with Brooke."

He nods like he understands, but there's a well of disappointment in his eyes. I know it has nothing to do with me not taking the listing. But I only have room for one man in my heart. Someday, I'll find someone. A friend, a lover, a person I can settle down with. A companion. Someone easy, someone I don't have to give too much, someone I don't have to love with all my heart. It could never be that way with Campbell. And if I loved him the way I should, the way I know I would, it would be a betrayal of Josh.

I get to my feet because I can't stay here any longer. The sheer depth of sorrow in the room is overwhelming.

"I'm excited for you," I say, trying to sound like the friend I hoped I could be, but now I realize there's too much between us for that to be possible. "You always wanted to travel. And this place"—I take one last look around—"when you're done with it, it'll go in a snap. It's beautiful, Campbell."

"Thank you," he says quietly. "I'll walk you out."

When we get to my car, no words pass between us, but there is a world of meaning in the silence. We both know this is it for us. Campbell is gone to me.

Chapter 30
Wedding Crasher

Shireen's wedding is today, and I'm playing the part of event planner, even though I have no idea what I'm doing. Brooke is in the kitchen making enough canapes to feed the city, despite me reminding her that there are only fifty guests.

The fog seems to have lifted, promising a sublime day weather-wise. Not too cold. Still, the guests have been warned to bring wraps and coats. June in San Francisco can be like Christmastime.

The chairs for the ceremony have been set up on the front lawn. In back are the tent and tables. Shireen has hired a string quartet to play both at the ceremony and the reception. They appear to be pros and don't need any guidance, leaving me to deal with the messier things. Like the wedding cake, which isn't here yet and was supposed to be an hour ago. Every time I call to check on the baker's ETA, I get "We'll be there in ten minutes." Ten minutes have come and gone three times now, and I'm about to lose my mind.

The flowers were unceremoniously dumped off in boxes this morning in front of the house. Silly me, I was under the impression that the florist was supposed to place the arrangements on each table and tie the leafy green garland Shireen ordered to the arbor and rows of chairs. This now falls on me? A person who has zero talent in this sort of thing?

Luckily, Josie came early to help the bride with her dress, and I foist the project on her.

"You were born for this kind of assignment," I tell her, and she gives me the finger.

But when it's done it looks spectacular, like something you'd see on Pinterest. I snap a few pictures for our portfolio, an idea I got from the leather-bound one in Shelby's office. Later, I'll sweet-talk Shireen's photographer into giving us a few glossy pictures with the promise to recommend him in the future. I've already begun collecting business cards of reliable vendors. As soon as this is over, I plan to throw away the ones from the florist and cake baker.

The bartenders show up, lugging crates of booze. I point them in the direction of the bar and let them do their thing. The bride arrives—she's an hour early. I send her upstairs to my parents' old bedroom and tell her champagne is on the way. Then I remember she's pregnant. Shit.

Brooke shoves a bottle of sparkling apple cider at me. The woman thinks of everything. I fill a lovely wine bucket I find in one of the cabinets with ice, grab a few crystal flutes and send Josie up with a tray.

"Keep her busy," I say.

Jo beams like a proud mama. "Look at you all bossy and shit. Girl, you've found your calling."

I don't have time to contemplate Josie's words. It's only three hours until showtime, and there's still a million things to do on my list, including sweeping the driveway for the valet station. I've hired a company that has a contract with a parking lot not far from here. Which works out perfectly.

I jog to the gardener's shed and grab the broom. On second thought, this calls for the big guns. I put back the broom and pull out the leaf blower. Johnny, Mr. Scott's replacement, was here yesterday. But the big oak out in front never stops shedding.

I'm out blowing when the Queen of Tarts—more like the Queen of Tardy—rolls up. I watch them carry Shireen's four-layer wedding cake to the backyard with my heart in my mouth. All I need is for them to drop it.

They make it to the round table Josie has decorated with rose petals from the garden and manage to hoist it onto the lazy Susan without incident. Done. One more thing I can check off my list.

Back to the leaves. When that's done, I remember the glass balls for the pool. As Mom predicted, they were in the attic. Brooke, on a break from the kitchen, helps me put them in the water. The effect is quite nice. Return on zero investment, priceless.

Brooke steps back and assesses the white tent, the pretty tables with their flouncy floral linens, the buffet stations lined up in perfect precision and lets out a sigh. "You've outdone yourself. Seriously, it looks like something out of *Bride* magazine."

I have to agree. I suppose I borrowed a little inspiration from my own wedding, which makes me all at once melancholy and proud that I can pass this on to someone as sweet and lovely as Shireen. Someday, her children will pore over the pictures from today and see how it started. I remember spending hours sifting through my parents' wedding photos. Unlike my mega wedding, they had a small reception with just family and a few friends on the East Coast while my father was in medical school. They looked so happy in those photos that they instantly became my role model for the perfect couple.

I try not to think of that now and only want to focus on the bride and her special day.

"Oh shit, the place settings. They're up in my room." Josie and I stayed up all night at her place, making them on her Cricut machine. Hannah even came over and brought pizza.

I dash upstairs, bring them down and carefully line them up in alphabetical order on the guest book table.

Shireen's parents are here. They've traveled from Minneapolis and stayed with the bride last night. But tonight, they're staying in the cottage with their son and daughter-in-law, who are also here from Minneapolis. Shireen and her new husband will be taking the pool house. And Brooke is making a big breakfast for the wedding party tomorrow.

I send them up to the bride's room and lug their bags—they've packed enough for a month—to the cottage. I go over my list one more time to see if there is anything I've missed, then check my watch. Only one more hour until the guests start arriving.

I check in on the bride, who is so calm and serene that I can't help but wonder if the fuss about bridezillas is an urban myth. Her fiancé is on his way with the best man, so I make sure their room is ready. It's the guest suite on the main floor with a view of the backyard. I stock it with champagne and snacks and a few toiletry items in case one of them forgets something. I read about doing that in an event-planning book. Very informative.

With my work done, I wander into the kitchen to see if Brooke needs help.

"Eat," she says and hands me a plate of canapes, like a Jewish mother, even though she's the ultimate *shiksa*. "You'll need your energy for the rest of the day."

I sit at the island, devouring the miniature crab puffs. "Whoa, these are good." I never ate breakfast and am starved.

I get up and pour myself a cup of coffee from the bottom of the pot. Another thing I'd forgone when I woke up at five in the morning in my quest to get everything done. I should be exhausted, but I'm pumped. Now I know why they call it an adrenaline rush.

I finish my canapes and load the dishwasher with all the dirty bowls in the sink. I start a second wash in the dishwasher in the butler's pantry.

"Give me another job to do," I tell Brooke, who is cutting vegetables for a crudité platter. She seems to have everything well in hand, but I'm out of chores.

"Could you check the oven to see how the roast is doing?"

"Sure. But I don't know what I'm looking for."

"Just make sure nothing's burning."

The roast looks like it's doing what it's supposed to. I grab a sponge and some disinfectant and wipe down the counter. "I think we're going to pull this off," I say like I still can't believe we're doing this.

"Of course we'll pull it off, O ye of little faith." I don't know how she manages to do it, but Brooke is always confident. Maybe it's working in the ER, saving lives. "And by the way, you need to start drawing a salary. This has become a full-time job for you, and we're making enough money for you to pay yourself."

"I'm living here free, Brooke." It comes out with me sounding indignant, which I am a little bit. Brooke said she was doing this for us, for future Gold generations to save my dad's legacy. Why should I profit from that?

She turns and forces me to meet her eyes. "I'm not paying you, if that's what you've got your panties in a bunch over. The house is. Part of your compensation package is free room and board."

"You know that's not what I'm saying." I stare back at her. "Let me put it this way, when we were kids, my parents, unlike other parents, didn't pay us an allowance to do chores around the house. It was their philosophy that everyone had to pull their weight. They didn't get paid to put a roof over our heads, so why should we get paid to make our beds? I'm just pulling my weight."

"I'm not suggesting you get paid to make your bed or to take out the trash, or any other menial chore. That's pulling your weight. What I'm talking about here is a full-fledged business. If you want to be a partner in it, you draw a salary. No one works for free. And for the record, it's my opinion that you enjoy this more than you do real estate, and you work a hell of a lot harder at it. So embrace what I'm offering you." She returns to her vegetable cutting, letting me know she's done talking about it. Take it or leave it.

She's given me plenty to chew on, but I don't have time to think about it now. Not with a wedding less than thirty minutes away.

I pop my head out the front door to make sure the valet company has arrived and is ready to receive guests. Then I climb the stairs, tap on the bride's door, and check in. Shireen's parents are sipping champagne while Josie is doing the bride's makeup. They don't need me crowding their party, so I take myself downstairs. The officiant is here, and I get him settled outside.

That's when my mother of all people pulls into the driveway. What is she doing here? My first reaction is to reach for my phone and scroll through my missed calls. Nothing. There would've been dozens if there was an emergency.

I watch her alight from her car in one of her crazy outfits. Flowy cropped linen pants, a dozen layered tops in various lengths and widths, and a pair of gladiator sandals. The ensemble makes her look both like a bag lady and a well-heeled customer at a Lilith closeout sale.

To my knowledge, this is the first time she's been to the house since my father married Brooke, and I can't imagine what she's doing here. She and the valet are talking. I'm too far away to hear what they're saying, but I can tell that he wants to take her car. The instructions are that all vehicles are to be parked offsite except for the groom's, the officiant's, and the photographer's. The delivery people are allowed to park just long enough to unload.

As I approach, I see the valet throw his hands up and my mother pocket her keys.

"Mom?"

She kisses me on the cheek. "What are you wearing, dear?" She eyes my work sweats with disdain.

That's the last thing on my to-do list. To change into black pants and a white blouse, the uniform Brooke and I have chosen. If I rush, I'll have time.

"You have leaves in your hair." My mother reaches up and pulls one out of my ponytail.

"Ouch." I pull away. "Mom, what are you doing here?"

"Is that the way you greet your mother?"

She knows how important it is that this wedding goes off without a hitch because for the last week that's all I've talked about.

The waitstaff pulls up in a minivan, and I'm momentarily called away. I direct them to the kitchen, and in that time my mother has managed to slip away. Damnit. I don't have time for this now.

I rush to the backyard, where I find Shana casually strolling through the party tent. "Mom, what are you doing?"

"You should switch that centerpiece with that one." She points. "The colors of the flowers go better with the tablecloth."

They're all the same, so I don't know what the hell she's talking about. But to appease her—and God willing, get her to leave—I switch them. And damned if it doesn't look better. How does she do that?

"Mom, you haven't answered my question."

She strolls over to the pool and gazes into the water at the glass balls that look like bubbles. "I told you they were in the attic. I like what you did with them. Very festive."

"Mom!"

"What? A mother can't visit her child every once in a while? You do live here, no? Plus, I wanted to see this wedding you've been so excited about."

I don't even...there are no words, so I say the ones I'm certain will penetrate. "Brooke is here."

"I assumed that. She lives here too, no? And you are hosting this wedding together, yes?"

"We're not hosting. This is our job. This is how we make money." I don't know why I'm quibbling over "hosting" when there are bigger fish to fry, like what the fuck is she doing here in the middle of an event? Or at all. But her la-di-da attitude galls me.

"I understand that. And if you need to work, don't mind me. I can entertain myself." She starts walking toward the guest cottage.

"Mom," I say through gritted teeth, afraid of making a scene. "You can't go in there. And guests are due to arrive any minute."

She shoos me with her hands. "Then you best get going." She eyes my dirty sweats again. "And, Rachel, put on something more appropriate. Oh, how I do love a good wedding."

I catch up with her and pull on her arm. "That's the thing, Mom, the bride didn't invite you."

She stares me down like she used to when I was thirteen and going through a rebellious stage. "I'm sure, Rachel, there is room for one more."

I throw up my arms in defeat and pray that she stays out of trouble while I rush off to change my clothes.

At the last minute I decide a quick shower is imperative if I plan to get within a few feet of anyone, and leave Josie in charge. By the time I make it to the front yard, the ceremony is in full swing. But Mommie Dearest is nowhere in sight. I hike down to the valet station where her car is still parked. Unless she took an Uber home, she's still here somewhere. But I don't have time to find her. Not now. So I do the best thing I know how. I call for reinforcements.

"HELP!" I tap in a text to Adam. "Mom's crashed the wedding. Come get her before I call the cops. Remember, you're her favorite. You owe this to both of us."

The officiant appears to be wrapping up the story of how the bride and groom met and seems to be moving into the vows section of the program. Time for me to motor to the backyard and get the trains running on party mode.

That's where I find my mother. She's behind the bar, helping the bartenders pour flutes of champagne for the pre-dinner toast. I want to throttle her. Instead, I slip into the kitchen to give Brooke and the staff the ten-minute warning sign that the ceremony will be wrapping up soon.

"Hey, do you have a minute?" I ask Brooke.

"Just a minute, but yeah, what's up?"

I beckon her to follow me to the dining room, out of earshot of the others. "I don't want to freak you out, but my mom's here. She just showed up and has taken it upon herself to help the bartenders. I'm really sorry, Brooke."

"What are you sorry about? We could use the extra hands. When she's done with the bartenders, tell her to get her ass in the kitchen."

My mouth falls open, and I quickly close it. "Uh...okay...if you're sure." I have no intention of getting my mother anywhere near Brooke. But I've at least done my due diligence. The two women are on their own now. I'm out of it.

I pop out to the front again. The ceremony is still going. The bride and groom have written their own vows and are reciting them to each other. It's lovely and painful for me at the same time. Josie's sitting in the front row on the bride's side in case there's a dress malfunction. I catch her eye and motion that I'll be in back.

There's nothing I can think of to do right now other than to wait to lead guests to the welcome table, where they can sign the wedding book and get their seating assignment. I'm exhausted and elated, too. Other than Mom, everything so far has gone smoothly.

I take a welcome break on the swing. The chains, thanks to Josie, have been wrapped with leftover garland. It's so whimsical and pretty that I think we should keep the swing like this all the time. I try to remember if Ran Gately did it for my wedding but have no memory of the swing. I think about Campbell and his wedding—the one he was supposed to have next weekend—and a flood of guilt washes over me. I was dreading that wedding to the point of coming up with an excuse to leave town on the day of the event. I know it's selfish and even mean. And that there's no good reason for it. I made my choice more than seven years ago to love somebody else.

I see Josie out of the corner of my eye. She's giving me a thumbs-up and mouthing, "It's over."

I race to the front yard again, wait for the bride and groom and their families to go off with the photographer for pictures before herding the guests to the backyard. Twenty minutes later, the guests are mingling, cocktails in hand, while the quartet plays a jazzy version of "Stand by Me."

I'm off to the side, basking in a self-congratulatory moment, when I see Adam walking toward me in a pair of shorts and an "I paused my game to be here" T-shirt. His hair is wet and slicked back as if he just got out of the shower.

"What the hell, Rach?"

I hadn't really expected him to come. "It may have been a false alarm," I say with an apologetic cringe. The last time I saw my mother, she was doing something innocuous like reorganizing the gift table.

"Now you tell me." He glances around at the party in motion, and it seems to dawn on him that he's woefully underdressed. He continues to take in the scene. "Nice. Sort of like the old times, huh?"

"Sort of. You want a drink?" *What the hell,* I think. The Golds never could resist a good shindig.

"Sure. Is that Hannah over there with Josie?"

I follow Adam's direction and shield my eyes from the sun. My sister, who is at least dressed for the occasion, is holding a margarita in her hand, laughing at something Josie is saying. Hmm, maybe she knows the bride through Josie.

"Holy Moses, don't look now," Adam says. "But Mom and Brooke are standing together, talking."

Oh, for the love of God, I knew this was going to happen. It was too damn good to be true. I make a beeline for them, hoping to head off a scene before it erupts in the middle of Shireen's reception. Adam comes tripping after me. I wave my hands at Josie to get her attention and point to Hannah, who has her back turned to me, motioning toward my mother. Calling all Gold reinforcements, this is a code blue.

But when I reach my mother, who has a drink in her hand (never a good sign), and Brooke, they smile at me serenely.

"So far so good," Brooke says, and for a minute I think she's talking about her and Shana. About how they're not trying to kill each other.

Then my mother raises her glass. "Kudos to the two of you. It's a beautiful party."

Adam is here, right behind me, as a witness. Hannah is a few steps behind us. When we're all huddled together like a mini football team ready to sack my mom, if need be, she gathers us in a group hug.

"Isn't this lovely?" she gushes, sloshing her drink on the three of us. "I have all my children together. Here. Where it all began." She flags down one of the servers. "Will you take a picture of us." But she doesn't have a phone, so I hand him mine.

We pose like we used to when my father was alive and we were still a family. Goofy smiles, Adam jostling to be in the middle, Mom fluffing her hair.

The waiter steps back, fitting us all in the frame, ready to snap the picture, when my mother does the one thing that has the power to floor me. She calls Brooke to join us for the shot.

Chapter 31
Change Is Good

I'm sitting outside of the Windham Real Estate Agency, reading a text from Dr. Booth.

"Want to do dinner this week to celebrate?"

Last month, I sold his apartment. It took about ten minutes, no exaggeration. There were four offers on the table, all of them over asking. Finding him a place, however, wasn't half as simple. But we persevered. In three weeks, if all goes well, he closes on a sweet townhouse near the ballpark where the action is.

Judging by his text, I get the feeling he wants to get out there again. I have no delusions that dinner isn't a pretext for us going to bed together. And the crazy thing is I'm actually considering it. I miss sex. All the physical and messy parts of it. I won't apologize for that. Not to myself—or to anyone else. I may be on the cusp of thirty-five, still in love with my late husband, but I'm not dead.

I deliberate for only a second before sending Dr. Booth a quick text that simply says, "Maybe." Then I walk into the office where I haven't shown my face in nearly a year.

Janney's eyes open wide at the sight of me. "Well, hello, stranger. I assumed you wanted me to mail your commission check, like I did last time."

"Nope. I came to get it in person and say hello to everyone." And goodbye, though I'm keeping my license current just in case the venture with Brooke doesn't work out. But I'm optimistic. More optimistic about this business decision than I've ever been about real estate. And markedly more enthusiastic.

Janney is hugely pregnant, and we spend time talking about names and how she doesn't want to know what sex the baby is until he or she is born. I swing by the coffee bar and fix myself a latte because why not? I will miss the excellent coffee here and may drop by from time to time for a cup.

Niki comes in, bringing her entourage with her. Last I heard, she has her own team now. Her gaze flickers over me. *Oh, it's you,* it seems to say. *Nothing to see here.* I flash her what I hope is a demonic smile. Then I wave her over.

"I have a lead for you."

She looks mildly interested but dubious that any lead I might have is worth her time.

"Remember that offer you advised me on months ago?" Niki gives me an imperceptible nod. "A dear friend of mine bought it and wants to flip it. He's a master carpenter, and what he's done with the house will take your breath away. I'd like you to be his agent." Of everyone I know in the business, she's the one most likely to get Campbell the biggest return on his investment.

When he asked me to be his agent, I couldn't. I can't watch him pack up his life here and leave. I know from experience how desolate and desperate that's going to make me feel. I know. Because the last time it happened, when I was just seventeen years old, it broke my heart in two.

"If I text you his number, will you give him a call and let him know I sent you?"

"I'd be happy to," she says, sounding as if she's doing me a favor. She is. But she stands to make a nice chunk of change in the process. So, *You're welcome, Niki Sorento.*

"And, Niki, not one of your minions." I glance over at the cabal that apparently now travels with her like she's freaking Beyonce. "You need to handle this one yourself, okay?" Something passes between us, and she acknowledges my request with a curt nod.

My work here is done.

* * * *

Group grief is meeting tonight at Vivian's house. She lives in Pacifica, kind of a schlepp. I had hoped that Brooke and I could carpool (i.e., she would drive) but she isn't sure she can make it. The ER is swamped tonight.

So it's just me, driving forty-five miles an hour on the freeway, a lot of people passing and giving me the finger. "Fuck you," I shout. "Bet your husband didn't die at the hands of a texting Tesla driver."

The GPS takes me off the interstate, to Highway 1, then onto a winding road with views of the ocean. Thank God it's not dark. But it will be when I go home, which terrifies me.

When I get to Vivian's, I'm a jumble of nerves. I force myself to get a grip and go inside. There's a sign on the entry door that says, "Come in. We're in back."

As I step into the front room, my first impression is this is a house well loved. There are toys on the carpet, one of Vivian's kids has made a tent out of the sofa pillows, and everything from the furniture to the décor has a beach theme. I note that Vivian's late husband's stuffed fish is once again above the fireplace, and a smile blossoms in my chest.

"We're back here," Raj calls and waves me into the kitchen, then through French doors to the backyard. The group is sitting around a lit fire pit. A set of solar lights strung through the trees have begun to flicker on as the sun starts to fade.

"Great spot."

Someone drags over an extra patio chair and squeezes it into the circle, wedging me between Doris and Raj.

"Brooke has a busy night in the ER and probably can't make it. She sends her regrets."

There's a collective murmur of disappointment. I don't know how she found the group or if the group found her, but I quickly picked up that she and Raj are the unofficial organizers, sending around the signup sheet for people to take turns hosting and making sure everyone knows where the meeting is each month. According to the others, sometimes they invite guest speakers. Therapists, grief counselors, that sort of thing. I haven't been to one of those yet.

"Everyone," Vivian says, "there's food on the table and coffee in the urn." She points at a small gazebo on the other side of the yard.

We all get up in unison and head to the table where there are trays of what looks like homemade cookies, banana bread, and blueberry muffins.

"Did you make all this?" The little I've ascertained about Vivian besides the fish story is that she works full-time and is raising two kids on her own.

"It's nothing special. I've made them so many times I could do it in my sleep."

"Impressive." I fill my plate, starved. After my visit to Windham, I spent the rest of my day running around, buying things like vacuum cleaner filters and Costco toilet paper, forgetting to eat.

Everyone wanders back to their chairs and to the fire to keep warm on a cold summer night.

"A little housekeeping before we start," Raj says. "We're taking a break next month. Too many people are on vacation. But I'm sending around a signup sheet for anyone who is available to take calls in case someone needs to talk. I know this group provides a lot of support, and I don't want anyone to feel abandoned." He passes a clipboard to me.

I bogart it, wavering on whether to put my name down. What wisdom do I have to impart? Not a day goes by when I don't think of Josh, don't miss him, don't wonder how I'll move on without him. And yet I have. Little by little, I'm emerging a different person than the one I was when Josh was alive. I've found a job I love—and more important, I'm actually good at it. In a lot of ways, Josh's death, even my father's death, forced me to find my independence. I'm the one who has to catch myself when I fall, and there is something incredibly empowering about that.

I put my name and number on the sheet and pass it to Doris.

"Can I go first?" Vivian asks.

"Absolutely," Raj says.

"I'm thinking of moving closer to my parents in Maine. I'd like my kids to spend more time with their grandparents, and frankly I could use the help. But this is the only house they've ever lived in, and it's a piece of their father." She wipes her eyes with the back of her hand, and Doris hands her a tissue. "Everywhere they look here, they can see Rich. The beach he loved, the tree we planted when Bobby was just eighteen months old, the gazebo he built with both boys. Even his old Dodge Charger is still in the garage. The damn thing doesn't run, but it's still here. How do I take them away from that?"

"Oh, honey, they have their daddy in their hearts," Doris says. "They will take him with them wherever they go. The three of you can't live the rest of your lives living with a ghost."

"I agree with Doris," Sylvia says. "You need to take care of your boys, but you also need to take care of yourself. When my Davis died, I wanted to be—I needed to be—closer to my children and my grandchildren. I left my home of forty years to move here to be near them, but I took my memories and my pictures with me. And you know what? This is where Davis would've wanted me to be. I know he'd be heartened by the fact that I'm surrounded by our kids. That they're here to take care of me. Rich would feel the same way."

"What is your time frame, Vivian?" Raj asks. "If you're worried about uprooting the children, perhaps you can ease into it by explaining that there needs to be change. Give them a little time to get used to the idea."

Vivian sniffles and nods. "That's what I was thinking. Maybe put it off until the new year. That way we can spend one last Christmas in the house."

Daishi, who's recently joined the group after losing his wife to a stroke last winter, pats Vivian's shoulder. "You should be with your parents. Change is good."

Change.

I remember the day not so long ago when I had to flee our apartment, how it had become a shrine to Josh, and I had become its prisoner. Yes, change is good.

More people go around the campfire. Daishi wants to start dating again. And Sylvia would like advice on whether she should hire a lawyer for a living trust. Doris wonders if it's unhealthy to have running conversations with her dead husband.

When it comes to my turn, I freeze. These people are warm and kind and in a way kindred spirits, but I'm not sure I can articulate the profound ways in which my life has changed since Josh died.

"Well," I say, clearing my throat, "next month will be the one-year anniversary of the accident that killed my husband. In my religion and culture, we have this thing called yahrtzeit, where we go to temple on the deceased's anniversary, say a special prayer, and light a memorial candle. I'm going to Chicago to do that for Josh with my in-laws." The group hums its support, and I suddenly feel emboldened. "In other news, I'm watching my sister's marriage disintegrate, I'm stalking my late husband's ex-girlfriend, and the man I've loved since I was twelve years old is moving to the other side of the world. Oh, and I'm thinking about sleeping with my father's former anesthesiologist."

The group goes silent.

Chapter 32
A New Story

I'm in the Mission on Monday at the butt-crack of dawn, waiting in line with a dozen other suckers at a well-known Mexican bakery that's famous for its *bolillo* rolls. Brooke wants them for *tortas,* Mexican sandwiches, her contribution to a bon voyage party for one of the nurses in her unit. She worked past midnight last night, so I volunteered to get them for her.

Big mistake. I had no idea the rolls were such a hot commodity and that the bakery usually runs out by eight a.m. There are five people ahead of me, and if they get whatever rolls are left, I'm screwed. The man behind me is talking incessantly, and I haven't had my coffee yet. He wants to know why a "beautiful woman" like me isn't married. Yeah, he actually uses that line while staring at my naked ring finger.

I took off my wedding set and locked it away after the Beth sighting at Les Puces. It wasn't just me lashing out at Josh for Beth, which I know is childish. It was time. It was time to stop pretending that I'm still married. Like Doris says, you can't spend your life married to a ghost.

The line inches closer to the door, and by the time it's my turn, there are only two dozen bolillos left. I take a dozen, leaving the now six people behind me to duke it out for the rest.

There's nothing like the warm smell of bread. Even though it's earlier than my usual breakfast hour, my stomach growls, and I can kill for a cup of coffee.

I'm only a few blocks from Josie's. It's a nice morning, so I decide to hoof it, stopping off at my car to stash the bolillos and then a coffee shop along the way. Shopkeepers are out, sweeping and setting up sidewalk signs. People are walking their dogs. One woman is walking her cat. On a leash. I've never seen that before.

On the street in front of Josie's studio apartment, there's a pickup truck that looks awfully familiar. But then again, don't they all look the same? I don't pay it a second thought while I try to juggle two lattes and a bag of almond croissants. I climb the stairs to Josie's studio apartment. The scent of fresh tortillas makes me hungrier than I already am. I'm discovering that I can get used to this morning thing. Everything is so vivid...and hopeful.

When I get to her door, I hear voices coming from inside. Two voices. And I recognize both. That certainly explains Stephen's truck out front, but not why. I twist the knob and it's unlocked, so I don't bother to knock, just walk in.

And what I find is my sister and Josie kissing. Like really kissing, kissing like they mean it. I manage to catch the carrier with the lattes before it drops. That's when the two of them see me and pull apart.

They both stare at me like I'm an apparition.

We stand there awkwardly until I say, "The door was unlocked."

Josie takes the coffee carrier from me and puts it on the table.

"I only got two," I say stupidly. "And croissants." I hold up the bag.

"I'll make more coffee." Josie busies herself in the kitchen, leaving me alone with Hannah. At least as alone as we can be in a studio apartment.

For a long time, the two of us don't speak.

"I guess mazel tov is in order," I finally say, breaking the silence.

"Are you mad?" Hannah asks, her expression contrite, the same way she used to look when we were kids and her friends would slam her bedroom door in my face, letting me know I wasn't welcome in their big-girl circle.

Adam may be disappointed. But I've always wanted Josie to be an official Gold. "Why would I be mad?" Though I am a little. Not mad, just scared that I'm losing them both.

"That we didn't tell you," Hannah says. "It's just...so new. I'm not even divorced yet. But I'm so happy, Rach." Joy radiates off her like the sun. Once, a long time ago, she used to smile like that whenever she was happy. Before Stephen.

There are a million questions I want to ask, like does this mean Hannah and Josie are serious? Does this mean Hannah is leaving Stephen for good (fingers crossed)? And what does it say about my sister's relationship with my brother-in-law? Was she also having an affair?

It also explains the matinee movie and why she and Josie have been spending so much time together. Without me. It's twenty kinds of selfish, but I feel like I've been cast into the odd-girl-out role in this new equation, a little like my best friend is being taken from me. Or my big sister has deserted me for my best friend. It's stupid, I know. And later, I'll be elated for them because I really am.

But as I stand here in the shadow of the glow from their happiness, these are the shitty things running through my head. And for no reason—or for all those reasons—I start crying.

"Is there even room for me?" I say, barely coherent, my nose running like the Trevi fountain.

Josie has come out of the kitchen, and she and Hannah rush toward me. I shield my face with my hands, trying to hide my tears.

"Rach?" Hannah reaches for me and pulls me into her arms. "Of course there's room for you. You're my sister."

"And you're my sister from another mister." Josie joins us, and we're locked in a group hug. All three of us crying like idiots. "You really think we'd leave you out? You've been my best friend since grade school."

"I know," I say, but it comes out like a hiccup. "I'm being a moron. I'm probably premenstrual."

"You're not a moron." My usually stoic sister hugs me tighter. "You've been through hell and back this year. I love you, Rach. I love you forever."

"I love you too, Hannah."

"What about me?" Josie says.

"You too, Jo." I start to clean my nose on my sleeve, but Josie gives me hers. "Uh-uh, it's too nice." I think it's angora.

And Josie does the one thing that lets me know for better or for worse that I'm in her life forever. She wipes my snotty nose on her fancy sweater.

* * * *

On my way home, I cruise by Campbell's house. His truck isn't parked in the driveway. Still, I don't dare get out of my car in case he's home. We haven't spoken since that day he told me he's going to Scotland. I guess we both figured there was nothing left to say.

There's a Windham for-sale sign on his lawn with Niki's name on it. I sit in my car, staring at his little Craftsman. The sunlight glints off the stained glass in the new front door. The house has been freshly washed in a coat of pale green and white trim. It's much more cheerful than it was before. The tiny front yard is blooming with flowers, and bright blue lobelia trails from tan-colored pots on both sides of the door. Two Arts and Crafts rockers, presumably handmade by Campbell, keep each other company on the front porch.

Realtors love to throw around the phrase "good bones." But this home has more than good bones. I can feel Campbell's soul here, even from a distance. He may be letting the house go, but he spoiled it with love.

I think about the Queen Anne on Vallejo and how my parents poured their hearts into it. How they took a decrepit old building and made it the essence of our family. The love is still there—you can feel it emanating from the halls, from the ceiling, and from the floors—but their love for each other is gone. I think about Brooke and how she's become the next steward of the legacy, a legacy that started with my mother. And I think about how I found a new beginning within that legacy's walls.

I think about Raj and Vivian and Doris and Sylvia and all the others in the grief group and their new beginnings. About Hannah and Josie. About Adam selling his business. About the end of one story and the start of a new one. I may not know what mine is yet, but I'm moving toward it. I'm moving toward it in my own sweet time.

Chapter 33
Anything Is Possible

I'm at San Francisco International Airport about to catch a flight to Chicago when I get the call. Mom has fallen down the stairs of her townhouse and is in the ER. Brooke, the duty nurse, was there when the paramedics brought her in.

I half drag, half carry my suitcase, zigzagging through the Delta gate, jostling between the crowds. It appears everyone is traveling today. SFO is crawling with people, families on vacation, business commuters. An entire group of teenagers and their harried chaperones are spread out, taking up all the seats and even much of the floor space. I maneuver around them like an obstacle course.

It's so loud I almost don't hear my phone ring. Adam's name pops up on my display. I deliberate whether to answer or push forward. I can call Adam once I'm in a cab, speeding toward San Francisco General. On second thought, I take it, cradling the phone between my ear and shoulder as I race through the terminal for the exit.

"I'm on my way," I shout to hear my own voice over the hubbub of the airport.

"Don't come. Hannah and I have you covered. Go to the yahrtzeit."

"What about Mom? Are you there? Is it bad? Brooke seemed to think it was bad."

"I'm looking for parking. But I talked to Mom on the phone. She's bitching and moaning, which means she's fine. We'll handle her. Go to Chicago."

I stand there for a minute deliberating on what to do. The Ackermanns will be disappointed if I don't come. But I don't want to stick my siblings with all the responsibility. Mommie Dearest can be a handful. Not to mention she's probably keeping score on which one of us is the better child.

"I'll get my flight changed and go later in the week," I tell him, even though I'll miss the yahrtzeit. If Josh were alive, I know he'd tell me to go be with my mother and forget the yahrtzeit. *Light a candle for me anytime you want, babe.*

For some reason this makes me cry, and I continue to rush through the terminal with tears dripping down my face. Thank God it's an airport and no one seems to think anything of the fact that I'm weeping in public.

My mother is still in the ER when I arrive. Both Hannah and Adam are around her bed in the tiny room where she's waiting to be wheeled in for X-rays. Her hip is blown up like a balloon, and the back of her head has a knot on it the size of a tennis ball where she hit it on the stair railing as she was going down.

"Oh, Rachel, you should've gone to Chicago," she says in a limp voice that actually sounds like she means it. "I'm fine."

"Honestly, Mom, you don't look fine." I'm betting money that her hip is fractured. And the ER doc thinks she has a concussion. "What's taking them so long?" I pop my head out of the curtain as if the action alone will somehow summon someone sooner.

"According to Brooke, they're slammed and understaffed," Hannah says.

"You think we could get a pizza delivered here? I'm starved." Adam plops down in the only chair in the room. Hannah and I look at each other and shake our heads.

"Go to the cafeteria if you're hungry," my mother says. "Bring something up for your sisters."

"The food's vile." Adam stretches his legs out in front of him.

There's a knock on the curtain, and Brooke walks in. "Not too much longer." She circles the bed, stepping over Adam's feet, to check my mother's IV bag. "How's everyone doing?" Her eyes meet mine, and I send her a silent thanks for calling. For involving herself even though it was probably awkward.

"What does not too much longer mean?" Adam bobs his head at Brooke. "Do we have time to order in a pizza?"

Brooke ignores him and goes about checking my mother's vital signs. The room is quiet, except for the hum of the medical machines. Hannah's texting on her phone. It's the middle of the day, so I assume she's updating her law firm, which reminds me to call the Ackermanns.

I step out into the crowded hallway. Mom was lucky to get a room, and I wonder if Brooke had something to do with that. I find a private spot and break the bad news to Pauline, who is both understanding and disappointed.

"I'll come as soon as I get my mom settled in."

"It's a shame you'll miss the yahrtzeit. Rabbi Naditch does a beautiful service. She's a woman, you know?"

"I remember you telling me that. I'm so sorry, Pauline. We can go to temple when I'm there. And I'll light the candle for Josh tonight. So he'll have one burning in both his homes. San Francisco and Chicago. I'll take a picture of the service and send it to you." I don't even know if that's allowed in a synagogue, but somehow I'll make it happen.

"That sounds very nice. Did you hear that, Saul? Rachel is going to light a candle for Josh in San Francisco." Saul says something in the background that I can't make out. "Tell your mother she's in our thoughts and prayers, and we're hoping for a quick recovery."

"I will. And I'll let you know as soon as I can come."

When I get back in my mother's room, there's a medical staff person in scrubs preparing to wheel her to radiology.

"Should one of us go with her?" I ask, directing the question at Hannah because Adam is pretty much useless in situations like this.

"I'll go," Hannah says, but the radiology guy stops her.

"We're good on our own, aren't we, Shana?"

My mother nods and graces the technician or whatever he is with a beatific smile. He just happens to be really nice looking, and Mommie Dearest is a born flirt.

"Don't worry about me." My mother holds out her hand and wiggles her fingers, showing off a French manicure.

While she's gone, Josie shows up with sandwiches. Adam grabs the pastrami and appears unaware that Josie and Hannah are an item. I haven't told anyone, as it's not my story to tell.

"What did the Ackermanns say?" Adam asks around a bite of his sandwich.

"I told them I'd do the yahrtzeit here and send them pictures of the service. Am I even allowed to do that?"

Adam shrugs.

"I doubt it," Hannah says.

"I'm pretty sure you can at my parents' temple," Josie says. "I know people have videotaped bar and bat mitzvahs. Why not a yahrtzeit? I can have my mom ask. You want to do it there?"

The Blums belong to the same synagogue as Dianne Feinstein. I think members of the Haas (aka Levi Strauss) family also go there. It's more than a bit swanky for the Golds, and even the Ackermanns for that matter. But since I don't belong to a temple, beggars can't be choosers.

"Yes," I say. "If they'll have me." I gaze around the room. "Will you guys come?"

"Do I have to?" Adam grins, and Hannah swats his head.

"Of course we'll come," she says. "Mom, too, even if she's in a wheelchair." Which I think will probably be the case.

We're the only ones in the ER eating, but that's the Golds for you. No place is too sacred for a nosh. The cute guy returns Mom to the room, and we wait for the doctor to come with her results.

Brooke pops in again, takes one look at our sandwiches and lets out an exasperated breath. "Any news yet?"

"Still waiting," I say.

Mom is dozing, which sort of worries me, given that we haven't exactly been quiet. Brooke checks her pulse on the screen and gives me a thumbs-up.

"It shouldn't be too much longer," she says. "I'm off shift. You want me to stick around?" It's her way of offering to help without intruding.

"Nah, go home and relax," I tell her and realize that it's not because I'm trying to rush her off or keep her at arm's length. It's because Brooke looks tired and the rest of us have got this.

"Okay, but call if anything comes up."

When she leaves and is well out of earshot, Adam says, "I guess we're all one big happy family now."

Not quite, I think. But something tells me that we're moving in that direction.

* * * *

Mom's hip isn't broken, just sprained, which seems like a miracle given all the swelling. The doctor said she'll have to stay off it until it heals. Treatment includes copious amounts of ice and elevation. Because she has a mild concussion, she can't take anti-inflammatories for a while.

"I think I'll take a shower," my mother says as soon as we get to her townhouse. I've been elected to stay with her tonight.

"I don't think that's a great idea. You're not supposed to be on your bad leg."

"So I'll sit."

I know better than to argue with her, so I help her to the bathroom, which is as large as most San Francisco apartments. Together, we get her undressed. Her shower is the size of a one-car garage and has a built-in bench. I manage to half lift her in, get her situated on the seat and turn the water on without getting soaking wet.

I find a fresh towel in the linen closet and make myself at home on her vanity stool while she bathes, occasionally pressing my face to the shower glass to make sure she isn't sprawled on the marble floor.

"How's it going in there?"

"It's delicious and just what I needed."

"Let me know when you want me to turn the water off."

"Five more minutes."

The mirrors are fogging, so I turn on the fan and open a window. "Are you hungry?" Unlike us, Mom didn't have a sandwich at the hospital.

"Maybe we'll order something from the Chinese restaurant down the street and have it delivered. What do you think?"

I'm not hungry but I say, "Sure" anyway.

"It'll be like a slumber party," my mother coos. "Were Saul and Pauline terribly disappointed?"

"I think so. But I promised to light a candle here, and that seemed to make them feel better about it. Josie volunteered B'nai Israel. You think if we borrow a wheelchair from someone you can go?"

"Oh, I can just hobble in on the crutches the hospital gave me."

I lean into the shower and turn the water off before my mother turns into a prune. "Time to dry off." I hand her the towel and go in search of pajamas. On second thought, a nightgown will probably be easier.

I find some kind of caftan thing in her closet. It reminds me of something Joan Crawford would've worn while smoking from a cigarette holder. Very Mommie Dearest. I help her out of the shower and into the caftan and find her a pair of slippers.

"Want me to call in that order now?" She really should eat.

"Let's have wine first."

"I don't think that's a good idea, Mom. Not with the painkillers."

"You're no fun," she says. "Well, then, I guess it's fizzy water for me."

"Come on into the living room and I'll get you some." I lend her my shoulder. Between that and a crutch, together we maneuver her to the sofa, where I stuff a bunch of throw pillows under her hip and hand her an ice pack to apply to the swollen area. "Keep it elevated, and I'll get you a drink."

I find her flavored seltzer water in the fridge next to a bottle of vodka. There isn't much in there otherwise.

"Mom, if I didn't know you better, I'd think you were a lush." I hold up the bottle of Hangar 1.

"It was a gift from a gentleman friend." She throws this out casually, but it's clear she wants me to know there's a man in her life.

"A gentleman friend?" I raise my brows, playing along, even though I don't want to. It seems my whole family is living secret lives.

"I'm old, not dead."

"Who is this friend? Do I know him?"

"Just a neighbor." She waves her hand in the air dismissively, then quickly adds, "He's a certified public accountant."

"Yeah? So?" My mother drops people's professions like some drop names. Once we went for a walk in her neighborhood, and she proceeded to tell me who lived in each house and what they did for a living. An hour I'll never get back.

"I'm just telling you about him," she says with feigned innocence.

"So, are you dating this guy?"

"I wouldn't call it dating." She's being coy and enjoying it.

Fine, I don't really want to know anyway. The idea of my mother dating... of my mother...Eew!

"Did you know Dad wanted to be a photojournalist when he was young?"

She seems put off by my sudden change of subject. "Where is this coming from?"

"The day before he died, he told me that he worked for the school newspaper at Yale and that one of his pictures made it onto the cover of the *New York Times.* Did you know that?"

Her lips turn up in a wistful smile, and just as quickly it's gone. "Of course. He was very proud of that photo. I had it framed, you know?"

I can't remember ever seeing it hang anywhere. Not in the house on Vallejo or even my father's office.

"But did you know he wanted to be a photojournalist before he wanted to be a doctor? That he chose medicine because it was a more practical decision."

"We talked about it." She readjusts herself on the couch. "We all have our phases. There was a time when I wanted to be an interior decorator. Then I had your sister and your brother and you. And that was out of the question."

I don't know why. Most of the mothers I know work. But I don't refute her comment.

"Your father loved being a doctor. Do you think we could've given you, your brother and sister the life we did on a photojournalist's salary?"

The question isn't really about us. What the question comes down to is my parents. What changed in their master plan that made my father reassess his decisions, including marrying my mother? What gave him regrets?

"Did he ever talk about backpacking around Alaska, visiting Denali?" I ask because it seems so counter to the man I knew. But maybe I never really knew him. Maybe what I knew was him and my mother as a unit.

"Frequently. Don't you remember that time we were debating whether to take you kids to Alaska for the summer or Hawaii?"

I don't remember any such debate. I do, however, remember going to Hawaii. Maui. It's when I realized I wasn't a beach person after days surfside, baking in the sun. I actually remember Adam and I being bored to tears and Hannah learning how to boogie board. She spent two weeks throwing herself into the sport like she'd found religion.

"How come he never did it? Alaska, I mean."

My mother lets out a long sigh. "I guess it just never fit in to our schedule."

Our schedule.

At some point, my father, as I suppose many of us do once we're married and have a family, morphed into a *we* and an *our* and lost his individuality. I wonder if it was Brooke who helped get it back. If Brooke was the bridge from the life he'd chosen to the one he'd always wanted. The epiphany makes me mournful and hopeful at the same time.

"Mom, do you think if Dad hadn't died, he would've left Brooke and come back to you? Do you think he thought he made a mistake?"

There's a long silence. My mother takes the ice pack, which is starting to melt, off her hip and puts it on the glass coffee table. "First of all, I wouldn't take him back if he did," she finally says.

"Because he cheated on you?"

Shana Gold has cut off friends and relatives for things far less egregious than my father's betrayal. She once went five years without talking to her first cousin for questioning whether my mother's engagement ring was a cubic zirconia.

But my mother surprises me by saying, "No. I would've made his life a living hell, but I would've taken him back. The fact of the matter is our love story had run its course."

I rear back. "What does that mean?"

"It means our marriage was already in jeopardy when your father began his dalliance with Brooke." *Dalliance?* It sounds so Victorian. Like Dad and Brooke were having tea behind my mother's back as opposed to Dad sleeping with another woman.

The thing is there were no indications to me that my parents' marriage was on the skids until my mother caught my dad sharing a room with his nurse at a medical convention.

"Mom, you loved Dad."

"I did and I always will. But by the time you went away to school, we'd fallen out of the kind of love we used to have for each other, which left our marriage on life support." She rolls onto her noninjured side and pulls herself into a sitting position.

I should tell her to continue elevating her hip but am too consumed by this new revelation and whether to believe it to focus on anything else. "Why is this news to me?"

"Because you weren't paying attention. And why would you? You had your own life to live and your own future to think about."

"I would've known if you were unhappy."

My mother gives me a penetrating look. "And yet you didn't." Her statement is devoid of blame. She's simply trying to drive her point home. "Honey, you know your father. Do you think he would've had an affair if he wasn't terribly unhappy?"

"I don't understand what you're saying." Or I don't want to understand it because it goes against everything I've ever believed.

"What I'm saying is that your father's affair set us both free."

"But you were devastated." I remember that crazy birthday party she threw herself at the Log Cabin. At the time, I thought she was putting on a big act. A big in-your-face fuck you to the curve ball my father had thrown her. Now, I'm not so sure.

"I was humiliated," she says. "There's a difference. Do I wish we'd had the courage to walk away from each other like two mature adults who knew when to call it quits? Absolutely. But we didn't. We didn't because everything we had, including ourselves, was so intertwined that leaving was too hard—and too damned devastating. Without realizing that it would come to this"—my mother waves her hand to indicate her townhouse, a symbol of their divorce—"your father forced both our hands when he cheated with Brooke. In the end, it's what we needed. It's what was best."

I'm reeling, but deep down inside I believe my mother. It would be so easy for her to say Dad was coming back to her. That Brooke had been a bump in the road of a marriage that came with twists and turns like any marriage. A mistake. But instead, she's laying it bare, telling the truth.

"Why didn't you ever tell us this? We thought it was all Dad. That he blindsided you."

"Oh, make no mistake about it. I was blindsided and hurt to my marrow. No one wants to lose their husband to a woman half their age and twice as beautiful. And he lied. In all our years together, it was the first time I'd known your father to be a liar. A cheater. That was the worst part."

"Is that why you hate Brooke?"

"I don't hate Brooke. But what she did—what they both did—was wrong. Your father may have been unhappy in his marriage, but he was still married. I don't forgive him, but I'm working my way to forgiving her."

"Why?" I ask, stunned. Because, again, my mother is not the forgiving type.

"Because she gave you a second lease on life. Even before Josh died you needed a jump start, and she gave you that. Because she's committed to saving the house on Vallejo for you and your siblings, because she's been good to all three of you. Because my children are more important to me than my resentment for her. She also made your father happy. I may have been angry with him. Hurt. But he was a good man, a wonderful father, and for more years than I can count, the love of my life. I'm beyond glad that in the last leg of his life he was with someone who made him truly happy."

"You didn't make him happy?"

"I made him happy, and he made me happy. And then we didn't," she says, a wry smile lifting her lips. "This may come as a big surprise to you, but I'm not always easy. And your father...don't get me started."

"But don't you think you could've rediscovered each other again if Dad hadn't died? I just don't understand how you could toss away a grand love like that. You and Dad were together since you were kids. He was your one. Brooke was just a footnote."

"Not a footnote, Rachel. She was your father's grand love for the man he'd become. I was his grand love for the man he used to be, the man I fell madly, deeply in love with. People change, circumstances change. It doesn't mean we don't cherish the past, but we move on to the future." She probes me with a look, letting me know we're not just talking about her and my dad anymore.

But I'm not ready to let the topic of this new side of my mother go. "Why did you let him buy you out of the house? You loved that house. You made that house."

"Uuck." She makes a guttural sound when she says it, like she just got off the boat from Russia, and tosses her head. "It was too much house. Even before your father and I split up, I wanted to sell it. You guys were gone, we were empty nesters, and I wanted a new project. Something different, something exciting. I now realize I wanted something I wasn't getting from my marriage. Anyway, I tried to talk your father into selling, buying a pied-á-terre in the city, so we could still be close to the three of you, and a fixer-upper in Tahoe, a home base for when your father retired. He wouldn't hear of it. He'd become so attached to that house he couldn't see outside its walls. I could've been spiteful and fought him for it, but I would've only been spiting myself. I'll give you and Brooke credit for turning the house into a business. Otherwise, it becomes an albatross. A symbol of how much love you can put into something and discover in the end that it didn't fulfil you as much as you thought it would or should."

I motion to my mother to elevate her hip, and I go to the kitchen for a new ice pack. I contemplate telling her about Beth Hardesty but nix the idea. This is her night for confessions, not mine. Besides, I'm still trying to absorb everything she's told me, everything that was right in front of my eyes, but I didn't see.

"What about Tahoe?" I ask, placing the pack on her hip. "Is that still an option?"

Mom does a 360 around her glamorous living room, so different from the Queen Anne on Vallejo. "Maybe." She takes my hand. "Anything is possible."

Chapter 34
Chicago

If Josh were still alive, he'd be thrilled to be held in memory at B'nai Israel. The synagogue is an architectural marvel, all concrete, glass and wood lattice. It's almost ostentatious in its sparsity. It has none of the stained glass and ornateness you would expect from a place of worship.

The sanctuary is a light-filled, round room with the bema in the middle instead of in the front, like in most synagogues. The windows, walls of plate glass, look out onto gardens of various varieties of fescue grass. And the ceiling is made from a series of wooden slats that appear to undulate like an ocean wave. I've never seen anything like it.

Raj, Doris and Vivian, the only members of grief group who could make it on such short notice, greet me with hugs and kisses. Brooke borrowed a wheelchair from the ER and has taken it upon herself to be my mother's keeper. I've decided to let those two deal with each other on their own and to stop running interference.

Josie's parents are here and have seated themselves next to Josie and Hannah. Adam brought me so I wouldn't have to drive myself. Before we came in, in a signature Adam move, he tried to talk me into smoking a joint with him.

Now, I wish I had, or at least lingered in the car.

The room is filling with congregants, and I find myself staring out to the gardens, disassociating. That's why I don't hear Campbell come up behind me until he brushes a light kiss against my neck. Adam must have told him. I didn't invite him because it seems unfaithful to Josh. Unfaithful to both of them. The whole point of today is to celebrate Josh's life and to reflect on how his death has changed me. How my soul is different now. I don't want Campbell to distract me from that.

I turn to him. "Thank you for coming."

He nods. "I better find a seat. The place is filling up fast." Before he leaves, he slips his hand in mine and gives it a squeeze. When he lets go, I feel so empty inside that I want to pull him back. Instead, I turn toward the bema and stare out the window again.

The B'nai Israel staff has offered to video tape the service and send me a link that I can send to the Ackermanns. In all the hoopla over Mom's fall, I forgot to light the yahrtzeit candle last night at sunset. This morning, I raced to the grocery store and bought a candle, then snapped a picture for the Ackermanns of it lit. Hopefully, they'll be none the wiser.

The rabbi starts the service. Today's sermon is coincidentally about grief. I reflect on the last year, about how in the beginning, the pain of losing Josh was unbearable. It has subsided over time but is always there, like a dull throbbing that never goes away. There are still nights while I'm dazed from sleep that I reach for him. And mornings when I start to tell him something and remember he's not here.

By the time the rabbi gets to calling off the names of the dead, including Josh's, and starts to deliver the mourner's kaddish, I have disappeared into a world of memories. Memories of Josh.

"Yitgadal v'yitkadash sh'mei raba b'alma di v'ra chir'utei; v'yamlich malchutei b'hayeichon u-v'yomeichon, uv'hayei d'chol beit Yisrael, ba-agala u'vi-z'man kariv, v'imru amen," the rabbi says.

"Amen."

"Magnified and sanctified is the great name of God throughout the world, which was created according to divine will. May the rule of peace be established speedily in our time, unto us and unto the entire household of Israel."

"Amen."

"I've got the world on a string...sittin' on a rainbow...what a world, what a life, I'm in love!" The song rings in my head and I smile, my heart so full that I can feel it bursting from my chest.

It's as if I can sense Josh sitting beside me, wearing one of his fedoras, whistling the tune while snapping his fingers like Sinatra or Sammy Davis Jr.

"Take care, my love," I whisper.

After the service, we walk out into a beautiful August day. No fog, only glorious sunshine. Even the temperature is balmy with a slight breeze coming off the bay.

Brooke invites everyone back to the house on Vallejo for refreshments, which is really kind of her. She's a good person, and my father was lucky to have her.

I head to Adam's car when Campbell waylays me on the sidewalk. "I'm not going to make it over," he says and looks away.

"Okay." It's probably better that way. Lately, Campbell has been taking up too much of my head space.

"How's the sale going?" I ask because it's easy, because I don't want to address what's going on between us. The heaviness.

"A lot of interest. Niki's taking offers next week," he says to answer my question, but I can tell the sale is the last thing on his mind. There's only regret and sorrow for all the things that might have been.

"That's good. She's the best. She'll get you top dollar," I ramble. My eyes start to sting, and I turn my face slightly, trying to pretend this isn't the man I've been in and out of love with for twenty years.

"Yep." He reaches out and brushes my hair out of my eyes. We stand like that for a few moments, him touching me, and then we pull apart.

"Look, I've got to get going."

"Okay." My voice is whisper thin.

Then he leaves without saying anything, not even goodbye.

* * * *

Three days later, I'm in Chicago, in the Ackermanns' lovely suburban home, the one where Josh grew up. His childhood pictures line the hallway walls like a haphazard art gallery. Him playing T-ball. His debate team. A preteen Josh, donning a bow tie (this one cracks me up). Prom with his high school squeeze, the lawyer. Our wedding portrait on the tree swing at the house on Vallejo. And about a dozen others. None of them in chronological order, just a stream of consciousness history of Josh's evolution from boy to man.

On Pauline and Saul's coffee table is the *San Francisco* magazine cover with the interior of Il Matto, the Mission District restaurant Josh designed the year before he died. Next to it lies *Architectural Digest* with a blurb on Rabbits. The burned-out yahrtzeit candle sits on the polished black lid of the grand piano no one knows how to play.

"Are you hungry, dear?" Pauline pulls a tray of cold cuts from the refrigerator and pushes a basket full of French rolls at me in their dated but sunny kitchen. It's the kind of kitchen that hugs you as soon as you walk in the room.

My stomach is a little off from the plane ride, but I take one of the rolls and a couple of pieces of salami to appease her.

"Josh loved hard salami," she says as if I don't remember her bringing a whole salami every time she and Saul came to visit. For three weeks after they left, we had salami on everything. Omelets, sandwiches, cheese and crackers, even stir-frys. It was a salami festivus.

"I know," I say. Our conversations are about as dry as those salamis.

It isn't that Pauline isn't a wonderful person, but she and Saul are...shall we say, less colorful than their son was. Definitely less colorful than the Golds, which isn't necessarily a bad thing. We can suck the oxygen out of a room in less than a millisecond.

Instead, it's like that scene from *Auntie Mame*. No matter what story my mother-in-law is telling, all I hear is "And I stepped on the ping-pong ball" in an upper crust accent.

I told Mom once. She erupted in laughter, then told me she'd had the exact same reaction. I never shared that special piece of cattiness with Josh, though. Some things were better left unsaid.

"Pauline, can I ask you a question?" Maybe it's the awkward silence between us, or maybe I subconsciously planned this all along. But as much as I want to make peace with Josh's past, I can't seem to let Beth Hardesty go. "Did you know Josh's girlfriend Beth? Beth Hardesty."

I catch Pauline off guard, I can tell by the slightly caged look on her face. Beth's name has definitely registered with her. Of course it would. Her son lived with the woman, for God's sake.

"I remember her," she finally says. "Why do you ask, darling?"

"No reason, really. I came across some old pictures and correspondence between her and Josh from a long time ago and wondered." I left out the part that I'd been regularly stalking Beth. "It's just that Josh never mentioned her before, and I was surprised."

"It was a short-lived relationship. I'm sure Joshie didn't think it was important enough to discuss." She raises her arms in the air like *what are you going to do?*

"But he lived with her, right?" I don't want to put Pauline on the spot, but this is my chance to answer the questions that have been keeping me up at night.

"Yes, and we weren't happy about it."

I know instinctively that it's because Beth isn't Jewish. The Ackermanns had no qualms with Josh and I living together before we were married. At least none that I know of.

The Golds have never had a problem with marrying outside of the faith. Don't get me wrong, my mother was thrilled that Josh was Jewish. But as long as we were happy, my parents were happy.

I don't press Pauline on this point and let her finish telling me about Beth.

"She ran off with another boy," she continues. "A boy in their circle of friends. At first, Josh was devastated. And then he met you." She cups my chin, and I feel the warmth of her touch and an affection that grabs me by the throat and makes my eyes tear. "He loved you so much, Rachel. You made him so very happy."

"He kept her old text messages all these years," I blurt, surprised that I'm confiding in my mother-in-law, a woman I've never been particularly close to. "I mean...I'm not saying he was still involved with her...only that it's odd that he never mentioned her before, don't you think?"

"Why would he?" Pauline hitches her shoulders like she's truly baffled by my confusion over Josh's hesitance to mention an ex-girlfriend. "She was no longer important to him. Why would he think she would be important to you?"

It seems so simple the way Pauline says it. But I know it's not. Or maybe I just want to make things complicated. Later, I'll take the time to explore that notion, but now I want to know what Pauline knows.

"Do you think Josh loved her?" I ask, afraid to hear the answer but needing it like I need my next breath.

She takes the stool next to me and kisses me on the cheek. "Josh had a big capacity for love," she says, her eyes sadder than I've ever seen them. She misses her son as much as I miss my husband. "But he knew better than to want something he couldn't have, something that was impossible. So, he let himself grieve for a while. But he had too much passion for life to not move on, to not look for love somewhere else." She reaches out again, this time wrapping her small hand around mine. "And then he met you, dear, and his whole world changed."

* * * *

On the plane ride home, I dissect my conversation with Pauline. Is the takeaway from it if you can't be with the one you love, love the one you're with? Or is it something different? I can't help but remember something my mother said. "People change, circumstances change. It doesn't mean we don't cherish the past, but we move on to the future."

Her words—and Pauline's—give me a new sense of clarity. I think I've been giving Beth Hardesty too much importance. Or maybe not the right kind of importance. The idea of a one true love is the ultimate romantic trope, but it doesn't account for the exigencies of life, like getting dumped by your live-in girlfriend or getting T-boned at thirty-five. Or for that matter getting pregnant at seventeen, miscarrying and upending all your plans. Had Josh seen Beth as his one and only, he never would've gone looking for someone else and he never would've found me, the next chapter in a great love story. Because it really was a great love story. And no one can ever diminish what we had together.

So instead of holding me back, the lesson of Beth is pushing me forward. And when I try to see my future, it looks a lot like my past, and I suddenly know what I have to do.

Chapter 35
This Is How it Starts

On the ride home from the airport, Dr. Booth texts me.

"How 'bout we finally get that dinner? Tonight? Tomorrow? You name the day and time."

I've been putting him off for weeks, coming up with every excuse under the sun. But only now do I realize that it's not out of loyalty to the memory of Josh that I have been evading him, it's out of loyalty to Campbell.

I hover over my phone in the back seat of the Lyft car that smells like disinfectant and Mexican food as I ponder my response. Then my fingers are moving. Swiftly. Confidently. And before I know it, I'm hitting the Send button. "Delivered," my phone says. It's done.

In the driveway, I stand beside my small carry-on suitcase as the Lyft driver pulls away and stare up at the Queen Anne. The sight of it, even after only a few days gone, lodges somewhere deep in my soul. I'm home.

I drag my bag to the back door, waving to the young couple staying in the guest cottage, enjoying their coffee poolside on the lawn. They wave back, and I go inside and climb the stairs to my bedroom. There, before I unpack, before I wash away my travels, I open my email and purge the selfie of Beth in the dressing room, the one I sent myself and have been carrying around ever since I found it, letting it hold more meaning, more weight, than it should.

I pull the scrapbook of Josh and me that I made after he died from the bookshelf, lie on the bed, and take a deep breath as I turn the pages, visiting the passage of years. Our years together, Josh and me. We made a good life. One filled with love, one filled with happiness. Even now, I can feel him everywhere I turn. All around me.

The melted yahrtzeit candle is on the nightstand, the flame long flickered out. I gather it up along with the scrapbook and Josh's laptop and tuck it away next to my wedding ring in a drawer. In the back of my jewelry box, I find the forever band Campbell gave me so long ago and watch prisms of color play off the gems in the sunlight like a new dawning.

I spend the rest of the morning cleaning my room, putting away my cherished past to make room for my future.

Then I stand under a spray of hot water in the shower until my skin wrinkles and the water turns cold. After dressing, I head to my car, drive across town and park across the street from Campbell's house. There's a sold sign where the for-sale sign used to be. He did it. He sold the house.

I guess I can say it's part of his cherished past, except it isn't. It was just a way for him to bide time until he found his future. I sit there for a while, imagining all the what-ifs the same way I did after Josh was killed in the car crash.

A long time passes before I start the engine and pull away from the curb. I make it all the way to Sunnyside before I remember that I'm afraid to drive.

The Scotts' house has the best yard on the block. A cottage garden filled with lavender, roses and sage. I stay in the car, summoning my courage, then climb the porch steps to the front door, where I ring the bell.

Mr. Scott is there to greet me and, without saying a word, enfolds me in a hug. I smell his chewing gum, the kind that tastes like violets. He used to give us pieces when we were kids, and I'm momentarily thrown back in time.

"He hasn't left yet, has he?" I ask, fearing that I'm too late.

"Come inside." He guides me into the living room, which would be a simple space if not for Campbell's furniture. Each gleaming wooden piece is more beautiful than the next.

But I only have eyes for signs of Campbell, that he's here. *He couldn't have left yet,* I tell myself. Escrow takes at least thirty days.

"He's gone, lass," Mr. Scott says, then insists I sit and have a cold drink.

My heart drops, and I'm paralyzed by loss. While Mr. Scott gets me a soda, I stare out the big picture window that looks onto the street. Even though it's not far from the bustle of San Francisco City College, it's a quiet neighborhood. Many of the modest turn-of-the-century cottages have been jacked up to two-story luxury homes, but the flavor of old working-class San Francisco is still here.

This is where Campbell grew up and where Mr. Scott chose to stay long after his landscape company grew prosperous. It's a good place. Safe and friendly, where the streets are thick with trick-or-treaters on Halloween, and everyone knows their neighbors.

A man comes up the sidewalk, his gait so achingly familiar that I know it's Campbell before I can even make out his face. I don't wait. I bolt out the door and run to him.

He catches me in his arms. "Hey, what's this?" He cups my cheeks with both hands and looks at me, studying each plane of my face. "What's wrong?"

"Your father said you were gone."

"I just went to the corner market." He raises the small bag, the handles wrapped around his wrist.

"I thought you'd left without saying goodbye."

"No, not yet." He runs his thumb over my wet cheek, then cocks his head to one side. "I thought we already said our goodbyes."

"What if I don't want to say goodbye?"

He looks at me again, this time with a mixture of confusion and wonder, then wraps me tightly in his arms. So tightly that I can feel his heart beating. And then his mouth is on mine, making my body tremble.

It's nothing like the impulsive kiss we shared in the little Craftsman on Liberty. Nor is it like the thousands of innocent kisses we stole from each other as love-struck teenagers. It's breathless and frenzied and filled with yearning.

He sighs my name, and I look into his moss-colored eyes, and I see it. Our future. Together. This is how it starts.

Printed in the United States
by Baker & Taylor Publisher Services